Rosenthal

KEYS
TO
HAPPINESS

A NOVEL

Anastasya Verbitskaya

KEYS TO HAPPINESS

A NOVEL

translated and edited by
Beth Holmgren & Helena Goscilo

INDIANA UNIVERSITY PRESS
Bloomington and Indianapolis

Abridged from *Kliuchi schast'ia: Sovremennyi roman A. Verbitskoi* (Moscow: Tipo-lit T-va I. N. Kushnerev, 1910–1913).

This book is a publication of

Indiana University Press
601 North Morton Street
Bloomington, Indiana 47404-3797 USA

www.indiana.edu/~iupress

Telephone orders   800-842-6796
Fax orders   812-855-7931
Orders by e-mail   iuporder@indiana.edu

© 1999 by Indiana University Press

All rights reserved

No part of this book may be reproduced or utilized in any form or by any means, electronic or mechanical, including photocopying and recording, or by any information storage and retrieval system, without permission in writing from the publisher. The Association of American University Presses' Resolution on Permissions constitutes the only exception to this prohibition.

The paper used in this publication meets the minimum requirements of American National Standard for Information Sciences—Permanence of Paper for Printed Library Materials, ANSI Z39.48-1984.

Manufactured in the United States of America

Library of Congress Cataloging-in-Publication Data

Verbitskaia, A. (Anastasiia), 1861–1928.
   [Kliuchi schast'ia. English]
   Keys to happiness : a novel / Anastasya Verbitskaya ; translated and edited by Beth Holmgren and Helena Goscilo.
      p.   cm.
   ISBN 0-253-33538-8 (cloth : alk. paper). — ISBN 0-253-21299-5 (pbk. : alk. paper)
      I. Holmgren, Beth, date .   II. Goscilo, Helena, date .
   III. Title.
   PG3470.V4K4213   1999
   891.73'3—dc21   98-48993

1   2   3   4   5   04   03   02   01   00   99

to
DR,
peerless colleague and friend,
and
JR,
our woman for all seasons

Contents

Acknowledgments	ix
Introduction	xi
List of Characters	xxxi

KEYS TO HAPPINESS — 1

BOOK ONE	3
BOOK TWO	69
BOOK THREE	131
BOOK FOUR	183
BOOK FIVE	223
BOOK SIX	249
EPILOGUE	291

Glossary	297

Acknowledgments

Our warmest appreciation to Susan Larsen, for sharing with us not only materials and astute insights, but also an irrational passion for Verbitskayan excesses, and to Louise McReynolds, a genuine pioneer in potboilers, whose essays on Verbitskaya and Nagrodskaya have set high standards of scholarship in popular culture. We also thank Irene Masing-Delic and the lively, hospitable Slavic Department at Ohio State University for having enabled us to rehearse our commentary on *Keys* during a Dynamic Duo presentation in unusually pleasurable circumstances in 1997.

As always, Janet Rabinowitch far exceeded the customary role of editor, and we have relied on her common sense, laughed with her at ourselves, and blessed the gods of publishing for her vital input into our work on *Keys*. During the two years we have struggled to anglicize and prune Verbitskaya's *magnum opus*, Donald Raleigh's critical intelligence, humor, and affection have played an inestimable part in our lives. So, with admiration and gratitude, we dedicate this volume to them both.

On a more intimate front, my thanks to RC for bringing Steinbachian moments to vivid life. And, above all, a loving "thank you" to Beata for confirming that *zweimal* improves on *einmal* when she's the peerless partner (HG). I give "extra credit" to our good-natured readers, Emily Koos and Kevin Reese. My greatest thanks go to my Stakhanovite partner-in-translation, whose stylistic verve, exuberant industry, and wicked sense of humor truly made this gargantuan project doable (BH).

Introduction

Who Was Anastasya Verbitskaya?

Anastasya Verbitskaya (1861–1928) does not register on the "A" list of Russian writers we've been assigned to read in college courses or exhorted to sample by worldly literary critics. Her name is not mentioned alongside those of Leo Tolstoy, the great chronicler of nineteenth-century Russian society, or Tatyana Tolstaya, the flamboyant conjurer of late-twentieth-century Russian dreamscapes. In experience and craft she sooner resembles Danielle Steel than Fyodor Dostoevsky. Her creative biography unabashedly crosses over from Russian highbrow to Western commercial models of artistic success.

Born into an impoverished family of noble descent, Verbitskaya trained as a classical singer at the Moscow Conservatory but could not support herself as a musician and, as her autobiography makes clear, would not do so as a governess.[1] After a halting apprenticeship in journalism, she found financial security and personal fulfillment in writing. Verbitskaya first ventured into publishing in the early 1880s as a proofreader and occasional contributor to the newspapers, but she made her name and fortune as a fiction writer. Debuting in 1887 with the novella *Discord*, she attracted favorable reviews for her feminist portrayals of heroines trapped in traditional marriages and family life. The overtly political realism of her early work reflected her lifelong commitment to socialism and earned her praise from one of the reigning powers of the leftist cultural establishment and the future father of Soviet literature, Maxim Gorky (1868–1936). Yet the blockbusters Verbitskaya churned out in the first two decades of the twentieth century—*Keys to Happiness* (1909–13) and *The Yoke of Love* (1914–16)—marked her as a bestselling author, the darling of the Russian reading public, and the target of highbrow attacks. Her wild success prompted no soul-searching and no change of artistic course. Instead, she reinvested her profits in translating and publishing other women writers, to become a one-woman industry.[2]

Verbitskaya's posthumous obscurity reflects, at least in part, the dynamics of the commercial market. A writer's popularity very often depends on her productivity and topicality. The "classic" may survive in print after its author's death, usually with the help of industrious academics, but the bestselling author must keep in constant contact with the reader, guaranteeing a recurring set of protagonists, themes, and values. Verbitskaya in particular promised to "process" current events for her audience, and to furnish them with charismatic role models. Yet, her popularity, in contrast to her Western counterparts', died prematurely, snuffed out some ten years before her actual demise in 1928 by a Soviet cultural establishment whose outraged disapproval of her heroines' high living and sexually explicit loving culminated in a ban on her books. After the 1917 Bolshevik revolution, Verbitskaya subsisted as a pseudonymous children's writer, while her blockbusters were forced to circulate underground.

Why Keys?

Why read Verbitskaya now? Why translate her greatest bestseller for today's English-speaking audience? To a certain extent we, like Verbitskaya, took our cue from the market. Russia's recent capitalist reforms not only completed the rehabilitation of politically repressed literature begun in the glasnost' period, but also restored commercial values in the publishing industry. During the Soviet era, highbrow literature dominated Russian society both officially and in dissident circles, patronized or persecuted by government institutions. The state publishing industry subsidized inflated print runs of politically approved classics, while the works of politically proscribed writers fetched high prices from rare book dealers and on the black market. Since publishing has passed from state bureaucracy to private firms, from patronage system to free market, publishers and writers have been experimenting, often desperately, to deliver a product that sells. Amidst the 1990s' flurry of translated Harlequins and Barbara Cartland "historical" romances, Verbitskaya's *Keys to Happiness* is one of the old chestnuts that new presses in Russia have reissued in a bid for a popular readership.[3] Suddenly Verbitskaya's commercial savvy matters to those eager to try out Russian variations on Western popular fiction.

What attracted us, however, was not the possibility of testing a fin-de-siècle Russian potboiler on the Western market (although the prospect of a lurid-covered *Keys* in the checkout line frankly thrills us), but *Keys* as a historical and literary phenomenon. Several prominent historians have highlighted Verbitskaya's "key" role in identifying and addressing her audience's aspirations and desires.[4] They remark on her appeal to a broad spectrum of readers, including members of Russia's nascent middle class. The success of her bestsellers signified not only the presence of a mass readership, but also the emergence of middle ranks that belonged to neither the newly educated peasantry nor the established elite, that dared to pursue their own special interests. Verbitskaya's novels recognized the needs of ambitious new professionals, insecure arrivistes, would-be intellectuals, and, perhaps most of all, women of all classes who felt stifled by societal and professional restraints. Her *Keys to Happiness* proffered a quite extraordinary mirror-gallery of aspiring, marginalized types ranging from schoolteacher revolutionaries and impoverished medical students to a Jewish tycoon longing to divest himself for a noble cause. For the uninitiated and underrefined, Verbitskaya's work furnished both finishing school and European tour. For the restrained and repressed, her bodacious heroines repeatedly articulated women's rights to sexual adventure and professional achievement.

Keys thus provides students of Russian history with a sensationalistic panorama of Russian society on the eve of World War I—a sort of popularized easy reader covering the period's dominant political allegiances, philosophical beliefs, cultural movements, and social types, attitudes, and lifestyles. Like Western middlebrow works, such as Margaret Mitchell's *Gone with the Wind* or John Jakes's *American Bicentennial Series*, *Keys* renders history a digestible package, a consuming read. The very accessibility that wowed Verbitskaya's readers a century ago may well lure today's students into a subject they otherwise might dismiss as alien or exotic. *Keys* refers to famous and not-so-famous historical names, dates, and episodes; perhaps more importantly, it conveys a certain contemporaneous worldview. In contrast to popular historical fiction written at a temporal or cultural remove, Verbitskaya's blockbuster can be read as an authentic document of its time and place. As our discussion of then current philosophies of gender, race, and sexuality will show, even the stereotypes and prejudices in which *Keys* abounds express popular perceptions, or misperceptions, of the world the novel presumes to reflect.

But what of its significance for Russian literature? Having pored over the novel's unabridged version, which numbers over 1400 pages, we fully admit *Keys*' considerable aesthetic flaws. To paraphrase the critic Korney Chukovsky's notorious attack on the author, Verbitskaya's novel is overlong, repetitious, at once melodramatic and formulaic in its development of character and plot, and all too often badly written.[5] Yet its strong attraction resides in what it discloses and how it engages and satisfies its readers. Western readers are accustomed to thinking about their culture as inclusive of art *and* entertainment, for the market dictates cultural value in our society more powerfully than any academy. Yet, perhaps because we have been following the lead of a Russian cultural establishment that positively revered highbrow writers and critics, we still tend to teach and learn about Russian culture by "classic" example. No one would presume to know American culture exclusively through its Hawthornes and Hemingways, but we have been operating for decades on this presumption in our transmission of Russian culture.

Verbitskaya's *Keys* amply fills the social, cultural, and sexual blank spots left by these "classics," unashamedly spelling out cultural references, indulging reader fantasies, and exploring taboo topics. It does so by means of a poetics we academics underestimate at our peril. The very formulae, repetitions, and excesses that once drew sharp critical fire also compelled Verbitskaya's audience to read and keep on reading. Brought out in six volumes over five years and avidly consumed by tens of thousands, *Keys to Happiness* proved to be a genuine pageturner. We urge today's readers, be they teachers, students, or non-academic fiction fans, to allow themselves to indulge in *Keys'* crass blandishments and incessant melodrama.

Moreover, Verbitskaya's novel piques our interest because it attempts to resolve, on a grand scale, the fascinating dilemma of Russian popular literature—its aspiring status in a society that worshipped its writers as real-life leaders and prophets. As prolific and pragmatic as any commercial author, Verbitskaya nonetheless always conceived of and presented herself as a "serious" writer disseminating a "serious" message. *Keys* combined inspirational role models and educational passages on philosophy and the arts with passionate love stories and incessant displays of beautiful bodies, opulent residences, and "exotic" locales. As we note below, it suggested to its upwardly mobile readers that they could indeed "have it all"—both an affluent lifestyle and social-intellectual prestige.

In short, this abridged version of *Keys* presents an enjoyable and even educational read, for which the following critical observations are offered as a selective reader's guide.

Politics in Keys

Although *Keys* focuses mainly on the evolution of its charismatic heroine, Manya Yeltsova, its action reverberates with the shock and aftershocks of the 1905 revolution, when Russia's various underground political parties joined ranks with a restive populace and managed to provoke and sustain significant workers' strikes and peasant uprisings in the major cities and throughout the countryside. The picturesque Ukrainian estates Manya savors during her summer vacations are swept up in the "unrest"; her lover-to-be, the anti-Semitic reactionary landowner Nikola Nelidov, is burned out of house and home; and she and her schoolmate-friend, Sonya Gorlenko, watch the bullets fly from their Moscow lodging. Once the general furor ebbs, *Keys* dutifully registers the continuing activities, both propagandistic and terrorist, perpetrated by underground radical groups disappointed by the revolution's outcome—the Socialist Revolutionaries (SRs), Social Democrats (SDs), and anarchists.[6] Most of the novel's sympathetic characters are drawn to leftist programs, although their involvement ranges widely from assassination attempts (Lika) to lip service in local debates (Uncle). Indeed, the self-sacrificing Sonya, despite her revulsion for political violence, epitomizes the female revolutionary in the making, a conscience-stricken gentry miss who would study her way to a medical degree and service for the poor, and thence to revolutionary agitation.

The 1905 revolt did wrest some concessions from the tsarist government, including the establishment of a Duma or Parliament with restricted power, yet its aftermath was overwhelmingly one of anticlimax, redoubled government repression, a splitting of the opposition, and societal restlessness. On a psychosocial rebound resembling that of a wildly self-indulgent Weimar Germany or flapper-era America, educated Russian society after 1905 sought nonpolitical diversions in high culture modernist experimentation and "boulevard" entertainment. If, as one historian surmises, the 1905 revolt constituted a period "in which libidinous impulses had shattered existing constraints, but were effectively subordinated to the cause of constructing a new political order," then these impulses, unharnessed, awakened diverse appetites and pursuits in a society accustomed to self-control and formerly united in its devotion to political reform.[7]

This post-1905 chaos is well represented in *Keys*, manifest in its many debates between dogmatic revolutionaries and committed aesthetes, and in Manya's incessant vacillation between "pure" artistic self-expression and art in service to the masses. Perhaps most of all, the tycoon-philanthropist Mark Steinbach demonstrates the era's much-divided loyalties with his contributions to different underground groups, artistic projects, and deserving individuals. Steinbach's will-less magnanimity, pallidly reflecting the actions of real-life Moscow merchant-patrons, generally expresses the delectating eclecticism of his era.[8]

What truly distinguishes *Keys* from countless contemporary discussions and illustrations of the politics-versus-art debate is its elaborated, effective assertion of feminist politics. The feminist movement per se never enlisted a large following in Russia, for, as even Sonya remarks, its political platform was dismissed as too narrow and self-serving, and its largely upper-class membership alienated many of its would-be beneficiaries.[9] A few radicals, most notably Alexandra Kollontai (1872–1952), agitated for a combined program of feminism and socialism, and Verbitskaya's works and beliefs certainly overlapped with their efforts. Yet, unlike Kollontai, who later assayed rather dogmatic political fiction about new Soviet heroines, Verbitskaya garnered enormous attention with her fictionalized feminist campaign. Perhaps because her politically astute heroines were engendered in a more permissive sociopolitical climate, they never sacrificed individuality or sexuality for their politics. In her art, Verbitskaya was to other female radicals as her protean Manya is to the self-abnegating Sonya.

Thus, the bestselling Russian "woman's novel" pioneered by Verbitskaya did not reprise its Western popular romance counterpart, but instead represented the potent packaging of feminism with socialist sympathies, modernist flourishes, and commercial strategies. Equating Verbitskaya with women romance writers in the west, authors who enjoy the same level of popularity, misses the

Introduction xv

radical core of her heroinism. As a market phenomenon, she surely indicated women's burgeoning power as consumers and producers, and her work spearheaded a short-lived boom in women's popular fiction before and during the First World War, a quite distinct publishing phenomenon emerging from a generally flourishing popular literature scene. In the last decades of tsarist rule, a host of new or newly amplified publishing concerns recruited and promoted new writers and products in an attempt to capitalize on a rapidly growing, diversifying readership.[10] But the boom in women's fiction, far from codifying a "woman's novel," masked important differences in the writers' ideological orientation, artistic ability, and sociopolitical ambition. Of the cohort of best-selling women authors in the early twentieth century—Nadezhda Lappo-Danilevskaya (1874–1951), Olga Bebutova (1879–1952), Lidia Charskaya (1875–1937), Evdokia Nagrodskaya (1866–1930), and Verbitskaya—the last three actually built their following on strong-willed protofeminist role models.[11]

Keys lavishly elaborates the *Bildungsroman* of the so-called New Woman—a fin-de-siècle type who asserted women's rights to equal education, professional achievement, political voice, and sexual freedom.[12] Manya, like her maker, at first seems doomed by poverty to a life as governess or dutiful wife, but she instinctively rebels at all forms of compulsory service, whether this be earning good grades in comportment or "having to kiss someone when she didn't feel like it." Fortuitously, dancing talent, a dreamer's temperament, and facilitating friends save her from drudgery and domestication. A chance acquaintance, the visionary anarchist Prince Sitsky (Yan), formally sets her on her grand quest for the titled "keys to happiness"—specifically, the ability to smash the "chains" of duty, compassion, and self-sacrificing love, and the strength to honor one's own dreams and passions.

The spoiled family favorite and perennial guest of her social betters, Manya is exempted from family obligations and prohibitions and somewhat miraculously relieved of the burdens of single parenting and making ends meet. Mastering both classical and interpretive dance techniques, intuiting her own critically acclaimed and audience-inspiring style, she excels in honoring her characteristically fin-de-siècle dreams. This New Woman, a Duncanesque artiste who reportedly surpasses her unorthodox model, is no mere beautiful body, but also choreographs, writes, and sculpts. As the next section will elucidate in detail, Manya's many passions, filtered through contemporary conceptions of sexuality, psychology, and biology, prove more difficult to honor and contain, but for much of the novel our heroine struggles valiantly to be mistress of her irresistible body and free in her affairs. Even after she bears an illegitimate child, she long resists the conventional refuge of marriage, and ultimately weds only to save Steinbach's life. Although her suicide certainly problematizes her New Woman status, signaling her regression to an "enchained" subordinate Femininity, it also finalizes the pattern of contrary willfulness that sharpens Manya's heroinic appeal and links her with her contemporary self-realizing, self-destructive star, the Russian émigré artist and diarist Maria Bashkirtseva (1858–84).[13]

Keys *on the Body*

Keys to Happiness belongs to the rich, canonically neglected fund of racy fin-de-siècle texts that include Mikhail Artsybashev's *Sanin* (1907), Mikhail Kuzmin's *Wings* (1907), Lydia Zinoviev-Annibal's "Thirty-Three Abominations" (1907), and Evdokia Nagrodskaya's *Wrath of Dionysus* (1910) and *Bronze Door* (1911).[14] All these fictional narratives blend philosophy and pseudoscience with melodrama, to promote individual freedom through sexual nonconformism or transgression. In that sense they polemicize with moralistic conclusions about sexuality expounded not only by Tolstoy in *Anna Karenina*, "Kreutzer Sonata," "The Devil," and "Father Sergius," but also by such mainstream misogynistic philosophers as Vladimir Solovyev, Nikolai Berdyaev, and Nikolai Fyodorov.[15] The nature and role of sexual identity and libidinal drives, in fact, seemed to obsess fin-de-siècle Russia, as well as the rest of Europe, and carried weighty social, political, and philosophical implications.[16]

In the era's anxiety-ridden confrontation with modernity, issues of sexuality were inseparable from the rapid and disruptive growth of cities and industrialization, the intensification of political agitation and class conflict, and the emergence of psychological theories grounded in biology.[17] Indeed, the period's biological metaphor for society as an organism, popularized by the psychologist Paul Bourget and the biologist Ernst Haeckel, facilitated an equation of individual behavior with social tendencies. Both, according to Max Nordau's massive, influential study, *Degeneration* (1892), suffered from a collapse of morality, skepticism of authority, a mood of pessimism, and an increase in physical and mental disease. Scenes of cafes, dance halls, cabarets, theaters, alcohol and drug addiction, "perversion," promiscuity, near-nudity, and violence proliferating in the art and literature of the time (e.g., Bakst, Serebriakova, Somov, Sudeikin, Andreyev, Blok, Bunin, Kuprin, Kuzmin, Rozanov, Sologub) disconcerted observers as demoralizing spectacles. They reputedly stimulated unfulfilled passions and courted morbidity, depression, hysteria, nervousness, and suicide—which, in fact, reached epidemic proportions in the 1890s and 1900s.[18] A widespread absorption with eroticism, sickness, and death was both a source and a symptom of fin-de-siècle anomie. Tellingly, the 18,000 Russian-language publications issued in 1908 were dominated by pornography and crime novels.[19]

Verbitskaya's *Keys* captures the decadent zeitgeist that dominated Russia and Europe during the first decade of the new century. Accusations of pornography were leveled at Verbitskaya (as they had been at Artsybashev and Kuzmin) primarily because her novel condensed "signs of the times," portraying multiple suicides, illicit sexual congress, rape, illegitimate children, public venues associated with the demimonde, insanity, and degeneracy. The specter of degeneracy and death hovers over *Keys* throughout, and reflects popular notions of advancing social decay, which postulated a physiological model to elucidate both psychological states and social development.

The psychologist Bénédict-Augustin Morel's influential concept of degeneracy as an inherited organic disorder with specific physiological and psychological manifestations underpins major aspects of the plot and the discussions in *Keys*. The belief that sexual profligacy, alcoholism, prostitution, and insanity have a biological basis not only fuels the impassioned debate between Steinbach and Nelidov—the two male protagonists competing for the heroine's favors—but also impedes Manya's marriage to Nelidov, with dire consequences: It renders her daughter Nina illegitimate, makes Manya's reprised intimacy with Nelidov adulterous, and ultimately leads to their deaths by suicide. As the reactionary, anti-Semitic spokesman for the droits de seigneur, Nelidov rapes and unknowingly impregnates Manya, but dreads contamination of their future offspring, for, according to the theories of genetic inevitability rampant at the time, the sexually triggered dementia of Manya's mother, which erupts as hysteria in the teenage Manya, may surface as full-fledged insanity in the next generation. A suspended threat for both Manya and Steinbach, the scourge of heredity nonetheless does not prevent their enjoying sexual intercourse with each other and different partners—episodes that bolster the novel's reputation for sensationalism.

Sexual relations with multiple men are integral to Manya's iconoclasm in *Keys* and Verbitskaya's sociopolitical agenda, and elicit two conflicting attitudes, both embedded within the novel. The more conservative segment of society, such as the gentry, largely concurs with Richard von Krafft-Ebing's hugely influential *Psychopathia Sexualis* (1886), which condemned sexuality outside monogamous marital relations as symptomatic of degeneration. According to Yan, the novel's ideological spokesman for the New Woman, however, separating physical intimacy from the "yoke of love" provides the title's keys to happiness, for it liberates women from a coercive middle-class morality that erroneously conflates the two. For Verbitskaya, the talented individual's personal autonomy and self-realization are paramount, and theoretically, at least, Manya, Steinbach, and the novel's bohemians endorse this quasi-Nietzschean philosophy of hedonistic egotism, which Manya pursues along with economic independence through her career as a dancer. Thus her relationships with Yan, Steinbach, Nelidov, Harold, and the secondary male characters whom she tirelessly captivates may titillate the reader (and certainly scandalized some contemporaries), but ultimately have a sociopolitical dimension. In fact, Verbitskaya had an available model for the articulation of radical politics through women's sexual freedom in arguably the most resonant novel of the mid-nineteenth century: Nikolay Chernyshevsky's *What Is To Be Done?* (1863), as well as the personal biography of the author.[20]

In advocating that women be extended the historically male privilege of sexual liberty, Verbitskaya engages gender politics and one of the era's seminal publications: Otto Weininger's *Sex and Character* (1903). This controversial thesis on sexual differentiation through quantitative verification rooted in the body made Weininger an international household name among European intellectuals and pseudointellectuals. By 1912 it had appeared in six Russian translations totaling more than 35,000 copies and provoked a deluge of comments from diverse readers, including Bely, Berdyaev, and, later, Platonov. Like Nagrodskaya's *Wrath of Dionysus*, *Keys* draws on several basic Weiningerian principles for its formulation of gender and "Jewishness."

Positing a chemically based universal sexual indeterminacy, Weininger sees femininity and masculinity as distributed in every possible proportion, dependent on the degree to which a person possesses female or male plasmic dominance. Verbitskaya's progressive visionary Yan incarnates the qualities Weininger labels Masculine: clarity of intellectual perception and articulation, potential for genius, ingrained respect for ethics, capacity for universality, and an active relationship to the environment. Defined negatively by antithesis, the Feminine embodies incapacity for "pure" thought, hence the primacy of feeling (incompatible with genius), organic mendacity (in crisis, manifested as hysteria), illogicality (which precludes universality), and passivity to the environment. Weininger views women as exclusively sexual beings, the two poles of their character represented by the mother and the prostitute, who share the trait of indiscrimination, seeking only to reproduce and to obtain sexual gratification, respectively. Woman, who represents matter and thus exists as the complementary object to the near-divine male subject, is mirrored in the Jew, for he "is soulless, and possesses neither ego nor individuality, personality nor freedom, character nor will"—all prerogatives of Christian virility. Weininger laments the profoundly feminine and Jewish essence of modernity. Clearly, such a vision of womanhood does not conduce to female emancipation, and Manya's struggles partially reflect her author's efforts to reconcile novelistically her own bifurcated convictions and allegiances.

Steinbach's Italian lecture in Book 2 of *Keys*, on Semitic and Christian cultures, essentially encapsulates Weininger's commentary on Jewishness and its deleterious effect on culture. The depiction of Steinbach the Jewish sugar magnate as a morose, languid, decorative presence, who in his relations with Manya enacts the traditional female role of obliging submission, derives from the same preconceptions. Manipulative, conciliatory, patient, and domestic, Steinbach, and not the male-plasmaed Manya, fulfills the maternal function for her daughter, ascribes a "masculine soul" to Manya, and accepts their exchange of conventional gender roles. Of the novel's three protagonists, Nelidov is the uncompromisingly virile "master," Manya oscillates between the masculinity of the New Woman and the fabled femininity of Eve, while Steinbach by *biological definition* is the feminized Jew. As receptacles of identity, their bodies determine their gender on the invisible level of plasma and project that identity on the visible level of features, expression, and gesture.

According to Verbitskaya's relentless body semiotics, certain features and gestures are an index of permanent, fixed identity grounded in race, gender, and "core" characteristics. Thus Manya's bottomless, mystical eyes and radiant smile convey her spiritual depth and richness; Steinbach's insinuating (*"vkradchivyi"*) Jewish melancholy and droopiness denote passivity; Nelidov's firm, light step bespeaks his self-assurance. Other physiognomical signs offer visible clues to transient internal states, melodramatically registered at every conceivable opportunity: people flush and pale, their brows contract, jaws clench, lips compress, and eyes flash as they shiver, quiver, and palpitate, in a hyperbolic manner favored by lofty Russian Romantics such as Mikhail Lermontov (1814–41) and Alexander Bestuzhev-Marlinsky (1797–1837) and by authors of Harlequin romances. The body also signals class and race, for Steinbach's ears (!) betray his Jewishness, Nelidov's lofty brow and small hands—his noble origins.

As befits a heroine whose profession demands corporeal expressiveness and sensuous embodiment, Manya affords the novel's most richly elaborated example of a physical text urging constant interpretation. As though orchestrating a "photo op" event, Verbitskaya frames her as an object of visual consumption for friends, lovers, family, colleagues, audiences, and the novel's readers. Spotlighting details of Manya's appearance, Verbitskaya makes her the cynosure of all eyes in established visual genres of the period: as human still life when Manya lounges on various couches; as daring fashion plate at social occasions; and as entertainment icon when she enthralls audiences through movements on stage and gazes out from photo-postcards advertising her persona as the dancer Marion. The novel's passion for visualization partly explains why *Keys* became Russia's first cinematic blockbuster when transferred by Iakov Protazanov as melodrama to the silent screen in 1913.

Bodily Blandishments and Female Dance

Manya's gifts as an "intuitive" dancer clearly were intended to dramatize her radical departure from the conventions of classical ballet, thereby certifying her revolutionary credentials in the sphere of art. Yet Verbitskaya's choice of profession for her heroine—one long associated with the demimonde—courted ambiguity in the context of the times. With fear of degeneracy and its manifest symptoms running high, an entire range of physical activities seemed proof of humans' animal nature, their regression to a precivilized state. Freestyle dance, favoring the "natural movements" of an Isadora Duncan as opposed to the rigors of balletic discipline, could be analogized with primitive instinct and even disease, such as hysteria, epilepsy, and madness (witness the term *Saint Vitus' dance* and the fin-de-siècle pictorial and theatrical enthusiasm for the bacchantes). Dance, like hysteria, was gendered, as attested by artworks depicting dancers that blur the boundary between madwoman and "child of nature."

If Isadora Duncan was the living example of regression to atavism, her cultural parallel was Salome, the focus of numerous literary, pictorial, and musical works of the era.[21] Whereas Book 2 of *Keys* concludes with Yan's recipe for woman's emancipation, Book 4 closes with a scene that captures the prevalent fin-de-siècle perception of woman's fearsome, inexplicable power. When the poet Harold, who later succumbs to Manya's blandishments, stares at her portraits displayed in a store window, beneath the female dancer he detects Woman the artful seducer:

> Manya lay on the ground in the pose of the Sphinx, her huge, mystical eyes gazing at him. [. . .] Her dark brows were tragically knitted. Slightly raised on her elbows, her chin resting on her palm, she gazed—*frightful, enigmatic, full of menace and challenge*—into his very soul.
> And Harold stood motionless, fully in *her power*.
> There she was—*Woman! Ever alien, ever inimical! A riddle comprehended by no one. An elemental, dark force. . .*
> Isn't it she who stands at all the roads and crossroads, *lying in wait* for the moment when one's weary, reading in the wayfarer's eyes his craving for rest?
> Isn't it she who with a *cruel laugh* at whoever lies in the dust *plants her foot on the chest of the vanquished?*
> Her hands are prehensile, and her lips thirsty. . .
> She is a *symbol of her sex, and the enemy of personality*. (Emphasis added)

This diatribe accords perfectly with the decadent image of the femme fatale/phallic woman as the agent of the instinctual unconscious, unleashing the eruptive forces of libidinal impulses.[22] That iconography of the thanatal temptress, in which the Sphinx, Eve, and Delilah merge, overran the literature and the art of the period. The identification of Manya with the Sphinx—in the myth of Oedipus, a monster with the head and breast of a woman, a lion's body, and the wings of an eagle, who killed all men incapable of solving her riddle—evokes simultaneously Freud's memorable question about women's desire and the ominous answer exemplified by such operatic ice-queens as Puccini's Turandot. The more pertinent, though unstated, parallel for the deadly, enigmatic, animalistic female who wantonly destroys males, however, is the dancer Salome, who inspired Flaubert, Huysmans, Wilde, Moreau, Beardsley, Richard Strauss, Bakst, Ida Rubinstein,[23] Alexandra Ekster, Sudeikin, and a multitude of lesser artists.[24]

The Biblical Salome in her modern version as the embodiment of aesthetic spectacle and the manipulator of a complex weaponry of seduction[25] incarnates visual-sexual enslavement of the male, doomed to dual decapitation. Losing his head literally and metaphorically, the male undergoes an annihilation of his "true self," defeated by the "enemy of personality."

What lends *Keys* spice while making it problematic is Verbitskaya's reliance for Manya's characterization on two conflicting paradigms of the era: the revolutionary socially conscious woman seeking material self-sufficiency via career, and the primordial, alluring siren whose physical endowments (thinly masked as art) ensnare every man in her orbit. Contradictions in the text arise from Manya's persona as both the New Woman and the nude on display. From the first page, when Manya as a child sits wriggling in the laps of her mother's sugar daddies, to the last book, where Manya greets visitors in a dress that discomfits even her loyal friend Sonya ("All the lines and forms of her body were visible through the thin fabric, as if Manya were undressed. But Uncle was in ecstasy"), readers, along with the male half of the novel's cast of characters, are invited to delectate Manya's bodily charms. And, as befits the modernist devouring Venus flytrap, she drains the life's blood of her enamored male victims, literally in the case of Nelidov, who escapes his sexual bondage only by blowing his brains out, and figuratively in the case of Steinbach, whose premature aging transforms him into a near-double of his demented uncle, for, as Uncle prosaically muses, "Life with Manechka is obviously not easy."

If Verbitskaya resorts to Gorky's *Znanie* school of physical explicitness and the decadent brand of fleshly transgression, she simultaneously strives to lend respectability to the cult of female sexual liberty by harnessing Manya's "no-holds-barred" libido to aesthetic depth and spiritual insatiability. Accordingly, after Manya's intimacy with each man, Verbitskaya invokes a platonic lexicon, whereby Manya's postcoital eyes are mystical and the site of her transports becomes the soul. This discourse of euphemism and deflection rhetorically elevates the genital to the metaphysical. Indeed, since the conviction that this debased world cannot accommodate transcendent aspirations and desires forms a cornerstone of Symbolist philosophy, the novel's conclusion allies it with highbrow sublimating trends. Taking her cue from Ivan Karamazov, Manya returns her keys, for they unlock doors to a flawed realm. Whether the fault lies with the keys, Manya's psychological makeup, or the specific historical moment remains an open question. But Manya's inability to disavow romantic love as life's prime mover places her solidly within traditional paradigms of femininity and their cultural forms.

Consumer Education in Keys

Much as Manya accommodates feminist, femme fatale, and Ophelia in her capacious image, so Verbitskaya depicts her charismatic characters somehow embracing consumerism and altruism. Her rich and famous do indeed have it all, even the exclusive right of condemning themselves for their good fortune.

Whether Verbitskaya deliberately engineered this contradiction or absorbed it from a society in great socioeconomic flux, such an ambivalent orientation surely enhanced *Keys'* consumer appeal. In the opening section, we compared the novel to American middlebrow blockbusters, and characterized it as a consuming read, literature effectively rendered a commodity. *Keys'* keen attention to decor, dress, and picturesque sights obviates its fulfillment of consumer expectations, for it proffers readers vicarious consumption of experiences and items available only to the well-to-do, functioning much like a catalogue or, as one historian asserts, a print department store.[26] The novel showcases, for example, the overwhelming opulence of Steinbach's manor house, which instantly alerts Manya to the "paltriness" of her friends' estates; through Steinbach's lectures to Manya it introduces readers, both descriptively and pedagogically, to the glories of Venice, Rome, Florence, Vienna, Paris, and London. Like any work of commercial fiction—the detective novel, Gothic thriller, popular romance—*Keys* imagines, advertises, and approves the considerable joys of consumption. That the novel itself generated a mini-boom in *Keys*-related entertainment demonstrates, at least in part, its formulaic success.[27]

Yet, despite its overt enticement of an audience presumably without higher education and avid for an upper-class lifestyle, *Keys* consistently critiques an unreflective consumerism and scorns the very notion of an all-consuming bourgeoisie. In so doing, it appealed to the same readers who bought it for its "shop windows." By the beginning of the twentieth century, Russian society was no longer clearly stratified into tiny educated minority, conservative clergy and merchantry, and vast peasant underclass. There were countless examples of upward and downward mobility in this era, as more peasants became literate and sought nonrural employment, a few highly visible merchants joined the sociocultural ranks of the traditional intelligentsia, the gentry overall was relinquishing its economic advantage, and many more members of all the so-called "estates" entered the professions. Nevertheless, as Western historians of Russia generally insist, this movement did not produce a self-aware, self-satisfied bourgeoisie. Plenty of Russians found themselves in the "middle," between estates in terms of financial means and cultural advantages, but they did not coalesce in a Western-style middle class.[28] Rather, this amorphous middle subscribed to a distinctly non-Western national system of class values, disdaining the implicitly philistine, mercenary label of a Western bourgeoisie, and aspiring to the intellectual, spiritual, and political status of the intelligentsia, a group formed of educated members of various estates and long recognized for its altruism, reasoned opposition to the repressive tsarist state, and felt obligation to serve the exploited masses. No self-respecting *intelligent* would be satisfied with the good life, and the same certainly held true for the would-be intelligentsia who swelled Verbitskaya's readership.

Verbitskaya engaged these "middle" readers, then, by at once indulging and expiating their consumerist impulses, and she managed the latter operation by ennobling the motives and experience of her two primary consuming heroes—Steinbach and Manya. It is important that these two symbolically cover the spectrum of consumption, with Steinbach serving as highly experienced and moneyed consumer guide, Manya flamboyantly acting the part of impoverished consumer novice, and both evincing the same attitudes toward worldly goods. Through Verbitskaya's manipulation, this pair variously metamorphoses into scholar and artist, or priest and goddess, authoritatively leading the reader upward.

Steinbach and Manya expiate consumption in ways ingenious and paradoxical. Both passionate devotees of the arts, and particularly the visual and material arts vaunted by fin-de-siècle modernism, they appreciate the stylish *self-expression* they achieve through their purchases, a principle that elevates mere acquisition into an art form. Steinbach is impressed with Manya's unerringly exquisite taste when she outfits her first modest residence in Paris. Her later Parisian abode, made possible by her stage success, literally realizes her dream of home as a temple for creative contemplation, adorned with marble statues, fresh flowers, and a tiger skin rug before the always-roaring fireplace. Steinbach's house in Moscow, which contrasts with the opulent showplace his father built, finds favor in Manya's eyes because the millions invested in furniture, vases, statues, paintings, and bronze "weren't oppressive" and "didn't obtrude," much as his discreet, expensive clothing unobtrusively frames his striking face and figure. In fact, Steinbach, the supposedly "feminine" Jew who repeatedly tries to house a nomadic Manya, proves to be the more gifted artist in interior decoration. Verbitskaya's narrator formally recognizes his achievement in the historic house he rents in Paris where he "surround[s] himself with beautiful things, creating the illusion of 'home' [the English word is used]—of an intimate life that reflects one's 'I.'"

More surprisingly in a novel that regularly genuflects before socialism, Steinbach and Manya refine consumerism by invoking the lofty examples and lifestyles of legendary aristocrats. They strongly intimate that real beauty and real style emanate from a blood aristocracy or, exceptionally and expediently, an innate royalty. The beautiful Nelidov, whose image Manya first encounters as she browses a picture book of legendary figures, descends from Russia's ancient Rurik dynasty. Steinbach, whose Moscow house Manya dubs "a genuine prince's palace," comes from the "Davidov line" of the old Jewish aristocracy. Manya herself, born into an undistinguished middle-gentry family, is proclaimed as a blend of bohemian and princess, a girl who disregards private property even as she presumes that the riches of the world are hers to enjoy and dispense. As her teacher-champion-housekeeper Frau Kessler patiently explains to Manya's less perceptive half-sister: "Things have no hold over her soul." Verbitskaya's accent on the aristocratic, of course, divests consumerism of any mundane bourgeois taint, and presents aristocratic acquisition and display as artistic masterpiece and encapsulated legend. Big spending and high living in a remote past inspire dreams rather than disgust. The same Manya who refuses to deal with fees and self-promotion in her daily life instantly locates romance in the artifacts and abodes of the noble dead.

In the final analysis, consumption for both Manya and Steinbach ideally serves as a bridge to the Beyond—of art, legend, the afterlife. Fine things and wondrous places prompt contemplation, revelation, and communion with ancient truths. Manya's first dance before Steinbach, which culminates in their lovemaking, is excited in no small part by the ancient cloth he bids her wear, a "faded fine silk fabric embroidered with gold" that once draped a Catholic statue stolen by Cromwell's forces. One idol's presumably "priceless" robe conduces the impressionable Manya to "feel like a goddess" and succumb to Dionysian inspiration.

Travel especially excites and underscores this aspect of the characters' consumerism. Early in their relationship, Steinbach forewarns Manya about the banal, vulgarized experience of being a tourist, relating in plaintive detail his ruined communion with the Pyramids and the Sphinx on account of money-grubbing Egyptian guides and a "herd" of bourgeois English tourists who "talk and talk and eat and eat," littering the majestic Sphinx with empty bottles, orange peels, and cigar butts. Thereafter, when Manya embarks on an unplanned European tour, Steinbach thoughtfully facilitates her unadulterated encounters with great buildings and artworks, and lectures her in the evenings about these sights' cultural significance. A consummate guide, Steinbach trains the relatively uneducated Manya to be a higher order of tourist and to experience sightseeing as a kind of soul travel. So Manya communes with portraits and statues of legends in Venice, Florence, Rome, and Paris; with nature in the Alps; and with history and the cosmos in Paris, where a visit to Versailles attunes her to a poignantly doomed aristocracy and repeated visits to the city morgue expose her to an afterlife gazing from the corpses' eyes.

In the end, however, having it all obligates these characters to give it all up. Predictably, the bohemian princess Manya is not satisfied by her wealth, fame, and domestic security, and, in a clichéd romantic gesture, she joins her long-lost love Nelidov in committing suicide. Steinbach echoes her act more responsibly, distributing his fortune to various worthy parties and projects before disappearing in the midst of a police dragnet. Enacting a strict sequence, *Keys* ultimately ennobles a renunciation of earthly wealth, beauty, pleasure, and success. The purity of the characters' consumerism, it seems, depends on the noble, willful death of the consumer. The sole heir to *Keys'* abandoned property must be the ever-nearing revolution.

Our Abridged Translation of Keys

This abridgement of *Keys*, taken from the second edition of its unabridged original, presents approximately a quarter of the novel and concentrates on decisive or eloquent stages in Manya's personal and professional development.[29] No publisher in this day and age would gamble on an uncut reissue of such a gargantuan bestseller, and we have worked closely with our editor to produce as coherent an abridgement as possible in a single volume. Since so much of the text has had to be excised in the interests of an affordable publication and an accessible read, we chose not to mark every excision, but to provide a summary in italics wherever untranslated sections of *Keys* contain information fundamental to plot or character psychology. These bridges also minimize the discontinuity caused by periodic omissions within any text, however meandering and tautological. Readers should be aware that sudden revelations and abrupt shifts between subplots are characteristic of Verbitskaya's novelistic technique, and our summaries frequently reflect these gaps and leaps in condensed form. In a few places, moreover, we have inserted line breaks so as to alert unsuspecting readers to a change of scene unannounced in the original text.

Disquisitions on culture and art, social commentary and political incidents, local color, peripheral characters, and innumerable repetitions have been omitted unless they illuminate the focal figure of the New Woman or pertain to the formative influences on Manya's life and chief participants in it. The primacy of heredity and degeneracy in the novel accounts for the inclusion of Manya's episodically related childhood and adolescence in Book 1, just as the importance of the woman's question necessitates the retention of female personae who illustrate the range of options at women's disposal in the early twentieth century: Manya's toiling sister Anya, her ambitious friend Sonya Gorlenko, the companion/governess Agatha Kessler, the committed revolutionary Lika, the professionless wife Katya Lizogub, the freewheeling journalist Lily, the naive music student Lia, the dance teacher Iza Jimenez, the successful writer Nina Glinskaya, the political activist Nadezhda Petrovna, and so forth. Our abridged version in no way dilutes the feminist impact of the original.

So as to convey the pervasive anti-Semitism of such characters as the older Gorlenkos, Nelidov, Manya, and Steinbach—individual instances of prejudice presumably typical of Ukrainian landowners, the Black Hundred, and self-deprecating Jews of the time—the majority of startling pronouncements about "Yids" that thickly pepper the novel appear in our version.

Since uncontrollable impulses and accumulation of experience matter to Verbitskaya's intents and entail a degree of repetition, we have tried to distinguish between repetition as device and as sloppy ineptness. Although we eliminated the most egregious instances of near-verbatim repetition, we preserved those scenes that introduce some variation on a general pattern (e.g., Manya's apparent irresistibility to men) and that foreshadow or mark a shift significant to the novel's thematic structure. For similar reasons we expunged most of the nonstop ellipses so dear to Verbitskaya. They seem superfluous because the rhythm of her sentences conveys quite adequately the breathlessness and fragmentariness of her characters' speech and thoughts. Notwithstanding our drastic abridgement and intermittent pruning of ellipses, our translation does not attempt to rewrite Verbitskaya's formulaic style. We have retained the repeated details and responses that code character features and emotions for the reader; the clichéd similes and metaphors designed to signal, if not achieve, a lofty style; and the melodramatic effects, both uttered and narrated, pedaled to create suspense and climax.

In the interests of readability we opted for a transliteration that enables correct pronunciation of names and places without appearing overly peculiar to the eye (e.g., Sonya, Yan). Thus the surname "Steinbach" appears in lieu of "Steinbakh," the given name "Semyon" in lieu of "Semen," and the patronymic "Sergeyevna" in lieu of "Sergeevna." Our text does retain the various Russian nicknames and abbreviated forms that appear in the original. Hence the reader will sometimes find Manya (already a diminutive form for Maria) referred to as Manichka or Manechka, and Sonya's Uncle is addressed in dialogue as Fyodor Filippych rather than the more formal Fyodor Filippovich. Our appended list of characters notes most of these variations. The glossary appended to the translation briefly identifies important items in the novel that might be confusing if unfamiliar to the reader. Parenthetical numbers following the entries refer to the book in which they first occur, and in the text are marked by an asterisk.

Notes

1. Verbitskaya's first edition of her autobiography appeared as *Moemu chitateliu. Avtobiograficheskie ocherki (Detstvo, gody ucheniia)* (*To My Reader. Autobiographical Sketches. Childhood, School Years*) (Moscow, 1908); its second edition was renamed *Moi vospominaniia (My Reminiscences)* (Moscow, 1911).

2. For a handy synopsis of Verbitskaya's life and works, see Alla Gracheva's "Verbitskaia" entry in the *Dictionary of Russian Women Writers*, ed. Marina Ledkovsky, Charlotte Rosenthal, and Mary Zirin (Westport, CT: Greenwood Press, 1994), 703–705. For a more concentrated focus on Verbitskaya's early work, see Rosalind Marsh's "Anastasiia Verbitskaia Reconsidered," in *Gender and Russian Literature: New Perspectives,* ed. Rosalind Marsh (Cambridge: Cambridge University Press, 1996), 184–205.

3. Two editions of *Keys to Happiness* appeared in 1993: the two-volume hardcover version issued in St. Petersburg by "Severo-zapad" in the "Zhenskaia biblioteka" "romance" series, and the drastically condensed one-volume paperback, containing only four of the novel's six sections, brought out in Moscow by "Planeta" publishers.

4. Cf. Jeffrey Brooks, *When Russia Learned to Read: Literacy and Popular Literature, 1861–1917* (Princeton: Princeton University Press, 1985) and Laura Engelstein, *The Keys to Happiness: Sex and the Search for Modernity in Fin-de-Siècle Russia* (Ithaca: Cornell University Press, 1992), both of which follow Russian high-culture traditions in their fastidious denigration of the novel as "literature." In the U.S., Brooks and Engelstein are responsible for first drawing attention to the Verbitskaya phenomenon, as are Rosalind Marsh in England and Alla Gracheva in Russia. For a wider-ranging analysis that examines the functions fulfilled by *Keys* for Verbitskaya's contemporaries, see the first-rate article by Louise McReynolds, "Reading the Russian Romance: What Did the *Keys to Happiness* Unlock?" *Journal of Popular Culture* (Spring 1998), 95–108.

5. Kornei Chukovskii, "Anastasiia Verbitskaia," *Kniga o sovremennykh pisateliakh* (St. Petersburg, 1914).

6. See the glossary for basic definitions of these underground parties.

7. Engelstein, 212.

8. For more information about the enlightened merchants who established themselves as major patrons of the arts, see Beverly Kean's book, *All the Empty Palaces: The Merchant Patrons of Modern Art in Pre-revolutionary Russia* (London: Barrie & Jenkins, 1983); also John Bowlt's article, "The Moscow Art Market," in *Between Tsar and People: Educated Society and the Quest for Public Identity in Late Imperial Russia,* ed. Edith W. Clowes, Samuel D. Kassow, and James L. West (Princeton: Princeton University Press, 1991), 108–30.

9. For an excellent history of the feminist movement in Russia, see Richard Stites, *The Women's Liberation Movement in Russia: Feminism, Nihilism, and Bolshevism 1860–1930* (Princeton: Princeton University Press, 1978).

10. For more information on this popular literary scene, see Brooks, Engelstein, and Louise McReynolds, *The News under Russia's Old Regime: The Development of a Mass-Circulation Press* (Princeton: Princeton University Press, 1991).

11. On the popularity of these authors, see Brooks, 160.

12. In "Achievement and Obscurity: Women's Prose in the Silver Age," *Women Writers in Russian Literature,* ed. Toby W. Clyman and Diana Greene (Westport, CT: Greenwood Press, 1994), 149–70, Charlotte Rosenthal remarks that the New Woman, as developed by fin-de-siècle Russian writers, "was usually an artist of some sort" (156).

13. Bashkirtseva's posthumously published diary, which flamboyantly asserted her artistic ambitions and personal desires, exerted a tremendous influence on Russian women at the turn of the century.

14. Most of these works have been translated into English: Artsybashev's *Sanin* by Percy Pinkerton (New York: Illustrated Editions Company, 1932); Kuzmin's *Wings: Prose and Poetry* by Neil Granoien and Michael Green (Ann Arbor: Ardis, 1972); Zinoviev-Annibal's "Thirty-Three Abominations" by S. D. Cioran in *The Silver Age of Russian Culture* (Ann Arbor: Ardis, 1975); and Nagrodskaya's *Wrath of Dionysus,* translated and edited by Louise McReynolds (Bloomington: Indiana University Press, 1997).

15. On the misogynistic utopianism of these thinkers, see Tatyana Osipovich's paper, "Pobeda nad rozhdeniem i smert'iu: ili zhenofobiia russkoi utopicheskoi mysli na rubezhe XIX–XX vekov," delivered at the January 1998 "Sex and Gender in Russian Culture" conference at RGGU (the Russian Humanities University) in Moscow; and Eric Naiman, *Sex in Public: The Incarnation of Early Soviet Ideology* (Princeton: Princeton University Press, 1997), 27–57.

16. According to the Symbolist Zinaida Gippius, for the Merezhkovsky circle, which boasted Bakst, Benois, Diaghilev, Dmitry Filosofov, Vladimir Gippius, Pavel Pertsov, and Rozanov among its members, "the unsolved mystery of sex" was a burning question. On Symbolists' rarified notion of sexuality, see Olga Matich, "Symbolist Meaning of Love," *Creating Life: The Aesthetic Utopia of Russian Modernism,* eds. Irina Paperno and Joan Delaney Grossman (Stanford: Stanford University Press, 1994), 24–50.

17. For an intelligent assessment of the period, with eloquent illustrations, see Shearer West, *Fin de Siècle: Art and Society in an Age of Uncertainty* (London: Bloomsbury, 1993).

18. In 1908 the Petersburg police reportedly registered fifteen hundred suicide attempts (Solomon Volkov, *St. Petersburg: A Cultural History* [New York: Free Press Paperbacks, Simon & Schuster, 1995], 151). On suicide in Russia, see Irina Paperno, *Suicide as a Cultural Institution in Dostoevsky's Russia* (Ithaca: Cornell University Press, 1997).

19. Volkov, 156.

20. For this aspect of the novel and Chernyshevsky's Sandesque domestic arrangement with his free-thinking spouse, Olga Sokratovna, see the groundbreaking study by Irina Paperno, *Chernyshevsky and the Age of Realism: A Study in the Semiotics of Behavior* (Stanford: Stanford University Press, 1988), especially pp. 110–33. The postpublication ban on the novel was lifted only after the Revolution of 1905.

21. Vasily Rozanov, whose anti-Semitism and notions of sex overlap with aspects of Weininger's pronouncements, wrote two fascinating essays on Oscar Wilde's Salome and Duncan's performing style. See "Religiia i zrelishcha" and "Tantsy nevinnosti," in V. V. Rozanov, *Sumerki prosveshcheniia* (Moscow: "Pedagogika," 1990), 316–24; 324–34.

22. See Deborah Silverman, "The 'New Woman,' Feminism, and the Decorative Arts in Fin-de-Siècle France," in *Eroticism and the Body Politic,* ed. Lynn Hunt (Baltimore: Johns Hopkins University Press, 1991), 144–63.

23. The likelihood of Verbitskaya's having attended Rubinstein's performance of the ballet in St. Petersburg in 1908 seems strong.

24. For the centrality of Salome to decadent aesthetics, see chapter 8, "The Veiled Woman," in Elaine Showalter, *Sexual Anarchy: Gender and Culture at the Fin de Siècle* (New York: Penguin Books, 1990), 144–68; also Bram Dijkstra's *Idols of Perversity: Fantasies of Feminine*

Evil in Fin-de-Siècle Culture (New York/Oxford: Oxford University Press, 1986), and his *Evil Sisters: The Threat of Female Sexuality in Twentieth-Century Culture* (New York: Owl Books/Henry Holt, 1996).

25. Silverman, 150.

26. Engelstein, 404.

27. In "Reading the Russian Romance," McReynolds lists unendorsed sequels, a film treatment, and even a waltz as evidence of the *Keys* phenomenon.

28. See, for example, Alfred J. Rieber, *Merchants and Entrepreneurs in Imperial Russia* (Chapel Hill: University of North Carolina Press, 1982) and also the following essays in the anthology *Between Tsar and People: Educated Society and the Quest for Public Identity in Late Imperial Russia*, ed. Edith W. Clowes, Samuel D. Kassow, and James L. West (Princeton: Princeton University Press, 1991): Samuel D. Kassow, James L. West, Edith W. Clowes, "Introduction: The Problem of the Middle in Late Imperial Russia," 3–14; Abbott Gleason, "The Terms of Russian Social History," 15–27; Sidney Monas, "The Twilit Middle Class of Nineteenth-Century Russia," 28–37; James L. West, "The Riabushinsky Circle: *Burzhuaziia* and *Obshchestvennost'* in Late Imperial Russia," 41–56; Bernice Glatzer Rosenthal, "The Search for a Russian Orthodox Work Ethic," 57–74; and Thomas C. Owen, "Impediments to a Bourgeois Consciousness in Russia, 1880–1905: The Estate Structure, Ethnic Diversity, and Economic Regionalism," 75–89.

29. This edition is entitled *Kliuchi schast'ia. Sovremennyi roman A. Verbitskoi (Keys to Happiness: A Contemporary Novel by A. Verbitskaya)* (Moscow: Tipo-lit T-va I. N. Kushnerev, 1910–13).

List of Characters

Anna Vasilievna (nicknamed *Attila*): teacher and radical, friend of Lika.

Dora: writer of feuilletons, occasional lover of the poet Harold.

Emma Vasilievna: Frau Kessler's sister-in-law.

Enrico: handsome, earthy Italian street musician hired as model for the sculpturing Manya Yeltsova.

Fyodor Filippovich (also *Filippych*): Sonya Gorlenko's dandyish, liberal uncle.

Fyodorova, Lina: classmate of Manya Yeltsova and Sonya Gorlenko, enrolled in the Higher Courses for Women.

Galagan, Natasha: eligible young neighbor of the Gorlenkos and the Lizogubs.

Glinskaya, Nina: radical Russian writer and activist residing in Paris.

Gorlenko, Sofya Vasilievna (usually *Sonya*): Manya Yeltsova's champion and closest friend, medical student enrolled in the Higher Courses for Women.

Gorlenko, Vera Filippovna: Sonya Gorlenko's mother.

Lady Hamilton: British society woman, former lover of Nelidov.

Harold (pen name for *Boruch Isaakovich Mendel*): the modernist artist, founder of the innovative theater *Studio*.

Izmail (also *Zyama*): violent revolutionary, devoted follower of Yan.

Iza Jimenez: Manya Yeltsova's passionate Creole dance teacher and soulmate.

Joseph Lvovich: Steinbach's crazy uncle.

Kessler, Frau Agatha: Manya Yeltsova's boarding-school teacher and pragmatic lifelong companion.

Lia (*Liubov Grinevich*): a young, tubercular violinist, in love with Steinbach.

Lika (*Lydia Yakovlevna Syromyatnikova*): radicalized daughter of a laundress, becomes a nurse and a revolutionary.

Lily: struggling fiction writer, erstwhile lover of Steinbach.

Lord Littleton: British nobleman infatuated with Manya Yeltsova.

Lizogub, Katya: frivolous country miss, eventually wife of Nelidov.

Natasha (also *Natalka*): the Nelidovs' comely maid and Nelidov's short-term mistress.

Nelidov, Nikolay Yuryevich (also *Nikolenka*): reactionary, anti-Semitic Russian nobleman, one of the novel's heroes.

Nelidova, Anna Lvovna: Nelidov's widowed mother.

Nils (*Pyotr Likhachov*): Manya Yeltsova's talented dancing partner.

Ostap: Steinbach's old Ukrainian caretaker.

Petro: Steinbach's stablehand.

Robert Yakovlevich: renowned doctor who attends to Manya after her suicide attempt.

Roza: a revolutionary.

Sarra: Steinbach's mother, a suicide before the action of the novel begins.

Semyon Nikolayevich: radical colleague of Steinbach's, at loggerheads with Harold.

Steinbach, Baron Mark Aleksandrovich: Jewish tycoon who finances both artistic and revolutionary causes, one of the novel's heroes.

Storozhenko, Nadezhda Petrovna: famous radical, friendly with both Yan and Steinbach.

Xavier: doctrinaire revolutionary, close friend of Yan.

Yan (Prince Mikolay Sergeyevich Sitsky): revolutionary philosopher, author of the treatise *Keys to Happiness*.

Yeltsov, Pyotr Sergeyevich (also *Petya*): medical doctor, Manya Yeltsova's half-brother.

Yeltsova, Anna Sergeyevna (also *Anya, Anichka*): Manya Yeltsova's half-sister.

Yeltsova, Maria Sergeyevna (usually *Manya*, also *Manichka, Manechka, Manka, Masha, Marie*, with stage name *Marion*): free-living, fabulously talented barefoot dancer, the novel's heroine.

Yeltsova, Nina (also *Ninochka*): Manya Yeltsova's daughter by Nelidov.

KEYS
TO
HAPPINESS

A NOVEL

FIGURE 1
A publicity shot of *Keys*' fashion-conscious author, Anastasia Verbitskaya. *Izvestiia knizhnykh magazinov tovarishchestva M. O. Vol'f,* August 1901.

BOOK ONE

There is more intelligence in your body than in your supreme wisdom. And who knows for what precisely your body most needs your supreme wisdom?

In love there's a measure of madness. But in madness there's a measure of intelligence.

—Nietzsche

In their modest Moscow apartment student Petya Yeltsov and his older sister Anya care for their insane mother, whose shrieks and occasionally violent outbursts arouse neighbors' suspicion and gossip. The siblings' younger sister, Manya, is currently away at boarding school, and ignorant of their mother's inherited madness.

Manya remembered her life as a three-year-old. She remembered her mother as young, beautiful, and lively. They had guests the whole day, all of them lively "uncles." Her mother would play the piano and Manya would dance barefoot on the rug, wearing nothing but a little shirt.

The "uncles" would be profoundly moved, and, shouting "Little angel!," would seat the child in their laps, kiss her ardently, and feed her sweets.

They lived well. She owned a lot of dolls and expensive toys and her playroom was big and light. One Papa left, another appeared. . . And the "uncles" kept bringing flowers, sweets, and toys.

Sometimes her "sister" would visit, a thin girl in a high school uniform, always melancholy, as if she'd been beaten. She'd sit on the rug, take Manya in her arms and, crying, would kiss her little face. A lanky, unattractive high school student with a gloomy face would turn up.

"Kiss your brother!" the nursemaid would instruct her. "This is your brother."

But Manya would shout capriciously, "Go away! I don't love you! You're yucky-gucky! Go away!"

Then she grew used to Petya. He'd hoist her on his shoulders and carry her around the room, tossing her high in the air. She'd gasp with pleasure and shout, "Again, Petya, do it again!"

Anya would tell her fairy tales and she'd doze in her lap.

"Don't go! I don't want you to! Don't go!" she'd plead when her sister and brother kissed her plump little hands, with their folds of baby fat at the wrists, as they'd leave.

After their departure she would sob uncontrollably. Then her mother would rush in, beautiful, angry, her bracelets jangling. "What's this? What is this? Take that! And that! Quiet! Be quiet at once!"

But Manya would fall on the floor and writhe in a fit. And she'd scream for a couple of hours until she turned completely blue, whereupon she'd fall asleep from exhaustion.

Her mother was erratic. One minute she'd spoil the little girl without restraint, the next she'd hit her for a trifle. She wouldn't see the child for days, abandoning her to the nursemaid's care. The little girl often fell asleep hungry and in tears, after her calls had gone unanswered, while the nursemaid would sit drinking with the kitchen help. Often the nursemaid would come in angry and flushed, a glass of vodka and a gingerbread in her hand.

"Here! Here you are! Drink up! Shut your gullet! You're not the least sleepy! For God's sake! Why are you howling? Why? Is it bitter? Never mind, drink it!

Chase it down with the gingerbread. That good? So lie down now and not a peep! I'm going to have my supper."

The little girl would cry at first, but then she grew to like the vodka.

When she was six she fell ill with a serious case of stomach typhus. When she finally regained consciousness, Anya was seated at her bedside. Manya smiled and drew her weak, shaky lips toward her. Petya was also there.

"Don't leave!" asked Manya. "I don't want you to. . ."

"Go to sleep. Sleep! We won't leave," Anya whispered, her eyes brimming with tears.

Manya fell asleep, but through her sleep she heard her mother enter the playroom. She must have been wearing her fur coat, for the room grew cold.

"How many times have I told you not to come in directly from the outdoors?" Petya told her sharply. Manya was so weak that she could neither move nor open her eyes.

"Is she sleeping?" her mother asked in a whisper.

"Yes," Anya replied. "Thank God! I think she's better."

"See? I told you it was nothing dangerous!"

"She was within a hairbreadth of death," Petya cut her short.

After a long silence her mother went up to Anya and kissed her. "My dear girl, you won't leave until she's up and about, will you? I have to go out again. You like it here, don't you? And I can be at peace. . ."

Anya kissed her hand in silence.

"Petya, please come tomorrow! And tell Father not to be angry. I'm so at peace with you!"

Much later, after she was up and about, Manya remembered those words: "Father? Tell Father not to be angry. . ."

Where was this angry father?

Some time later, Anya came, wearing a black dress with a white stripe, with a long black veil on her hat. She was crying as she and her mother hugged each other. But Anya cried quietly, whereas her mother kept shrieking, wringing her hands, running around the room, and beating her head against the table. When she left, Manya asked her sister, "Why are you crying?"

"Your Papa's dead!" Anya sobbed. "Your poor Papa. Pray for him!"

"What Papa? Nikolay Ivanych?"

Anya suddenly flared in anger. Manya had never seen her look so cross.

"You won't go away now, will you? Will you?" the little girl kept asking her. "And Petya will stay with me too?"

"No, dear! We can't stay here. Don't ask us to! Don't torment us."

Then something dreadful happened. Her mother fell ill. She took to crying and roaming about at night. During the day she would lock herself in her room and chase everyone out. For weeks she wouldn't comb her hair, but went around disheveled, her robe unfastened. She kept complaining about her head and repeating, "Misery." Then she began falling into a trance; she'd come into the playroom and sit down, stare off somewhere, and sit like that for an hour or more. Sometimes she'd whisper something.

Once Manya went up to her mother, who was sitting sunk in thought in the playroom, her collar undone, braid disheveled. For a long time the girl gazed at the woman, struck by the change in her appearance, as if she were a new, alien mother.

"Oh!" she exclaimed suddenly and clapped her hands. "You know what, Mama? You've gone gray! See how many gray hairs. . ."

She didn't finish and leaped back in horror.

Before her was a distorted face, teeth bared in a convulsive grimace, the gaze wild and glittering. . .

"Aah!" her mother uttered a long, menacing groan.

The little girl gave a shriek and fled into the kitchen.

Once Manya was awakened in the night by wild howls. She heard a clatter, a door banging, the sound of a struggle, and a muffled, desperate scurrying. Then the despondent moans of someone crying and the yelp of an enraged beast. Trembling, Manya sat up in bed.

The nursemaid was listening intently as she stood by the door, holding onto the handle. "My luckless one! My poor little orphan!" she cried, rushing in tears to the child.

By morning things had quieted down. Anya arrived, her eyes frozen in a look of horror, and told the nursemaid to get Manya's things together.

"Mama?" was the little girl's first question.

"They've taken Mama to the hospital. She's sick."

"Did they beat her during the night? Did they?" Manya gave a cry and burst into tears.

Her face contracted in spasms, Anya started comforting the child. Upon learning that she was going to visit Petya, Manya calmed down.

She grew used to being without her mother terribly easily. But she missed the nursemaid and above all the apartment. Petya's was so cramped and shabby, only three rooms on the fifth floor. Every day the little girl demanded pastry and sweets, turning her back on the kasha and cabbage soup. She was a lot of trouble, but Petya and Anya never lost their tempers. They didn't shout, as her mother had, nor did they hit her. Whenever she got angry and flew into a rage Anya would try to talk her out of it with imperturbable restraint. And each time Petya would gaze intently at her with a strange expression. Sometimes he would sigh. "Poor child!" he'd say. "It seems you can't escape heredity." Manya was ten when they enrolled her in a boarding school.

Petya and Anya retire to Gruziny with their insane mother after she is released from the nursing home. Petya, formerly unloved by his mother, who'd abandoned the family for Nikolay Ivanovich—Manya's real father—now devotes his life to the madwoman he has always adored. He alone can calm her, especially when, using the musical talent he inherited from her, he plays Mendelssohn's and Schumann's "Song without Words" on the piano. Heeding Petya's warning that insanity is hereditary, Anya renounces her love for her brother's friend, but grows irritable and petty.

Meanwhile, Manya causes a scandal at school. Told by her German teacher, Frederika Fyodorovna, to conjugate German verbs, she refuses, claiming a headache. When the teacher attempts to drag her to the headmistress, Manya collapses in hysterical convulsions, ultimately losing consciousness. At the meeting of the school council convened to determine Manya's fate, the priest and the women advocate expulsion, but the inspector, citing Freud's Psychopathology of Everyday Life, *argues for tolerance on grounds of inherited mental instability. After Petya and Anya visit the school to explain the family situation, the council decides to keep Manya, transferring her to a lower class, under Frau Agatha Kessler's tutelage.*

What a mysterious and endlessly novel book! During leisure hours the tousled curly head was wholly engrossed in its treasures. . .

Here was a Rhine castle ruined by the hand of time. A bandit's nest perched on a high cliff from which barons pursued and pillaged merchant ships. And here was the legendary and dread White Lady in a Mary Stuart cap. Or the long-nosed Strusensee and the charming queen in love with him.

"How could she love such a freak? That touching Beatrice Cenci, with her half-parted lips and innocent eyes. Why did you have to die?"

And further on. . . The little fingers feverishly leafed through the pages and paused at the portrait of the mad Ioanna of Castile. What a beauty! Her eyes gazed enigmatically from beneath heavy lids. A veil fell from the fillet around her head onto her shapely swanlike neck.

And further on. . . The pages rustled. . . Oh, how her little heart pounded! At last! With a deep sigh the girl dropped her little hands, gently clasped as if in prayer, to her knees, and sank into blissful oblivion.

Here was a painting by a Hungarian artist. An angel with a magnificent manly head bore the soul of a girl away from the devil, who snatched angrily at her garment. Oh, how proud the angel's profile! How implacable his gaze! How marvelous his hair, swept up above his wide brow!

In blessed ecstasy the girl gazed at this face for a long time, then pressed her lips to the page. . .

"Miss Yeltsova. . . Maria. . . Repeat the problem, please!" said a rasping voice. And the mathematician's gray face smiled meekly.

The slender girl rose. An entire universe gazed out of the large, astonished eyes turned upon his gray face, a universe closed to pedagogues, like the book of the seven seals. Oh, from what a height her soul had just plummeted!

"You're 'absent' again, Miss Yeltsova? Be seated!" said the papier-mâché figure meekly and gave a hypocritical sigh.

"He gave her an 'F' . . . an 'F' . . ." the class whispered.

A smile flitted across the girl's face. But the next moment her eyes watched in rapture as the last ray of the setting sun trembled and glowed on the window ledge. "Dear, dear sun! Good night!"

A year later Anna Sergeyevna sat drinking coffee in the cozy room of Frau Kessler, the Bavarian woman who ran the private school. The Frau was a strong, cheerful, pretty brunette of about forty. An artist's widow whose children had died, she did not feel old and was ready to start life anew.

"I'm so happy that you love Manya, Frau Kessler!"

"Everyone loves her, mein Fraulein! You can't help it. Marie is a charming little woman. A real woman. And now she knows her worth."

"And how is she doing now, Frau Kessler?"

"Neither well nor badly, as you say in your country. She's a child with a vivid imagination. . . She learns what she likes. And she's very capable. But don't expect any awards from her! She's too absentminded, and she lives in her own world."

Anna Sergeyevna clasped her hands fearfully.

"You needn't be afraid! Children who have their own world are fortunate. They can't be bored and they're not earthbound. Not earthbound," the German woman repeated, making a sweeping gesture. "Marie doesn't know the meaning of envy or pettiness. She's a born princess. Why are you looking at me like that, mein Fraulein? There are three types of women in the world: cooks, governesses, and princesses. Marie's eyes contain an entire book of magic tales."

But Anna Sergeyevna found no comfort in these arguments. She stirred her coffee, staring myopically at the pattern on the cup, then asked timidly: "But what about her conduct, Frau Kessler?"

"One can't call her exemplary. She's very vivacious. Mischievous. Volatile, stubborn, egotistical. . ."

"Oh, how terrible! Is there no way to change her character?"

"Oo-la-la! Character? Was ist denn das? If character means that she has whims and passions, then she has one. Marie doesn't hesitate between desire and satisfaction. If she likes something, she must have it at once. If she can't, then there'll be tears and sorrow, as with a grown woman."

"You're really upsetting me, Frau Kessler! This girl will be unhappy."

"Who knows, mein Fraulein? To want something very much—isn't that already happiness? They say that the person who never suffers and never weeps never lives. And I can't hide the fact that Marie has enemies."

"E-ne-mies?" Anna Sergeyevna's eyes filled with horror.

"Ha, ha! Really, it's not that terrible. And Marie knows how to get revenge. Have you ever seen her caricatures? Oh, she has talent! They're of our 'ex-empla-ry stu-dents,' the ones who get the highest marks in comportment. They can't stand Marie."

"Why?"

"Because Marie is a bohemian."

"What's that?"

"A bohemian is untidy, careless, unconventional. Oh, yes! She has no discipline! Just look at her desk!"

"Oh! She's always been that way."

"Well, of course. She can't be any other way. She loves medallions and earrings. Everything that shines and looks pretty. She'll persuade you to give it to her, and then put it on, and forget to return it."

"Frau Kessler! What are you saying! This is terrible!"

"Calm down, Fraulein Anna! She doesn't steal these things. She simply has no sense of private property. But those 'ex-em-pla-ry stu-dents' have petty bourgeois souls, and they don't forgive Marie her forgetfulness."

"No, this is terrible! How can you put up with this, Frau Kessler? This vice must be rooted out!"

The German woman laughed gaily and patted Anna Sergeyevna on the shoulder.

"Oh, liebes Fraulein! It's easier to reverse a river's course than to root out an inborn trait! Don't you know that?"

Anna Sergeyevna hung her head, as if the bridge over the abyss had finally given way.

"This makes Marie superior to many of us: things have no power over her soul. A few days ago Sonya Gorlenko gave her a beautiful turquoise ring. We have a poor girl here—Karaulova—who pays no tuition. When she saw that ring she began to cry out of envy. 'Do you want it?' Manya asked. She took off the ring and gave it to her. The whole class gasped. Only princesses behave this way."

Anna Sergeyevna stood up. Her cheeks were blazing.

"I can't allow this! She shouldn't accept such gifts! This isn't the way we do things. Her brother will never forgive her if . . ."

"Come, come! Prohibitions and punishments won't help! If you take away her presents today, she'll get more tomorrow. This is the age, Fraulein Anna, at which the instinct of love first awakens in us. And it unerringly draws us to the one who was created for that love. Strong passions will stir Marie all her life. What's so surprising that her friends love her? It's natural, even beautiful. . . And I can't prevent it!"

"You're making a big mistake. . . Forgive me, Frau Kessler! Manya's a poor girl, and has a modest future ahead of her. . ."

"As a governess?" the German surmised. "Oh, liebes Fraulein! I repeat: Marie was created for happiness. When told she must study for an 'A,' she answers, 'Why? I know I'm pretty. I'll be rich, get married, and won't work!' And she's right."

Anna Sergeyevna's face grew morose.

"Girls without a dowry don't get married, Frau Kessler. She has to get these thoughts out of her head. She's headed down a slippery path."

"Forbid a flower to smell sweet, or a lark to sing. You're asking a miracle of me, Fraulein," the German woman said sarcastically. "I'm just a poor woman who loves the sun and children and happiness. And I give children only what I have..."

When Anna Sergeyevna was about to leave, she drew a green note from her old pocketbook.

"Frau Kessler, here's money for Manya. I don't want her to go without! These are my earnings, and I've worked hard for them. When I was a student" (and even now, she wanted to add, but restrained herself), "three rubles spending money was a fortune. And I don't want Manya to get used to extravagance. But her ease in accepting everything from other people frightens me. Goodbye, Frau Kessler! Think about what I've said!"

Nighttime. Profound silence. Everyone had long been asleep in the dormitory when Manya silently slipped from her bed and knelt down. Tears of exaltation shone in her huge eyes as she prayed. It was so good to suffer and shed burning tears that drained away her strength!

Sonya Gorlenko suddenly awakened as if someone had touched her. "Again?" she whispered in horror. "Manya! You're killing yourself. What are you asking of God? Why are you crying?"

Clad only in her nightgown, Manya had grown chilled on the cold floor. She was keeling over from fatigue. Sonya lay next to her under the blanket.

"I'm asking for death... I dream so of dying! To die..."

"Be quiet! Quiet!" Sonya embraced her head and kissed her eyes and forehead. "Do you want to kill me? How can I live without you? And why should you die? Are you truly unhappy? Do you want for anything? You're surrounded by admiration and love."

"I'll tell you my secret," Manya said in a half-whisper. And her voice was so full of import that the tranquil Sonya's heart began to pound in anticipation of something new and wonderful.

"Listen! I love my dream... An angel in a German book. I'll show it to you tomorrow..."

"So?"

"I'll never meet him on earth. Angels don't come to earth. Don't you understand?"

"What craziness, Manichka! This is the reason you haven't slept for nights on end and don't study! You've gotten so thin! Look at your hands! You've melted away in a month."

"Ah, that's good!" Manya said with a blissful smile. "I've given myself three months to live. And I'll die the first day of Easter... I know I'll die!"

Sonya began to sob.

But Manya could not share her grief. Her soul was far removed from earthly things!

For the benefit of the poor high school students, at Shrovetide the head-

FIGURE 2
An example of dancing instruction at an exclusive girls' school, the Smolny Institute for Daughters of the Nobility. Central State Archive of Cinema and Photo Documents, St. Petersburg.

mistress organized a pageant, a concert, and then a ball. As a woman with artistic tastes and initiative, Frau Kessler was entrusted with organizing the pageant.

"I'll give you an idea, madame," she told the headmistress. "We'll have one number that will set Moscow talking about us. And we'll have to repeat the evening at higher prices."

"Frau Kessler, you're a genius!"

"Listen, madame. Do you know that little Marie Yeltsova is a marvelous dancer?"

"Yes, the dance teacher—"

"Ah, that's not what I mean! That would be too simple. That child is a living symbol of musical rhythm. She's a talent. Her relatives made a great mistake in not dedicating her to the stage."

"You've got me interested, Frau Kessler. What does she dance?"

"Everything and nothing. Have you heard of Isadora Duncan? She's not visited Russia yet, but there's a lot written about her! It's a new kind of art . . . a return of sorts to ancient dance. Manya also expresses all the movements of her soul, all her dreams, in dance. She dances unconsciously. But it's a creative activity. It's improvisation."

Manya had come back to life. Her sunken cheeks grew pink again and she laughed once more, her dimples flashing. Life beckoned her. Her dream of wondrous Hungary filled her days and nights.

Sonya learned Brahms's Hungarian dances, and after lunch Manya would move to their sounds through the dormitory in a madly wild dance, disheveled, cheeks and eyes ablaze, eliciting cries of delight from her classmates.

"That's what you'll dance," Frau Kessler told her. "That and something from your dreams . . . soft and aerial . . . to the adagio from the Moonlight Sonata."

Ah, what an evening! What rapture!

Forgetting the audience that filled the hall to capacity, responding to the sobbing sounds of Beethoven, Manya glided along the stage illuminated by the moon as a stageprop. Clad only in a tunic and sandals, she glided like a phantom, wringing her hands, stretching them skyward, to her distant dream. And her small, pale face, with its inspired eyes, was full of stupendous drama.

To the burst of unanimous, mad applause she ran backstage. Frau Kessler, radiant and triumphant, hurried after her into the washroom. She quickly unfastened the white tunic and threw a red one over her. All of it—both tunics, the inevitable tights, the sandals, the short light drawers and the batiste shirt, fine as silk—had been bought and sewn by Frau Kessler herself. It was also she who'd arranged Manya's luxurious braid into a Greek hairstyle, she who'd made up the girl's little face. And Manya had become a beauty.

There resounded the exotic sounds of Brahms's Hungarian dances, melancholy one moment and wild the next, conveying the despondency of solitude and the anguish of unrequited passion, the sweep and sizzling heat of the Asian desert.

From behind the curtain the girl ran rapidly onto the stage, and paused... She inclined forward, tense as a musical string, eyes shooting sparks... She seemed to be listening attentively to the wave of creativity gathering momentum within her soul...

A moment, and then she began to swirl, to whirl about on the stage, elusive, tireless, sparkling and bubbling with life... The pins spilled from her hair, and it fell loose, covering her shoulders. She resembled a rusalka* spinning in a gray mist above the swamp. She resembled a forest elf dancing on a moonlit night beneath an oak on the edge of the forest...

When she ran off backstage, she collapsed on the floor almost unconscious.

But the audience summoned her, called for her non-stop. Her name was on everyone's lips. The next day the whole town would be talking about her.

Pale and subdued, Pyotr Sergeyevich, who'd received a free ticket, sat in the first row. He was an aesthete at heart, an aesthete who, whatever his ascetic way of life and his harsh fate, was shaken and thrilled by the beauty he'd witnessed.

Who'd have expected such strength from little Manya? Yes—for surely such power over a crowd was strength? Such elemental ecstasy? Such an abundance of creativity? His own tears, which stung his eyes?

"This child is made for love and happiness," Frau Kessler told him.

"Thank God!" he thought. "Now she's got something to which she can devote her life and soul. She has somewhere to escape from love. And to find her happiness outside the stereotype. Let her go her own way! Art will set her free."

Petya wishes to send Manya to a theater school, but Anya, who hopes that Manya will study medicine, insists that she complete her general education. Manya's dancing triumph transforms her into the school idol and earns her the admiration of the class star, Sonya Gorlenko. The latter invites Manya to stay the summer at Lysogory, the Gorlenko family estate in Ukraine. When Manya expresses her horror at spending holidays in the dark, gloomy apartment where Petya and Anya tend to their demented mother, she is permitted, despite her poor exam performance, to join Sonya for the summer.

*As the two girls journey south by train and coach, Manya's imagination is fired by the bounties of the Ukrainian countryside. Sonya's mother, Vera Filippovna, and Petro the driver discuss the famine in the area, which the landowner Steinbach has attempted to alleviate. Because of Steinbach's recent illness, his son has been summoned from abroad. Sonya protests her mother's use of the anti-Semitic word "zhid" ("Yid") when referring to Steinbach's Jewishness. While Vera Filippovna ruminates on the gradual shrinkage of their family property, Manya finds herself falling passionately in love with Little Russia.**

Manya quickly came to feel at home in the idle, noisy household of the hospitable landowners. It was as if she'd been born "in a nest of gentlefolk."* The place continued to keep alive legends about the ferocious magnate, Vera Filippovna's grandfather. He'd kept his mistress, the wife of a neighboring petty estate owner whom he'd abducted, languishing in an underground vault in the depths of the forest. Manya was shown the extant remains of the underground prisons, with chains and grilles, for the members of the nobility who'd been found wanting. A hundred years ago people here had led such a dissipated, free, and wild life, which recalled the mores of the German robber barons!

Manya establishes close relations with Vera Filippovna's brother, Fyodor Filippovich, a stylish, cosmopolitan egotist, whose neighboring estate now belongs to Steinbach. As a "talented dilettante" in art and music, he teaches Manya and Sonya art, marveling at how different they are. Attracted to Manya, he paints her portrait.

The girls also learn about life on the estate. Local unrest erupts among the peasants and is reported in the papers. Sonya explains to Manya about how animals mate, and regales her with the story of her uncle's love for the family maid Oksana, whose pregnancy led to her dismissal from the estate.

Manya paled suddenly. Her troubled, awakening soul gazed out of her huge eyes.

"You think . . . Wait! I don't understand a thing. That means you think that people also . . . that love . . ."

Sonya blushed and turned away.

"I don't know, really. . . Perhaps, yes. . ."

"Quiet! Be quiet!" Manya cried violently. "No! No! It can't be! It shouldn't be! . . ."

"Stop it, Manya! Why are you crying?"

"Oh, why did you tell me about it? Why did you shatter my dreams? Oh, how repulsive! Now I don't want to love! I don't want to live! I can't stand to see your uncle!"

"Manya . . . Forgive me! Manya . . ."

"No! I don't believe you! After all, we're not animals, but people. It can't be! You hear me? It shouldn't be!"

Every evening Sonya and Manya would go to an elevated part of the estate grounds to enjoy and admire the sunset. Manya loved this time of day to distraction, when the colors glowed, only to become extinguished like a flame beneath ashes. And the southern night would fall quickly, without any dusk.

Wearing light dresses and with wreaths of cornflowers, their braids loosened, they'd sit on the hillock.

The sun was setting.

Suddenly there was the sound of distant hoofbeats. Someone was riding along the road. On the horizon, against the sun, the rider's silhouette seemed gigantic.

"Who is it?" Sonya asked in perplexity.

The rider drew near. He wore a sailcloth blouse, leggings, and strange headgear resembling a Greek warrior's helmet. His horse was a fine English thoroughbred. Drawing level with the hillock, the rider removed his helmet and proudly bowed to the girls.

A cry was torn from Manya's breast—a tremendous mad cry of terror and ecstasy!

She recognized the proud profile, the splendid brow, the implacable glance.

She leaped up. Her mad heart raced in pursuit of her nocturnal vision. Her hands seized her breast. . .

The rider disappeared. The sound of the horse's hoofbeats hung for a long time in the dust it had raised.

"How good-looking he is! Who could it be? Manya, dear, you surely can't be crying? Manya, dear, what's the matter with you?"

Manya had fallen face down on the dry hillock and was sobbing.

Back at school, Manya has a particular attachment to the many-windowed room in which Professor Wolf gives piano lessons.

She sat on the windowsill, her eyes raised, gazing at the last rays of the sun. Scarlet patches of light played on her dusky complexion, with the blushing down of an apricot. At sixteen, Manya had the same rebellious curls at her temples and brow. Her profile was irregular, her vivid mouth a trifle too generous. Her dark eyebrows flared in a capricious, uneven line, one arched higher than the other. But her dark eyes flashed and sparkled. And in that original face they were all one noticed.

Leaning against the door frame stood another girl, thin and dark, with burning eyes and a haggard face.

"Manya, I love you," she said softly, with adult passion. "Have pity on me! Give me a kiss! I've been begging you for one for so long. . ."

"Leave me alone! I don't like kissing. You know that."

The dark girl burst into passionate sobs and showered Manya with reproaches.

Manya kept silent until the last sun ray had vanished. She closed her eyes, so as to retain the reflection of the fiery disk in her mind's eye. Then, as if reminded of something annoying, she turned to the sobbing girl.

"I just don't understand you. Loving is happiness. And if I've given you this happiness, you shouldn't abuse me. But I don't love you. Don't cry! I don't love anybody. Did you ever see me chasing after any students? Worshipping any teachers? Then why do you want me to love you? Aren't you just like everyone else?"

"Sonya Gorlenko doesn't know how to love, yet you're friends with her!" the brunette shrieked jealously.

"Sonya doesn't torment me with kisses and jealousy the way you do. And I hate it when people are jealous of my feelings. What rights do you have over me?"

"My love!"

Manya laughed contemptuously.

"Surely I don't have to thank you for your love? I didn't ask for it, did I? I lived without it all those years, didn't I? Go away! If you can't love me from a distance the way others do, go away!"

"I won't survive! I'll die!" the brunette said, gesticulating hysterically.

"Then die!"

Manya's eyebrows, with their capricious sharp curve, arched over her flashing eyes. She turned away and once more gazed through the window.

That very night, when the girls in the boarding school were fast asleep in the dormitory, on their hard beds separated by the small closets, the thin, dark-haired girl with the haggard face and ardent eyes, dressed only in a nightgown, stole her way to the corner where Manya slept.

Her heart pounding, she fell soundlessly to her knees. . . After a long inner battle, with a stifled moan of passion, she pressed her lips to the scarlet lips of the half-open mouth. . .

Manya's face glowed with ecstasy. Her arms passionately twined themselves around the thin neck. Completely in the grip of her ardent dreams, she kissed her friend without opening her eyes.

"Oh, what bliss!" the blackhaired girl breathed, and, sapped of all strength, sank to the floor, covering her face with her hands, as if blinded by lightning.

At that moment Manya awoke. Propping herself on her pillows, trembling with revulsion, she gazed on the girl's bent head without hearing her whispered words or tears. Manya's eyes were full of sorrow and affront. . .

The caress intended for her life's dream had come from a wretched girl, who'd stolen it in Manya's sleep.

They'd already read everything on the quiet: Zola, Prevost, Loti, Knut Hamsun, Przybyszewski, *Homo Sapiens*, and *Pan** had made an especially strong impression. The blinders had been removed. There was no mystery now. At least in theory. For those who had married sisters, like Lina Fyodorova, everything was already simple. And with revulsion they talked about how little poetry there was in marriage! How bored their sisters were with marriage! How, with the first child, the horizon closed in for a woman.

"I'll never marry!" Manya said. "What filth all these relations are! Especially if you fall out of love. I can't even imagine it! To have children . . . one . . . five. . . No! I'm going to go on the stage. I'm so disillusioned with love that I'll never fall in love!"

The bucolic scene in the glen haunted her, especially at night in her sleep. That repellent mystery of nature, which she had secretly espied. Ah! It was absurd to call it a mystery, when everything was done so openly, without any shame! But she constantly kept seeing those images, and awaking with her heart pounding . . . all heated and tormented. . .

Sonya also decided to pay no attention to men. She was dreaming of signing up for courses and was angry at Manya for her dreams. To go on the stage, and, moreover, as a dancer! It was shameful! Who respected dancers? Who went to look at them! Old men and officers! Was it really worth devoting your life to that?

For a class assignment, Manya writes a composition on the topic of "a scene from classical life" that pits the worth of an individual life against ageless Beauty in Art. When the teacher reads her composition aloud, Sonya angrily attacks the notion of

Art's superiority and champions the value of human life, "à la Tolstoy." A parallel argument later takes place among the schoolteachers themselves.

My God! What a scandal!

They wanted to expel Manya. The headmistress's favorite, the nurse Maria, found an album with caricatures of the teachers and administrators. The drawings were so talented that it was impossible not to recognize the faces. And it was difficult to restrain one's laughter.

At the meeting of the pedagogical council the album passed from hand to hand, and they all bit their lips, shaking their heads. The headmistress sniffed smelling salts. She was outraged that the inspector was powerless to do anything to defend his pet. And only the fact that Manya had just one year of studies left prevented her expulsion. But her diploma would be ruined. For behavior she would receive only ten out of twelve points, the fatal "good" instead of "excellent." The door to teaching would be closed to her. She wouldn't be accepted either as a boarding school teacher or as a class matron.*

Anna Sergeyevna wept bitterly.

"What paltry ideals she has!" Manya thought.

"Anichka, that's enough!" she said to her sister. "It's not as though I ever dreamed of becoming a class matron. Ha! Ha! What do I need that paper for? I'll conquer life even without it."

If it weren't for the tears shed by Anya, whom she loved and pitied, the whole incident would only have been funny.

But Petya said nothing. Not a word of reproach. Ah, how interesting and wonderful Petya was! She loved him profoundly, much more than she did Anya. There were a lot of people like Anya. . .

Both Manya and Sonya start frequenting the apartment of Lina Fyodorova, who, upon graduating from high school, had spent the summer in Switzerland and now is enrolled in the Higher Courses.* Groups of young people who meet at Lina's discuss new ideas. Manya and Sonya deliver packages for her, presumably containing political propaganda, and Sonya constantly criticizes Manya for her flightiness in the midst of political change. Lina and her brother are jailed, demonstrations take place in the streets, and the high school becomes invaded by delegates as the country experiences large-scale unrest. Fearing for his sister's safety, Petya arranges to have Manya and Sonya move in with Frau Kessler's brother, a married doctor. One day, after the girls help to erect a barricade across the street, an old man is killed in the shooting that ensues. As the girls listen in the darkness of night, they hear bold footsteps in the empty streets.

Who was coming? Who dared to walk openly that night, when even the walls didn't offer people reassuring protection?

The girls involuntarily grabbed each other's hands and huddled together . . .

Rapid steps. . . Closer. . . Someone young and daring was walking with a buoyant step. . . Someone full of strength . . .

And suddenly the night trembled as a powerful baritone unexpectedly resounded beneath the windows . . .

"And you'll be tsaritsa of the world . . .

The first friend . . ."

Tra-ta-ta-ta . . . cracking sounds punctuated the darkness. Catty-corner from them sparks flashed, then went out. . . There was a resounding ring as a corner window shattered, and with a dry crack the bullet hit the wall of the room.

The girls fell to the floor . . .

A moment passed . . . another. . . Perhaps half an hour?

The night was silent. Blind and treacherous, it concealed betrayal and death.

The city slept . . .

Life becomes less violent, but Manya often dreams of that night with the bold singer and wonders who he was. In the summer the two girls return to the Gorlenko estate in Lipovka, where signs of political and social protest have also appeared.

Again the lofty sky . . . and the black night . . . and enormous stars blinking like eyes . . .

But here, on earth, everything had undergone an elusive change: the estate owner's mood, relations with the workers and neighbors, even intimate life. The flower garden was overgrown with weeds. There were no longer any roses. The gardener had been discharged. Beauty was not on people's minds. The wonderful fruit orchard was rented out. Some strangers or other, the children of the renter, scampered about the orchard and gaped beneath the windows.

Alarm was in the air. People tried to stifle it, but it persisted. It gazed from the hostess's eyes and the host's confused gestures. As before, he spent entire days in the field, dressed in a landowner's jacket and high boots. But now he not only didn't change clothes for dinner, but often would sit down at table without remembering to wash his hands. And only Uncle, correct as ever, *tirés à quatre épingles,* as the French say, fastidiously looked askance at his dirty nails.

Vera Filippovna was indifferent. Life had become so hard! That Steinbach, the deceased owner's heir, had hardly arrived in the area when the masses seemed to turn rabid. He raised the prices so high that there were no working hands. They had to treat the peasants carefully, and it was far from easy to get along with them now! Now the landowners had to look over their shoulders and think before speaking. And who could say what all the dissatisfaction that had accumulated would lead to? "Jacquerie,"* Uncle predicted darkly. It was fine for him to joke when he had nothing to lose! And then there were all those newspapers! The duma!* Talk of land. . . Surely they wouldn't actually take everything from the nobility? Ruin them? Beggar them? . . .

Worries prevented the landowners from sleeping well.

"Don't go too far from the house, girls," Vera Filippovna asked. "All kinds of people are roaming the streets. You could be accosted. . ."

But Manya waited for the horseback rider on the estate grounds every evening. She would sit on the hill, gazing into the distance. And her entire soul was in that gaze. . .

A series of suspect fires break out in the area, but no culprits are identified. The governor visits Lysogory, and during an after-dinner discussion, Sonya's father, Gorlenko, displays his conservatism and anti-Semitism, whereas Sonya's uncle demonstrates his liberal leanings. The atmosphere grows increasingly tense, and relations between Gorlenko and his workers worsen, as do Manya's with Sonya. Manya is fascinated by Izmail, nicknamed Zyama, a local incarcerated for political activity at Kiev University, now released from prison.

The sun had set. Manya and Sonya were going home from a distant part of the estate grounds. The wind that had started blowing as the sun set scattered the sounds of their light steps. At the empty drying shed, which was open wide but still permeated with the aroma of last year's tobacco, stood Zyama. At his side stood a small, frail-looking blond. Like Gorlenko, he was dressed in a jacket and tall boots. He wore a student's service cap, but that proved nothing. It was the fashion. All the young fellows in the village wore the same kind of cap.

He had a purebred, refined face, with a virginal, light brown beard. The eyes of a poet. The small, white hands of a gentleman who'd never known hard labor.

"No, I like that kind of life," he was saying in Ukrainian. "I love flowers."

"But you don't know anything about gardening!" Zyama interrupted him in a sharp, gutteral voice, speaking in jargon.

"Why do you think that? I read a lot. At least I know enough to ward off suspicion. I'm studying the life of orchids right now." (Zyama gave an angry snort.) "No, it's interesting! Flowers have such complex lives! Such mysterious souls! Have you read Maeterlinck? Ah, yes, you don't like him. . ."

"Now's not the time to read that nonsense!" Zyama interrupted. And passion flared in his voice. "Ah, Yan, you really upset me! The city certainly changed you in those six months! I prayed for you. . . I was ready to kiss the hem of your clothes. . ."

"I don't need that, Izmail! I'm opposed to fetishism."

Zyama suddenly pricked up his ears. The girls were approaching, and though the tall forest of sharply scented hemp hid them from view, they could hear everything.

"I'm very tired," Yan said in his soft, almost feminine voice. "Don't judge me too harshly, Izmail! Not to have shelter for six months, every minute expecting arrest and death. . . You better than anyone else can understand my psychological state. I need to rest. Believe me, if not for Steinbach. . ."

"Yan! Quiet!"

Zyama seized his companion's arm in a grip like a vise. Keen as an animal's, his black eyes attempted to penetrate the gloom.

Two figures emerged from the dusk of the fields.

All four gave a start and stood motionless . . .

Yan raised his cap. Zyama didn't stir. With a soft exclamation the girls moved on, almost at a run.

"Who are those charming girls?" Yan asked pensively.

"Charming girls also have ears," Zyama responded through gritted teeth. "What did they hear? And what didn't they?"

Yan shook his head proudly.

"A woman can't be a traitor!" he said with conviction.

Uncle drove the ladies to Lipovka to look around the park, and at the castle, if the young owner was absent.

Midway there, between the two estates, was located the cursed spot. Not a single Ukrainian would venture past it at night. It was a small oak grove on the steep slope of a muddy precipice. Once the corpse of someone who'd been strangled was discovered there. No one recognized him, and whether he'd been killed or committed suicide remained a mystery. The body was buried at the edge of the grove, and a gloomy black cross erected above the anonymous grave.

When nightfall engulfed the sky in fire, the cross was starkly silhouetted, tall and gruesome, against the horizon, and seemed to loom even higher. When the moon silvered the steppe, one involuntarily recalled Gogol's "Terrible Vengeance"*—any moment the cross would sway and the corpse would rise from the grave. And with a howl it would raise its hands to the moon . . .

Beneath the hill was a ravine, also an accursed spot. A pond was there now, where formerly there had been a river. With a forest of reeds, cold springs, and deep, treacherous pits on the bottom. But there was nowhere to bathe except in the pond, and so every year children and livestock drowned in it.

The carriage stopped at the railing to the park.

"Can we go in?" Uncle asked the guard.

The latter removed his cap and energetically rushed to assist the generous landowner.

"The owner's away?" Uncle asked, adjusting his clothes.

"We're expecting him any moment, your grace. He's expected back from Kiev. Excuse me. . . You can't go into the castle now. But you're welcome to walk in the park!"

Manya instantly lost the power of speech. She hadn't imagined it possible that such buildings were to be found in the backwaters of Little Russia.

"The architect was an Italian. It's the eighteenth-century style," Uncle explained. "Girls, do you remember the painter Borisov-Musatov?* I showed you his work in a journal last year. He used to paint palaces like these in the distance, between the walls of hundred-year-old tree-lined walks."

The entire linden-lined alley leading to the house was carpeted with flowers. In the middle of it water spurted from a fountain decorated with horns that held a smiling marble nymph.

"Can we go in the greenhouse?" Uncle asked.

"Please do. The new gardener will show you around."

"Ah, girls, you should see the orchids here! The late Steinbach was a man of taste. He loved everything rare. He bought this house from the Nelidovs when they lost all their possessions. Everything was neglected. Tall weeds used to grow here instead of these carnations and gillyflowers. And now the park has such marvelous exotic blooms! To think that the person who acquired all this splendor doesn't even live here. He's more of a visitor!"

"Where does he live, then? Where?"

"He's a cosmopolitan, Manichka. One day in Moscow, another in Venice, yet another in London. Lucky man! I don't envy anyone the way I do him. Watch out for your hearts, girlies, if you should ever meet him! He's handsome. . . To the point of unpleasantness. . ."

"Handsome? You haven't seen him, have you, Uncle?"

"Just once. At a dinner party given by the old man, the late Steinbach."

"He's a Yid," Manya said, wrinkling her nose. "Yids can't be handsome."

"Obscurantist!" Uncle laughed and shook a threatening finger at her.

The light inside the hothouse was pleasantly dim. The scent of some flowers made the air stuffy. The gardener was busy, squatting over some tub.

"Hey, there, my good man!" Uncle said superciliously, drawling the words. "Where are the orchids?"

The gardener looked around and rose to his feet. He had a refined face with a light brown, virginal beard, the eyes of a poet, and the small, white hands of a gentleman who'd never known hard labor.

Manya's eyes dilated, the pupils diffused with excitement. She poked Sonya with her elbow, and her friend blushed deeply. She also recognized the stranger.

"Follow me," he said softly and peremptorily, and led the way.

What wonders! Blossoms shaped like slippers quivered on tall stems. It looked as though butterflies of all colors were dozing over the flower pot, as though strange, alien, gigantic insects had attached themselves to a branch. . . They looked like anything but flowers! The most whimsical fantasy could not have created such mysterious shapes, such diverse colors.

In a gentle voice, his small hands gesturing absently, the gardener told them about the various species, calling each type by its Latin name. He spoke beautifully and poetically, describing the distinctive features of the mysterious plants as if he were revealing the dark soul of these flowers. Uncle was astonished. In mute excitement, the girls kept their eyes fixed on the gardener's face.

"You talk about flowers as though they're people," Sonya observed quietly.

His own eyes seemed to shine as they gazed simply and directly into hers.

"Yes. For me, they're closer than people," he replied.

Uncle was embarrassed. The change that he had prepared as a tip jingled quietly as he let it drop back into the bottom of his pocket.

"You're a recent arrival here?"

"Yes," the answer sounded reluctant and cold.

They stood a moment longer, at a loss. Uncle was the first to raise his panama respectfully.

"Thank you!" Sonya said timidly.

With a gesture full of dignity the gardener touched his cap. And he stood motionless, watching them leave.

"Mikolay Sergeyich! Where are you? Mikolay Sergeyich!" shouted a boy running up to the hothouse. "You're wanted in the office. Khfyodor's come from town with the seeds . . ."

"Coming."

With eager eyes Uncle and the girls watched the man called both Yan and Mikolay Sergeyevich cross the yard with a light, elastic step. Small, graceful, fragile . . .

"What a delight!" Manya said. "You can tell, can't you, that he's a prince in disguise?"

And they laughed unrestrainedly as they recalled Uncle's summons, "Hey, my good man!"

"At times I think we're not alive, but asleep. And we have dreams," Manya said in the park. "Don't you agree, Uncle? This 'prince'. . . And then there's our worker Iskra. Have you noticed him? He's also in disguise. And don't you think that this is only a prelude to some sort of enchanting spectacle?"

Uncle quietly pinched her cheek.

"Clever girl! No question! Only let's hope the devils don't carry us all off in this enchanting spectacle!"

For an hour they roamed around the park, admiring the trees. The huge crypt with Steinbach's grave captured Manya's imagination. It was an Indian pagoda of sorts, with a marble facade and a pyramid of flowers inside. Wreaths made of silver, porcelain, laurel, palm branches, with ribbons and inscriptions, hung on the wall. In the depths was a full-length portrait of the deceased, with orders, both Russian and foreign, on his chest. It was an arrogant, shaven face with a predatory profile and thick, arching eyebrows. The perceptive and young eyes, which seemed alive, followed all the strangers' movements.

"A good portrait!"

"And an interesting face!" Manya said.

They all involuntarily lowered their voices.

"Yes, he was a prominent man. A plebeian, but a talented one, who owed everything exclusively to his own efforts. And he was an exceptional personality. He had control over the whole region. And he did a lot of good. You should have seen his funeral! The entire district came to the funeral reception. The governor from Chernigov, many journalists from Kiev, landowners. . . Yes, he knew how to live, and he lived to the full. He loved women, my dears, was a real connoisseur of them. And he was in love with this estate, he squandered about a million on it. What a pity we can't go inside the castle. He has a small cabinet of carved oak there with a depiction of the Annunciation. Work from the thirteenth century, a church piece. Bazilevsky offered him half a million for it, but he refused to give it up."

They slowly walked around the pond, big as a lake, with little islands, bridges, and swans.

"I'm tired. Let's sit down!" Uncle said.

"Shh! Someone's singing!" Manya whispered. "Perhaps it's something from an enchanting spectacle again?"

They waited. . . Footsteps sounded on the gravel. Light, decisive, full of an elusive rhythm.

Around the turn screened by the thick trees, about fifty feet from the bench, a woman was walking along the tree-lined path. She was singing a long love song in a clear, true voice.

"Now she'll stop," Uncle thought. "She'll see us and be embarrassed."

Imperceptibly, he drew himself upright. His eyes gazed penetratingly at the stranger.

But she continued to sing as she approached. Small, thin as a girl, with short curly hair and a pale face. "Chiffonne," Uncle instantly labeled her. She had a short upper lip and her small teeth gleamed rapaciously. Her large light blue eyes were narrowed contemptuously.

Utterly ignoring the trio seated on the bench, she continued to sing as if she were alone in the park. Not a single facial muscle moved when she rounded the turn onto the straight tree-lined path. She didn't speed up as she drew closer to the bench. Pronouncing the words of love coldly and clearly, she slowly passed by them in her old skirt and chintz blouse. Pensive and distant . . . as if shut off by a glass wall from the people who were superfluous to her. And her small footsteps were as firm and rhythmic as before. Her face was as calm, her high voice as true.

She vanished from view at the next turn.

"Isn't she something!" Uncle said, comically throwing up his hands. Although they all laughed, they felt uncomfortable.

The stranger had made an impression.

"How magnificent she is!" Manya laughed.

"No! I like her!" Sonya said. "You have to have a lot of courage to walk by people you don't know like that. Anyone else would have fallen silent in her place."

"Uh-huh. Evidently to her we're not people."

In his heart of hearts Uncle was unpleasantly impressed.

"How are we worse than she? How?" Manya was angry.

"Bourgeois, ma chère! That's clear."

Sonya flushed. Manya clapped her hands.

"What do you think, Uncle, who is she?"

"I think she's the new medical assistant at Steinbach's hospital. I heard that she'd arrived. A Ukrainian."

"That's probably right," Sonya whispered.

They made their way back to the carriage, which was waiting for them behind the cast-iron grating.

Ah, what a railing! How beautiful were its dark, severe lines and the gilded coat of arms at the top!

"This is what I appreciate about the old man. He didn't succumb to fashion. He didn't put up a railing in the style moderne. You know, my dears, where this design is from? All the ancient castles in France are enclosed by exactly such a railing. The Tuilleries, Versailles . . ."

The guard suddenly removed his cap respectfully. A figure had emerged from the lower story of the castle and slowly, like a phantom, made its way along the flower garden awash in the rays of the setting sun.

They saw a strange, deathly white face with a dark curly beard as long as Moses's. Silver threads of gray hair gleamed in it and at his curly temples. There was a velvet cap on his head. He had the regular, refined features of a rare beauty. His bloodless hands rested on a cane, and his head was bent. A long, black, tightly buttoned frockcoat covered his tall, bony, stooped body and he wore shoes.

The man's whole figure seemed lifeless, impassive and remote, as though he were a wax doll. His gait bespoke aimlessness.

"Ben-Akiba?" Manya whispered.

"Worse. The eternal Jew*. . ."

Manya could not explain the strange premonition that seized her. The dark figure moving indifferently along the flower garden flooded with sunlight beneath the scarlet rays of the sunset, amid that glittering beauty—the contrast was frightful!

When he drew level with them, he raised his eyes. Those enormous eyes—black as though bottomless, without sheen or awareness—rested for a moment on Manya's face. It was only a moment, yet she winced. Her eyes followed the dark figure, hunched over, as if crushed by the invisible phantom of grief resting on its shoulders. She had seen these eyes before. . . Yes, yes! Strange as it was, she'd already seen them somewhere.

"Who is that?" Sonya asked in a whisper as they got into the carriage.

"That's young Steinbach's uncle. The brother of his late mother. And the nephew looks amazingly like him! A really romantic figure, don't you think?"

"Uncle, dear, why are his eyes like that? Why is he so . . ." (Sonya searched for the right word.) "lifeless? Did you notice how he walks? He's not like us."

"No wonder. You're right in your observation. His entire family was killed in Odessa in a pogrom. And he went mad. . ."

Manya paled. She tried to grasp something, to recall something. . . And the black wings of melancholy descended on her soul. They were silent the whole way back.

An irresistible force draws Manya to the Steinbach estate. She takes to visiting a ramshackle summerhouse on the edge of the park, quite close to the cross, from which the grounds are visible and where she dreams and at night reads her favorite poems by Baudelaire, Verlaine, and de Musset in the original. From that vantage point she overhears an argument between Zyama and Roza, a fellow "revolutionary." Roza initially criticizes Zyama's attachment to Yan, but after Zyama lists Yan's activities against the privileged class, Roza worriedly predicts Yan's imminent doom.

Manya became emaciated in one week. Her eyes grew large and blazed feverishly. She was in love.

Yes! Yes! Strange as it might seem, if love means dreaming about another day and night... If love is a yearning to hear his voice, see his face, hands, and movements... If love is a yearning to be together and to tear away the darkness jealously concealing from us the other's soul, then this was, indeed, love...

For the first time, the face of the stranger riding along the road a year ago at sunset and the angel's face with the implacable gaze paled and were overshadowed by another face, purebred and refined, with the eyes of a poet.

Now Manya needed to see Yan. No matter what it cost! She needed to speak with him. She would go to Lipovka, directly to the greenhouse, and would say... What would she say?

In the meantime she sat at the cross in the cursed spot, on the edge of the grove. From there she could see the roofs of the castle and everyone who drove or walked to the estate. With a book in her hand, she lay on the grass and inwardly willed Yan to come out from behind the railing.

All was quiet. Only the geese were making their creaky sounds, the white splotches of their bodies spread in the mud of the ravine. The water of the pond, overgrown with swamp weeds, sparkled brightly. The black of the half-broken cross showed clearly against the pale blue sky.

Deeply sunk in reverie, Manya did not hear the light footsteps in the grove. Suddenly she looked around and uttered a cry... Yan stood before her.

"Did I frighten you? Forgive me!" he said, removing his cap and giving her a worldly bow.

She sat up and pulled her skirt over her black-stockinged legs, which had been exposed to the knees. Her cheeks were brightly flushed. Her eyes resembled stars. And Yan was taken with this beauty.

"No... Yes... You did. I expected you to come from there!"

She nodded in the direction of the estate.

"You were expecting me?"

Yan's faltering voice expressed endless surprise. His eyes darkened and a slight flush burned in his cheekbones.

And Manya didn't know where to hide from shame. But suddenly she laughed unrestrainedly with her characteristic boldness. And, gazing into Yan's eyes, she said: "Yes... I've been expecting you for a long time. Sit!"

Yan sat down with a smile.

"What a marvelous, marvelous smile!" she thought.

A long pause ensued. Greedily, naively, Manya examined his face, hands, ears, lips, and nostrils. Everything about him appealed to her. Everything! He looked like a fragile shepherd made of Sèvres china. At first he was embarrassed at her curiosity. Then, still smiling, he started to examine her face and figure.

She laughed freely. Her laughter was clear, sparkling, bubbling with life.

"She's like a wave shattered by an oar on a sunny day. When every scale glimmers and sparkles with gold," Yan thought.

"I'm waiting," he said quietly. And his voice was so caressing that Manya felt as though he had touched her cheek.

"I know who you are!" she said solemnly.

"I know who you are, too. . ."

"No, I don't mean that. I know your secret. . ."

It was a good thing that not a single muscle in his face twitched at her words!

"You're a prince in disguise! Ha! Ha! And your name's Yan."

He continued to smile. But his eyes narrowed and grew cold as metal. Bravo! Others would have lost color, but not he. He could not be like everyone else!

"Ah! I know something else about you. Something absolutely incredible. You're a robber chief and are alive only by a miracle. . ."

They gazed into each other's eyes without saying a word.

Suddenly Manya hugged her knees and rested her head on them. In a pleading voice, her soul dimmed, she said, like a provincial child: "Don't be angry with me! I overheard it by chance. Izmail was speaking with Roza and I didn't understand everything. But when I heard your name . . . I couldn't not listen. But don't be afraid of me! I know how to keep quiet. No one knew what I was dreaming of either in childhood or now in high school. Or what I want. . . You're not angry? You're not, are you?"

She extended her hand. With the same smile Yan gave her his.

"Oh, what a marvelous touch!" she thought.

"I'd really like us to get to know one another. Do you want to?" she asked in impassioned tones. "Come here every day! I'll wait for you. All right? Ah, if you knew how I was dreaming of meeting you! What joy that you've come! But it makes no difference! If you hadn't come here now, tomorrow I'd have gone myself to the greenhouse. Come on, sit down! Closer! Why are you looking at me like that, Yan? Ah, yes! Can I call you that?"

"When we're alone," he said, smiling.

Her arm in the muslin sleeve, bared to above the elbow, a thin and swarthy girlish arm, unconsciously reached out to him. And he, also unconsciously, obeyed the pull of an irresistible attraction. Taking her hand, he held it in his, softly squeezing it.

A happy sigh escaped Manya's breast.

"You must know me, surely?" Manya suddenly asked. "Do you?"

"Yes," he replied in a whisper.

"Who am I? Who?"

"You? A fairy tale . . ."

She laughed in delight.

"I knew you during my childhood when I read Andersen. And I still like to read him."

"I do, too. Do you remember the fairy tale 'Rusalka'? You're like the prince in disguise."

"I lack his cruelty. I couldn't break Rusalka's heart."

"Really? You really aren't cruel? Is that so?"

"No, I'm not."

Manya was a trifle disillusioned.

"How's that possible? Yes. . . So how can Izmail say that the gallows are awaiting you? What for? That means you've not killed anyone?"

"I killed people out of necessity, defending myself. The way people kill in any war."

Manya gave a sigh of satisfaction.

"Did you kill many people? A lot of them?"

Yan smiled.

"No, really . . . How many?"

"What a child you are! I didn't count."

Manya was satisfied. It was a genuine criminal facing her, without any falsification.

"Izmail, now, is cruel! I don't like him," she said completely illogically. "Poor Roza!"

For a long time they didn't say a word, caressing each other with their eyes, smiling trustingly with joy. A profound silence surrounded them, as happens only in the steppe. Only the sound of the water splashing and the geese's creaky calls reached them from time to time.

"How nice it is!" Manya blurted out.

"How old are you?" he asked, without releasing her hand.

"I'll soon be eighteen. I'll graduate in a year. And I'll come here. Will you be here in a year?"

"I don't know."

He looked sad. Manya's heart contracted.

"Is your mother alive, Yan?" she asked quietly.

"Yes."

Sadness was audible in his voice. Oh, what sadness!

"Do you love her?"

"I've caused her a lot of grief. And she doesn't believe in my love. . ."

Manya grew pensive. She recalled her own childhood. The face of a lovely woman tenderly leaning over her. Then, through an elusive association, her memory conjured up the bloodless face of the dark phantom floating soundlessly along the tree-lined walk in Lipovka. Why did she recall him? How strange!

With an involuntary shudder she drew her hand over her eyes.

Somewhere the clock on a church tower chimed, the sounds carrying monotonously.

Yan got up. His face and eyes looked different now. He shyly kissed Manya's hand. And her breath caught fire from happiness.

"We need to go our separate ways, Maria . . . Maria . . ."

"No! No! Call me Manya!"

"Izmail will be here any moment. I don't want him to see us. You'll go this way. . . Come on, I'll show you."

"Will you come tomorrow? Will you? For sure? When?"

"At the same time," he replied softly.

Joining hands, they walked along.

"Good bye, Manya," he said.

"Until tomorrow, Yan! 'Til tomorrow!"

Oh, what a marvelous life! It was a waking dream. They were together every day from two until four. The secrecy drew them closer together. Manya kept her word. Even Sonya could not understand what filled her soul and days, why the expression on her face had changed so much.

Now they would sit side by side, shoulder to shoulder. And they constantly talked of literature. Yan would bring books and read out loud. He had a very distinctive way of reading—chanting the words rhythmically and monotonously—but the effect was of something unreal, remote, and full of sorrow. And Manya appreciated it.

Yan liked only the modernists—of the poets, he preferred Briusov and Blok. All of it was new to Manya. Now she read *The Crossing* and *The Golden Fleece** and, like Yan, she found other journals boring.

"Are you reading *Sanin*?"* she asked once, interrupting his reading.

"Oh, yes. With great interest. What about you?"

"We're also reading it on the sly. The family subscribes to the journal. Fortunately, the older folks haven't got to the novel yet. They don't have time to read in the summer. And Uncle is only interested in the classics. You know, I hate Sanin! He's such an animal!"

"I see a brilliant protest against fossilized moral values in the book, Manya. And as such the novel has social significance."

"Sonya is so strange! She argues that Sanin respects women!"

"It's true. There's more said in defense of the individual there than in all West European literature. Your Sonya interests me."

"Can we sit like this?" Manya asked once, and laid her head on his shoulder.

Yan shyly put his arm around her and she clearly heard his heart pounding.

The book lay forgotten on the grass, while, eyes closed, they listened to their souls.

Another time Manya placed her hand on *The Golden Fleece*, as if to say: enough reading!

"I want to ask you . . ." she whispered.

"Ask!"

"Have you ever loved anyone, Yan? Have you loved anyone the way . . . Phall* loved women?"

"No," was the firm, tender response. "Never!"

"Ach! That's so good! I felt it. You're not like him. What happiness! Yan! Kiss me!"

On an uncontrollable impulse she flung her thin arms around his neck and, closing her eyes, raised her face to his.

He tenderly kissed her cheek. Timid though this contact, it burned her. With a cry she fell, face down, on the grass. And tears of happiness gushed from her eyes.

"Manya . . . Dear Manya! Did I . . . disillusion you?" he asked in fear.

Her fine brows arched in a mournful, sharp curve. He tried to force her around to face him.

"No! No! I love you, Yan! Oh, how I love you!" she said. And with selfless passion, as naive and primitive as a bird's song, she nestled against his chest.

In Yan's bright, clean room Zyama sat at the window, nervously biting his nails.

It had rained, and his dirty boots have left tracks on the floor. That depressed him. He loathed this cleanliness, in the midst of which he felt alien. Even more than that, Yan's habits, his high degree of culture, behind which Zyama saw the whole span of his past life, mysterious, full of experiences about which Zyama knew nothing, indescribably irritated him. He called these habits lordly. And he infused this word with all the bile of his restless soul.

Yan was late. He was the one who'd specified when Zyama should come, so why wasn't he there?

A young owl sat on a perch in the corner. Each time Zyama moved, the owl started tilting its round head, with its feline face, from right to left and back again. It was as though it were sneering at him, the miserable thing! Its unseeing yellow eyes gazed persistently at the visitor without blinking. And Zyama felt terrible.

Yan came in, his cloak wet, but his eyes were shining with rapt joy. Just one glance at his eyes made Zyama's heart contract. How acutely painful! Why was Yan happy? And why didn't he say anything? Zyama would have liked to be the one to account for all the joys in Yan's life. And now he was suffering.

"I dirtied your floor. Forgive me!" he said gloomily, biting his nails.

"It doesn't matter. We'll have some tea!" Yan replied affectionately. And he called the teenage Gritsa, who put on the samovar in the entrance hall.

Yan walked over to the owl, stroked its head, and placed the bird on his shoulder.

"Where did you get this good-for-nothing?" Zyama asked.

"Oh, that's a whole story! I have insomnia and the owls keep calling at night. Strange as it might seem—imagine!—I'm afraid of the owls' night calls! I'm a mystic by nature. In short, my nerves were so affected by the noise that I decided to shoot them. And I did. I hit this poor thing. She's still very young. But when I heard her struggling in the grass—you won't believe it, Izmail, but I felt so sorry for her. I brought her home. She was hit in this foot. I took care of her and now she's domesticated and doesn't want to leave."

"What sentimentality!" Zyama's lips twisted.

"What can I do! I really love animals. Hunting, like any other pointless killing, is repulsive to me."

"And do you love people, Yan?" Zyama asked thickly.

"Yes, only not the current generation. I love those of the future, daring, free, and harmonious. But I do love children."

There was a long silence.

"Where did you get the Baudelaire?" Zyama asked, hostile fingers touching the book in its sumptuous binding, with gilt-embossed initials.

"From Steinbach's library. He gave me the keys to it. It's a very valuable library, Izmail. I love reading in that room. Do you want me to show it to you? There I'm in the company of an aristocracy of the spirit—the only aristocracy that shouldn't be rejected. By the way, I need to exchange this book for another one."

Zyama shrugged his shoulders with hatred.

"You don't want to come with me?" Yan asked coldly. "If you're not interested, I don't insist."

"No, why not? Let's go."

Yan and Zyama talk in Steinbach's sumptuous library. Yan reminds Zyama about the need for absolute secrecy in their conspiracy. He also warns Zyama not to dismiss the Steinbach family and especially the son, Mark, to whom he owes his life and who is underwriting his book. Yan admits that terror is sometimes a necessary evil, but it's more important to fight with ideas and not individuals. He wants to create, while Zyama is drawn to violence and vengeance.

Manya had just left the grove. Zyama was already waiting for Yan in the conservatory, where Yan had gone to water the flowers.

"How much money do you need for the commune?" he asked somewhat grudgingly, leaning against the door and looking scornfully at this kingdom of bright colors.

"A great deal, Izmail. Around five hundred rubles is needed at the start, I think."

"When the money's here, let's go to America, Yan! Or to England. Ah, it's so hateful for me here. It's been that way all my life."

"No, Izmail! I want to create a kingdom of love and peace right here in your charming homeland. The Ukrainians are so poetic. Their souls are so easily set afire. It will be my first experiment. Then I'll move on."

"But you shouldn't stay here!"

"Why? No one here knows me."

They were silent for a long time. One could hear the water gurgle in the pump and the faded flowers greedily drinking it up.

"But why do you like Steinbach?" Zyama asked as if they had been speaking only of Steinbach.

"He has a beautiful soul. The soul of an Aryan. I don't like the Jewish soul, Izmail. There are many such souls among us Christians. And you must know what I mean by this."

"A soul? Ha!" Zyama interjected bitterly. "Does Steinbach have a soul? I doubt it! If the soul is the presence of faith, temperament, and convictions, then he has none! I'm telling you! In his youth he was a Zionist and during the revolution he joined the SDs."*

"He's still an SD."

"Ha! Then why doesn't he treat us as the enemy?"

"Leave that question to me, too, Izmail! Be consistent!"

"What SD would give us so much money? And I know that Nadezhda Petrovna . . ."

"Who?!"

"It doesn't matter." Zyama flushed visibly and waved his hand. "Anna Nikolayevna also counts on him, and she apparently has nothing to do with the SDs."

"She's a Bakuninist,*" Yan interjected gently and pensively.

"Are you laughing at me, Yan? What sort of SD would risk his hide to shelter a Bakuninist who's being hunted throughout the district?"

Yan thoughtfully explains to Zyama that he values Steinbach's indecisiveness and melancholy, for such types harbor a creative potential missing in goal-oriented men. Zyama, just such a goal-oriented man, declares Steinbach a bankrupt libertine, and leaves.

"Do you like Hamsun?"* Manya asked.

"Very much . . ."

"You know, Yan, when I read *Pan*, I wanted to die. What a creature that Glahn* is!"

"Why?"

"If he loves Edvarda, then why does he fool around with Eva, the blacksmith's wife? Can you really love two people at the same time? He's even worse than Sanin, and Sanin didn't really love anybody. I need to ask you a question. . . Give me your hand! Do you hear how my heart is pounding?"

"I'm listening," he said hoarsely. And his eyes burned.

"Yan . . . are *all* of you like Glahn?"

"No, Manya. Not all."

"Dear Yan! That's wonderful! My soul was so bitter! There's nothing worse than doubt! I've dreamt of eternal love since I was a child. I wept over the poems about Toggenburg. I adore Dante for loving Beatrice. But then there's this Glahn, this Phall. That repulsive Karsavina, who is simply used like some object! And she's not upset about it, she doesn't protest, even though she loves another! I felt dirty. If *that's* love, then it's not worth living!"

He was silent and thoughtful for a long time, his fine brows knitted. There was such significance and silence in his face that Manya's heart fell in dread.

"Listen to me carefully, Manya! Humanity has blundered into a thick fog, and it's so used to the darkness that it fears the sun. It timidly hides itself behind the walls of a musty, dark temple and prays to old gods out of inertia. And then great artists appear who overturn the idols—often unconsciously, with a single stroke. They're tearing down the walls of the old temple. And there, up above, you'll see a piece of blue sky! Their feat is to boldly disperse the fog into which our souls have blundered and to shout to us: 'Here's the sun! Even if you're blinded by the pain, have the courage to live with your eyes open!' Yes, with one vivid book an artist will break the laws of conventional morality more surely than the philosophers and sociologists—sometimes not even knowing he's doing so. He speaks with the masses."

Yan quietly kissed Manya's hand. Her large anxious eyes gazed into his soul. Her own soul lay open to him like the fresh calyx of a flower.

"We're living through a strange epoch in the liberation of the flesh. This is the dawn of a new day. It's indubitably a revolution. The wave of revolt has surged. Not everyone acts like Glahn, Manya. But the difference lies only in temperament and worldview. The instincts are the same, and these do not lie. Prepare for a blow, my little Manya. There is no eternal love."

"Oh, Yan! Why?"

"It doesn't exist if we understand love as passion, as desire. The Greeks deliberately depicted Eros with wings. There's a profound meaning in this myth. Attachment remains. Passion passes away. Our desires are holy, but they have no *tomorrow*. Love can live on for years, evolving and changing, after it has lost its desires. But that which gave it color disappears, succumbing to mysterious and unfathomable laws. Glahn loves one woman and desires another, and in this there's no deceit, no vulgarity, no filth. Perhaps life will present you with the same dilemma, Manya. And if you're genuine and daring, then you'll do the same."

"No! What are you saying, Yan?"

"Open your eyes, Manya! Look up! The sectarian and the slave are speaking in you now, and for them the word 'freedom' is terrible. Oh, if I had a daughter like you! I'd keep her away from today's sentimental and false petty-bourgeois literature. I'd give her Knut Hamsun, Gejerstam, Maupassant, Boccaccio and the naive literature of the Middle Ages. With one blow I'd strip away her illusions in the bud, and so lead her to freedom. Yes, Manya, it's a thorny path! But it's the only way out of slavery!"

He said nothing for a long time. She whispered as she peered into his face:

"What are you thinking, Yan?"

"I feel the breath of a new morality. This force is being born somewhere in the sleeping depths of the human soul. A new world hovers before me. This world must be created!"

Manya and Yan continue to meet, and their feelings for each other intensify. Manya is the more demonstrative, Yan is reserved, trying to control his great passion for her. Yan is ecstatic that Steinbach has given him money so that he can arrange for "certain things." But he delays on Manya's account, waiting until she leaves. When his accomplice Zyama urges him to bed her rather than mentor her, Yan retorts:

"As a Semite, you scorn women and see them as sinful. It's hard for you, Izmail, to fight yourself and to respect the individual. But that's the foundation of the new edifice! How do you expect to build without that?"

"I don't want to build anything! I only want to destroy! . . . You go and build! But I'll clear a space for you on this earth. That's my mission."

"When this girl is with me," Yan said thoughtfully, "my whole soul trembles. Her way of thinking is a bright hymn to life. There's so much possibility and potential in her! I urge you to look in her eyes, Izmail! Have you noticed her capricious brows, and how her left eyebrow is higher than the right?"

Yan smiled dreamily and blushed, at that moment resembling a girl.

Zyama stood up with darkened face.

"This girl will be the death of you, Yan!" he said as he walked out.

Yan tells Manya that he's written his mother that he's alive, but he is wary of his mother's pity. Pity only enslaves the strong. He also tells Manya that he has finished his book, and in so doing has conquered death.

It was raining. Manya sat at the table in Yan's room. The towheaded, barefoot Gritsa had set up the samovar.

This boy loved Yan, and Manya loved him for it. Yan was teaching him reading and arithmetic. When Yan went into the village, the children crowded around him and begged him to tell them fairy tales.

Everyone feared and hated Zyama.

The curls at Manya's temples and nape had grown tighter from the damp. But her rosy cheeks had paled and even her eyes had dulled.

Gritsa left, having laid out the bread and milk.

"My fairy has been crying?" asked Yan, pressing her hands to his chest. "Do fairies even know what tears are? Rautendelein* didn't know how to cry until she fell in love."

"Oh, Yan, I feel bad! I didn't sleep last night. Sonya and I were talking about love again. And Sonya thinks and feels as I do. Of course, you're cleverer and, of course, you're right. But I can't feel any differently. I long for eternal and mutual love! I'll die if I'm disappointed by you, dear Yan. If I knew that some beautiful Ganna came to you at night, I'd never see you again!"

"No one comes here, Manya. Until I met you women had no place in my life."

"Yes?! Oh, Yan, look how my eyes are shining again! It's as if your smile made a stone fall from my heart."

"It's hard to liberate women, Manya!" Yan said sadly.

But she was not listening. She was too self-absorbed. Pressing herself to his chest, she whispered:

"And what is . . . debauchery?"

"The buying and selling of the body and affection, whatever kind of sanction society may give the transaction. . ."

"And what is infidelity, Yan?"

"There's only one infidelity, Manya. To oneself. And there's only one virtue—to do no one evil. But what is evil? If you fall out of love with me and fall in love with another, don't worry about my suffering! That's not evil to me. But if you deny your attraction, then you are doing evil to yourself. Manya, everything I'm telling you is only the basics of what should become a common truth. The earth keeps moving, and we're just mortals. But the real horror is that people renounce this truth even though they know and feel it... No one dares to take charge of their lives! People fight for power, money, political rights, and territory. Women fight for the right to work, for a voice in Parliament. No one thinks to break the chains on their soul in order to smash the chains on their lives. For a thousand years priests have forged these chains to enslave a free-born human being. And you women meekly love and kiss your chains. Manya, do you want to be mistress of your life?"

"Oh, yes, Yan! Teach me! I so want to be happy!"

"Good. I'll give you the keys to happiness. Happiness lies behind seven seals. And poor humankind lost the way to it long ago... Listen, Manya. The most valuable things in us are our passions, our dreams. Pitiful is he who denies them! Out of fear of public opinion, that is, the opinion of people who are remote and alien to us; out of a feeling of duty to one's dear ones; out of love for children and family we all trample and disfigure our souls, which are eternally young, eternally changing, in which mysterious and plaintive voices resound. One must heed and believe only these voices. *One must be oneself!* Oh, don't think it's that simple! From your very first steps, when your little body is still wrapped in diapers, loving people are already diapering your awakening soul. The Hindus disfigure the newborn's skull in order to give it the perfect shape. The Chinese disfigure women's feet. We, cultured people, do the same with a child's soul. From the very first day an iron hand lies on your breast, and you can't remove it until your dying hour. You don't dare to flee this guardianship. Everything is calculated and foreseen for you, everything is decided and fitted into set frames. You're given a name, you're chosen a school, your profession is predicted, your convictions decided, your path set. This is a broad well-beaten path, everyone's path. And once you've understood yourself, when you've realized your own calling, it's too late! You can't begin again! And you apathetically walk along the path laid out for you, fatally repeating others' mistakes. And when you suddenly look around, your youth is gone. Your strength has disappeared. Such is life."

"Yan! This is terrible! I don't want such a life! It's slavery."

"Little Manya, you felt this. Keep up your protest and respect your agitation! It's the key to liberation! Don't give up your dreams and desires out of fear or duty or compassion! Let them stone you for the fact that you dare to speak, feel, and act outside of convention! Let them vilify your name! Follow the road you've chosen and don't be afraid to be alone! It makes no difference if the one you've left behind perishes from loving you! Move forward to the promised goal: to creativity, art, science, beauty. Don't let your soul shudder from shame or repentance! Remember: this is just the clank of old chains. If you kiss me in the morning, and in the evening your desire drives you into another's arms, heed your desire! Know that the liberation of the flesh is the door into the temple of freedom, where gods and ideals higher than the cult of love await you. These are bright and joyful gods unknown to the woman enslaved by passion. Remember this, above all: Your body, your feelings, and your life belong only to you. And you have the power to do with them what you will. *But do not give your soul to love!* That is my testament! I'll make a poem of your life! May it be filled with lyricism, or, as in Dante's poetry, may it be a hymn to freedom! Try to live beautifully! Rise to the heights inaccessible to cowardly souls. And if the slow descent into the valley seems to you sad and long, don't forget that death lies in your power. We all die like pitiful animals—senselessly and randomly or after a long illness and agony, with horror and sorrow. But isn't death a miraculous secret filled with promise? It would be so good to leave life voluntarily, at its zenith, to sacrifice it rapturously to a higher aim. Yes, one must know how to live beautifully. But it's even more important to die beautifully. My dear Manya, you're looking at me with such big, naive eyes! Your soul is as pure as a child's or a savage's. You haven't yet been corrupted or crippled. What delight awaits that soul! Kiss me, Manya! I've presented you with a treasure."

"Oh, Yan! If I act the way you've taught me, will I be happy?"

"Hardly! But there is a higher goal, Manya. You will be free!"

While waiting for Manya one fateful afternoon, Yan rushes off to save a drowning child in the accursed pond and drowns in the attempt. Arriving only in time to witness Zyama's search for Yan's body, Manya collapses on the spot. Yan is buried, and Steinbach returns for the magnificent ceremony. Zyama disappears and Roza weeps. Manya remains so shaken that she cannot be left alone and is provided a nurse, the young woman Lika Yakovlevna Syromyatnikova, who'd passed them, singing, during their visit to the Steinbach estate. Uncle becomes infatuated with Lika, who is a laundress's daughter and has had a rough life as a result—attending school on fellowships, serving time in prison, and joining the SRs.* Steinbach saved her from exile and arranged for her job. Lika's life story rouses Manya from her depression.

The girls were off to Moscow with Uncle. He was glad to be having a holiday in the capital. Lika had given him so many messages to deliver! Delicate and intimate, for family members and for the party. . . Uncle felt young and in love and was proud of Lika's trust. He was ready to lay down his life, let alone his freedom, for their friendship.

He walked along the open platform, waving his cane and limping slightly.

The sun poured down on the little station, but there was shade beneath the big poplars. The girls sat on a bench, waiting for the train, and looked out onto the distant steppe.

"Steinbach!" Uncle said suddenly as he hobbled up to the bench.

"Where?" Sonya jumped up.

"He just rode up in his landau. He'll be riding on the same train."

"Manya, wake up! Let's go! I've heard so much about him from Lika!"

"My children, guard your hearts! He's a real King Solomon!"

Sonya laughed happily.

There he was. The stationmaster inclined his body toward him respectfully, explaining something. The guard and the bartender peered out from the station entrance.

He listened, but it was as if he'd heard nothing and was thinking of something private.

How tall he was! He wore a dark coat and an artfully styled panama. Manya saw his proud profile, his ivory-pale skin, and his pointed black, fashionable beard, like Uncle's.

He squinted absentmindedly into the golden distance where the train was due to appear.

"What beauty!" Sonya whispered, squeezing Manya's hand painfully.

"Who does he look like?" Manya thought. "Where have I seen him? In a picture? A dream? In a crowd on the street?"

Then he turned, and Manya froze with half-open mouth. Yes, he was regal in appearance. But where did his charisma come from? What distinguished him?

"What brows!" Sonya whispered.

Why, of course. It was the most striking thing about his face, what gave him significance and individuality. What gave him soul. Almost joining in a single line above his nose, they spread wide and boldly across his pale forehead, as if an invisible hand had drawn a mysterious arabesque on that face, an arabesque that hid a vague threat.

"Fateful beauty," thought Manya.

Uncle hobbled up, agitated. He was offended that Steinbach hadn't recognized him, and he didn't feel like being the first to bow.

"Rembrandt, don't you think?" he said to the girls, trying to joke.

"Oh, I've gone crazy," Sonya said as if in a dream, and clasped her face, laughing.

The train rushed in.

At all the big stations where the train stopped for eight minutes, Sonya hastily got off onto the platform, with Manya and Uncle in tow. Sonya was searching for the first-class wagon-lit. If only he'd get out for a walk!

No! He didn't appear.

In the evening, when an enormous red moon had risen on the horizon and the steppe wind whipped up after sunset, the train stopped at some big station with electricity and a buffet. A huge crowd of locals came to look at the express. The young people flirted with each other. The ladies laughed loudly. Ukrainian speech sounded like music to Manya's ears. She stood next to Sonya, who seemed to be conjuring, leaning against the wall without taking her eyes off the wagon-lit and willing Steinbach to come out.

At long last! He descended slowly and lazily, and walked aimlessly through the crowd.

He was met with ecstatic looks and surprised cries and whispers. People parted before him. They stopped and watched him go by.

"What a cold face! What exhausted movements! Such a man can't be happy," thought Manya. "But why is someone so rich and handsome unhappy?"

And curiosity flared up in her soul. To probe the secret of this indifference, this fatigue! Such an immeasurable abyss separated them, as if he were the inhabitant of another world!

Her heart contracted with a sense of injury and alienation.

"Let's follow him!" whispered Sonya. "I want to read the expression in his eyes."

The station seemed a different world where the electric light ended. It was dark and mysterious under the garden poplars. It emanated the aura of the steppe, solitude, and the quiet of a desert. A strange loneliness. Here the moon rose, scarlet and eerie, from the dark blue mist that had settled on the horizon. The moon as yet shed no light.

The girls slowed their pace. They hid noiselessly behind a tall figure. It was quiet here. The locomotive stood behind them.

Steinbach stopped and looked at the moon.

"Yes, he's looking, but does he see it?" thought Manya, greedily drinking in his profile. "What's he thinking about? Why is he sad?"

Steinbach was as motionless as a dark statue.

"Now I understand. He's in love," thought Manya. "Hopelessly in love. Why else would he be so unhappy? But I'd like to see the woman who's enthralled him! What's she like—tall, dark-eyed, a brunette? No, she's probably a blonde and married to another."

And Manya was glad that he was suffering and had been rejected. It gave her a strange satisfaction.

The second bell sounded. The girls shrieked and ran back laughing, disconcerted by the fact that Steinbach had looked around.

It was already late at night, after Uncle had ordered their beds to be made up, that the girls went to buy postcards at a large station with a buffet. They secretly hoped to glimpse Steinbach again.

What luck! There he stood by the bookstall, distractedly perusing the book titles. The vendor, naive and open-mouthed, stared at his brows.

Sonya nudged Manya, and they both froze while still several steps away. But they soon forgot all social niceties and their pride and shame. They wanted to get their fill of this profile, its tragically joined and precisely drawn brows, its exotic matte skin.

"What amazing hands!" thought Manya.

"What do you want?" the vendor asked, suddenly noticing the girls.

At that moment Steinbach glanced around. His gaze, dispassionate and weary, passed indifferently over their young faces.

But Manya's whole body was shaking.

"I'll take this one," he said, pointing to a book, and walked off after paying for it.

The second bell rang. The girls ran out of the hall without buying anything.

In the doorway they almost bumped into Steinbach. His coat caught on Manya's shoulder.

"Excuse me!" he said. And again his gaze rested briefly on her face. It was so quick, so superficial. But the blood rushed to Manya's face, and she ran off in a daze. She was shaking from a strange, new, painfully sweet feeling.

"Did you see? His eyes are bottomless!" Manya said, catching her breath as the train started moving and made its way into the dark night. How eerie!

Sonya smiled blissfully. They were silent for a long time.

When Uncle was already snoring lightly and their fat female suite-mate was asleep, the girls kept talking in their top bunks.

"I want him to visit us," Sonya whispered. "Let Mama get acquainted with him and invite him over!"

"Don't! It's not worth lowering ourselves. Don't invite him! Why? What do we have in common?" Manya suddenly interrupted heatedly.

"What? I don't understand!" Sonya was angry.

"Good Lord! What little sensitivity you have! Did you see how he looked at us? I look that way at little insects when I stomp on them, without even noticing them. We're flies to him, not people."

And, choking with hatred, Manya fell face down on the pillow. She was ready to cry.

But Sonya smiled in the semidarkness.

At last! Here was the old Manya! She'd woken up and shaken that strange paralysis from her soul. She was laughing and getting angry.

"Thank you, dear, marvelous Steinbach!"

The train rushed along. It was already two o'clock. They weren't asleep. Standing in the corridor, they gazed out on the black night. Here and there the sky blazed. Here and there an evil scarlet light tore through the darkness of the summer night, like some troubled, far-off promise.

Had the evening light lingered in the sky and was only slowly dying out? Was it moonglow?

"Fires," said Sonya, remembering everything she'd talked about with Lika. "They're burning the landowners' estates."

And her deep eyes reflected her serious thoughts.

"How beautiful!" Manya sighed, running from window to window. "Ah, how beautiful!"

Manya saw Steinbach in her dreams.

"We'll enroll in the Higher Courses together," Sonya said firmly and importantly.

"Cour-ses?" Manya asked. She stood with her hands behind her head, gazing into the distance with half-closed eyes.

"I'll major in medicine and you'll major in history. With your abilities, you'll distinguish yourself right away."

"His-to-ry?" Manya repeated as if in a dream.

Sonya got angry. "Why, yes! Why do you keep repeating my words like a parrot? Are you off in dreamland again? You've an impossible mind!"

Manya stretched her entire body with a kind of languor. A smile parted her lips.

"No!" she suddenly said firmly and deliberately, dropping her hands and looking at her friend. "I don't want to study! I'm through."

"Now you say so! But just what do you want?"

Manya was silent for a long time, staring into the distance.

"I want to . . . live."

She put so much meaning into that short word! Her voice and face breathed such mysterious promises that Sonya instantly fell silent. She grew pensive and . . . recalled Steinbach.

Out of boredom Manya studied assiduously and, without effort, ranked third in her class. Sonya won the gold medal. Twice a week either Anya or Petya visited their sister, and it was a holiday for all concerned. It was so good to be loved, to be *everything* for people! Manya didn't know whom she loved more—her family or dear Frau Kessler.

Time passes slowly for the Yeltsov family. Petya is working on his dissertation, and Anya has aged into an old maid. Manya has finished school and Anya is upset about her possible future. They see in her the former beauty of their mother. They hesitate to tell Manya of the madness she has surely inherited and allow her, still ignorant of her dire fate, to summer again with the Gorlenkos.

Manya was at Yan's grave in the park. The past had welled up again, and its high cresting wave of sadness had flooded her soul.

What a marvelous spot! There were two gravemounds, one large and one small, on the green meadow under the chestnut trees. Marvelous, extraordinary roses ringed the dust of the one who had loved them so.

There was neither name nor prayer on the marble slab, only a prominent gold inscription:

A KNIGHT OF THE SPIRIT

And beneath it, in smaller script:

"I love the man who builds above himself, and so perishes . . ."

Steinbach had done this. And that dark feeling of malice toward him melted in Manya's heart.

She came here every day from two to four, sometimes with a book, just as she had kept their rendezvous. She believed that Yan had called her. She was no longer afraid. Contact with his immortal soul only brought her happiness.

She sat on the bench by the grave, her eyes closed. The book lay on the grass. The roses gave off their lovely scent. The silence all around echoed and breathed. And it seemed to her that very soon Yan's voice would resound in her soul.

"If you kiss someone in the morning, and in the evening desire pushes you into another's arms, heed your desire! This is the path to your soul's liberation!"

Footsteps sounded on the gravel path. Manya opened her eyes. Steinbach stood before her.

She so lost her head that she didn't respond to his bow.

He slowly walked on. His head was lowered and his steps sounded furtive and faded away beyond the gate.

Manya watched him go. And her heart pounded stormily, anxiously.

"I won't bother you if I sit nearby?" he asked, smiling just barely, with one corner of his mouth.

She nodded. She was so agitated she couldn't speak. This was the third day she'd been waiting for him by the grave, and she'd known he'd come today!

He watched her lowered head and rapidly heaving breast from the side, with half-closed eyes. "What a lovely little head!" he thought coldly.

"Do you like this park?" he asked with a sad overtone of indulgence.

Her eyelashes suddenly fluttered and her look burned him.

"Why do you speak to me? Why did you sit here? What business do you have with me? You don't think that I came here for you? Why did you imagine that you could make me happy by indulging in a conversation? Did I ask you to come?"

She jumped up and stood before him, stamping her foot. Her face was aflame and her eyes sparked.

"Leave me alone, please, and be on your way! Oh, yes—this is *your* park. I forgot. Well, what of it? The public isn't forbidden to come here. And you're not obliged to entertain the public. You may go!"

"Why are you driving me away?"

Steinbach smiled. This was the first time in his life that someone had yelled at him. He liked it. It aroused his curiosity. A badly bred, but charming girl. Life itself!

Manya didn't answer, but looked at him intently with a naive lack of ceremony, as if she were studying a portrait.

God, what marvelous brows! But he had an unpleasant smile. His lips were crooked and his eyes remained gloomy, as if they belonged to a different face.

She suddenly lost heart and sat down far away from him, on the end of the bench.

"You can stay! I don't care," she said two pitches lower, with exaggerated coolness and avoiding his insistent gaze. She picked up her book and held it upside down. Her blood was raging. Her heart seemed to be pounding in her throat, and something burned her eyelids. As long as she didn't turn scarlet! That would be a scandal!

Steinbach looked at her book and then at her reddening cheeks.

"What are you reading?" he asked ingratiatingly. "What strange script!"

Manya's eyes opened wide. She noticed that the book was upside down. And suddenly she began to laugh loudly and uncontrollably. She should have gotten angry, but she was choking with laughter.

"You're not angry?" Steinbach guessed. He waited a moment until Manya calmed down, then said shyly and tenderly, so shyly that Manya's anger dissipated: "Would you like to get acquainted?"

She was silent, on her guard, listening with her whole soul.

"I've been waiting to approach you for a long time now, but I couldn't make up my mind. You're wrong to fault me for arrogance. I'm afraid of people. I'm very shy."

Manya impetuously wheeled about. The book fell on the path. Manya believed him immediately, not so much by his words, but by his tone.

"You? Shy?"

"Yes. Why does that surprise you?"

Manya was lost in admiration and forgot the question.

"What brows!" she uttered aloud.

He smiled his bad smile once again.

"You like them?"

Manya flushed. "What have I done!" But in an instant she was boldly shaking her curls.

"Yes!" she said proudly. "I like them very much. I'm always thinking about them."

He wanted to bow in jest, but she quickly raised her hand.

"For Christ's sake, don't be banal! Don't thank me for 'the compliment.' You'll destroy my illusions and I'll never forgive you for that!"

He looked at her with growing interest. She'd addled him. All of the clichéd gestures men use with women and never change out of laziness were superfluous with her. And that "never" was full of promise. Did this mean that the girl, unbeknownst to him, had already admitted him into her life?

She said: "Here I'm sitting beside you and it seems like only the continuation of my dreams. I have marvelous dreams. Much more beautiful than life itself. And I often speak with you. And you? Do you like your dreams?"

"N-no. . . They're boring, like my life."

Manya again fell silent, stunned. What truth was in that voice! What sorrow!

"Can you really get bored? You're so rich! If I were rich I'd constantly be traveling from one country to another. What joy to see India, fakirs and serpents, Egypt, the pyramids, Jerusalem, Mount Sinai and Golgotha. To see Mexico, virgin forests, the Amazon."

Her voice sparkled like champagne. He listened and savored this unfamiliar, stormy, bright thirst for life.

"I've seen all that!" he said with a sigh.

She clapped her hands together and moved toward him.

"You've seen them? My God! How lucky you are! What I wouldn't give to see the East!"

He gazed silently into her eyes. Her trusting and naive gaze conveyed an indescribable charm. His heart suddenly began to pound and he involuntarily lowered his long eyelashes, which cast a shadow on his cheeks, and sketched something with his cane on the ground.

"I don't want to disappoint you," he said sadly. "Maybe your rich youth would be able to find the magic threads that could veil all that is ugly, tasteless, vulgar, and banal, that torments us tourists and mocks our dreams. But I was searching for solitude and contemplation, and I've found this nowhere except in this park. For this reason I love it now."

"And in the desert? At the pyramids?"

Steinbach laughed. How his laughter marred him! It was malicious, caustic laughter, and his teeth were small and sharp like those of a predator.

"I went to Egypt on a ship full of tourists. Mainly English, and that's a curse. Tourists poisoned for me all the beauty of art and culture in Europe. One couldn't be alone in a museum or a cemetery or in the mountains. There was a crowd swarming everywhere, with its flat, insatiable soul. It shouted in the Medicis' crypt and in front of Michelangelo's *Night*. It whistled in the moonlit Coliseum, in those hours when you think that hungry lions will rush out from its dark maw and tear apart phantoms wavering in the moonlight. It guffawed in the strange cemetery of *Campo Santo* in Genoa, and halloed in the Roman Forum and on the streets of Pompeii. It held nothing sacred, and feared silence. It only understood the movements and feelings of the herd. It defiled all the roads and temples, and talked and talked and talked. And ate and ate and ate."

"How awful!"

"You understand?" Steinbach surmised. "Although you're a child, I feel you understand me. When I thought of the East, I thought of it with the same passionate sadness that I hear now in your voice, and I longed for one thing—to be face-to-face with nature. To hear silence and the beating of my heart, to live through my daydreams in reality, to be happy in forgetting. But I didn't find this. When the train brought me to the pyramids . . ."

"A train?"

"Unfortunately, yes! The entire train was filled with English. They brought their own knives, plates, glasses, bottles, and entire baskets of provisions. And they talked and talked, and ate and ate. The guides met us (another unavoidable curse!) and treated us like prey. They had the unctuousness of priests standing near the source of the mystery and above the ignorant crowd. They were rude, disdainful, and greedy, and they herded us about. Everyone had to listen when they explained things. We walked about and looked at everything like a herd. Then this human herd, laughing loudly, would climb up the pyramids and scatter. There was the inevitable group photo. Then they took their provisions out of their baskets and opened their bottles. And they ate and ate, while the guides with criminal faces divided up their money, greedily cursing at each other. They were dividing up the usual spoils."

"Oh!" Manya burst out. She covered her face with her hands.

"I returned to the hotel. You must understand how I longed for the moment when I would look at the face of the Sphinx! I told myself: 'Let it be at night when the tourists are asleep.' When the moon had risen high above the desert, I left. My heart was full of anxiety, as if I were keeping a rendezvous. It was cold. I would have frozen in my coat if my blood hadn't been burning with passion. And there I saw it in the distance. My heart began to pound. A huge shadow lay on the chilly sand. I saw the profile of the Sphinx, disfigured by human meanness. Suddenly I heard voices and laughter. 'An illusion,' I thought. But, unfortunately, no! A group of tourists sat on the ledges. People had gathered like flies at its base. They talked and talked and ate and ate. Cigar butts, empty bottles and orange peels were strewn all about. The guides were playing on some kind of eastern instrument. It produced a senseless, primitive, and sad buzzing reminiscent of flies in the autumn-time. I almost shouted out of resentment, out of the pain of a defiled silence, a disfigured Sphinx. The next morning I left."

Manya was silent for a long time.

"Why did you tell me this?" she exclaimed at last with sorrow.

"Such is life."

"No! You shouldn't have told me! You've robbed me of my beautiful daydreams."

"You like to daydream?" Steinbach guessed.

"Yes. I don't value what life gives me, but what it promises me. And also what I find in books. I wouldn't need books if my heart didn't already pound from fear or ecstasy."

"Are you a romantic? Realism is alien to you?"

"It must be. I don't like pictures of flowers to look like ordinary flowers. They can be strange! I love the fact that bushes and trees can have a soul and that walls and houses can have faces and voices. Have you seen Borisov-Musatov's pictures?"

"I own some."

"Yes? Then you must understand me."

"Do you like to read?" Steinbach asked quietly, biting his walking stick and not taking his eyes from Manya's profile.

"Yes. Only not about the peasants or pogroms or contemporary life. That's so gray and flat! That doesn't stir my heart. I don't want to find familiar faces in novels! Whether they be worse or better, I just want the heroes to be different! I forgive books everything but poverty of imagination."

"This girl has a brilliant temperament," Steinbach thought.

"You're demanding. Insofar as I know, you should like the modernists."

"Yes. I don't need brilliant colors or sharp contours and expressions. I like to seek things out and get excited when I read. For instance, have you ever happened to get lost in the pattern of a balcony or a street railing? No? I always look for the resolution of some kind of lost thought in those strange lines of the *moderne*."

"Unfortunately, the modernist period is over. They're already going back to realism abroad. You see this especially in the Paris exhibits."

Manya sadly clapped her hands.

"That's terrible! You know, Yan taught me to love that school."

"Who?" Steinbach interrupted quickly.

"Yan. He valued no one more highly than the modernists."

Steinbach looked at her intently. His brows formed a single line.

"Who are you talking about?"

Manya pointed to the grave. The silence lasted for a second. And Manya squirmed under the stare of those dark, bottomless eyes.

"You knew him?" he asked softly.

She raised her head proudly.

"He loved me."

"Ah!"

"That's good! Go ahead and look! Now you won't ignore me!" she thought.

"Excuse me. You've quite astounded me with this news. Did you know that you weren't supposed to use that name for him?"

"Yes . . . but, after all, he's dead now."

Oh, how he stared at her! His eyes wanted to pierce her through! "A-ha! You'll have to reckon with me now!"

"Can you tell me about your acquaintance?" he asked quietly, with a new shade of respect.

And Manya told him. It was such a pleasure to talk about Yan here, two steps from his grave! As she talked, hugging her knees and looking at the blue sky between the dense lime trees, the past—so brilliant and so wonderful—stood before her as if it were yesterday. It was sweet to tell a stranger what she had hidden from Sonya and preserved deeply and jealously in her soul, much as the Miserly Knight hid his gold. Some unfathomable force drove her to speak about love, about how she had kissed Yan as they sat in an embrace, about how she had laid her head on his breast and heard his heart beating.

Her voice trembled with tenderness, with an engulfing thirst for love. Her pale face was now turned toward Steinbach and wordlessly uttered what she had not yet resolved to speak.

When she spoke about his death and their last meeting, a spasm suddenly constricted her throat. She shrieked and sobbed despairingly, dropping her head on the back of the bench. It was as if only now, a year later, she fully understood what a treasure life had taken from her.

"My child! My poor child!" Steinbach whispered, shaken by the directness and freshness of her sorrow. It had been a long time since he'd witnessed such stormy tears and sincere joy!

His hand involuntarily lay on the curly head and caressed it. A forgotten agitation warmed his soul. He felt like doing something for her. What? All his millions were powerless to recompense her for such a loss.

She rose suddenly. Her nose, eyelids, and lips were momentarily puffy. Tears spoiled her beauty, and she didn't like to cry. But right now she didn't care. Those tears had been so sweet!

She gratefully gazed at the stranger who unexpectedly had given her so much. And her eyes were so marvelous that Steinbach saw them alone in her tear-stained face.

"Excuse me. . . Don't laugh at me! Goodbye!"

"Wait! When will I see you again?"

"Tomorrow! No! Don't follow me! There's no need."

She left very quickly, with a determined young step and without looking back. She almost ran along the path.

Steinbach watched her, pensive and agitated.

"If I were an artist, I would paint her portrait full of movement and call it *Spring Wind*. She bears hope and agitation along with her, like that wind, and some kind of troubled possibilities. . ."

He sat for a long time by Yan's grave, contemplating the mood that had engulfed him.

How incredibly long ago had such moments abandoned him!

"Ah! You're already here?"

"A long time ago. I've been waiting for you more than an hour."

She laughed, flashing her teeth, eyes, and dimples, as if she were all afire. She gave him her hand in a friendly fashion.

"I couldn't come earlier. There were guests. That stupid Katya Lizogub came. She talks about anything. And laughs at decidedly everything. I can't stand such people! Do you know her?"

"A lit-tle . . ."

"You like her? Tell me. Do you like her?"

"I don't remember her face."

Manya laughed wickedly and gaily.

"I don't want them to know of our meetings!" she said seriously. "That will destroy their charm, don't you think?"

Her soul emanated such springlike feelings that he felt as young as he had the day before.

"You're a little magician!" he said. "Just now as I was waking up and before I was fully conscious, I felt a sense of joy. I felt that something had entered my life. Something new and bright."

"I did, too!" she said naively and triumphantly.

"But you're young. This is natural for you. I'd forgotten this feeling."

"And are you really old?" Manya asked. She sat down, tilting her head to one side and looking him over attentively.

"Like a bird!" he thought sadly. "You idiot, why do you talk about age and dig your own pit?"

"I'm almost forty."

"For-ty?"

"Ah, such disappointment! Am I right? Yes, with little exaggeration I could be your father. And Yan was so young! So bright and at peace!"

"What? What did you say? Repeat it!"

She was aquiver.

What eyes this girl had! Steinbach couldn't look into these burning and innocent eyes without agitation.

"I loved Yan very much. Despite his complexity, he was very much at peace. He affected me like the mountains. You're surprised? I love the mountains. More than the sea. The sea troubles and irritates me. It's so like our soul—turbulent, changeable, treacherous. But the mountains are silent. They're full of mystery and grandeur. They're the steps to the gods."

Manya sighed deeply, and he found it pleasant. He felt that a mood had been created.

"I always go to the mountains to get away from people. It's only there that you understand quiet and fresh air. I've climbed so high that even the bees don't drone below. And as I lie there for hours at a time I forget about injuries and disappointments. I spent an entire year in a hut in the Caucasus mountains."

"This means that you don't like people?"

"No. Yan loved the man of the future—free, daring, and magnificent. I don't believe in such a man. Of all the creatures on earth, man is the cruelest and most egotistical. And if the millennia haven't changed him, there's nothing to hope for. I reject miracles. People like Yan come along only once in a century in order to show us what the ideal man could be. But the world won't accept this ideal."

"For God's sake, don't talk that way! I'll start to cry."

He quietly took her hand and lifted it to his lips.

She trembled. His touch was tender, but it seemed to burn her. She withdrew her hand, and, stunned by her feelings, looked at him with fear and almost with hostility.

"Forgive me! I didn't want to offend you," he said timidly.

"What pupils! What eerie, dark pupils! Listen. . . May I? You'll not be offended?"

"What is it?"

She went up to him.

"I'm terribly drawn to look into your eyes. . ."

"Then look."

His lips twisted into a smile. A rapacious, sarcastic smile. So be it! It didn't matter. She placed her hands on his shoulders and looked up into his eyes. Their faces were close. Their breathing commingled.

Steinbach's nostrils quivered, and his heart began to pound. What long forgotten bliss!

"Am I still capable of infatuation?" he thought.

"Your pupils are completely invisible. It's as if I'm looking from a lighted window into black night, with my face pressed against the glass."

He watched as her lips moved. She was probably sensual. What a rarity! And so valuable in women. If . . .

He was terrified that she would notice his agitation. Desire made his face old and unappealing. But he wanted to please.

"Why did she turn so pale? Why is she breathing so heavily?"

She moved away, sad and subdued. "What fateful, terrible beauty!" She did not think so much as she felt this with all her being.

It was exactly as if something wavered and perished in her soul. Would a new feeling be born? Had the old feeling vanished? Ah, she knew nothing! For that brief moment it was as if she'd been drowning in the darkness of his eyes. She'd looked into the abyss, deceptive and terrible.

He was silent, waiting.

"Yes, you're completely different," she said in a kind of broken voice. "Yan was like a spring day."

"And I'm like an autumn night?"

"Yes. You're not angry?"

"No. I know it myself."

Now Manya felt sorry for him. She unconsciously moved nearer. When he was this way, she had completely different feelings for him—simple and tender feelings.

He read this in her soul.

"Sit with me as you sat with Yan!" he whispered shyly, like a boy. "Do it if I'm not repulsive to you."

She hesitated for an instant. Then she laid her head on his shoulder. He quietly embraced her.

Her eyes were closed. She didn't realize that her heart was pounding deafeningly. Her head was spinning and she couldn't breathe.

She pulled back sharply.

"No! I can't! You're not Yan. Don't be angry, please! But I feel something completely different for you."

"Revulsion?" he prompted. And his upper lip lifted, showing his teeth.

"He doesn't think that's a smile?" She studied his face attentively and coldly. Yes. There his temples were graying. And his hair was curly like that terrible uncle's. In ten or fifteen years he'd be just as terrifying. What a resemblance! How had she not seen it right away?

The enchantment was disappearing. What a pity! No! It was even good. That enchantment had been too strong. She needed to get a grip on herself. "Lord, help me! Otherwise I'll fall hopelessly in love with him and run after him like a pupil after her teachers. And he'll speak condescendingly to me again and secretly scorn me as he does the others. But his brows! They'll drive me mad!"

Steinbach shrank from her gaze and involuntarily lowered his lashes.

Now she saw him in profile and there was nothing predatory, nothing typically Jewish about him. What marvelous satiny skin, without any glow or ruddiness! What nostrils!

Suddenly . . .

Manya herself didn't know whether she was upset or happy. She saw the flaws in that face. The ears. Small, pretty, but pale. Deathly pale and transparent as if . . . How revolting! And the bluish eyelids, dead somehow. She shuddered involuntarily. She recalled the eyelids and ears of little Poznansky. "A Yid!" someone said loudly in her soul. How could she forget that?

When she stood up, cold and distant, Steinbach felt that all was lost.

He was destroyed. There was nothing to ask. Her face was too expressive.

"I'm too old for her," he thought, and his heart sank. For the first time he'd encountered a woman's scorn.

It was the end!

He didn't even ask her to return the next day as she walked off, indifferent to him. She was cruel as only the young can be. And all the power of his millions could not capture the fantasy of this girl or buy her caresses.

He sat hunched over on the bench, feeling the dead weight of his expended life on his shoulders. He listened with a kind of fatalistic humility to her light, fading steps. She'd come like the spring. And left like youth.

All was finished.

"Hello, Steinbach! Ha, ha! Why are you trembling? You weren't so lost in thought that you didn't hear my footsteps? What were you thinking about? Can you answer me? Didn't you expect me? Or had you forgotten me?"

An entire cascade of laughter and words, as always! And you don't know what to answer.

He jumped up, forgetting the sadness of yesterday evening, of the sleepless night and his bitter thoughts just now. . . He stood, squeezing her hands and embracing her with his hungry gaze.

How he needed this girl, with her laughter, her youth, her lust for life! She was like a fresh oasis in a burning desert, like sleep after a fatiguing journey, like wine when one needs to forget. It was a gray day, about to rain. But she had come and brought the sun with her.

"I thought you wouldn't come back."

She looked rapturously at his brows.

"Ha, ha! You think that I'm so sated with impressions that I don't value another meeting with you? I've dreamt of you so much that I won't be so quickly satisfied. You needn't be afraid."

"She hasn't a shred of coquetry! It's frightening."

"I'm afraid to believe you. Have you really . . . *thought* of me?"

"Oh! Both Sonya and I have. We've talked about you an entire year. And I've seen you in my dreams almost every night!"

She told him of their meeting at the train station.

"Do you remember? I pushed you. Your coat caught on me and you said, 'Excuse me'."

"N-no. Forgive me. How did that happen? Wait a moment."

Her face lengthened and grew pale. Once again she saw, clearly and sharply, the great difference in their social positions, the deep chasm that separated their lives and over which only her fantasy had cast a flimsy bridge.

She withdrew the hand he'd been holding all the while.

"You don't remember? I see that's so. Please! Your delicacy is out of place. I sense you don't remember, and what's strange about that? What are Sonya and I to you? We lived a whole year off this meeting. And you? Let go of my hand! Leave me!"

"Are you angry?"

"That's an understatement! 'Are you angry?' I hate you! I hated you then an entire month."

He suddenly laughed.

"How dear you are!" he said unexpectedly and softly. "I'm so happy that you hate me!"

Everything got mixed up in her soul. It was as if the sun peeked down through the chaos. She laughed, all dimpled, her teeth sparkling and her eyes shining. At that moment they were again comrades, equal and close.

"It's so strange!" she said, yielding her hand once more. "The Steinbach I saw at the station and you are completely different. Two different faces. Have you noticed that this always happens? No one resembles what we think and expect of him when we first see him. That's why I don't like to get to know new people. I only like to dream about people."

"Blessed be your mistake this time!" he whispered, greedily admiring her.

But she didn't notice her power over him. She was completely self-absorbed.

"What power!" he thought. "She has taken my heart into her hands. She holds my life. And I have no idea what she'll do with it. Will she drop it on the path, like that handkerchief? Step on it as she walks away, indifferent and cruel, as she did yesterday? Or summon me again. . . God! I don't even know who she is! What's her name? One morning I met her on this bench, a person as mysterious and sudden as my fate. And I'm ready to accept sorrow or happiness from her hands. Even death! Without a murmur or regret."

Rustling noises filled the park.

"It's raining," Steinbach said disappointedly. "How can we stay? Where's your umbrella?"

"Ah, it's in tatters! I'm always without an umbrella. I'm not afraid of rain."

"But you'll get soaked and catch cold. Would you like . . ." (he froze for a moment, frightened by his own daring and joy) "Would you like to wait in the house?"

"Where?"

"In my house."

"Oh, that would be fine! I've long wanted to see it. Is it far from here? Let's go right away!"

"What splendor!" Manya said, stopping in the study before the original paintings of Rembrandt, Durer, and Van Dyck.

FIGURE 3
How Steinbach might have lived. The Gothic study of the Moscow "new merchant" A. V. Morozov, designed by Fyodor Shekhtel, with painted panels by Mikhail Vrubel. A. V. Shchusev State Museum of Architecture, Moscow.

"Father especially loved these artists. My mother's family was from Holland. This is in her memory. In general there's nothing here of mine. All these show the tastes and passions of my father. The imprint of his strong soul lies on everything. I'm as much a guest here as you are."

He sat down on a soft ottoman at her feet and took her hands.

She was silent, overwhelmed by impressions. She'd never seen such wealth even from afar. The decor of the Gorlenkos and the Lizogubs seemed so paltry now! And how freely this *yid*—as Vera Filippovna would say—moved and breathed here. "There are people made for wealth. But I'm a Cinderella," she told herself. "My skirt and shoes are awful in contrast. How is it he doesn't notice this?"

She daydreamed. It was so strange to sit here on this ottoman covered with Persian rugs. Just as in a dream . . .

No, she was not Cinderella. She was a princess. And here was her vassal at her feet. Handsome and a little frightening. But obedient, like a kite on a chain, ready to extend his talons.

"What's your name?" he asked her as if in a play.

"Verbena."

"N-no, seriously. Tell me, who are you?"

"Why? It's better this way. I have a vulgar name. And it's so good that we know nothing about each other! Neither about the past nor anything else!"

He smiled.

"You think I have no past? And Yan?"

She arched her left eyebrow. What a capricious little face!

"Oh, yes! That's an awful lot!" he said seriously. "He enriched your soul. He knew how to give."

"Explain!" She moved towards him, and her dusty old shoes left dirty marks on his knees. But the closeness did not bother her now. When they spoke of Yan, he was here with them. Love for him brought their souls closer and created an atmosphere of light and trust.

"There are people who are fated their whole lives to give their souls to those around them. There are few like that. Of those who only know how to take from others, there are millions. Yan was as generous as a prince. His nature was a treasure everyone scooped up by the handful and joyfully made away with. That's why we should never forget him."

"And you?"

"What about me?"

"Do you . . . give? Or only take from others?"

"My life is a complete irony. Fate gave me little talent, energy, joie de vivre, desire. I'm the descendant of a degenerated family, the last of my line. We Jews quickly degenerate. Perhaps that's why the struggle to live comes too hard to us. Although one can't say that about my family. Already by the twelfth century my mother's ancestors, the Davidsons, were lending money to kings and lords. And during Elizabeth I's reign they were in favor at court. We never knew humiliation or need, those curses always hanging over Jewry. Nevertheless, the poison of degeneration tainted our blood. And I was doomed from the cradle."

Manya feels terribly sorry for Steinbach and weeps. She at last divulges that her name is Manya.

"And what's your name?"

"Mark."

"Mark. Mark . . ," she repeated, listening intently and nodding her head like a little bird. "That sounds good. It reminds me of Rome. And your other name? No, don't say!"

She put her hand to his lips.

"I'm afraid it will be Mironych, Lvovich, Borisych—something impossibly Jewish. Ha, ha!" she burst out. "You're not offended? Angry?"

"You don't like Jews? Don't answer. I feel it."

"For God's sake, don't be offended! But it's true. I'm always trying to forget that you're a Jew. And I'll manage to. You're so fine! So aristocratic. . . You know, there was a student in the village with the bizarre name of Izmail. And these tasteless yi-"

"Yids," prompted Steinbach.

"Forgive me! It's a bad habit. Everyone talks that way at the Gorlenkos. But these Jews called him *Zyama*. They have no sense of flair. And why do they always use diminutives? Sasha Schneider. That's so absurd! *Zyama*. It brings to mind something flat, something that crawls like a worm. And he has such a fiery soul! But what a shame they didn't name you Izmail!"

Manya asks Steinbach why he doesn't like people.

"They treat me without pity. In childhood I had a timid and tender soul. They made me into a cynic. With the rudest flattery, the rudest neglect of my own personality. Insatiable greed. Absolutely bare-faced calculation. That's what I saw around me in those years when you seek a friend and believe in people and wait for love. If I had been poor, perhaps I would have found friends, love, people interested in me. But I was a moneybags. No one expected anything from me. No one asked for anything but gold. Individuals and entire parties fought over me, as if I were the highest prize in life! Everyone aimed to get power over me, but they didn't seek me out. Even women loved me through the prism of my millions. All these long years I didn't meet anyone who came to me without calculation, with deep interest in my soul. I was met everywhere with predatory looks and whispers. But I know the cost of this attention. 'There goes Steinbach, the millionaire Steinbach . . .' they'd say in my wake. If only you knew how painful it is to cling to illusions, and lose them suddenly! On account of one unintentionally dropped word, a flash of the eyes, unconscious mimicry! If you knew what it means to kiss a beautiful face in a mindless thirst for oblivion! To hear words of love and—to believe nothing! My life is an irony. I mean nothing without wealth. And I curse this wealth. My father got satisfaction from power over others. He got drunk from it. But is *this* really power? Yan—poor, ragged, and without a roof over his head—reigned in the souls of men. And his testaments resound even from the grave in the hearts of those who embraced his faith. I am a beggar before Yan. And I've long been a bankrupt. How eager I'd be to throw off these golden chains! But am I really the master of my life? There is no slavery more terrible than mine! Every person has the right to come to me at any hour when I want to be alone, when I want to dream, when I want to rest. Everyone has the right to spoil my mood with a vulgar lack of ceremony and to lay out his requests. Everyone demands something of me. But I must hear everyone out, look at their flat faces, shake their unneeded hands. My position requires it! It's been this way since my university days. How many times that year did I dream of ridding myself of the factory! Of selling it, giving it away. No! Your hair would stand on end if you knew what a mountain of obligations lies on my shoulders! Obligations before society, the people, the district, the authorities. What rumbling and grumbling! The admonitions of the governor, the amazed glances. 'Of course, I'm ill? It's all nerves. I ought to rest for the good of the country!' My God! I'm bound hand and foot by every possible obligation. No matter where I go, I'm followed by telegrams, requests with deadlines, business letters. How much I have to read every day! How many answers to write! There are stewards everywhere, but they've no initiative. My father held all the strings with an iron hand. They're all used to subordination. I was happier when my father was alive. I could go away and live abroad incognito. Ah, I'm tired!"

Without releasing her hands he drew her nearer, and his voice trembled and stole into her soul.

"Little fairy! You don't know what a pitiful beggar sits before you! You don't know how hungry his soul is, how poor his life is! You don't understand with what torment he envies your spontaneity and belief in yourself! You're so rich! You're so lavish! People have given me nothing but a profound weariness and revulsion! You've returned to me my beautiful dreams, my timid and pale hopes. Let me be deceived, and wake again tomorrow just as alone and poor as I was before I met you! Nevertheless, I'm made happy by this deception. In exchange demand anything of me, including my life! And I'll lay it with joy at your feet!"

Manya looked into his pupils, the way one looks into an abyss. Her head was spinning quietly, and her heart sweetly skipped a beat.

A terrifying bliss . . .

"Do you love me, Mark?" she asked in infinite amazement, as if in a dream.

"Oh, Manya . . ."

And nothing more. Not a single vow, not a single confession.

What need did she have of them? His voice pierced her soul. All her nerves trembled from his glance.

She believed him. She was happy.

He embraced her very quietly, and quietly drew her to him. His inspired face was beautiful and tragic.

She took his head in both hands, and kissed his forehead and sorrowful brows. Then she pressed her cheek to his head.

He was motionless beneath her caress.

They sat motionless, with eyes closed, and listened to the sonorous silence of their souls.

It rained every day. Manya, dressed in a hooded raincoat, arrived at the appointed hour in the grove where Yan had once waited for her.

Now Steinbach waited there. He would carry her off to his home in his cabriolet and then return her to the grove.

Manya was upset. Vera Filippovna was alarmed by her walks in this weather. Someone had seen her on the road to Lipovka.

She trembled for her secret! How terrible if it fell into someone else's hands! They would gossip, joining their names together with a smile!

"Yes. Life is vulgar!" he said. "You don't even understand everything they can say about us. People have no imagination and no need for beauty. They're only happy when they can drag your soul through the dirty street. That's what they call 'public opinion'!"

Manya said sadly, "Come to the Gorlenkos now and make my acquaintance! There's nothing left for us to do. The barometer has fallen. The rain may continue for two weeks. Come tomorrow. But remember that we don't know each other! Actually, that's true. We won't be the same in different circumstances."

They were silent for a long time, depressed.

"Mark, they talked about you at dinner."

"They criticized me, of course?"

"Just imagine, not too much. They said, rather, that you were a talented lawyer."

His lips twisted.

"You think, perhaps, that that's a smile?" she asked him sternly. "It's simply a grimace. I can't bear you when you smile!"

"Forgive me! I won't."

He was already laughing.

"And now I hate you!" She stamped her foot. "You have such a cynical, repellent laugh!"

"No, Manya. I completely lack talent. If I had to win some prize in life with eloquence—love, for example—even then I wouldn't be able to do it. A good lawyer without temperament and creativity—that's a contradiction. That's just what I am."

"Too bad. It was pleasant to hear. This means that you have no temperament?"

"Absolutely none. Like an amphibian."

"How disgusting!" Manya laughed. "But what do you have?"

"Monstrous sensuality. That's in Semitic blood."

Manya mused. "And what's the difference?"

"Yan and Zyama had no sensuality. Or it was dormant... But deep passions ruled their souls and drove them to great achievements or crimes. An idea, a woman... All this filled their souls, and submerged them like a mighty wave. And they acted and loved with daring and clarity, without calculation."

"And you, Mark?"

"I? I love a woman's body and the feelings it gives me. Sometimes some turn of the head or a single line in a face or figure drives me insane. Sometimes a way of laughing, or a manner of . . . caressing. There's a mass of nuances here. Each woman is deeply individual in her love. But I'm terribly cold and poor in spirit. Passion, Manya, is lightning that blinds and often burns another's soul. Sensuality is a will-o'-the-wisp. With sensuality, it's just as dark and terrifying. And cold. You run after it and it disappears."

"Stop!" Manya had pricked up her ears and was concentrating. "This means. . . You do love women?"

"Very much," he said, and his curved lips twisted.

She suddenly felt wretched.

Why was she here? Why were they sitting in this embrace? Such cold emanated from his words! And how infinitely remote he was from her soul! What a tormenting feeling! Where did it come from? She felt like crying.

She rose, dispassionate, burned out. Even the corners of her mouth turned down in a kind of deep apathy.

"Where are you going, Manya?"

"Nowhere. I'm bored. Take me home!"

He shrank down and didn't dare ask her to stay. This girl's soul was a mystery to him.

The entire way home she was silent and withdrawn.

When she was getting out of the cabriolet at the edge of the grove, he wanted to kiss her wet hand.

"Leave me alone! Don't you dare!" she suddenly said with passion. Her eyes glittered with hostility. Her curls had escaped from the hood and were curled more tightly from the damp. Her eyelashes were wet.

Why? Were these drops of rain . . . or tears? Her downy cheeks were burning. "Oh, dear little face!"

"Are you angry?" he humbly asked.

"Oh! Am I angry? I hate you! Never dare to kiss my hands, do you hear? If you kiss them just once, it's over between us!"

She walked off without looking back. He sensed that she was crying.

Already unhappy, Manya becomes jealous when she learns that Steinbach is married, and his past is closed to her.

Manya rode on horseback despite the muddy roads. She was seeking oblivion. There was such a burning pain in her soul!

The sun set beautifully in the haze. Clouds had risen. It would be sunny tomorrow, but that would not drive away the shadow on her soul or heal this first wound.

When she returned, night had already fallen.

All the windows were open, and a fire burned in the hallway. The heated horses were snorting in the courtyard. There was an unfamiliar carriage . . .

"We have guests?" Manya's heart fell.

"Shenbok," said Petro secretively and joyously, plucking her from the saddle.

Manya stopped in the doorway, her heart pounding.

Someone was singing. What a marvelous voice! It was "Evening Star," Wulfram's song from *Tannhäuser*.

Yes, it was he, and he was accompanying himself.

They turned to look at her, hushed her. She froze in the entryway. Here were the Lizogubs, Katya, Sonya, everyone. . . They had such new, beautiful faces!

"He's noticed me," Manya sensed suddenly.

It was as if Steinbach's voice took fire:

"Bright angel, dear angel// Who shines in my hateful life . . ."

His eyes gazed on her beseechingly and passionately. His sorrowful, fiery confessions rang in her ears. Her lips trembled from an insane desire to weep, as if a stone had fallen from her breast.

"Allow me to introduce our pet." She heard Vera Filippovna's voice in a dream. "Manya Yeltsova, my daughter's friend."

He bowed low before her. "As before a princess," Manya thought.

Katya Lizogub flared up in envy. Uncle was amazed, Sonya on guard. When Steinbach lifted his head, he saw that Manya's eyes were full of tears and promises.

The next day the sun shone in the sky and in Manya's soul.

She was angry with herself for the joy that pulsed in her breast, but she couldn't overcome it.

"I'll see him in a moment! He's probably waiting at the grove. And if not? Then it's the end—of everything! I'll never ask for anything. Should I go? Stay? I'm going. I'll look. I'll look coldly. But I won't go to him for anything! And I won't go into the park."

There he was—standing by the forest's edge.

"What are you doing here?" she asked haughtily.

"Waiting."

"How arrogant you are! Why did you think I'd come?"

His nostrils twitched as he restrained a smile.

"You did come," he said barely audibly.

"But this proves nothing!" she flamed up and stamped her foot. "I'm out for a walk."

"Allow me to accompany you!"

"Not for anything!" she said carelessly. But then without any logic she took his proffered arm and they silently walked together into the park.

His humility had undone her.

No. It wasn't even that. Why lie to herself? She could only scorn him and ignore him at a distance. His nearness intoxicated her nerves and a sweet, terrible passivity bound her soul. How new it was! And how oppressive. And this strange dissatisfaction and anxiety. It had been entirely different with Yan. With Yan it was so peaceful and light! These two men had given her two separate worlds.

"What a voice you have! And what a sensitive artist you are! Why aren't you on the stage? Why didn't you tell me that you sang? When I heard your voice I forgave you everything."

"Forgave me? Am I guilty before you?"

She was silent, hostile and guarded.

"You know, you're right," he said sadly. "The past does not die."

She did not speak all the way to the house, and was distant and hostile.

"Tell me about your wife," she said, sitting with her legs on the ottoman in his study.

Steinbach was next to her; only an embroidered pillow separated them. But for him this was a wall that obscured Manya's soul. Her face was new, even her voice was new . . . and alien.

"Is she very pretty? Do you love her very much? Why isn't she here? And why are you unhappy if you're married? Wait! What's she like? A blonde or a brunette? Well, why don't you say something? And please don't look at me! You confuse me when you look at me. Lower your eyes and stop grimacing! You're repulsive when you smile! No, that's not so—you may laugh! The worse you look the better! Well, sir? I'm listening. What's she like? A blonde?"

"Yes."

"A Jew?"

"Yes."

"Why, of course," Manya guessed with disdain. "Uncle says that a Jew can fall in love with anybody, but only love another Jew. And only take a Jewish wife."

"Fyodor Filippych, one must conclude, is well informed in this matter. Is he also an anti-Semite?"

"What do you mean by 'also'?"

"I meant to say, like you?"

"I myself don't know what I am!" Manya said angrily. "I can't stand Yids . . . Jews! But I loved you."

He made an abrupt gesture and grabbed her hands.

"You loved me?"

"Why are you so happy? I don't love you, I *loved* you for several days or hours, perhaps. And not even you, but your face, your brows. Take your hands off me! And please don't kiss mine! I need nothing from you now! All the enchantment has vanished."

"When?"

"The third day. Mark, Mark, have you gone mad?"

"I'm happy! God, I'm so happy!"

He took her hands and placed them over his eyes. His lashes were trembling.

And suddenly the little bridge on which Manya held fast slipped out from beneath her feet. It was swaying and the abyss appeared below. Her heart fell. She almost fainted. Something fatal and terrifying stared at her from those eyes, that face. She felt like running away.

Or was this fear really joy that flooded her soul? Oh, to touch his face, his brows, his lips! To drown in this feeling, in this smell of his skin and hair. Completely unaware of what she was doing, she grabbed him by the shoulders and, closing her eyes, pressed her face to his lips.

"Oh, kiss me! Kiss me!" she said through her teeth, and shuddered.

When she regained consciousness, her face was bathed in tears.

He was kneeling at her feet. His face was hidden in the folds of her dress.

What had just happened? Where? In what new unknown world was her soul wandering?

His fingers had plunged convulsively into the velvet ottoman. She took his hand and placed it on her trembling heart.

He raised his head. Oh, how beautiful and terrible his face was!

"Mark," she said very quietly. "Dear Mark. . . Why do you have such wild eyes—like the dog Gnedko's when he's about to bite? Why do you feel so new? Wasn't that true happiness? It seems that you're suffering, and something's frightened me. . ."

"My child! Don't be afraid of me!" he said brokenly. "You are too dear to me. I'd sooner my heart break than deprive you of one of your illusions! I won't make an irreparable mistake. I couldn't survive your disgust."

She tried to penetrate the dark meaning of his words, the meaning of all that had taken place.

Something between them had collapsed. She felt this. Some sort of barrier that kept her from touching him. Now she felt as though she had known him a long time.

"Hold me! Sit close to me, like this. . . Oh, what bliss, Mark! You love me! Tell me that—every day, every hour. I so want to be loved, loved eternally! Your kisses are heaven! How could I live without knowing you!"

Suddenly her heart leaped with searing pain, as if she'd been stabbed. And the magic seemed distant.

She moved away. Her face seemed older.

"Tell me about *her*," she said in a voice utterly unlike her own. "Do you love her very much?"

"I love you, and not her," he replied timidly, as if before a judge. And Manya was just as implacable.

"Where is she now?"

"Abroad."

"Why isn't she with you?"

"We separated long ago."

"Why? Why?"

He was silent, his eyes with their bluish transparent lids downcast. Manya's anger grew.

"Why don't you answer?"

"That's my secret."

"Oh, it's that way! You keep secrets from me?"

Despair flooded her soul once more, and she stood up as if to go.

"Stop!" He said this hollowly, with great pain, and caught her hand. "I'll be frank. Sit beside me and listen. I married when I was twenty-five."

"For love? Did you love her? Passionately?"

"Yes. Not as I love you now. That was a different feeling. I didn't love her as an individual. She was colorless, like most women. . ."

Steinbach explains that they were happy together as man and woman, and they had a son. But after a year their boy died from meningitis, and their life seemed to him like a garden destroyed by a storm. They also had a daughter, who seems to him like Manya, and this prompts him to foretell Manya's future happiness and probable motherhood. But he warns that she will not be happy with him because, he hints, there is hereditary madness in his family, and that is the reason he left his wife after giving her a fabulous allowance and complete freedom.

Manya subsequently reports to Steinbach that someone has seen them meet, and she is upset that this may be their last rendezvous. She reports the family quarrel over this "impudent Yid's" intentions, with Sonya rising to his defense and claiming that if his feeling is serious, he'll divorce his wife and marry Manya. . .

"What about. . . What do you think of that, Manya?"

"What nonsense! I don't think any . . . such thing. Why should I? What other people say about us pains me to the point of tears!"

Steinbach had gone so pale that Manya felt frightened.

"My child. . . There should be no misunderstanding! I'll never stop loving you, but I can never marry you, even if you wanted or demanded it. Will you hear me out?"

"Yes."

"Above all, this isn't meant to insult you! I reject marriage. I've always rejected it. But my wife could not help being unhappy. She's very religious. If I demand a divorce, then I'll inflict on her an undeserved and profound pain that will poison her life. She's a stranger to me now. But she loves the name I gave her and she clings to the pathetic tie that remains between us, that phantom shade of being a family. Lastly, I won't do this to my daughter. So from the point of view of today's morality, Gorlenko and Fyodor Filippych are right. I'm a scoundrel to you! And if you believe this . . ."

"No! Be quiet! I love you, Mark, and I believe in your love. Forget everything I told you. I shouldn't have told you! You know, I never dreamed of marrying. I somehow never thought about it. I dream about the stage, about art. And then Yan told me so much about this, you know? Now I simply scorn marriage. Just think that I'd have to kiss someone when I didn't feel like it or bear children when I don't need them at all. Or not go abroad without my husband's permission. In general, be dependent on someone else. My God! What could be better than freedom? I was born a gypsy, Mark. That's what dear Frau Kessler said. And if I got married, my husband would hang himself from indignation or throw me out of the house. I'm a terrible egotist, Mark! I've been that way since childhood. Obligations are abhorrent to me and I can't bear force."

Manya is still suspicious that Steinbach has other women, but he assures her that "there is no one in the way people expect." She asks him to recall what he was thinking of that night in the train station while he stared at the moon.

Her voice resounded with triumph. He laughed heartily. It was so strange to hear his first genuine laughter.

"There's nothing funny about that," she said seriously. "I've lived so long on these memories! And I've invested so many dreams in them."

"Senta,"* he interrupted her, smiling quietly. "You're a real Senta."

"Who's that?" Manya started.

"Have you seen Wagner's opera, *The Flying Dutchman*?"

Suddenly Manya jumped up, clapping her hands and twirling around the room.

"I have it! Now I remember who you look like! You're the Flying Dutchman!"

"A crawling Dutchman," Steinbach whispered gloomily.

"How so?" She halted abruptly in front of the ottoman, her eyes wide open, her lips parted, utterly expectant.

"My soul has no wings. I'm a crawling Dutchman."

Manya burst into peals of laughter until tears rolled down her cheeks. Even her dimples were laughing. Catlike, she leaped lightly onto the ottoman and wound her arms around Steinbach's neck.

"Be so kind as to think back! You were standing at the edge of the platform and looking at the moon, and we hid behind you like shadows. Who was in your thoughts?"

"I don't remember."

"It wasn't that you were in love with a petite blonde married woman? Hopelessly in love?"

"I don't remember!"

"God, what a terrible memory!" Manya said angrily and punched the pillow. "Well, make up something! Don't you see that I long for the extraordinary?"

"I have no imagination. I'm boring, Manya," he sadly replied.

"And you had no sense that we were sneaking behind you? That you . . . had taken over our souls?" Her eyes suddenly grew big and deep. "What a strange thing life is, Mark! Only a year ago we stood a few steps away from each other and that was such a distance! And how could I think that you—so proud and exceptional—would fall for me?"

Impulsively he drew her to him.

"I was insane, Manya!" he said hoarsely, with painful passion. "I don't remember what filled my blind soul in those moments. Probably something insignificant and prosaic. My soul felt no sacred presentiment that there beside me stood my Fate!"

He threw her head back and gazed deep into her eyes with his bottomless pupils.

Then he pressed himself to her lips. And once more the abyss parted soundlessly beneath their feet and looked on them with mute eyes. It summoned them.

And time stopped.

Vera Filippovna wants Manya to cease meeting Steinbach, and Manya, chastened, agrees. Sonya defends her, guessing that Manya loves him (for Sonya herself nurses an unrequited love for him). Vera Filippovna is horrified by Sonya's seeming approval of free love, and predicts Manya's future as a kept woman.

Manya was writing:

"I love you, Mark! I love you madly. Now that I can't meet you because I've given my word I realize that my whole life is in this love, in our meetings. I'm giving in, because otherwise I'd have to go to Moscow. And what will I do there without you? Oh, if only we didn't have to part!

"They say that you'll ruin me. What does that mean? If ruin is your love, then let me be ruined! It's better to live one year in mad happiness than drag out a long life without Beauty.

"Death? Oh, I do fear a long bedridden illness and the smell of medicine. I'm afraid of a gradual decline and the weariness of those around me and the alienation that rises up like a wall, imperceptibly and terribly, between the dying and his loved ones. Do you remember *The Death of Ivan Ilyich*?* And how people strive to die in their own apartment, their own bed, and in the bosom of their family die 'of a long and grave illness' as they write in the papers? But a voluntary and sudden death... What happiness! Yan used to say: 'Yes, one must know how to live beautifully. But it's even more important to die beautifully.' If you fall out of love with me, then I'll mount the barricades and perish joyfully and beautifully. I've dreamed so often about this sort of end over the last two years! What have I to fear if even death is in my power? If I never know weariness and loathing?

"Mark, I'm writing you because my soul is so full. Everyone is asleep. It's night. Please come tomorrow without fail! I'll savor your brows. You'll sing and I'll forget how it pained me when strangers trampled the flowers of my soul. They're yours, Mark! Pick them! Get drunk on their scent! And throw them away if that is how it must be—if love passes, as Yan told me. Then I'll die, without tears and without curses, as do butterflies who live only one day."

The threesome sat in the summerhouse: Manya, Sonya, and Steinbach. Sonya looked shy. Such a tender smile. "Dear girl!" Steinbach thought. "It's a comfort to be with you!"

Suddenly she rose, remembering something.

"Excuse me! They're serving tea now and Mama docsn't know where the keys are. I'll be back."

At last they were alone!!

Manya threw herself on Steinbach's chest and pressed her entire body against his in a mighty, passionate embrace.

For a long time they did not speak. Manya's eyes glistened with tears of ecstasy.

"Did you read my letter, Mark? Did you?"

"Yes. I have it with me, close to my breast. I'll never part with it!"

"Are you happy, Mark? Does my love make you happy?"

"I bless you, Manya!" he uttered sadly. Then he suddenly remembered something and moved away.

"I'm leaving tomorrow to go abroad."

"What?"

"I'll return, my child. I'll be back soon—in two weeks, and perhaps even sooner. I received a telegram this morning. My daughter's sick."

"Are you going to *her*?"

"I'm going to my sick daughter."

"No! No! I won't let you! Mark, don't go! Don't break my heart! If you go that means that you haven't loved me a single minute!"

"You're cruel. Hear me out!"

"You're returning to *her*? Oh, why did I write you that letter! Why did we meet? Give it back, right now! I don't love you anymore! I hate you!"

He had grown pale, as if someone had threatened to take his life.

She turned away and sobbed, her head fallen back on the bench, and she forgot about everything else in the world. He quietly slipped to his knees to humbly beg forgiveness. He promised to think about her every minute.

She impulsively turned around and hugged him around the neck.

"Mark! Mark! You're so mad! Why are you going away? Why aren't you afraid to go! Oh, you shuddered! You understand me? How can you tempt fate? I have a foreboding that we will never meet again."

"Manya, don't say such things!" he whispered in superstitious horror, hiding his face in his hands.

A minute later she seemed to have calmed down. She had stopped crying and was thinking about something.

"Mark, when everyone is asleep tonight, you must come back to the summerhouse."

"When?"

"At midnight. Will you come?"

"I will."

"Swear to me! Swear, Mark!"

"I swear."

"Manya! Tea is served!" Sonya shouted in the distance.

"Let's go now! Do my eyes look very tearstained? Is my nose puffy? No! Better you not look! My nose is my cross to bear! What I wouldn't give for a classic profile!"

During teatime Manya dreams of the upcoming night, while the assembled company talks about their neighbor, Nikolay Nelidov (Manya's "angelic" horseman), remarking on his loving relationship with his mother and his affair with the British Lady Hamilton. They also gossip about Nelidov's plans to buy up Steinbach's estate. In private Sonya tells Manya more about Nelidov, the first man in the district in comparison with Steinbach because he's not a Jew.

Oh, what a sultry, dry night! Huge, passionate, golden eyes sparkled and flashed between the branches of the poplars and lime trees.

What delight to wait for this moment, to steal out clad only in a housecoat and to stand stockstill on the creaking stairs! Stupid Barboska hadn't recognized her and barked. How frightening to think that you might stumble upon the old man and he might shoot his rifle at you, mistaking you for a *thief*. No, what sort of thief moves noiselessly in a housecoat with loosened braid? He might take her for a mermaid or a witch and run away without a backward glance. And the next day, shaking with fear, tell the whole village about his encounter with evil spirits.

She waited, pressing her breast on the wattle fence, her eyes piercing the gloom. It was so dark under the trees, but the road was visible for some distance. Why wasn't he here?

She leaped quietly over the collapsed fence near the stump where Roza had once sat with Zyama. Then she walked slowly along the familiar road. Her heart was knocking in her breast and made listening difficult.

Someone was riding along. Yes! Someone was coming. You couldn't see him, but you could hear him. What if it was a stranger?

She hid behind a roadside poplar.

"Someone tall? It's he! His shoulders!"

In one catlike leap she jumped into the road from behind the tree, laughing happily. The heated horse reared up.

"Manya! Careful! You could be killed!"

"At last! Mark, I'm breathless from happiness... Come this way! Watch your step!" she whispered, leading him to the fence. "That's the way! One more step ... and we're here!"

The horse, tethered to a tree behind the fence, snorted.

"Oh, Mark, how I waited for you! Kiss me ..."

"Manya, let's ride to my place! I'll put you in the saddle and in ten minutes we'll be there."

"You want to carry me off?"

Her voice rang out ecstatically.

"Yes, yes, for an hour or two. I'll bring you back. I grabbed a cape. No one will notice you."

His voice was so impassioned! Or did it seem that way because he was whispering? She couldn't make out his face beneath the trees, and his kisses made her head spin.

"I'm not afraid of anything. Let's go! This is our last night, and then come what may!"

It was so strange, as if they were in a fairy tale.

Donning the cape, she sat mounted in front, his arms around her. The horse slowly picked its way along the cliff, past the cross and past the grove where Yan used to wait for her. Steinbach kept kissing her hair, her temples, her ears. Fire and ice coursed up and down her back and through her whole body.

This must be a dream from which she'd soon awaken.

Here was Lipovka. He jumped off before they reached the railing and lifted Manya down.

"Wait for me here one minute, in the shadows. I'll give the groom my horse."

It was so strange to sit and wait here alone in the dark road! The black cape blended her silhouette into the night gloom. How high the sky was! How bright the stars!

"And what will become of me a year from now?"

He was coming. How well she knew his footsteps, his insinuating gait! He took her by the hand. They walked along, embracing.

At the gates a dark figure materialized.

"Is that you, Ostap?"

"Yes, Mark Leksandrych."

"Go to bed, Ostap! I've no need of you."

The old Ukrainian lazily put his hat back on and shuffled back to the lodge.

What business was it of his who stood there in black? Boy or girl? Let 'em be! For fifteen years he'd served the late Steinbach faithfully and truly, and now he served his son. A lot of people came to the master at night, and many of them stayed the night through. They came at night and left at dawn. Not so long ago some woman stayed there about a week. He was the only one who saw the master lead her into the palace. So if the whole district was searching for her, what business was it of his? The masters paid him well, God preserve them! Like princes they paid. And old Ostap knew how to keep his mouth shut, and his eyes didn't see what shouldn't be seen.

In the study the fireplace glowed, shielded by a tall Japanese screen.

There was no light. The heavy blinds were drawn. Even the shutters were closed. It was so mysterious, as if they were cut off from the world . . .

The house was asleep. Besides, who lived in this house aside from Mark and his terrifying uncle? One never saw the servants and everything was done soundlessly, as if by magic.

Each minute was filled with meaning.

He drew her into his arms. His hand rested high on her body, almost at her breast. It frightened her somehow. She quietly removed his fingers and pushed them away.

"Manya, tell me about yourself! About your childhood, your schooling, your first daydreams. Let me gaze into your young enigmatic soul, into that forbidden world of girlish dreams! Think out loud, as if I'm not here."

And Manya spoke obliviously, in a delirium, half-whispering . . . about how she had loved a picture of an angel with an implacable gaze and a proud profile. How she dreamed of him for years on end, and was in torment waiting for him. And how she believed that they would meet someday after death, in the next world.

"And I wanted to die. During a hard frost I opened a window and leaned out naked and shivered . . . and just ended up with a cold. I remember that I set myself to live only three months more, until Easter, and then I'd die the first day of Easter. And I began to lose weight and melt away and became so apathetic. My strength was ebbing with each passing day."

"That's terrible! You really might have perished. What saved you?"

"Ha, ha! You won't believe it. A concert. Yes . . . a concert in which I danced to music. . ."

"Character dances?"

"No! My own. Oh, Mark, I have a singular talent! I'm a born ballerina 'with a striking sense of rhythm,' as my teacher would say. When I hear music, I feel like moving! It's an irresistible need, a passion. At first everyone laughed at me. But then they were in raptures."

"I understand. You dance your own creations, like the famous Isadora Duncan?"

"Oh, don't speak to me about her! I can't bear to remember her dirty heels! Frau Kessler bought tickets for herself, Sonya, and me with her own money. At first we were charmed, and it seemed like my dream come true. But then she twisted her arms about so unaesthetically! She has such a hypocritical and artificial smile! She has such a poor figure!"

"And you?"

"Oh, my body is beautiful, Mark. I know this. I've studied its lines so often in the mirror! I think that if I studied I'd be somebody. I'm much more graceful than this famous Duncan, and no taller than she is. Cleo de Merode is my ideal of beauty. What a tragic, inspired face she has!"

"You'd like to see her?"

"Madly! But she's in Paris."

They did not speak for a long time. He bit his lips, uncertain about expressing what filled his soul.

"It's strange," Manya whispered thoughtfully. "At one time I thought that I'd always love my dream—that face of an angel—and that I'd live only to meet him. I believed that this was my fate. But then I saw Yan's eyes and forgot that face. When Yan died I also believed that my life was over, that my soul would never blossom again. But here I've met you. And Yan is forgotten. Mark, what does this mean?"

"Life . . ."

She pressed her face to his chest.

"Does this mean there is no eternal love?"

"No."

"Oh, Mark, how painful that is! Do you feel the same way? I hear such sorrow in your voice!"

"You're more fortunate than I am. It's easier to begin life without illusions than to lose them as I did."

"No, Mark, no! Maybe that's life, but I'll be stronger than life! I will love you forever!"

Oh, marvelous, unforgettable words!

His heart pounded as he ran his fingers through her hair.

"And that . . . other man?" he asked hoarsely.

"That one? He's also forgotten," Manya calmly replied.

"Senta! My dear Senta. . . And if you meet him some day? Your dream?"

"I've already met him," she answered softly.

Steinbach trembled.

"Yes. It happened two years ago. Sonya and I were sitting in the meadow, and he rode by on a gray horse."

"Was this a dream, Manya?"

"No. I see his face even now. The crown of golden hair, the high forehead, the proud profile, the gray, hard eyes, the little beard. I see his clothes, his leggings. His helmet. He removed it and bowed to us, like this. Mark? What's wrong? Why are you so pale? Why are those marvelous brows furrowed in sorrow? Is something hurting you?"

"No, nothing. It will pass. A little prick of the heart. Manya . . . I know him."

"Whom?"

"Your horseman. I know him. I've guessed. . ."

"Dear Mark! Forget about him! What need do I have of him? Silly me, why did I tell you this? I don't want you to suffer! Don't you believe that you're my only love? Let ten horsemen appear before me! I renounce them all for you. Don't you believe me?"

"There's a good proverb, Manya: a spring path is not a road. All of us in the labyrinth of life are feeling our way to our true path. And often when we think that we've found a way out of the labyrinth, we come upon a dark dead end. A woman's soul wanders even more helplessly in that gloom. You don't love me, Manya. And you didn't love Yan. Love is still to come."

"Don't speak that way!"

"You don't think this confession comes easily to me? Unfortunately, I don't have the sort of temperament that can blind and deceive me. And, unfortunately, I love you too much."

She concentrated on his strange words.

"Manya, can you fulfill a request of mine?"

"Anything, Mark! Anything you want! I only want you to be happy!"

"Dance something of your own for me now!"

FIGURE 4
Lev Bakst, costume for "Wilde's *Salome*: Dance of the Seven Veils" (1908).
A member of the fin-de-siècle group World of Art (Mir Iskusstva),
Bakst created costumes and stage designs that combined decorative,
kinetic, and erotic elements. State Tretyakov Gallery, Moscow.

She stood up impetuously, with darkened eyes.

"Yes, yes! That would be good! Will you play?"

"On the zither. Remember Turgenev wrote that the old soul of the Jew lives and weeps in the zither. That may be why I love the instrument. I'll play something sad. Something that matches my mood."

"Oh, Mark, this is impossible! I'll get all tangled up in this shapeless dress!"

"Take it off! Over there by the fire, behind the screen. I'll turn around. I'll give you a marvelous old cloth. Do you want to try it on? You can wrap yourself up in it any way you like."

He went over to an ancient carved locker made of oak, and drew from it a faded fine silk fabric embroidered in gold. It wafted forth the odor of decay, of the irrevocable.

"God! What splendor!" Manya said, plunging her face into the silk. "Are these imperial robes, Mark?"

"They were taken from a Catholic statue stolen by Cromwell's forces. Thousands of lips have touched its hem. Do you see the traces of dead kisses?"

"Mark, this fabric is enough to create a mood. I already hear music in my soul. I see images. Mark, turn away! I have to undress. It's so thrilling when this cold cloth touches my shoulders! Give me a pin! Why are you trembling so, Mark? Why can't I recognize your face? Turn away now!"

"What are you doing, Manya?" he asked thickly, not turning around.

"I'm taking off my shoes . . . and I can't dance in my stockings! Why are you talking through clenched teeth? Are you in pain again? This fabric caresses my shoulders so delightfully! Mark. . . Sit down and be quiet. . . I'm ready. . . Where is your zither? I'm coming out. Begin! I feel like a goddess. . ."

When Steinbach was far away, Manya often recalled that night.

She could still feel his kisses on her legs, and see his new and terrible face.

The fiery ring encircled them both and drew tighter and tighter, constricting their breath.

And then she fell into the abyss that stared out from Mark's eyes. The mystery of life suddenly unfolded before her.

Mark tore down those veils!

Would she ever forget him? Is it possible to fall out of love with the man who first held the poison of pleasure to one's lips?

But he wouldn't forget her! No! For now she knew her power.

At night tears flowed onto her hot pillow.

"It's nothing," Manya told herself. "I've got to control myself! Somehow these two weeks will pass and he'll return. He can't not return now! And we'll be together. We'll go to Paris and never part. Only death will separate us. But death is glorious and bold, like our love!"

BOOK TWO

Steinbach hadn't come back. His promised date of return had long since passed. When he'd departed the roses were blooming. Now the gold of autumn flamed in the trees, and leaves died meekly beneath one's feet. The evenings were brisk and the days shorter . . .

She was tired of watching the road, tired of waiting . . .

What had been between them? Had there been anything at all? It had melted away like her dreams, like a cloud in the dying sky.

Now she was tired of living. The cold of indifference held her soul in a iron embrace.

Had she really suffered? Had she really loved? Every passing hour carried off some of her soul, a bit of her youth and life. She didn't remember the past. She didn't look into the future. She was sleeping.

"Manya! Yoohoo!"

Sonya was calling, but Manya didn't have the energy to shout back.

Sonya ran into the summerhouse. A weeping birch dangled its green arms by the very entrance and permitted no one passage, catching everyone by the hair with its long branch. Sonya impatiently brushed it aside, her eyes mysterious and her smile strange.

"Manya, come quickly!" she said in agitation, gesturing strangely. "Do you know who's come? You won't believe it. That rider. . . Remember the one we saw in the meadow two years ago. It's the very same one. And imagine, that's Nelidov!"

Manya sat down, brushing heavy curls from her forehead. Her dulled eyes flashed. Her heart pounded and then stopped.

It wasn't a dream? And happiness would return?

She stood up. Sonya spied an awakening soul in those enormous eyes that had been empty only yesterday—the mysterious soul of a woman. Joining hands, they ran off.

There on the terrace Vera Filippovna was at the samovar, festive and beaming. Uncle was stubbing out his cigars in the blue haze. And there was someone else. Strong shoulders. An unfamiliar voice, with clear, almost childlike laughter.

Manya made a sign to Sonya, and they hid behind the old lime tree.

"Well, yes. Now everything's clear!" Vera Filippovna said happily. "But we didn't know what to think. Vasya, do you hear?" She turned to Gorlenko, who had just returned from the fields. "Nikolay Yuryevich has come into his inheritance. He's been to Petersburg twice and spent an entire month there."

"And so? Did you get a lot?"

"It's really nonsense. But at the moment this money is for us . . . you understand."

He rose. He was tall, handsome. Manya could see his shoulders, his curly fair hair, his proud profile. He shook his host's hand.

"Of course we do! Who doesn't need money? My congratulations!"

"And what was of interest in Petersburg?" Uncle mused.

Nelidov turned around, and the girls saw his face. It was fine, well-bred, with a small, reddish beard and a high forehead. He seemed bright-white from the dust that covered his thin cheeks.

"You know what? I could have been in Timbuktu for all I noticed. With all these formalities and problems, I scoured the city like a hound for days. And this at the height of the growing season!"

He laughed. His teeth were small, even, and white.

"What a pretty smile!" Sonya whispered.

Yes. It was *he*, the one who'd filled her girlish dreams, who'd given her her first stormy tears of then unfamiliar desire. The first powerful, unforgettable rapture. She didn't listen to a word, only the sounds of his voice and laughter. She gazed at him as if she were memorizing his movements, the turn of his head, his quivering fine nostrils, the gestures of his small refined hands. He was so unlike everyone else! She was staring at the one bright spot in a series of forgotten days, at the face of an angel with an implacable gaze, for whom a child's heart had burned and pounded.

"Manya, Sonya, come here!" Vera Filippovna shouted, seeing their white dresses in the park.

Nelidov was relating something to Uncle as the girls walked up the steps. Suddenly he saw Manya's face, the expression of her wide-open eyes that seemed at once ecstatic and terrified. Her gaze drank him in greedily and provocatively. He suddenly fell silent, and slowly stood up.

"My daughter . . . Manya Yeltsova, her friend."

Without bowing his head or body, he raised their hands to his lips. It was a dry, careless kiss. The usual ritual you don't even notice. But its unexpectedness shook Manya's entire body. And he saw this, and a terrible, dark wave suddenly flooded his mind.

In vain Nelidov sought to control himself. It was a good thing that Uncle was at last bestirring himself and dipping into his inexhaustible store of memories. He could remain silent. What had just happened? Why was his heart pounding so painfully, as if in fear? "I've probably turned pale." But who was she, this girl with eyes like stars? And what did these amazing eyes want from him?

He was afraid to raise his lashes. He felt her hungry, taunting stare. He didn't notice Sonya.

Once she'd finished her cup of tea, Manya walked down the stairs and sat down on the step, half turned away from their guest. She looked at the garden, the sky. But she didn't see the sunset, and didn't even listen to the conversation. She was entirely in the thrall of her feelings.

Her long lashes were sharply delineated against the bright sky. "An entire forest of lashes," thought Nelidov. He gazed at her hot, dark cheek, the irregular line of her profile, her bright lips that resembled a flower. Her disheveled dark curls shone red now in the light of the setting sun, like an aureole around her small head. But she herself was straight, pliant, and strong, like a young birch. With growing agitation he stared at her luxuriant braid, her narrow back in its light blouse, her nervously trembling shoulders.

A dark whirlwind churned up his soul—a mysterious and terrible whirlwind. It took his breath away, sped up his heart, fired his blood with unbearable longing. Why? Never, not even in the years of his demanding and avid youth, had he known the sort of burning desire now aroused in him by a single glance at these arrows of lashes, these bright lips, these trembling shoulders in a white blouse.

He rose. They joyfully urged him to stay to dinner. He thanked them and said no.

"Mama worries when I'm late. She still hasn't recovered from her stroke. . ."

"Ah, in that case, of course. . . But do come to dinner on Sunday. Without fail. You'll come?"

"Thank you. I'll try," he answered absentmindedly, shaking everyone's hands, and quickly kissing the fingers of his hostess and Sonya.

Then he was standing before Manya. She stood up, and he suddenly paled from the full force of his attraction. They gazed into each other's eyes . . . no . . . into each other's souls. Her hungry, taunting eyes stared straight into his soul. They told him: "I've waited for you my whole life, only you . . ."

And his rough, dark gaze answered: "You will be mine. I want you so."

Sensing his power, this time he took her compliant hand and raised it to his lips. And now his lips were hot, and the kiss was full of significance.

His bay beauty of a horse softly neighed, tossing its slender head at its master. Petro respectfully led it into the courtyard.

Everyone spilled out onto the porch. Nelidov jumped into the saddle, as if he had become one with his horse. Uncle looked on with delight and envy. Ah, in his day he looked grand on horseback! If it weren't for his leg. . .

"Goodbye!" they cried as he left.

Manya turned around and went into the park. Everything had been a lie, everything had been a dream until this day, this meeting. She hadn't loved. She hadn't lived. Had there really been anything? Let it sink into the abyss—needless torments, pitiful tears! The only truth was in the joy that flooded her soul with light and drove away the darkness with its fire. The only truth lay in what they'd said to each other with their eyes on the porch. . .

The young people, including Lika and her colleague Anna Vasilievna (nicknamed Attila by Uncle), take to gathering at Uncle's to talk radical politics. During one such evening, they argue vociferously about Nelidov, Uncle defending his "conqueror's strength," and the young women, with the exception of Manya, attacking him for his obscurantism, cruelty, and arrogance. Manya ponders what everyone is saying and doesn't care who Nelidov is. She simply loves him as lord of the earth. Inspired, she dances in a mad fury for the assembled and disturbs them deeply.

In the meantime, Nelidov has become obsessed with Manya.

Manya watched the road, her breast pressed against the wattle fence. At last! The rhythm of hoofbeats blended with her beating heart and she ran from the summerhouse into the house. The table was set on the terrace. Dinner was ready.

He was already in the courtyard. Hiding behind the pillars on the porch, she delighted in all his movements. How well he wore his clothes! How firm and proud was his gait! How beautiful were the restrained, spare gestures of his shapely hands! He was a "prince," just as Yan had been.

With his sharp sight he'd already espied Manya there, in the courtyard, but he went up to her last and everyone noticed how his thin cheeks quickly flushed. He did not kiss her hands this time, but looked her straight in the eye, cruel and full of desire, the way a savage looks at a woman he is about to carry off. Manya answered him with an innocent, naive, and ready gaze. And her face was beautiful and touching.

Sonya's heart fell. Now Manya's secret was revealed to everyone.

"Oh, hell!" Uncle thought enviously. "That's the reason. . ."

At dinner Vera Filippovna seated Nelidov between herself and Sonya. Manya sat opposite. They served the appetizers. Gorlenko raised a strange dusty bottle.

"Let's drink up, Nikolay Yuryevich! This is my grandfather's old vodka."

"I don't drink, thank you."

"I know you don't drink. But in this case you can't refuse. There are only two bottles left."

Their guest smiled drily and made a gesture of refusal. Uncle clinked glasses with the host and noticeably brightened.

Although Nelidov demurs, both Sonya and Manya partake of some homemade liqueur and become quite lively. During and after the meal, Manya teases Nelidov about being a rank obscurantist.

"But is that really bad—to be an obscurantist?"

"It's terrible!" Manya clasped her hands together comically.

"Manya, écoutez . . . au nom de ciel!"

"Don't worry, Vera Filippovna. Mademoiselle . . ."

"Yeltsova, Manya Yeltsova."

"Mademoiselle Yeltsova is a charming child."

"Ah! She's completely mad. When she gets like *this,* she turns the whole house upside down!"

Nelidov's nostrils quivered. Manya's coquetry was as artless and sparkling as champagne and it acted on him spontaneously. He felt he was drunk without wine.

"She's still a girl," he thought, "and she has such a naked thirst for love! She's summoning me with her laughter, her voice. Her laughter is like the snorting of a young filly untethered for the first time. It's just as silvery and enticing. Ah, I'd so love to embrace her, to melt into her! And destroy her in one burst of ecstasy! My God! She's so marvelous, and this feels so new! It's so hard to control myself!"

"You know, I've heard a great deal about you!" Manya said provocatively, and looked at him boldly and mercilessly.

"What? Tell me! I'm as curious as a woman."

"Manya, Manya," the hostess shouted from her seat and stamped her foot, forgetting herself.

Gorlenko moved restlessly on his chair, which creaked under his weight. Uncle winked at Sonya and chuckled.

"What have you heard? Something good or something bad?"

"Ah! Unfortunately, only bad..."

Uncle and Sonya laughed loudly.

"My God! Don't listen to her, Nikolay Yuryevich! Manya, I'll send you from the table."

"What exactly have you heard?"

"You're cruel. You're a bird of prey. You're an Achilles who knows no compassion."

"Ah!" he said shortly. "I've nothing against this assessment. Life is war, and I don't want to be the conquered."

"Manya! Have some water. It's simply stupid, Fedya, to make a child drunk. Pour her some water!"

"We're used to it," Sonya said naively, but loudly.

Her father shot her a fiery glance. He was always gloomy in his cups.

"And wasn't it your suitor who taught you this nonsense?" he asked Manya angrily.

Nelidov raised his brows.

"Mademoiselle Yeltsova *already* has suitors?"

"What does *already* mean?" Sonya joined in, in defense. "She'll soon be nineteen. She's finished her courses."

"And she's succeeded in snaring Steinbach!" Uncle interjected.

There was a pause. Nelidov lightly pushed back his chair and stared at Manya's burning cheeks, her lowered head. Sonya clearly saw a grimace pass over his features. She suddenly paled and her heart began to pound.

Nelidov kept staring fixedly at Manya's burning ears, watching how her blush crept even to her tender neck and how her tousled, seemingly guilty head bent still lower.

There was a strange silence at the table.

"You... and Steinbach?" Nelidov uttered this weightily and quietly, as if thinking out loud.

Sonya dropped her fork. She spoke with restraint, but hostilely.

"How strange that sounds! One could translate your question as 'a rose and a toad,' yes?"

"Almost..."

"That's enough! He's an Adonis! Well, Manya, why don't you say anything? After all, you think he's an Adonis, too."

"She's even in love with him," Uncle put in innocently.

Without looking up, Manya felt his insistent, cold gaze on her.

"He's a Yid," Nelidov dropped between clenched teeth. "That says it all."

"That's disgraceful!" Sonya shouted and noisily moved away from their guest. She was almost suffocating. Her agitation was so unexpected and her hostility so evident that her parents became flustered.

"She's found a fine victim to defend," Vera Filippovna exclaimed in amazement.

"Mama! He's an exceptional person. He does so much good."

"For his own?" Nelidov replied.

"No, for Russians, and for Ukrainians."

"Philanthropy is evil. It corrupts those who give and those who take."

"That's easy to say! And where were you when there was a famine here? You were calmly pursuing your diplomatic career in London. But here Steinbach's father donated fifty thousand rubles to the Red Cross and for two years his son funded soup kitchens in Elkiny and Lipovka. Now he's helping the unemployed. . ."

"Sonya, Sonya . . ." the hostess said as she came to her senses.

Gorlenko sniffed gloomily.

At the word "Lipovka" Nelidov's face trembled as from physical pain. He said hoarsely, "His millions are the people's flesh and blood."

Sonya laughed impertinently. "You know what? We won't argue about who bears the greater debt to the people, Steinbach or we and you."

"Eh, Sonya! It's clear Steinbach has turned your head as well," smirked Uncle, very pleased with this little scandal in a good family.

Sonya flushed and became flustered.

Nelidov spoke slowly through his teeth: "In giving away that 50,000 Steinbach of course counted on a decoration, or perhaps admission into the gentry. Many of them have attained that honor."

Sonya laughed scornfully.

"What's membership in the Russian nobility to him, when he's already a baron, and his ancestors are older than our and your lines. Pardon me! I forgot that you belong to the Rurik dynasty."

"That's it!" Uncle interposed. "I told you that he was of the Davidov branch. His mother's name was Davidson. He's of royal blood. No wonder the late Steinbach and Baron Girsh were agitating for the establishment of a Palestinian kingdom."

Nelidov didn't notice Manya now. He looked to one side or above her head. She no longer existed for him. Manya felt as though she'd been stripped naked and laid on the table. If only it would end soon!

She ran into the summerhouse, wringing her hands. Hatred for Steinbach suffocated her.

Sonya came in. "Go! They're drinking tea," she said gloomily.

Manya rose silently and moved off like a sleepwalker.

"She's silent, as if her mouth were full of water," Sonya grumbled along the way. "A fine love! They're insulting him."

"I don't love him," Manya burst out candidly.

"Wha-a-t? What's this?"

"I don't love him."

"Are you mad? You loved him only yesterday!"

"No. It was a long time ago. Now it repels me to remember that we . . . ah, leave me alone! Don't say one word about him!"

Sonya stared at her almost fearfully. For the first time Manya's soul seemed to her a bottomless chasm.

"What a weathervane! Whither the wind blows, there goes she. I've guessed right that you're in love with this obscurantist?"

Manya raised her lashes. How sorrowful and profound was her gaze! It was as if she'd grasped some wisdom of life that was closed to others. And her face and silence were so expressive, so full of meaning, that Sonya was suddenly overwhelmed by repentance.

"Manya, forgive me! I was so sorry for Steinbach, and for that reason I was rude to you. But how did this happen so fast? Ah! I've never understood you."

Nelidov calculates how to extricate his estate from debt. We learn that he hates everything that seems to him to be Western: workers' strikes, parliamentary debates, feminist caucuses, the Salvation Army in London. He bids adieu to the Gorlenkos, befuddling Vera Filippovna, who had dreamed of matching him up with Sonya.

Back at home, Nelidov tells his mother that Sonya is not his type, but he admires the family and is grateful for their aid to her during his absence.

Manya had fallen silent once more, and again spent whole days in the summerhouse. But this was not the slow snuffing out of a fading soul. In her silence and solitude the white, regal lily of her first love bloomed luxuriously. All that Yan had tossed into her dreaming soul and that slept in its mysterious depths, all of Steinbach's dark passion and the magic of inflamed sensuality that had been powerless to summon her to life now awoke from a single glance of the one her soul awaited.

There was no past. It was dead. Life began only now. Yan and he . . . they were links in the same chain. The same joy. The same brilliance. And between these two lay a dark gap, an abyss out of which a pale and now alien face stared at her.

For hours Manya watched the road and waited. Her star-eyes, big and voracious, penetrated the distance, calling and promising. . . And *he* was coming again. . . How could he not come, when her entire soul and every fibre of her body called and waited for him?

Nelidov arrived in a charabanc. He drove himself. A marvelous autumn evening beckoned them out for a walk. The sunset was blinding.

Manya rushed from the summerhouse into the courtyard like a whirlwind. The barking dogs raced to the charabanc. But the hostess was in the garden and the host in the orchard with his tenant Leyboy. Sonya flung open the window and looked down.

What happiness! They were alone. Manya silently nodded. With blazing eyes and a bright smile, Nelidov removed his English helmet and greeted her.

"What a splendid horse!" Manya whispered and stroked the steed's neck. The horse snorted and looked sidelong in fright at her scarlet blouse.

"Do you like horses?" Nelidov asked. His voice trembled so, and had such a strange tone, as if he had said: "Do you love me?"

"Madly!" Manya replied. And her declaration burned in her voice.

He understood. They were silent and confused, with downcast eyes. The profound sense of these trivial words was clear to them both. He struggled to control himself. It was as if the ground were swimming beneath his feet.

"Perhaps . . . you'd like to take a drive?" he whispered with lips suddenly gone dry.

She heard the words. But what was in them? His voice summoned her into the Unknown and the Inevitable, down the mysterious paths of her fate.

"Yes!"

She raised her lashes. Oh, what eyes! How much they promised! And again they stood together without moving, thunderstruck. They were both pale and speechless, without understanding what they had to do next.

Sonya came to their aid, walking up and greeting the guest.

"Let's have some tea! Petro will take the horse."

"Pardon . . . Mademoiselle Yeltsova wants to take a drive. Vera Filippovna won't object?"

"Oh, no, of course not! You'll be back in an hour? Where are you off to, Manya? At least put on another blouse or take my scarf."

Standing on the porch, Sonya watched as the charabanc drove out of the estate gates, accompanied by the dogs' loud barking. And some unaccountable anxiety scratched at her heart like a mouse.

The horse ran at a round trot along the familiar road. The steppe embraced them with green arms, significant and silent, and shut their mouths. Wind blew into their hot faces and whirled dust along the road. They both were gazing so intently into their souls that they didn't notice their silence for a long while.

The charabanc was cramped. They sat shoulder to shoulder, leg against leg. And this contact seared Nelidov. His consciousness fogged. His knees shook. And he was afraid that she'd feel it.

"Wait, wait," an inner voice told him. "In another minute . . . when we're in the forest."

The forest sailed up to them. It was a forest of oak and spruce, black and cool, somehow entirely gloomy. Likhoy Gai.

The road gradually descended into a ravine.

At last!

Obeying the familiar hand, the horse slowed to a walk. On one side was the forest, on the other a steep clay wall.

They were alone.

With an exhausted sigh Nelidov turned to Manya. He took her hands in his. How it hurt! A cry died on her lips, but something grabbed his throat. And what, indeed, could he say to her? He had never been so helpless, so powerless, before his desire. But so be it! He was ready to pay for this moment with his life.

With the terror of happiness Manya looked into his cruel eyes. A cry, a staggering cry of joy and pain, suddenly burst from her. She fell on his chest. Her outburst decided everything for them both.

He kissed her silently, greedily, rapaciously, like a wild man. Roughly, painfully, and somehow primitively, he caressed her shoulders, breasts, and knees, and with a single blow of his blind and mighty desire destroyed all that had separated them yesterday, even a moment before. What did it matter to the dark force ruling him that one week ago he hadn't even known this girl existed? She was made for him. He'd understood that from the start. Hadn't he lived for this meeting after two years of abstinence? Hadn't he preserved his soul for this first love?

Manya was stunned, depressed. She lay her head helplessly on his shoulder, her eyes closed. Her hands fell to her knees helplessly, their rosy palms turned up.

She hadn't expected this. She hadn't wanted it. She was crushed by these stormy, crude, unfamiliar caresses. Something cried out helplessly and protested in her soul. Was this really necessary? Now? So soon . . .

He'd taken her into his arms like booty, and made off into the woods. She, like a slave, had succumbed to his desire.

She herself was submissive and dispassionate. She felt that he'd wanted to destroy her in his embrace, that this wasn't even love, but some kind of blind hatred. But so be it! Even if he strangled her, she wouldn't raise a finger to stop him.

It was getting dark.

He came to himself. He silently gave her his hand and led her out on the road.

She waited, trembling, for his first words.

But the silence lasted a long time, such an infinitely long time. And Manya's heart was barely beating. How cold it was! God, how cold! She shivered.

Suddenly he dropped the reins and clasped her shoulders.

"At last!" her soul cried. She hid her face in his breast. Her hot tears ran down like spring rain. She felt neither shame nor regret. Her protests drowned in profound tenderness. He was as dear and near to her as if she'd known him for decades.

"Marie . . . Marie . . ." he whispered and kissed her burning face, her wet cheeks. "Forgive me! I don't know how it happened. Don't despise me. I'm ashamed of myself."

"No . . . No! Be silent!" a heated cry tore from her breast, and she put her fingers to his lips.

He kissed them, again and again. He unconsciously bit them. His blood was still raging. He hadn't sated his tormenting desire. . . Ah, if only they could throw caution to the winds and spend one more hour together. But night was already coming on. They were expected.

He took her head in both hands and kissed her on the lips. He bit them painfully so that they bled. And Manya cried out in torment.

"Ah, forgive me! I'm losing my head."

"It's nothing!" she said quickly, and stroked his hand. But tears trembled in her eyes.

The charabanc halted at the gates to the estate. Nelidov silently and somehow hastily kissed Manya's hand.

He was completely extinguished and cold. He didn't even promise to come back the next day.

For a long time she heard the beat of the wheels on the road.

Of course, it was good that he had gone away. Was it really possible to have supper and carry on banal conversation after such moments? But if he'd only uttered one tender word! And that alien formal "you." . . If there had been only one shy kiss . . . tender . . . as Steinbach and Yan had kissed her.

Sonya's white figure suddenly emerged from the darkness.

"Manya, is it you? But we've been waiting. . . You didn't. . . Why are you crying? My dear . . ."

Hugging Sonya by the neck, Manya sobbed on her breast. She sobbed as passionately as a rich man who'd been robbed in a dream and awakened a beggar.

Sonya finds out what has happened, and is further shocked to learn from Manya that Nelidov doesn't love her. Manya knows that she loves Nelidov completely, but he loves only her body. And she admits to Sonya that Steinbach truly loved her.

In the morning Sonya scrutinized her friend's features with a new feeling of alienation and envy.

"When is *he* coming, Manya?"

"I don't know. I didn't ask. He didn't say."

It rained all day. The girls sat upstairs in the attic. Manya was pale, but seemed calm. Sonya was filled with inexplicable anxiety.

"Manya . . . did he promise to marry you?"

Manya turned around and stared with big eyes. Sonya suddenly lost her temper.

"Well, why are you looking like that? Did I say something strange? Of course, any decent man would marry under the circumstances."

"I will never marry," Manya replied.

"Well, those are your views, of course. But he should propose to you. He doesn't reject old customs. On the contrary . . . he has a pious nature."

"Ah, be quiet, Sonya! For God's sake! What does it matter? I want only to see him for the rest of my life. I'd like to be his slave, some thing he touches with his hands. I envy his servant, his horse, the pillow he sleeps on. Sonya, he has such downy, tender cheeks! I so want to stroke them. He's still so young, Sonya, and I'm young. We're a pair. He calls me 'Marie,'" she whispered pensively, and smiled tenderly at her visions.

Sonya was confused.

"But what will come of all this? If only he loved you as Steinbach does. . ."

Manya made a magnificent gesture of disdain.

"If Steinbach laid his kingdom and fiery love at my feet, and Nelidov promised me only poverty and humiliation . . ."

"You'd choose Nelidov?" Sonya cried.

"Oh, yes, of course!"

Sonya stood, dismayed.

What a mystery life is! And what a mystery was Manya's soul! A dark, bottomless well.

Nelidov is deeply disturbed by his rape of Manya and reflects that it is out of character, for he is a man who can control his considerable passion. Moreover, he intends to marry a woman as pure and noble as his mother, and he knows nothing of Manya's background and suspects her of a "temperament" that simply should not exist in a good girl. He sometimes hates Manya for her "sorcery" and feels he does not love her.

"Mama . . . would you hear me out?" Nelidov asked his mother the next evening when they remained alone after dinner.

"Gladly, my dear. . . I've long waited for you to speak."

He sat on a soft ottoman at her feet and tenderly kissed her palms. Then, leaning on his knees, he put his head in his hands so that his face was not visible.

"I must get married, mama," he said slowly and hoarsely, after a long pause full of significance. The old lady's eyes shone, but she bit her lip and waited in silence.

"Forgive me, but this happened so unexpectedly. I'd always thought that I'd first come to you for advice and your blessing, but fate has decided otherwise . . ."

"But who is she?" The quiet question was put after another pause. "Sonya Gorlenko?"

"No, mama! It's her friend, Manya Yeltsova."

"Ah!"

He uncovered his face and looked tormentedly into his mother's eyes.

"Do you love her very much, Nikolenka?"

"Ah, mama! I don't know if it's love or not. I only know that she's as marvelous as life itself, and that I was entirely in her power. Don't ask me anything, dear mama! I must marry and soon, so as not to lose the right to your respect and my own self-respect."

She listened with knitted brows, trying to understand.

Suddenly she bent forward, took her son's head into her hands, and kissed his forehead.

"It's fate, Nikolenka. You can't go against it. God grant you happiness! But I'm glad, you know. My soul ached for you these last two years. It's wrong for such a strong young man to live like a monk. That's tempting fate. Your uncle Andrei also shut himself up on his estate and entered into a liaison with a woman, and you know how that ended?"

"I know, mama."

"Of course, you can't refuse the dying their last request. We all recognized his marriage and his children. But I wouldn't want you to be so humiliated."

"Oh, mama! Were you really afraid of this?"

He recalled Natalka, their maid, and his face flamed.

"No . . . not now, while you're young and I'm still alive. But I'll soon be dead and you'll be alone here."

"Mama! Dear, please don't speak that way."

"That's why I've dreamed so fervently about your marriage. It doesn't matter who your bride is! Only that she not be bourgeois. My soul is open to her. I already love your Marie. Bring her to me as soon as you can! I must see her."

"No, mama. Don't be in a hurry! All of this is too unexpected. Let me get used to it!"

The Gorlenko house is in an uproar, as they guess about the romance between Manya and Nelidov. Vera Filippovna still considers him a fine match, but the two men think he'll drive a wife into the grave and they are positive that he will only play around with Manya.

Nelidov spends the next two days in torment, worrying about the passions Manya arouses in him, but then is calmed by the fact that he is obliged to marry her. He pays the Gorlenkos another visit and acts so simply and tenderly with Manya that he succeeds in charming the skeptical Sonya.

After dinner, the discussion at the Gorlenkos focuses on Nelidov's marrying and elicits his strong views against divorce and his desire for a pretty, meek, and perfectly healthy wife—a wife who neither works nor studies.

After a little pause Nelidov continued as if he were thinking aloud:

"Only physically healthy people have the right to marry so as not to threaten their children with consumption or epilepsy or madness or suicide—with not one hereditary curse."

"Ah, there you're right! Now I understand you."

Vera Filippovna's face was aglow. Hadn't she always been healthy? Hadn't she passed her happy constitution on to Sonya?

"How can you know that?" Gorlenko asked suddenly.

Everyone looked at him. He became confused and fell silent. His big, fat fingers played uncertainly on his stomach.

Nelidov sat down, putting his elbows on his knees, and his head in his hands.

"Degeneracy," he said in a completely changed voice. "What a horror! And how little we think about it! And who of us isn't guilty of this crime? You, Vera Filippovna, just now caught on immediately, as a woman and a mother. What torment to bear children who are already doomed! To wait hour by hour for the sword of Damocles to drop on their heads. My brother fell in love with a girl who had hereditary consumption. He knew about it, but his passion overrode his caution. He has just buried his third child, and his wife is dying a slow death before his very eyes."

"Poor man!" Vera Filippovna exclaimed sincerely.

"When I lived in London, I became friendly with Lord Fife, a marvelous fellow. He passionately loved the daughter of an alcoholic, who was also a lord and a baronet. And his beautiful and loving wife became an incurable drunk by the age of twenty-five and their only child an idiot... My friend has devoted his life to conceal this shameful family secret, this 'skeleton in the closet,' as the English say. But still he loved this woman madly. When she began to suffer from drinking, he shut himself up on his estate and gave up a career in politics for her sake. He was very talented—even prominent!"

"I'd've hanged myself in his place," Gorlenko murmured.

Nelidov lifted his head and stood up.

"Yes, we need to be brutal if we are to sober up our society and save humanity from degeneration. We need to outlaw marriage to neuropaths, and severely punish those who violate the law, the way we punish someone for debauchery or murder, because this amounts to the same thing."

"Hold on!" Uncle suddenly grew irritated, remembering something that clearly pained him and made him forget his manners. "I wouldn't obey anyone who prevented me from marrying the woman I loved. I'd send them to the devil!"

"Uncle! You're a marvel!" Sonya rushed over and kissed him.

"But this is egotism, Fedya. What about the children?"

"There'd be no children . . ."

"Ah!" Nelidov exclaimed coldly and raised his eyebrows. "But for me marriage has no meaning without children."

Uncle whistled. "Who has the right to deny me the happiness I want?"

"We're not savages."

Suddenly Uncle went scarlet. "In the interests of society, you'll say? Enough, Nikolay Yuryevich! All that is nothing but fear of life and suffering. Your fear for your own precious hide is speaking now. Imagine now if some wonderful being fell in love with you, and her only flaw is that somewhere five generations removed someone went mad or killed himself? You'd give her up for this?"

"I'd give her up."

"But if you loved her?"

Nelidov was silent. He grew pale, and everyone saw it.

"I'd still give her up," he said hoarsely.

"Bah! That's abysmal! Now that's real brutality—to destroy your own and another's life on account of some future shadowy misfortunes. That's cowardice, Nikolay Yuryevich!"

"What's wrong with Manya?"

She'd jumped up, her mouth open wide as if she were gasping for air. Deathly white, she clasped her hands to her breast and then suddenly waved them about. An hysterical, half-choked cry burst from her throat. She ran off, and Sonya ran after her.

Everyone jumped up in confusion. They could hear wild hysterical wailing in the distance.

"Light the lamps!" cried the hostess, rushing into the dark rooms upstairs.

When she returned, Nelidov stood motionless with pursed lips. He soon said his goodbyes and did not even inquire about what was wrong with Manya. No one detained him.

Hunched over, pressed to the pommel of the saddle, he galloped home, driving his horse so hard that it seemed the Gorgon head was chasing him. "I must forget her as soon as possible!"

Manya and Sonya have guessed that Nelidov was talking about Manya, and Manya fears there is madness in her family.

Nelidov comes back once more, knowing that he must marry this girl. When he sees her, he is enraptured anew. He interrogates Vera Filippovna about Manya's family, learning of her mother's strange paralysis.

At this point Steinbach returns. Sonya urges Manya to tell him the truth, and declares that their friendship will end if Manya chooses to insult him. Sonya then informs Steinbach of what has happened in preparation for his meeting with Manya.

And here they were, together again. Sitting beside each other. But completely apart.

He bowed low before her, doffing his panama as he had the first time they met. His face was inscrutable.

She angrily gave him her hand. Her fingers were inert. She was merciless as only a woman can be who has fallen in love with someone new and feels burdened by an old love she no longer needs. She sat down at a distance from him, her eyes downcast. Her cheeks flushed and then paled. It seemed she would never be able to look him in the eye. Had *he* really kissed every part of her? Had he. . . Sitting next to him, she was ashamed to remember those intimate, torrid pictures she'd fantasized about a month ago. Oh, if only nothing had happened . . .

But why was he silent? It was obvious that Sonya had prepared him. All the better! Explanations weren't necessary! No need for hints about the past. He was so repellent to her that it seemed she'd scream with disgust if he touched her.

But he didn't think to do so. Alien and aloof, he frowned coldly, as if he were studying her face.

"Sofia Vasilievna said that you'd been sick. You've really changed. What's wrong with you, Manya Sergeyevna?"

"He hasn't fallen out of love with me? Have I really changed for the worse?" Suddenly Manya lost the last remnant of her self-control.

"No. Why do you think so? I'm fine, only I have a headache. But I'm . . . very happy!" she said with a challenge in her voice. And for the first time she looked him in the face clearly and hostilely.

His lips twisted.

"I'm very happy for you. Congratulations!"

He averted his eyes and traced something with his stick in the damp ground.

Manya, of course, didn't expect this. She peered at him sideways with curiosity. "He's repulsive, repulsive . . ." she told herself. "Alien."

But she kept looking at his profile. Involuntarily she noticed everything—he was thinner and very pale. His skin was just like ivory... His pale ears... His transparent bluish eyelids... "He's repulsive! How could I have loved him? But his lashes are fine—long, dark... and those eyebrows. Yes. He is handsome. Whatever Nelidov said, he is handsome. He has an interesting face. A terrifying face. But why did he congratulate me? What does he know?"

Suddenly he lifted his head and their eyes met. Manya blushed and turned away and immediately got angry at herself. An instant later she became agitated. Steinbach's indifference seemed strange to her, impertinent. He's fallen out of love? Cooled off?

"Have you been back long?" she asked with forced calm. "Did you have a good time? Was it interesting to live there? Were there pretty women? Vienna is an exciting city, yes?"

She poked her toe into the ground. Biting his stick, Steinbach stared at her shoes and knees. She blushed to the point of tears and hid her foot. Suddenly she had the feeling that she was falling from a tower with outstretched arms. She turned full face to him. Her eyes burned. She'd lost control.

"Why don't you speak?" she cried sharply, almost rudely. "What do you mean by your silence? Why do you torture me? What do you expect of me?"

He didn't look at her. He listened greedily, trying to understand. His nostrils quivered.

"I'm waiting for you to tell me... about your happiness."

"For me to tell you?"

Something caught her throat.

"Don't I deserve your trust?"

"Why?" she whispered in uncomprehending terror. "Why should you know?"

His eyes were cold and impenetrable. He shrugged his shoulders imperceptibly.

"A strange question, if you haven't changed. I have not."

"Be quiet!" She raised her hand. "Not a word about the past! It's gone, do you hear? And don't you dare speak to me in such a tone!"

She'd forgotten that she'd been offended by his indifference. Now his reference to his love seemed to her the most terrible insult.

"Yes, yes, I forbid you! You don't think you've wronged me? Do you think I'll ever forgive you..." (my tears, she wanted to add, but refrained). Then she asked sharply, with hatred: "Why did you stay away so long? I don't believe in your daughter's illness, do you hear? It was all a lie."

"My daughter died."

Manya stared in silence. There was horror in her eyes. They said nothing for a long time. There was a profound stillness in the park. Only in the distance one could hear singing in the garden. An apple in the nearby orchard thudded softly into the grass.

Suddenly Steinbach raised his head and looked fixedly at Manya. Then he took her hand very quietly.

She was pale. Her memory of those past feelings was vivid. She couldn't put them to sleep. His touch was so timid, but her nerves were shuddering and aching blessedly and fiercely. And the past rose up from the abyss where Nelidov had tossed it.

"You waited for me, Manya?" he asked in a barely audible voice.

"Yes . . . I waited for you."

"You waited too long," he said bitterly. "Life doesn't wait."

Her heart fell. My God! Why did she feel this chaos in her soul once more? Why did she pity him? She needn't!

"You wrote me nothing, not a single line. I thought I was forgotten. I thought . . ."

"I've forgotten nothing!" he interrupted hoarsely, with bridled passion. "I can't forget. But what was I to write you? Words of love that could fall into another's hands and give away our secret? I thought you believed in me. I considered what happened between us so important and profound."

She stood up in horror.

"Be quiet, be quiet!"

"Don't be afraid of me, Manya! And don't try to justify yourself. You're in no way guilty before me. Flowers should spring up under your feet. You deserve to fall asleep with a smile and wake up in joy. But I gave you tears and suffering. I alone am guilty."

She sat down, instantly faint, and covered her face in an unconscious gesture.

"To love, to love, as I did before!" This beat in her temples, rang out in her heart, pounded in her brain. She could no longer hate. She felt no repulsion, just a terrible lack of will. It was a familiar feeling. And that mad, forgotten attraction that so intoxicated her at one time . . . yes, yes . . . this shook her body. Why did it waken? Out of what abyss did it rise up? It was summoned by his voice, his gaze, the simple touch of his hands. So soon? So easily? But, after all, she didn't love him. All these days she had loved another and didn't dream of him, didn't wait for him. Nelidov's face rose before her, haughty, with a disdainful grimace.

"Ma-a-nya! Te-eatime!" Sonya's voice carried from afar.

"No . . . I must end this! I have to put a stop to it. Should I insult him? We can't meet!"

She moved away and smoothed her hair. He could see that her hands were trembling.

"Sonya, of course, told you everything," she said hoarsely, without lifting up her eyes. "I love another. And you yourself understand, Mark . . ."

She stopped suddenly. She'd forgotten his patronymic.

"Aleksandrych," he prompted very quietly, watching her from below and pressing the head of his walking stick to his cheek. Manya's face was aflame to the roots of her hair.

"Everything is over between us!" she said brutally, insistently staring at his ears. "I hope you'll abide by my decision, and respect my will?"

"Have I ever not respected it?" he asked quietly.

Her heart began to thump stormily in her breast.

"You understand perfectly well what I want to say!" she cried nervously, losing her head. "Don't you dare stand in my way! Don't you dare ask for a rendezvous with me. Don't you dare request . . . ah! You know exactly what I'm talking about . . ."

"Why shouldn't I give you the pleasure of refusing my requests?"

She jumped up. Her little shoe stamped the ground.

"Don't you dare laugh! What right have you? I hate you, do you hear? You're repulsive to me. And if you're not a dishonorable man, you must forget everything."

Her eyes glittered like diamonds. She was beautiful. He looked at her hungrily from below, and his thin nostrils quivered.

Their eyes met. And once again her heart fell.

He lowered his eyes. The lids were bluish, transparent. He wrote something on the ground with his stick. The longer the silence lasted, the greater her anxiety grew.

"Your tactics, Maria Sergeyevna, are familiar to me. But you won't succeed in insulting me! He who loves has no pride. And you're worried for no reason. Mr. Nelidov will never learn about this fleeting romance in your past. You've torn it out, and that's enough. The rest involves me. Will I continue to love you? Will I remember what bound our souls and lives? What concern is that of yours? That will remain between the two of us . . ."

"But I want no secrets between us!" she burst out in despair.

Quickly, with a kind of predatory gesture, he threw back his head and looked straight into her eyes. Without a shadow of smile and with a strange threat, he said quietly and distinctly: "Even the gods are powerless to change the past."

The color drained from her face. She stared into his eyes, as one stares into a bottomless well, and lowered her lashes, breathing heavily.

"What? What did he just say?"

"Ah! There he is, our traveler!" Uncle cried in the distance and waved his hand. He hurried to the rescue.

Steinbach stood up and went toward him. They halted about twenty steps from the bench and chatted about something.

"Manya. They've been calling you. It's teatime. Aren't you going?"

"I'm coming, Uncle. In a little bit."

They walked away, their steps and voices audible for some time.

She was alone. She uncovered her face and looked around. Before her on the damp sand were these clearly written words: "MANYA WILL BE MINE."

She stared without moving. Her heart was pounding.

"Never!" she said after a moment, and stood up.

"Never!" she shouted in a rage. She looked around. In a fit of madness she began to stomp the ground and erase these angular, sharp, gothic letters with her heels.

When she returned to the terrace, her face was on fire and her eyes held a challenge.

"Oho!" Uncle winked at her from behind the samovar. She turned away angrily. Steinbach cast a sharp, fleeting glance at her and continued the conversation. Uncle was saying:

"Nelidov says that the workers in the London strike were defeated because the owners decided to recruit the unemployed Italian proletariat. He was openly ecstatic about it. He said 'there was no longer a worker's question!'"

"He wasn't speaking seriously? I'm afraid he's celebrating victory too early. If only it were that simple . . ."

Manya agonizes over Steinbach's return and Nelidov's prolonged absence. When she hears Steinbach singing later that evening, she is transfixed and ultimately yields once more to his caresses, but the next morning she insists that she still would renounce everything for Nelidov. Steinbach, in turn, invites the whole district to a grand birthday picnic. During the festivities Steinbach stays close to Sonya, who basks in his attention. Manya is jealous. They paddle about in boats, Steinbach sings to everyone's delight, and there is a magnificent display of fireworks.

By the end of supper there was no sober person at table except the host. Even Sonya's head was spinning, and Roza's face was on fire. Everyone talked at once, without listening. Manya was silent. She was looking into her soul. The daytime Manya, who was full of doubt, repentance, and anxiety, was dying away. In her place there rose up a new Manya—enigmatic, dark, and strong.

Steinbach watched her face intently. It had already changed, grown inspired. The eyes had deepened. When had he last seen her like this? Ah, he remembered! That night she had danced . . .

They served coffee and soda water.

"Show me your house, your pictures," Sonya said.

Steinbach got up. Manya unconsciously rose, looking at him.

Oh, the naive gaze of those gleaming eyes! For a moment Steinbach was flustered. The promise of bliss beamed at him from those dark orbs. They told him: "I'm yours!"

"Your hands, mesdames!"

The three of them toured the palace.

Again Steinbach did not look at Manya and was preoccupied with Sonya. But what of it? She felt no more jealousy. To the new, dark, strong Manya everything was clear.

"Ah, Mark Aleksandrych!" Sonya said, standing before the door to the study. "I won't forget this evening. You sang so . . ."

He kissed her hand. "You're an angel!" he said. "You are my only friend in the enemy camp."

Manya saw that kiss and the ecstasy on Sonya's face. But her eyes remained as deep and her face as inspired. Nothing mattered in comparison with what forever bound her to Mark!

They were in his study. Steinbach looked around and stared silently at Manya.

The circle of memories was complete. She stood still, and her memory silently and quickly wove its web, enveloping her frozen consciousness.

Had *something* really taken place between *now* and that evening? Something real, valuable?

Like a phantom, like the shadow of a shadow, she saw before her Likhoy Gai, Nelidov's cruel face, the confusion of a misunderstood soul, her timid tears and her love's poor setting.

A proud smile slipped across her face. Her soul's dark voice had summoned her here, to this room, where the secrets of life had unfolded before her and where she'd shed her first tears. From whence her triumphant, joyful cry had flown to the heavens.

It was getting light outside. The guests rose from the table and scattered onto the terrace. Steinbach did not move away from Manya. He was waiting.

Manya stood at the door to the terrace. Steinbach furtively took her hand.

"Yes, yes!" said her inspired face, her eyes, her scarlet lips. Oh, the tormenting thirst for happiness! She wanted to fall as soon as possible into the abyss from which those dark eyes stared at her. He squeezed her hand and suddenly stepped back. The heavy portiere fell behind them.

"Mark, Mark, what bliss!"

"This is love, Manya."

"Love . . ."

"Everything else was a dream."

"A dream."

"Only death shall part us."

"Death."

After their passionate interlude, Steinbach is called away on urgent, presumably political, business. He leaves word for Manya that he will be back in two days.

Nelidov returns to Lysogory three days after the picnic. He has aged in that time, and says he was sick. Acting aloof with Manya, he asks her whether she enjoyed herself at the picnic, then rides off in a fury.

A letter from Manya to Nelidov

"You, of course, are thinking: She's a crazy, ill-bred girl. But I don't care! I've suffered so that I'm exhausted! I've nothing to lose. But I just heard that you are going away. Where? When? Won't we see each other? After all, I'm leaving in a week's time.

They say that sorrow ages you. That means I'm already a hundred years old. Happiness flew away long ago.

No, that's not it. Where can I find the words that will touch your soul?

Nikolenka, did you love me for even an instant? I'm afraid you didn't. But if that's so then you won't be moved either by my pleas or the tears that, forgive me, make my letter such a mess.

Oh, I know that I don't deserve your love! You're a fairy-tale prince, like Yan.

And I'm Cinderella. And I'll never marry. That was Yan's bidding. If you've thought of that at all, forget it, Nikolenka! I don't know what sort of family I come from, if it's normal or not. What difference does that make to you? I only want to love you. I ask very little of you, Nikolenka. I don't even need what was. Do you want me to tell you the truth? *I didn't want that.*

In a strange way you remind me of Yan, my first love. No, rather, he was the foretaste of love. Because all that death took from me then—the unspoken words, the unformed dreams, the caresses that trembled in my heart and sought release—all that I gave to you, My One and Only.

I have such strange desires. I imagined love (with you, because I've dreamed of you since childhood) as some marvelous bond between souls. The sort children and angels have. I dreamed that we'd sit beside each other for hours in an embrace, with my head on your chest. That I'd hear the beating of your heart, feel your lips on my eyelids and hair, touch your downy, dear face with my cheek. There's so much beauty in these refined caresses! A world of poetry. Nikolenka, give me my radiant dreams! That's so little for you!

Now that my soul has completely opened up, now that I've grown a head taller after meeting you—I understand how sweet it is to love. Not to be loved, but to love, Nikolenka. I've said goodbye to the past. I'm starting all over. I was a mermaid without a soul. My love for you has made me into a woman. A treasure has opened up in my egotistic, stubborn, odd, and disobedient nature. It's tenderness. I don't know if this is how a mother loves its child. But I'd like to protect you from sorrow, as if you were a child. I'd like to snatch happiness for you from fate, even if I paid for it with my last drop of blood. Little one, do you feel this great pity? I'm crying, but these are happy tears. You gave them to me. And I can never forget you, I can never stop loving you. Your injuries, your insults . . . I foresee and forgive them in advance!

When I loved Yan, life seemed dear to me and filled with sunshine. We walked hand in hand into the golden distance, and flowers nodded their little heads at us and the lark sang its wedding hymn high above us.

But why have I never seen us together in a dream walking hand in hand along that road? Why is my love filled with sadness? Don't I love you so wholeheartedly because you'll pass through my life like a daydream?

What will I do without you, Nikolenka?

Can a mother survive the death of her son? A poet the loss of inspiration? Will I ever want to live in a desert?

If only I had a child by you! With the same face, the same little hands! You, Nikolenka, in miniature! Maybe then I'd survive our parting and your cooling off.

I don't know what you want of me, what you demand of me. I'm yours. The only thing that's not necessary is obligation. We will respect the love that picked us out from thousands of others. This is a holy mystery, Nikolenka, and we should kneel before it. There is no *yesterday*. There is no *tomorrow*. We won't tempt fate! I'm afraid, Nikolenka, afraid . . .

Love me as Goland loved Mélisande!* He found her in the forest. What did he know about her past? But he pressed her to a heart full of divine compassion. And did that mystery really disturb his happiness?

Can you love me this way, Nikolenka? Unquestioningly? Without doubt?

I'll wait for you at midnight. That's the witching hour when real life is over and unknown forces conjure. I believe in them. The gods still live on this earth. May they whisper sweet spells to you! May they intoxicate you with memories! You'll come, Nikolenka, if you love me just a little. Ride along the old road to the big poplar. I'll meet you there and lead you into the summerhouse. No one will see us. No one will hear us. We'll forget about conventions and be like gods. The fairy tale will come true . . .

Your Marie"

"You'll receive this letter during the day. Perhaps you'll crumple it up and angrily say 'no!' But wait until nighttime . . .

At night the 'I' dies away that lived, suffered, struggled, and repented in the daytime. At night our other 'I' lives—the one we don't know, the one we fear. But it's stronger than we are. It's marvelous, bright, triumphant. Oh, I know this, Nikolenka!

Read this letter in the evening. Go out on the road and look up. Have you ever seen a starry sky? Not in passing, the way everyone sees it, but with real concentration? Then you know that feeling of trembling before the Infinite.

Look at the stars and understand how short our life is, how fleeting our happiness.

Nikolenka, you'll come! I'm waiting for you!"

And he was coming. How could he not? This little piece of paper, wet with tears, all smudged, so funny-looking with its childish handwriting, had aroused him, had turned his soul upside down. He felt it as if it were life itself in his breast all day. It burned his fingers when he read and reread it.

"Yes, she's a lunatic. Without a doubt. What mature feeling! What profundity of thought in such a child! But what can I do if I love her?"

"I'll be sober and severe," he told himself, shaking feverishly when the old poplar loomed out of the darkness. "If she's in a fit of passion, then I'm in a normal state, after all, and can keep myself reined in. I'll tell her now that if . . ."

"It's you!" A passionate, ringing cry greeted him.

The horse reared.

"Marie! Get back! She'll kill you."

He turned and galloped off like a madman.

She smiled in the darkness, pressing her hand to her heart.

He'd come back. Happiness would return.

Yes, there he was, walking his horse. He stopped and jumped off. He's coming. "Oh, those dear, light, firm steps! Such a distinctive gait . . ."

They enter the summerhouse. Nelidov struggles to control himself as Manya tempts him with tenderness.

"You are the first, the only," he said passionately, taking her by the shoulders, leaning toward her face. "Oh, I love you! I'm helpless before you."

Manya sighed deeply. A smile spread across her now thin face. She closed her eyes.

"But, Marie! You're making a big mistake if you depend on the strength of my feeling for you. There's something in my soul that's stronger than that and you. It may be that I'll marry you. But we might part strangers the next day, no matter how painful that is for me."

"I don't care. I love you."

She wound her arms around him and pressed her cheek to his. "Oh, his cheek is so hot! That's my third dream."

He shuddered and lost his train of thought.

"Wait, Marie! Dear Marie! You're preventing me from thinking. I need to say so many important things."

"Will you come tomorrow?"

"Tomorrow? Here? No! I won't come!"

"You'll come, dear one! I'll wait for you."

"This is madness! What do you want from me? You're tormenting me!"

"I'm tormenting you? My God! I love you so."

"No. We can't meet here. Leave me alone!"

"Why can't we?"

He clenched his teeth, cracked his knuckles, and covered his eyes.

"Understand. . . I'm not a piece of wood. I can't vouch for myself. Oh, Lord!"

"Ah, don't drive me away, Nikolenka! I can't live without your caresses!"

He grabbed her hands. A cry of pain and joy died away on her lips.

"I mustn't, until everything has been cleared up, I dare not. . . My God! Understand that I don't want you to have a child . . . now while . . . I'm tormented by the thought that you might even now. . . Have you noticed anything, Marie?"

"I don't care, Nikolenka. I love you."

She didn't understand. She was so far away from his thoughts. Oh, that passionate, primitive refrain—direct and complete, like the singing of a beloved bird! He listened to the sound of her voice with delight.

But she was saying, "Defile me, if you want. Reject me! You'll fall out of love with me then. Do I hold you back? Do I ask anything of you? Love is free and so am I. You won't be guilty of anything. Why do you fear happiness? Why do you spoil my life and yours?"

He emitted a groan. Shaken to the secret depths of his soul, he covered his face with his hands. But a dark instinct of self-preservation remained vigilant.

Quietly, timidly, she placed a hand on his shoulder. After a long pause he removed that hand and brought it to his lips.

"Little pagan," he said softly and hoarsely. "You'll never understand me. I see that my torments and vacillations are wild and strange to you. I've learned your letter by heart. In it you revealed yourself to me and that's all the better! In truth I understand you, and that's why at times I'm afraid of you. Yes, the way children are afraid of what's hiding in a dark room."

"Dear one, little one! Say more. It's so good to listen to you. I love your voice."

"It's your good fortune, Marie, that you've come to me! I cannot, I organically cannot, do something vile to you! But, my God! It would be so easy for you to perish from your impulsiveness! Marie. . . Now you must be more careful. You are bound to me, and you need to take yourself in hand. You know what they'd say about you if they knew."

"Who?"

"Why, who? Gorlenko, for example. The Lizogubs. My mother. That's the main thing. They'd say: 'She's throwing herself at him.' Oh, Marie! It would be unbearable for me to hear that!"

"It doesn't matter to me!"

"No. You mustn't say that!" he burst out proudly. "We're not savages. We live in society. We need to value ourselves, Marie! We need to have pride."

"Little one, why do you tell me all this? Look around you! It's so good! Don't we love one another right now?"

He fell silent, crushed by her ingenuous logic. Under her trusting caress, a wave of tenderness flooded his soul again. They sat in a close embrace, shoulder to shoulder, leg to leg, their breath intermingling.

Unconsciously, succumbing to an insistent instinct, she passionately wound her arms around him. Her lips roamed over his face, seeking his lips. They found his ear, such a tender, velvety little ear . . .

He uttered a thick cry, unable to think as the reins of control snapped.

Day was breaking.

The pattern of branches and the outline of the bench were visible, as were their faces, pale as though transparent.

The last star on high flickered weakly through the net of branches. The timid chirping of stirring birds could be heard.

Her arms had no desire to break their clasp. They wouldn't release him.

Oh, the dream was realized! The fondest dream. . . What could life give her that was more elevated than this moment? She had only to die now!

But his heat had waned again. And his soul cooled like a campfire that had gone out. It was smoky. Awkward. Needless.

"It's time to go!" he said, looking around. And he listened intently to his horse's quiet neigh. "Look, Marie . . ."

"Look!" she interrupted peremptorily.

"Look how light it is! The workers will be up soon. We're insane, Marie!"

And there was sorrow and remorse in his voice.

"I'm not keeping you," she said with a sigh, and thought: "I hate the dawn!"

"Goodbye, Marie!" He kissed her hand.

"No! No! Not like that. Hold me tenderly! We were close and happy, weren't we? Don't be sorry about anything!"

"That's not the way one behaves with the girl one wants to marry," he said bitterly.

"Nikolenka, shh! Not a word about marriage! I'll bring you only unhappiness. I can't be your wife."

"It's too late to talk about that now! You will be, no matter what awaits me afterwards."

"I kiss your hands, my little one. Your dear hands. Don't be stern and distant! Look me in the eyes and give me a smile!"

"Marie, it's hard for me. I despise myself . . ."

A sigh escaped her. For her he was an inhabitant from Mars with an enigmatic soul.

She took his hand and led the way out. At the entrance the young birch showed white, like a phantom. Its bedewed branch caught on their heated young faces.

And Manya suddenly recalled Steinbach. Without any pain, shame, or remorse.

"All the same, that was a mistake! This is love. . . The real thing."

She drew the branch aside and shook the dewdrops from her face as though she were wiping off the past and all its forgotten joys.

"Wait! I almost completely forgot! Who's Yan?"

"He's dead."

"Ah! But who was he?"

"An anarchist."

"Are you serious?"

"Why are you addressing me formally? Have you fallen out of love with me?"

He squeezed her hand.

"Where did you know him from?"

"Oh, it would take too long to go into it. He lived here as a gardener under an assumed name."

"Did you love him?"

"I thought I did."

"Did the two of you kiss?"

"Yes . . ."

"Get away from me! Don't touch me!"

"My little one! I didn't know then that I'd meet you, did I? Don't be angry! Don't be jealous. It was such an elevated feeling between us. He was like a brother to me."

"Wait. . . What else did I want to ask you? My God! I still don't know anything about you, just as I didn't yesterday. Marie! Tell me the truth! What's the nature of your mother's illness?"

He felt her grow guarded and still. And that confirmed his conjecture more clearly than did her words.

"I don't know anything, I swear to you!" she said in a deep voice that again penetrated his soul like a sword. "But why do you need to know about that? What can your family or my mother take from or add to this night? Have you forgotten that we've been happy? Have you forgotten everything, Nikolenka?"

"Yes, it essentially makes no difference!" he said in cold despair. "Neither you nor I can change anything in our fate. And what's written in its book will come to pass. Farewell, Marie! I know . . . I feel that you'll be my misfortune. And yet . . ."

"You cannot repudiate me?" she cried out in rapture.

"No, I can't . . ."

"Oh, Nikolenka!!!"

She stood for a long time at the wattle fence, listening to the dull clatter of the horse's hooves. Her hair, damp from the dew, curled tighter around her face. The wind played with it. Tears of joy streamed down her pale cheeks.

Let life bring her nothing more! But she did have this night!

Half the region gathers at Vera Filippovna's birthday party, but to Sonya's dismay Steinbach does not attend, instead sending orchids, a palm, and a letter, delivered by a revolutionary posing as a worker. Nelidov and Manya have a rendezvous, during which he declares his hatred for Steinbach and demands that she never see him. They quarrel and he stalks off.

She sat down on the bench, burying her face in her hands. A moment later she was already in the summerhouse, lying face down. She had offended him. He wouldn't forgive her.

She had no recollection how much time had passed since they parted. Then, the sun had spilled over the bench, on which the shadows of the birches had swayed and danced. Now the sun had sunk behind the linden. It was cool and shady all around. In the distance there was the sound of laughter and voices, while here it was quiet.

Suddenly, footsteps . . .

Manya sat up, her body straightening. She listened, craning her neck. Someone was coming. To the summerhouse? Yes, yes . . . Was it he? Of course it was. He'd forgiven her. He loved her . . .

She rushed headlong to the entrance, pushing aside the birch branch. And almost fell onto Steinbach's chest.

"You? It's you?"

"Unfortunately, yes."

With a wry, sad smile he raised his panama. His eyes looked directly into hers without a smile or sparkle.

She felt as though the blood in her veins were freezing, as though she no longer had a heart.

"May I come in?"

She sat down on the edge of the bench. A ray of sunlight from behind the linden gilded the back of her head, the curve of her cheek, the long arrows of her drooping lashes.

"May I sit down?" he said timidly, and sat down at some distance from her.

"Did anyone see you as you were coming here?" she asked quickly. Her eyes entreated him.

"Mr. Nelidov is playing chess with Fyodor Filippych in the study."

"Did you see him? Did you?"

"He didn't see me. I walked by."

"He hates you, Mark. He hates you."

"I know that."

"Why did you come?"

"That's cruel, Marie. I wanted to see you."

"There's no need for us to meet! If you love me, stay away from me. He's jealous. He'll never forgive me. I'll lose him."

Steinbach was silent.

"What are you thinking? Mark, why don't you say something?"

She timidly laid her fingers on his sleeve. He quietly took hold of her hand and kissed her fingers one by one, slowly and sensually, inhaling the scent of her flesh.

She started trembling.

"Mark . . . I beg you. . . If you love me, leave! Forget about me! There's no room for the three of us on this earth, Mark! Try to understand! Between the two of you I'm suffering unbearably. I don't understand myself. Yesterday I forgot about you. You didn't exist for me then. Then when you came in here I felt hatred for you. And now . . ."

He turned her hand over and kissed the palm.

"I can't stand this! Go away!" she said, panting. "I don't know what it is in you that draws me to you . . . irresistibly. . . Go away! I can't . . . I'm trembling. . . But you're not the one I love. And you know that."

"It makes no difference, Manya. It makes no difference now."

"Let go of my hand! Wait! Will you leave? Will you? You're noble, Mark. . . Magnanimous. Will you leave? Otherwise all will be lost. I can't live between the two of you any longer . . ."

"Did you give yourself to him?" he asked barely audibly.

"Yes . . . yes . . . yes . . ."

She tore her hands from his and hid her face in them. Her shoulders bent over, as though she wanted to disappear. Her ears and the curve of her cheek were burning.

Suddenly she felt his hand touch her hair, softly stroke her head.

"I divined your secret a long time ago. From Sonya's first words when I returned. From the confusion on her face. From your merciless cruelty that evening."

"You? You guessed?" She stared at him, big-eyed. "Why, then . . ."

He laughed quietly.

"Surely you don't think it could change my feelings for you? You're the same person you were before, aren't you? And can there really be a power in the world that could erase the past?"

"I've finished with it. Yes, really, I swear to you, Mark! Everything's over between us now. After what I've experienced with another. . . No, I'm not saying any more! Don't look at me. I won't say a word. But I won't be dreaming of you now the way I used to. I'm happy. And you should leave, Mark. There's no room for you in my life any longer."

He released her hand and stood motionless. His shoulders hunched over and his head sank onto his chest. His lids were half-closed.

"Just like Heine," she thought. But she did not feel sorry for him. No. She looked at his ears and eyelids. She didn't love him at all.

"All right," he said quietly without looking at her or changing his posture. "I'll obey. I'll disappear."

"Mark!"

Touched, she placed her hand on his shoulder.

He raised his head and looked her directly in the eye.

"But you'll give me your word that . . . if he repudiates you, you'll call me."

"He? Repudiate me? What for?"

"We often answer for others' sins. In the Holy Writ it says: 'His blood is on us and on our children to the seventh generation!'"

The sounds of his voice died away, but she continued to listen for a long time. She was listening with her soul to those enigmatic words, mouth half open, eyes wide, as if delving into their dark significance.

Suddenly a current of cold ran over her body.

"Mark?" she moaned weakly.

"Manya. . . My dear child. . . You heard the footsteps of fate just now. Of ineluctable fate, the same for us both. So what if I'm not the one you love! Leave a small corner of your life for me! Don't be cruel. You're rich, and it's a beggar asking you. I throw my love beneath your feet. Trample on it if it can't be any other way. But don't repudiate me!"

She rose, full of melancholy and alarm.

The sounds of the gong could be heard throughout the park. Dinner was waiting.

He slowly followed her along the tree-lined walk.

Suddenly Manya halted. In the distance, at the end of the walk, she saw Nelidov. True, only for a moment. She saw his gesture of amazement, his haughty expression, his tightly compressed lips. He'd been coming to her . . .

It was all over now. He disappeared.

She gave a cry like a wounded animal's and ran forward.

Pensive and despondent, Steinbach slowly came out onto the terrace. His gaze fell on Nelidov. Finally!

Nelidov was speaking with Uncle. For a moment he lost his self-control. He paled so dramatically that Uncle looked around.

"You don't know each other, gentlemen?" he asked, raising his brows.

"We've met," Steinbach said coldly, bowing from a distance. He raised his panama slightly.

Nelidov nodded haughtily without stirring from his place.

Uncle smiled. "A really splendid moment!"

Oh, what a nightmare the day was! And the whole evening that followed . . .

Those assembled at the Gorlenkos argue heatedly about Darwinism and socialism—Nelidov upholding Darwin's survival of the fittest, and Steinbach quietly countering with various socialist theorizers.

"Communism and socialism are utopias," said Uncle. "But surely there's no equality in the world, in nature? Take ten leaves from this linden tree here. Are there two identical ones among them? And you want to make people equal?"

"You're wrong, Fyodor Filippych," Steinbach intervened with a smile. "The basic task of socialism is not equality, but equal rights. Give everyone the right to develop in the same conditions, and then we'll see! It's not the well-to-do who'll triumph, as is the case now. And often not the one who's 'adapted' and is limited. But the one who's genuinely strong. In the best sense of the word."

Nelidov unexpectedly turned round and said, his body craned forward:

"I'm taking you at your word, Mr. Steinbach. If the strong must survive and triumph in the new order, then all the same, in the end this is based on the destruction of the weak, as in nature. Isn't that so? And what of your famous socialist philanthropy? What will happen to it?"

"According to moral law," Steinbach said slowly and weightily, "everyone has the right to happiness."

"I'm sorry! Outcasts don't. That's a natural law. The weak and ugly perish without leaving progeny. Nature clears the way for everything viable. Nature doesn't make mistakes and commit crimes. People do that. They interfere with nature. Their philanthropy is an artificial and criminal multiplication of outcasts at the price of the healthy . . ."

Nelidov spoke with such force and passion that his argument's dark but important significance was clear to everyone who knew about his relations with Manya.

"He's merciless. Oh, how angry he is!" she thought. "He's insulted Mark. And he wants to hurt me too . . ."

Steinbach made his objections calmly, his eyes narrowed on Nelidov, his eyelids twitching just perceptibly:

"The human race has only one road to progress and it's unchanging. It substitutes an ethical law for your ferocious natural one . . ."

"And in doing so lowers the race. Yes! That's right!" Nelidov caught him up defiantly. "In the name of passing interests, so as to please a shortsighted and cloying sentimentalism, your so-called progress sacrifices the fates of all humankind. This leads to degeneracy."

"So what do you suggest?" (Steinbach's smile was almost sick.) "A Tarpeian rock* in each city? In each village? Do you think there is some selective right to existence? And that life isn't varied?"

Manya's heart sank, her eyes moving from the face of one to the other. One could sense that more than just the clash of two inimical worldviews was at stake here. A woman was involved. Love, rivalry. The desire to justify future cruelty. The impulse to defend one's beloved.

A haughty smile flitted across Nelidov's features.

"I remember a book by Lapouge, the famous specialist in selection," he said slowly and weightily. "I read it when I was in my teens, ten years ago. It made an impression on my imagination. The author proposes segregating all degenerates into a separate city, opening all the taverns for them, all the gambling halls, all the dens of pleasure. Left to themselves, they'll quickly disappear from the face of the earth. Humankind will be saved from degeneracy."

"Outrageous!" Sonya suddenly said loudly from her corner.

Steinbach cast a cursory glance at Manya's pitiful face and continued:

"And can you guarantee that with these degenerates Beauty also won't disappear from the world? Won't all possibilities disappear? The wealth of ideas? Creativity? Progress itself?"

"You consider that the work of outcasts?" Nelidov smiled insolently. Rather, he thought it was a smile, but his upper lip simply lifted, baring his teeth.

"Oh, without any doubt! The kingdom of mediocrity will come. The normal family will create it."

"That's interesting," Lika said, and her blue eyes flashed spitefully. "What do you, Mr. Nelidov, call degeneracy? And who will be the deciding judge in these questions? Well, for example, among us sitting here: who's strong? Who's weak? According to justice, who should be thrown off the Tarpeian rock? You? I?"

"Lydia Yakovlevna," Uncle shook his head.

"Mr. Nelidov, do you really think that degeneracy isn't first and foremost the result of the class struggle?" Steinbach asked insinuatingly.

"Science answered that question a long time ago," Nelidov turned to Lika. "Epileptics, alcoholics, hysterics . . ."

Nelidov sat down and turned directly to Steinbach:

"Do you insist that in moving toward progress humanity follows epileptics and hysterics like a herd?"

"I'll refer you to Charcot, Ferri, and Krafft-Ebing.* Genius, talent, madness, degeneracy—these are all links in a single chain."

"That's what Lombroso* says," Uncle got into the act.

"Excuse me," Steinbach said, "Lombroso is a hopeless petty bourgeois. Just look at his views on prostitution . . ."

"No. That's precisely where he's right," Nelidov interrupted decisively.

Steinbach shrugged his shoulders. "Mr. Nelidov, if you took the trouble to trace the course of a working girl's life in Berlin, Paris, and London . . ."

But Nelidov suddenly left all the verbal attacks unanswered and stubbornly shifted the conversation to what was troubling him.

"The human being is a sophisticated animal," he said. "Dissolute and sensual. He will never curb his passions in the interests of higher goals. His propagation should be regulated by law."

"Campanella!* Oho!" Uncle laughed. "My dear Nikolay Yuryevich, you've made a fatal return to socialism . . ."

"Come on!" Lika cried out, leaning across the table. "Do you want the government to interfere even in one's personal life?"

"Yes, yes, and yes! Laws should protect society from degeneracy. Only the strong and healthy should mate and love . . ."

"Excuse me," Steinbach interrupted with a malicious smile. "We're not in a stable."

A burst of laughter erupted around the table. Nelidov rose again.

"He'll hit Mark now. . . He'll hit him!" Manya thought in horror.

"Ah, you eccentric! And what will you do with love? The right to choose?" Uncle asked. "You're joking, of course, Nikolay Yuryevich?"

"I'll pose the question differently," Steinbach joined in, lips twisting. "What will happen to the degenerates then?"

"Oh, a great deal!" the schoolteacher Attila said suddenly. She spoke so forcefully and passionately that everyone turned round to look at her with curiosity. "Surely you don't think that people have no other task besides this propagation? What of art? And creativity? And the struggle for freedom?"

"You're right." And there was agitation in Steinbach's voice that only Manya understood. "A normal person won't relinquish property. He won't repudiate his family. He won't join the ranks of the socialists. He won't get carried away by anarchistic utopias. That is the lot of those whom fate has tossed overboard."

"Oho!" Uncle laughed and winked at Manya.

"Normal people are the united majority against whom Shtokman fought. A hopelessly petty bourgeois herd, obtuse and self-centered. It hates innovators. It casts stones at prophets. In all of humanity's efforts, in all its impulses to happiness and justice, degenerates are at the forefront. They alone speak for progress. They are the forerunners of the dawn of . . ."

"A la bonne heure!"

With this exclamation Nelidov pushed back his chair and went up to the hostess.

"What? You're leaving already?"

"Yes. I'm abandoning the field of battle," he said with a haughty smile.

"With your shield or on it?" Uncle asked insidiously.

"Whichever you like. I'm not chasing after the opinion of the 'united majority.' And I'm not afraid to hold onto my own opinion. I do think, however, that this position is less precarious than . . . the role of a degenerates' advocate . . . whatever motives may be at work here. Goodbye!"

He shook the host's hand and bowed to all the guests. For a moment his glance intersected with Steinbach's malicious gaze. Then he left.

Everyone stared wide-eyed at everyone else. Loudly pulling back his chair, Gorlenko hurried after his guest.

Manya seized the moment just as Nelidov got into his carriage. Standing at the gate, Gorlenko looked at her. So what! It made no difference now.

"Nikolenka!" she whispered, her voice full of tears, rushing to the carriage. And she stretched out her arms.

Nelidov looked at her as if she were a stranger.

"I don't know you," he said haughtily.

The guests disperse, while Manya retreats to her room in despair. When Sonya tells her that Steinbach wishes to say farewell, Manya sends the message that she hates him.

In Lipovka, Lika and Attila listen as Grigorii Morozov—in reality a Social Democrat whose life has been shattered by the 1905 Revolution, but who in the guise of a worker earlier delivered Steinbach's birthday gifts—recounts his flight across the country during freezing temperatures. They all gather in the annex to the house, where Sonya is waiting for them, and Morozov plays the mandolin, to everyone's delight. He is eager to see Manya again. As he sings, she, in turn, recognizes the song and the voice of the solitary hero who during the memorable night of armed conflict had daringly signaled his corevolutionaries. Anna Vasilievna confirms that Morozov has sacrificed everything, including his intelligentsia roots and connections, his love life, and any stability, for the Cause.

From Nelidov to Manya

"You're leaving, of course. And this time I'm not trying to keep you. Let thousands of miles, a difference of interests and of life conditions, new encounters, my worries, your joys and my sufferings, which will end sometime, separate us, and the sooner the better. Leave and never return to this wilderness! That's my sole request to you.

But in memory of the past, which can't be obliterated, I find it essential to explain my behavior to you.

I considered it my honorable duty to marry you, despite all my ominous premonitions. My mother knew of this. The only question was whether our lives would proceed along the same path, side by side. I had to come for you, see your brother, clarify the nature of your mother's sickness—in general, the mystery that surrounds you. I won't lie. I loved you so madly—until yesterday—that I was even ready to disregard the premonitions and threats that have tormented me this whole month. I was ready to devote my whole life to you as to the first woman whom I came to love with that feeling that one never experiences twice.

But you didn't appreciate this feeling. You're a flirt. I made that discovery yesterday and it's a good thing that I made it in time! I don't wish to be made a fool of. I need a self-abnegating love, selfless and profound. That's the kind of love I give, and I demand the same in return. Not an iota less! I need the care and feminine kindness of a healthy, strong, and calm woman. Definitely calm and balanced. I need peace. Otherwise I can't work. I need a companion. I need a faithful friend. Because I'm poor and my life is harsh. To compensate for all the deprivations that fate has brought my way, I seek solace in love and a family.

But can you really provide peace? Do you really have a sense of duty? Are you really capable of fidelity? You are a pagan through and through. Men don't marry such women. Perhaps you'll say that my behavior toward you is low and cowardly? But who can condemn a person who draws back with horror from an abyss that suddenly yawns under his feet?

I won't dot all the i's. You'll understand anyway why now I don't believe in your love.

It's my misfortune that I belong to the type of person who loves only once. And it's not easy for me to forget you. But in moments of weakness I'll remember yesterday. You had the temerity to toy with me. I shall try to erase you from my memory.

Nelidov"

At the bottom, already in a different handwriting, changed and weak, was the postscript:

"If you discover you're pregnant, write to me. I shall marry you to give the child a name and to protect you from need."

They were in Moscow, staying in two rooms at a hotel.

"What am I to do with her?" Sonya said in a low voice, as she sat in Uncle's room. "She's abnormal somehow. She lies around in bed for whole days, and doesn't eat anything . . ."

"She's always been abnormal."

"No, Uncle. Don't say that! I'm frightened for her. She didn't say a word the whole way. And here she's silent for the third day. I took care of her application to the courses myself."

"As though she has any need of your courses!"

"Ah, Uncle! You're irritating me! What, in your opinion, should she do?"

"Give birth, my dear . . ."

"What??!!"

" . . . and then we'll see . . ."

"Uncle. What on earth are you saying?"

Sonya clasped her hands and blushed so violently that even her eyes blazed.

"Ah, my dear! It's the most common story with these reckless maidens. Surely you've noticed that she . . ."

"Shhh! For God's sake! She'll hear you."

"I just don't know from which of the two she got pregnant. More likely from Steinbach. But Nelidov wouldn't miss the chance either. Wait, wait! What's the matter?"

Sonya had sunk into an armchair and, her face hidden against the back of it, was sobbing passionately.

Uncle got flustered. He ran for water and splashed some of it from the glass onto Sonya's knees. He tried to kiss her on the head. She pushed him aside hostilely with a kind of repugnance.

An hour later, having calmed down somewhat, Sonya firmly closed the door to the room where Manya was lying down, and sat down opposite Uncle, her face angry, ill-looking, and full of determination. Uncle would have been happy to disappear, but it was awkward.

"How did you find out that she. . . In short . . . why do you think . . ."

"Perhaps I'm wrong . . ."

"No! No! Don't play the fool, Uncle! I have to know everything."

"Well, you see . . . there are specific signs. . . She's terribly changed, you know. Lost her looks . . ."

"Yes . . ."

"And this revulsion to food. And then . . . remember yesterday? And in the train?"

"Yes . . . Yes . . ."

"But, I repeat, what we need is a doctor. What can I do?"

"I'll take her to Frau Kessler. She likes her. So that's why she doesn't want to be seen at home. Wait! What did I want to say? No . . . I know for sure that she understands as little about all this as I do. She's devastated by the break with Nelidov. She doesn't want to live. She hasn't a drop of energy left in her . . ."

"That's her own fault. If you love one man, don't play around with another!"

"Wait a minute, Uncle! You're being unbearable right now. And do sit down, for God's sake! Why are you bobbing about? Listen. . . Why do you think she . . . and Steinbach . . ."

"O sancta simplicitas! And what did they do all June when she kept running to him in the park? I'm not condemning her for it the slightest bit. That's her business. For whom was she to save herself?"

Sonya paled and didn't say a word for a long while.

"She never told me anything about it."

"I should think not!"

"But why . . . when she and Nelidov . . ."

Suddenly she blushed, then fell silent.

"See? Consequently, I guessed right. It's all clear now. Nelidov discovered her secret. And doesn't want to forgive her. And, you know, my dear, not a single man would marry her in the present circumstances. What about me? You know my views. And even I'd think twice about it."

Sonya squeezed her temples.

"Wait! My head's spinning. Surely... Surely you don't think she... lived with both?"

"Oh, no, my dear! First with one, then with the other. It's all so simple. Now all that's needed is for this whole incident to end quietly and without a trace. She has her whole life ahead of her. Is it really worth grieving on account of such nonsense!"

They found an apartment. Frau Kessler promised to arrange for them to live with her sister-in-law, Emma Vasilievna, in two weeks, when the woman returned from the Crimea. She was so pleased to see the girls!

"Manya's sick. What's wrong with her?" she asked, stroking the girl's haggard little face, which looked as if it had melted away.

Manya had been waiting a long time for a sign of affection. Her soul had languished in solitude, and she wept on Frau Kessler's breast.

"My dear... Don't ask... I'll tell you later..."

With autumn, Sonya starts attending courses, while Manya abandons them after just two classes, to lie around aimlessly. Steinbach arrives in Moscow, and Uncle goes to negotiate with him for the payment of a debt that the Gorlenkos cannot meet because of a poor harvest. Uncle admires the luxury of Steinbach's house, while his host, who admits to having used <u>opium and hashish in his youth, offers Uncle both</u>. The two men discuss art, Steinbach expressing his preference for the contemporary, especially Rodin's "Love." Distressed at the Gorlenkos' worries about their debt, Steinbach reassures Uncle that they need not concern themselves with it, and returns the I.O.U. to them, torn in half and accompanied by a letter of apology. Sonya, upon learning that Steinbach mentioned her kindness when reassuring Uncle about the money, betrays her love for Steinbach in front of Uncle and Manya. She sends Steinbach a letter offering her services and declaring her readiness to die for him if necessary, as well as informing him that Manya has moved to her brother's apartment.

Manya arrives at her brother's in early October.

"Where's Mama?" asked Manya, taking off her outerwear.

"Mama?" Anna Sergeyevna looked distractedly around her. "Mama's sleeping. She only just fell asleep. We'll speak more quietly!"

She had lowered her voice as soon as she'd stepped back into the house. And Manya caught herself also speaking more quietly. She recalled that even on the porch, in the first moment of apparently spontaneous and lively joy, Anya seemed to be afraid of something. And her shout of joy seemed muffled, and even the joy itself was only halfhearted.

"Ugh! How gloomy! And how can they live in this silence, the poor things?"

"I've come for a short visit... Sonya's found a room in the apartment of Frau Kessler's brother. Remember, where we lived then? It'll be free in a week," Masha said, removing her hat. "Both of us are enrolled in courses, you know. We'll be living together. Give me shelter for just a short while. I don't want to crowd Sonya. We've got a small room."

Her brother and sister exchanged glances.

"We'll put you in the corner room in my study," he said. "I'll bring your things there right away. Anya, lend me a hand!"

"The basket's heavy. You'll strain yourselves. Call the cook."

"No! Why? We'll do it ourselves. We always do everything ourselves."

"Ah, what a pity you didn't let us know ahead of time!" Anna Sergeyevna wailed.

They disappeared, dragging the basket with them.

Manya looked around with a strange feeling.

From a world of incredibly vivid, fantastically wonderful experiences she had descended here, to this wretched life. She was alien to and distant from everyone, like a Martian. While she had loved, suffered, enjoyed herself, and become a woman, nothing here had changed.

She recognized the old, completely faded furniture; the velvet, half-worn tablecloth; the china ashtray and red table lamp, the album. These objects exuded the old melancholy of her childhood, just as fur clothing smelled of camphor for a long time, even when it was already spring.

There were strange sounds next door. Not where her siblings were moving furniture in the other room, but right there, close to her. They resembled a whisper or a rustling and sighs . . .

Manya got up and went out into the corridor.

No one. . . There was a light coming from somewhere. She took a couple of steps and turned the corner. And a scream froze on her lips.

In the corner, with her back to Manya, stood a woman in a nightshirt. Barefoot. Disheveled locks of gray, short hair fell untidily onto her wrinkled neck. She stood, bent over, as if examining or looking for something on the floor. And she was whispering.

Who was this old woman?

Suddenly she looked around and turned to face Manya without seeing her. And Manya recognized her mother.

Yes, she did recognize her, although in this ghastly old woman's face nothing remained of the captivating image of Mrs. Yeltsova. But the frightening expression in her eyes, which had imprinted itself on the child's soul, was unchanged.

The light from the dining room now fell brightly on her face.

"Mama . . . Hello!" Manya's voice shook.

The old woman only now saw her daughter, and laughed. Her front teeth were missing and her mouth resembled a black hole.

"Shhh!" she said suddenly, raising a finger and shaking it threateningly, with a mad smile. "Don't tell anyone. . . Heavens preserve us! It was the pencil, you know? A pencil popped out."

She approached Manya, gesticulating and nodding as she muttered something senseless and disconnected.

"Anya! Anya!" Manya shouted wildly, and hid in the corner behind the door.

The old woman winced, but Anna Sergeyevna was already there. Seeing her older daughter, the old woman suddenly flew into what seemed groundless anger.

"I don't want to! I don't want to!" she screamed and waved her hands.

"Mama . . . You can't. You can't come in here!" Anna Sergeyevna mumbled and seized the madwoman's arm and dragged her into the bedroom.

The short, mute struggle lasted for a few seconds. A key turned in the lock and Manya was alone. She emerged from the corner, her entire body trembling.

The hanging lamp brightly illuminated the table. Manya slowly approached it and passed her hand over the tablecloth.

"It's ready," Pyotr Sergeyevich said as he entered the room. "It'll be fine there for you!" He suddenly stopped speaking, astonished.

"I just saw . . . Mama."

Manya spoke quietly, with difficulty, and immediately sat down.

Pyotr Sergeyevich kept looking at her, growing paler by the second. Manya also didn't shift her enormous, voracious, piteous eyes from him.

"She's changed dreadfully. A completely old woman. Still, I recognized her. Petya, what's the matter with her?"

Every drop of blood receded from her face as she awaited his reply. Pyotr Sergeyevich had never seen such eyes on Manya when she was a little girl—imperious, beseeching, and threatening. Threatening whom? "How alike they are!" was the thought that struck him.

"What's the matter with her, Petya?"

By then Anna Sergeyevna had returned and now stood by the table, pale and silent. Glancing at their faces, she understood everything in an instant.

"Mama? You're asking what she's sick with? But you know, dear. She's suffering from a nervous breakdown . . ."

Head lowered, Pyotr Sergeyevich withdrew to the window.

"And . . . is it . . . serious?"

"Very."

"And . . . incurable?"

"Yes."

"How did this . . . happen?"

Anna Sergeyevna was silent. The reply came in hollow tones from the direction of the window:

"It's hereditary. It's useless to fight against it. It's inevitable, like death."

Manya drooped over the table as if crushed. She lacked the courage to continue the questions.

She retired early. And the heavy silence continued for a long time in the dining room.

"Petya. . . Did you notice?"

"Yes."

"Why has she changed so much? Was she frightened?"

"I don't know."

"How thin she's grown, the poor thing! And so pale. The truth killed her, Petya."

For a long time they didn't say anything. Then came the whisper:

"I was right to fear this . . ."

"Me, too."

The following morning Manya receives a telegram from Nelidov, who proposes marriage and announces his imminent arrival in Moscow. Manya has hysterics. Petya visits the hospital and learns some devastating news, presumably about his mother's condition. Manya's news about Nelidov's offer elicits cold responses from Anya and Sonya. Steinbach appears on the street opposite the Yeltsov apartment, and is noticed by both sisters. Manya goes out to confront him, and consents to give him one hour of her time.

"Where are you taking me?" Manya suddenly asked as if awakening. He quietly squeezed her hand.

"Don't talk against the wind. You'll get a sore throat."

She fell silent, incapable of getting angry and protesting. But in that familiar helplessness there was such a frightful enchantment!

They rode in silence to the gusts of a storm that was brewing. And Manya beseechingly gazed in alarm at the wonderful profile reminiscent of Heine's, at his sad, white countenance.

The carriage suddenly halted in front of a tall iron grating. Through its finely wrought carving one could see, in the depths of the yard, a magnificent two-story house—austere, stylish, castle-like. Beneath its towers swayed the bare trees of the garden. Yellow walks and faded flower beds could be glimpsed. Lacy blinds jealously masked the windows. To Manya it seemed like a dream.

They crossed the yard. Instead of ringing the bell, Steinbach opened the door with his own key. There was no one in the brightly lit vestibule, neither a doorman nor a footman. Somewhere there was the sound of hurrying footsteps and a distant door banging shut. Then there was complete silence.

The house seemed uninhabited. It was as if it knew something but was hiding, intent on holding its peace.

They went upstairs along the wide carpeted staircase. They walked past one room, then another, full of paintings and statues; past a round concert hall, completely white, with overhead lighting; past a series of guest rooms, a luxurious library and an enormous dining room.

"In here," Steinbach said.

It was a study. A huge Italian window looked out onto the garden and created the illusion of isolation from the city. The fireplace was lit, just as in Lipovka.

Manya looked around. No, it was better here. There wasn't that oppressive wealth, masses of valuable things that nonetheless seemed unnecessary. Everything was austere, in one color, sad, even somber. "Like his soul," Manya thought. But it was a genuine prince's palace. The millions accumulated here in the furniture, in the vases, statues, paintings, and bronze, weren't oppressive, didn't obtrude. The uninitiated wouldn't notice them.

FIGURE 5
Another glimpse of how wealthy Russians lived at the beginning of the twentieth century. This study was located in the Shtatny Lane mansion of A. I. Derozhinskaya. A. V. Shchusev State Museum of Architecture, Moscow.

It was clear to Manya that one doesn't bring the past into such chambers. Here everything was sufficient unto itself. Again an evocation of the tales of Scheherazade, where one had to rid oneself of everything that weighed upon one. To open one's soul to new impressions... The marvelous face of a woman gazed at her from a frame. She had to understand that face. She sat down in an armchair of black wood encrusted with mother-of-pearl. Its armrests were worm-eaten, the colored-silk upholstery faded. Blood princesses used to sit in these armchairs. Perhaps Lamballe herself had penned billets doux to her beloved Marie Antoinette at the writing desk of rosewood, elegant and airy, with carving on the mirrorlike cabinet and with countless secret drawers. One couldn't approach such treasures with a thin layer of dust on one's shoes and in one's soul! These things emanated the beautiful sorrow of a life vanished forever. One had to know how to respect that sorrow. One had to know how to preserve silence.

Steinbach sensed that the mood was set.

"And all this is yours," she said in a whisper.

"Yours, Manya," he answered strangely and just as softly.

She shook her head as if trying to shake off an impending nightmare.

"Is this your favorite room, Mark?"

"Yes. Here, in this house, there isn't a single thing chosen by anyone else. But this room—it's my 'home.' No one comes in here."

"But Uncle? And Sonya? Surely they must have been here?"

"No. I received them in another study. You're the first who's entered here."

Manya's cheeks flushed. "And—your wife?"

"She was never in this house."

Manya settled back with a profound sigh and an unconscious smile.

"Ah! I haven't taken my coat off yet."

With an insinuating movement he helped her remove it.

Suddenly she noticed an attractive couch in the form of a shell, also, like the desk, from the eighteenth century. And a small table in front of it was set for two, with wine and fruit.

"We'll have some dinner. All right?" And he rang a bell.

A silent servant in livery appeared unexpectedly, as if in a fairy-tale play. He brought in silver dishes full of steaming food, then disappeared.

That meant that this dinner à deux had been planned in advance? Again a suppressed irritation started growing in her breast.

She ate, nonetheless, for she was hungry. And it all smelled so tasty and was so exquisitely served! But she blushed... There were certain dishes that she refused, for she simply didn't know how to eat them. If only he didn't realize that. And why wasn't he himself eating? It inhibited her.

Suddenly she paled and pushed her plate away.

"You don't like it?"

"Be quiet! Don't ask! Give me some water . . ."

She lay for a few minutes with eyes closed. Then she smiled palely.

"You feel better?" he asked insinuatingly.

She blushed hotly and and sat up.

"Yes! Yes! Pour me some wine!"

"Isn't it bad for you?"

"Why?" she asked challengingly, avoiding his eyes. "Why should wine be bad for me?"

He quietly shrugged his shoulders. "You should know that better than I . . ."

"What's he thinking? What does he know? Surely he can't have guessed? I'll die if he has. It's my secret. A lifelong secret. I'll tell no one but Nikolenka. No one else in the world . . ."

The golden liquid, fragrant and thick, rushed to her temples. She felt as if her blood were on fire. It was pleasant and terrifying.

"Oh, how delightful! What is it?"

"Lacrima Cristi.* . . This wine is fifty-two years old."

Manya gazed pensively at the strange, dark jug.

"More?" Steinbach's eyes posed the question, and he poured her more without waiting for her response.

Manya suddenly put down her glass without emptying it.

"Mark . . . Mark. . . Where are you? It's dark. . . I feel unwell, Mark . . ."

When she recovered, she was lying inside a room with antique screens embroidered in gold, on a wide couch, of the sort seen only in theaters, in Maeterlinck's* play about knights. The couch was wide, and a heavy antique brocade cloth was thrown over it.

The next instant Manya saw it, the screens, and the face of a falcon bent over her. And those brows that she loved so much. But she saw it all with a different vision. Her consciousness was still slumbering.

"Where am I?" she whispered.

"With me. . . Don't be afraid of anything," came the whispered response.

And the bottomless, lusterless eyes gazed into her own so very close, and their breath mingled.

She clasped his head in a powerful drive for happiness. Even if he'd wanted to pull away, she wouldn't have released him. . . Her dark, slumberous soul palpitated with a premonition of joy, of divine joy, which she hadn't experienced for so long. . . So endlessly long! Her lips sought his mouth and fastened onto them greedily, as to a fresh spring in the burning desert. . . Oh, self-oblivion! To experience ecstasy. . . Once again to feel herself a god on earth . . .

A clock chimed.

She awoke, but kept her eyes closed.

Where was she? Why did she have the feeling that someone close to her, someone she loved, so strong and hot, had been lying beside her? And even the pliant lines of her body still seemed to retain his touch, his caresses . . .

"Nikolenka?" she whispered, and smiled.

A spark suddenly ran through her body. She instantly straightened and sat up. She'd remembered everything.

Steinbach sat at her feet, an embroidered cushion beneath his elbow, his chin resting on his hand. He was gazing at her avidly, predatorily, almost motionless, with an avid question lurking in the mysterious depths of his pupils.

When the word "Nikolenka" broke loose from Manya's lips, his features contorted. Only for a moment, however, before he was back on guard again, predatory and insinuating.

Their eyes met.

"My God!" Manya said, and in despair buried her head in the cushion.

He gently pressed his lips to her free hand.

She seized his face angrily and pushed him away from her. Her nails hurt him, but, with an effort, he managed to remain smiling.

"What time is it?" she asked rudely.

"It's after nine."

"Nine?" She leaped up. "What have I done! My God! What have I done? What will I tell them at home now?"

"You'll tell them you were at Sonya's."

"Oh, please, don't teach me! I know myself what I need to say."

"I thought you needed advice."

"I don't need anything from you!" Manya burst out with somber hatred.

"Totally like a man," he said quietly, as though to himself. But she heard him.

"What did you say? Say it again! What did you say?"

"Nothing offensive to you. You love like a man."

"And that means . . . ?"

"We don't need to dot the i's. You've attained a higher wisdom, Manya—being yourself. And your despair strikes me as strange."

She subsided, pondering his words.

"I despise you," she said suddenly with cold melancholy. "What am I? Someone without will. Without convictions. Without pride. I don't even know how to love . . ."

"Oh!" Steinbach emitted the exclamation, but immediately bit his lip painfully. Without understanding, she continued:

"I don't know how to. What kind of love is it? He'll be right to repudiate me if he does. And . . . I sometimes think that you despise me . . ."

"I??"

"Yes, you. Because . . . I'm behaving immorally."

"But surely you sense, Manya, that we're on the threshold of the future, when the meaning of this word will change? And of many others, too?"

With trepidation she wordlessly attempted to grasp this idea.

"I wouldn't judge you even if you were the last word in those women who sell their favors. So do you want me to despise you for having given yourself to me in love?"

"That's not true! You yourself know that I love another . . ."

"But me too."

"You? No. . . You're a stranger to me."

"Don't slander us, Manya. Your burst of passion was wonderful! Both now . . . and then. . . Weren't you happy? Can you really feel shame about such a moment? Get rid of all those imposed ideas, all that's alien to you! Let your soul appear before mine in its divine nakedness! And tell me: did you really not love me just now?"

"Oh, Mark!"

He felt the doors to her soul slowly open again beneath his timid hand.

"I don't understand myself, Mark! I don't. . . And it's torture. Is it really possible to love two men? Is it possible . . . to live with two of them? Oh, what a vulgar word! But I don't know another one. I feel that everyone, even Sonya, would turn their back on me if they knew the truth. They'd say that it's . . . depravity. Oh, Mark! But you know, don't you, that that's not what it is? You know that every drop of blood in me is dying for you during those moments?"

"I know, Manya. . . I do."

He walked across the room and timidly sat down beside her on the ottoman. She spoke quietly, slowly, as if in a dream.

"How strange it is! I have two souls. I realized that only recently. One is realistic, cowardly, and submissive. It's an ungrateful soul, Mark. It doesn't feel any tenderness for you or compassion for all the happiness you give it. That's the Manya whom everyone knows. The other one . . ."

"I alone know it?"

"Yes. It awakens suddenly. It's bold, bright, and strong. It's impossible to fight against it, for it instantly stifles the other one. And it moves to its goal and takes what it needs. It lives in darkness, Mark. It doesn't like the light, noise, and people. It doesn't know any doubts or hesitation. It sees everything clearly."

"Like the Sibyl?"

"Yes! And I love it, Mark. I'm afraid of it, but I love it . . ."

"I do too . . ."

He nestled his face against her hands and whispered:

"And this bright, daring, strong one—does it love me, Steinbach?"

"Yes, Mark. But it lives only in your arms, only on your breast. Like a sorcerer, you can summon it with your voice, with a glance . . . sometimes with a gesture. . . Without you it doesn't exist. Can someone understand me, Mark, if I don't understand myself? Only you. . . And . . . with you I have no shame!"

"But surely you're happy at times, my child?"

"Yes. . . When my nocturnal soul emerges . . ."

"That's everything, Manya! That's everything."

There was a long silence.

"My child, what are you thinking? Your face has such a wonderful look . . ."

"Shhh, Mark! Don't frighten off this moment. Your words pierce my soul like golden arrows. . . There's light in this darkness, where I've been wandering for so long. . . Oh, in such despair! I feel a premonition, Mark . . ."

They sat side by side, her arms around his neck, her head lying trustingly on his shoulder. Her eyes were closed. It was warm. Cozy. So quiet... Not to move, not to go anywhere, to die that very moment! She was so tired...

She raised heavy eyelids. What was the face gazing on her from the golden frame? So proud and sad, it seemed alive. Blue-black hair with a proper bandeau framed the severe oval of the matte white cheeks. In the extended brows, in the tense, mournful lines of the mouth there was an eloquent element of tragedy, a touching submission to fate. The bottomless eyes, filled with gloom, were narrowed proudly, as if threatening...

"Mark. This is your mother, right? You're incredibly like her! The same eyes. The same lips. She passed her beauty on to you."

"And her curse."

"My God, what beauty! It's difficult to tear yourself away from that face. But she was unhappy, Mark, right? I can feel it. Tell me about her... at some later time..."

Steinbach's heart beat quietly. Without being aware of it, with that short phrase she herself had marked a future for them.

Several hours later, they quarrel when Steinbach tells Manya that Nelidov will not come for her because he is involved instead in business negotiations that will bring him considerable money. He informs her that she is "a new woman," while she acknowledges that she loves both him and Nelidov and vows that thereafter she will lead a new life.

She placed her hands on his shoulders. Her voice trembled.

"I'm remembering... There wasn't a single moment between us for which I could blush. I'll go even further, Mark: my meeting with you fills the most magical, most beautiful pages in the book of my fate... But all the same I'm breaking off with you and I shall be Nelidov's mistress."

"Do you mean wife?"

"No. Mistress. I myself am choosing this role. I prefer it. What he said about marriage filled me with such fear... I'm like a bird, I can't live in captivity. If he cools, I'll leave. But I needed his desire, his decision to marry me as a proof of his love. I'm going after him. I'll live some place close to him, in the village. I'll earn my bread by drawing caricatures for magazines. They pay a lot for them. Frau Kessler promised to find me work. I told her everything. It'll be a quiet, obscure existence, but I love him and I'll be happy. And now... kiss me..."

"Are you forbidding me to see you?"

"Yes! Yes! I ask you... I beg you! Don't ever seek me out! Don't ever go back there! I want to be at peace, Mark. I want a tranquil and ... simple happiness, like everyone else's. Where's my pin? Ah! how pale I look! How late I am! Still, it makes no difference! I've burned my bridges. Mark... Come here and let's ... say farewell..."

He came up to her. She stood on tiptoe and laid her hands on his shoulders.

"You've given me a great deal of happiness. And I'd be a worthless woman if I erased you from my soul. I'll never, ever forget you, dear, wonderful Mark!"

She clasped his head and kissed his eyes and brow.

His hands held her when she tried to pull away from him. She saw his malicious expression. And her good mood faded.

"I'll be waiting for you," he said coldly and calmly, as if he hadn't heard anything she'd said. "Every day between six and nine in the evening, I'll be waiting for you."

"Listen... Is your goal to tease me and drive me crazy? Let me go! Do you hear? Let me go this instant! Give me my blouse!"

"Remember my address, Manya. Prechistenka, Steinbach's house."

Her hands froze on the buttons that she was fastening and she looked at his motionless face, his menacing eyes.

"What have you thought up, Mark? I'm so... so angry this moment that I'm ready to hit you! It's all over between us. And he'll be coming... the day after tomorrow."

"Fine. You'll come to tell me how your meeting went, how you love him. I'll be waiting."

Her eyes flashed. She turned round and went to the writing desk, where she'd left her gloves.

"Your father was an alcoholic. He went on a drinking spree when your mother left him. Did you know that?"

"N-no, I didn't. Why are you telling me this? And why do you know about it?"

"I know everything. Even your mother's mysterious illness, what it's called. I've been making inquiries for two weeks. I saw your landlord. I know the doctor who's taking care of your mother."

"Be quiet! Quiet! I don't want... I don't want to hear any more!"

"And I won't say any more."

He smiled, but only with his lips. As before, his eyes held a latent threat.

"My mother has a nervous disorder," Masha uttered abruptly. He didn't reply and looked at her, eyes narrowed. Their glances intersected and locked for a moment.

Manya's eyes shifted unconsciously to the portrait of the Jewish woman. The same bottomless, narrowed pupils stared menacingly at her from the gilt frame.

Manya quickly lowered the veil of her hat and went out.

Steinbach caught up with her on the staircase. The house was empty and silent, like a vault.

"Mark, I don't know now what to think of you. Surely you're not capable of telling him about my father... and about our family in general?"

"What do you think? Am I? Or not?"

"I don't know a thing!" she said in despair.

"And is it really a crime to fight for happiness?"

"Oh, be quiet! I'd sooner die than come back here! I hate you! I don't want happiness with you!"

The whole way back they didn't say a word. The wind blew off their hats, blew out the streetlamps, tore at the trees in the garden, and caused the signboards to rattle. The side street was empty.

Finally, a carriage with a driver pulled up!

"You'll allow me to see you home?"

She didn't reply. She was so tired. . . He seated himself beside her in the carriage under the closed top.

As they drove onto the public walk he took her limp hand and said:

"You can sleep peacefully, my child. I'm not capable of seeking happiness through cunning, force, or trickery. Long ago—long before I met Yan—I learned to respect other people's individual selves. And even passion won't make me betray that principle. And why do it? I won't be the madman who plucks an unripe fruit. I'll wait until it falls of its own accord, ripe, into my hands."

"How presumptuous you are! The Jew in you is noticeable now."

"No. I'm merely a fatalist. Nelidov won't learn the tragic history of your family from me. That will surface by itself. And it's essentially immaterial. It's even possible that you'll get married . . . and that his love will triumph over the pettiness of his soul . . ."

"Be quiet! I forbid you to abuse him!"

"I know one thing for certain: Manya Yeltsova, the girl with bright lips, no matter whose name she may bear, will be mine again. It's only a question of time. But I'm a Jew. I'm patient. I know how to wait."

"You're insolent!" she said proudly. "You seem to have gone mad."

His lips twisted.

"Not yet," he replied with a strange sadness.

But she wasn't listening. She was anxious.

"Driver, stop here! Take the money. Here's our side street. I'll get out here. I don't want you to escort me, Mark. Goodbye! Don't be angry at my harshness. But you yourself are to blame. Don't ever run into me on the street! Don't ever write me! Don't pursue me, for God's sake! You know I'm helpless when I'm with you. But I still believe in your magnanimity, Mark. I beg you to keep away. Goodbye!"

She tore her hand free and ran off.

"Au revoir!" he responded clearly and calmly.

With a wince she looked back. He raised his hat high in farewell.

She ran on without looking back.

The end . . . the end . . . the end of everything!

At the family apartment a telegram from Nelidov warns Manya that Steinbach is in Moscow and tells her not to see him. Meanwhile, Steinbach in a letter asks Sonya not to leave Manya alone for a second, for she may contemplate suicide. Manya moves in with Sonya. When she asks her siblings not to tell Nelidov about their parents, Petya warns her that their mother's sickness could manifest itself in the next generation. He advises Manya to forget Nelidov and go on the stage, and upon learning of her pregnancy, urges her to have an abortion. Predictably, she insists on her right to live her life as she wishes and storms out.

Nelidov arrives in Moscow to pay a visit to the Yeltsovs, and there, during Manya's brief absence, learns the awful truth about the mother's "folie circulaire," *what appears to be manic depression eventually subsiding into "feeblemindedness."*

Seizing his head in his hands, Nelidov ran out into the hall.

The door banged behind him. The snowstorm hit him in the face, the wind tore off his hat, knocked him off his feet. His legs trembled. He stood for a second on the porch, at a loss, unaware of his surroundings. Then he set off at a run . . .

"Nikolenka! Is it you?!"

A figure emerged from the darkness. A woman's hands grabbed him by the shoulders.

"O, what joy! We almost missed each other. I ran as fast as I could . . . I couldn't wait. . . I had such premonitions. . . Nikolenka, my joy! My dearest little one. You're trembling. . . Let's go, let's hurry . . ."

"Marie. . . Is it you? How horrible, Marie! Your mother . . ."

"Be quiet! Oh, do be quiet! You know. . . Now you know everything. But don't push me away, Nikolenka! Surely I'm not to blame? We love each other, don't we? Don't tell me anything! Spare me."

The pair take a carriage to Sonya's place.

They arrived at the apartment. Manya rang the bell, and the door opened instantly, as if Sonya had been waiting at the window.

After one glance at Manya's glowing face, Sonya gave a profound sigh of relief.

But Nelidov looked terrible! He was incredibly pale!

She left the two of them alone and went into the dining room.

The house was empty. Emma Vasilievna and her husband were at the theater. How lucky!

They sat on the couch, their arms around each other.

He was so shattered, that all the desires that had tormented him while he and Manya had been apart, the desires that had broken his pride, vanished now, as if he were sick. And he felt unbearably good—to the point of tears—from her closeness and her caresses. Those tears had trembled all the time in his breast. His nerves were so shattered! He hadn't known a moment's peace since writing that cruel letter to her!

But that was forgotten now, like everything else that had preceded the break and prompted it. The black shadow of madness had spread its wings over them. And everything that had recently separated them was swallowed up in its darkness—forever, it seemed.

"Marie!" he said after a long silence. "I won't go back home without you. We'll get married and leave. The wedding should be soon. I've decided. I can't live without you . . ."

"Oh, Nikolenka . . ."

At a loss for words, she took his hand and kissed it.

"But I have one condition. I've imposed it on myself and I demand it of you. You must help me by not tempting me. We shouldn't have children, Marie. Ah, don't look at me like that! Don't think me immoral, Marie! A month ago I'd have found such an agreement criminal and such a marriage senseless. But now . . . after what I heard. . . Oh, what a horror! Marie, have you ever . . . seen your mother during one of her attacks?"

Manya moved away and adjusted her disarrayed hair.

"Why do you ask? Surely you didn't . . ."

"Yes, yes, I did. Just now I heard that screech . . . that howl."

She laid her fingers against his lips. "Don't! Don't!"

"Marie . . . God will forgive us for what we're doing. If I had the strength to forget you, I'd leave after this evening. The future terrifies me. . . But do I really have a choice? What am I left with? But I'll be inflexible in this. Your brother's right. We shouldn't commit a conscious crime. And when I think that we succumbed to pleasure so recklessly. . . And that you could already be. . . But you're not, right, Marie? If you were, you'd have written me, wouldn't you?"

Her eyes fixed, she stared at one spot in front of her, as if not hearing him.

Fear crept into his soul.

"Marie. . . What are you thinking?"

"Nothing . . . "

"Are you . . . feeling all right, Marie?"

She turned her vacant eyes to him.

"Yes. Don't worry. I'm well."

"Oh, thank God. I was so afraid of that. Now we're going to be sensible, Marie! We're going to be restrained. You won't drive me mad with your caresses. And I'll rest, let my nerves recover. You sapped my health, my sleep, my strength. I became contemptible, pathetic, insignificant. Put your arms around me! Tell me that it will all pass. Well? What's got into you?"

"It's nothing . . ."

"Marie. . . It won't be easy for you with me. I'll be demanding, jealous. I'm an egoist, Marie. You'll always have to be even-tempered, cheerful. I need your laughter. I expect you to make me forget all failures. You'll have to be my fairy tale . . . always . . ."

He kissed her again. She was motionless.

"Oh, to start this life as soon as possible! To get into the rhythm of it! If you only knew how I'm afraid of everything new, everything that doesn't resemble yesterday! I'm a slave to habit. Only in the midst of a regular and peaceful life can I work and be cheerful. Marie, will you give me this peace? I'm so afraid of you! Your moods, your idiosyncrasies. And there's another condition: my mother has to like you. That won't be easy. She's as demanding as I am. She's jealous. She's spoiled by my love for her. And while she's alive you'll have to play a secondary role in our home. She has complete power over the household and will continue to do so . . ."

Manya seemed to wake as if from a dream.

"Nikolenka, I won't be your wife. I've already decided that."

His eyes darkened. "You're . . . rejecting me?"

"No. I simply will go away with you. Tomorrow. . . But that's all."

"You mean. . . In what capacity will you go away with me?"

"I love you, Nikolenka. But to be your wife. . . No . . . I don't want to be liked by anybody. I don't wish to try to ingratiate myself with anyone. I love my freedom. I love it too much to exchange it, even for what you're offering me."

"Marie, I don't want to hear this!"

"Nikolenka, don't be angry. Try to understand."

"Is this your pride speaking? You don't want to be subordinate to my mother?"

"No. I simply can't do otherwise. I feel terrified at the thought that we'll have to live as a threesome, to laugh when I don't want to, to always be ready for everything . . . to be a fairy tale. And if . . . tears are rising in my breast? If I'm tempted to go out into the field, while you're waiting for dinner? If you want to sleep, whereas I want to roam through the swamp? I love to roam about at night."

"This is childishness!"

"No, this is a whole world that lives within me. My world. It's dearer to me than anything. But you don't give it a thought."

"A serious woman should forget girlish dreams. These are bohemian habits. You'll have responsibilities . . ."

"No, Nikolenka! If I betray my dreams, my joy and my laughter will die. Everything that you like about me and what I value in myself. And I'll become worthless. I don't want happiness at such a price!"

"That means you've fallen out of love with me?"

"No, on the contrary. I love you too much! I don't want to lose this feeling. Move closer. Give me your hand! Hear me out and pay attention. You say you'll be demanding? Well, so will I, Nikolenka. I want poetry from love. Ecstasy. Poverty doesn't frighten me. But I won't be able to endure the prose and the habits that you value. Don't be angry! In you I love . . . my dreams. And if they're deceived, my love will die."

"Are you threatening me?"

"Oh, no! How can you think that? I'm merely opening my soul to you. You don't know me, Nikolenka."

"No, I don't," he said bitterly.

"Where are you planning to live?" he asked after a pause.

"Near you, of course. Somewhere in the village. I'll rent a room. And I'll make a magic cozy corner of it. I'll earn a lot. I've already thought about this. And we'll love each other. We'll meet not at dinner, not in the married couple's bedroom, nor at specific hours, but when our souls burn with desire and our hearts are torn by a thirst for happiness. You'll never come to me gloomy, irritated, tired, and you'll never see me listless, angry, half-dressed, slovenly. We'll remember our trysts with ecstasy. And we'll dream with trepidation of the next meeting..."

He rose and began walking around the room. As always, his eyes were clear, while his soul was turbulent.

"Not a bad picture," he said restrainedly. "But it's missing several details."

"For example?"

"At those times that the door to your dwelling will be closed to me when I'm tired, gloomy, and irritated, someone... cheerful, jaunty... perhaps will be knocking on your window?"

She quietly sat up straight. Her heart thumped.

"Who?"

"How do I know?! Some other man... some Harlequin with a zest for life..."

They gazed into each other's eyes. With amazing clarity she realized at that moment that the end was imminent. The end of everything. But she didn't try to change anything in her fate. She met it halfway.

"Whom are you asking about?" she said very, very quietly.

He gave a spiteful, uneven laugh.

"Perhaps you'll be living in Lipovka?"

"The end," her inner voice said clearly.

He sat down beside her again, his hands tenaciously holding her wrists. He gazed closely into her eyes, full of despair.

"Now you must answer to all the things that I thought about during these days. I suffered unbearably. I'm surprised I could have forgotten it and didn't ask earlier. You know what they're saying about you and Steinbach? DO you?"

"N-n-no..."

"They hinted to me that you... No! I don't even want to pass on to you these shameful rumors. They reached my mother. I thought I'd kill the slanderer. But then I realized... He was too far from the truth. He didn't know that I love you. But there's no smoke without fire. There was something... Are you going to deny that you used to go to the park? Everybody's talking about it. Is it true?"

"Yes."

"Why did you go? Did you like him?"

"Yes."

"No. That's too vague. I want to know the truth. Surely you didn't... kiss him?"

"Yes... yes... yes!"

He moved away from her and rose.

His expression was haughty. He went toward the window and in silence looked out onto the street.

The silence stretched frighteningly long.

"Do you despise me?" she asked, finally, unable to endure the uncertainty. She was racing headlong to meet her fate.

He turned round and looked at her with clear eyes, his lips tightened. Haughty and merciless.

"Men don't . . . marry women like you," he said quietly, through his teeth.

"Ah, I know! And there's no need to! But why despise me? Didn't I love sincerely? First him, then you? How was I to know that I'd meet you? Have I questioned you about your past?"

"You're a savage. Don't you understand the difference between us?"

"There is no difference! None!" she cried fervently and got up. "Nikolenka! Shed your prejudices! This is a question of your happiness and mine. Of my life, in fact. Surely you don't think that I'll go on living if you push me away? Think, think before leaving! I can feel that you'll be leaving any moment. Nikolenka! I swear to you that I wasn't flighty! I was never insincere or good-for-nothing. I swear that I gave myself in love! Only in love . . ."

"You? You gave yourself? To him?"

She saw his furious, leaping pupils right close to her face. His white, contorted, dreadful, alien face. He grasped her shoulders. He was ready to kill her, she could feel it. But she looked fearlessly into his eyes. She felt no guilt now. Her soul was pure.

"Yes, of course. After all, I loved him!"

Teeth gritted, he shoved her away from him as hard as he could. She fell and hit her head on the back of the couch.

He ran to the door.

But all his strength suddenly left him. He sat on a chair and buried his face in his hands. Tearless sobs convulsed his shoulders. She rose in horror, then sat down again.

"Nikolenka. . . Surely you wouldn't rather I'd have kept quiet? Surely I shouldn't have lied?"

"You did lie. You fooled me . . ."

"No! No! No! You didn't ask me anything. Remember! You took me . . . the way people pluck flowers along the road. And I love my past. It's mine. I'm not obliged to report to anyone!"

"I thought you were honorable . . ."

"Am I dishonorable, then? Why do you insult me?"

"Oh, my fears were justified. Listen. . . If you have even a drop of decency, tell me right now: did you meet with him here?"

"Yes!" she said proudly and gazed challengingly directly at him.

He covered his face with his hands, but only for a moment. Then he uncovered it, and though it was contorted with suffering, his eyes were now cold. She could tell that he had made his decision.

"Thank God it's not too late!" he said as if thinking aloud. "And you . . . perhaps you . . . again . . ."

"Yes!" she interrupted firmly. And her face paled. "I gave myself to him again. Because . . . at that moment I loved him more than you . . ."

He rose, his hand at his throat. He hadn't expected that.

She rose too, her eyes blazing. And she didn't notice that her whole body was trembling.

"And I have no reason to be ashamed of my impulses. They were sincere and wonderful. You hear? I'm not afraid of your contempt. Isn't love free? Isn't my body—these hands, these lips—mine? Oh, what blindness! Why are you repudiating me? Am I not, after all, breaking with the past? Am I not giving myself to you with ecstasy? Am I refusing to go off with you? Am I not promising love and tenderness toward you while I love you? And fidelity. . . Yes! God sees that I dream of you alone. I love only you while you're with me . . . when you don't torment me. You look at me with horror and . . . revulsion. . . As if I weren't always sincere and truthful. As if I'd sold my caresses. You pitiful man! Why are you pushing me away? You'll suffer when you're far away from me. And I'll die from despair here. And what actually happened? Just now you were kissing me, pressing me to your heart. Have I really become someone else? Tell me, what's changed? I offer you love—bold, free, wonderful, and true. . . What was it you wanted from me?"

"Nothing," he said hollowly, and his upper lip twitched convulsively, baring his gums. "I don't need anything from you. It was all . . . a mistake . . ."

While she was speaking she could see quite clearly that the person in him who had loved her and been close to her was dying. Revulsion was replaced by fear, fear by coldness. Feeling gradually died in his face, which then grew rigid. It left him the way the sun leaves the house at dusk. And when indifference tightened his features like a mask, everything in it became dull, dark, and lifeless.

She understood then and suddenly fell silent.

He looked around for his hat and saw it on the table.

Her dilated eyes followed all his movements.

At the door he glanced around. An inborn propriety, instilled by years of upbringing, made him pause on the threshold. His cold eyes slid over Manya's face, and he gave a haughty nod.

The door closed behind him.

His footsteps resounded in the drawing room, then the dining room. Not springy or light, as always, but uneven and heavy, like a sick man's.

Manya waited, sitting motionless. A minute later the main door slammed. A little later the noise of the access door closing could be heard upstairs.

Manya rose.

Sonya stopped playing the Schumann piece without finishing it, and listened intently.

It sounded as though the access door had closed. Surely Emma Vasilievna and her husband hadn't already returned from the theater? They couldn't have. It had just turned eleven.

Who was walking about in the dining room? There was the clink of a spoon . . .

She closed the lid of the piano, blew out the candles, and went into the hall. Her hand moved over the table, but Nelidov's hat wasn't there.

She flew to the switch and turned on the light.

His coat wasn't there either. Had he left?

As if someone had given her a push, she rushed to her room . . .

Manya was sitting on the couch and slowly, wincing and grimacing as she did so, was finishing up some jam. An empty glass stood beside it. There was a peculiar smell in the air.

Why did her eyes look like that? Where was she looking?

"Manya, has he left? Why so early?"

Manya turned round. Her face was strangely calm, both remote and unearthly.

Sonya suddenly understood, and, seizing the glass, sniffed it. Her eyes rolled with horror. She suddenly fell to her knees.

"Manya . . . Manichka. Why? Why?"

Manya has attempted to commit suicide by eating poisoned jam. Manya's brother, Frau Kessler, and Steinbach all rush to her bedside. She lies near death for hours on end. Ultimately, a "celebrity" doctor, Robert Yakovlevich, who has been urgently summoned by Steinbach, pronounces that "there is hope."

A profound, agonizing silence. And in the room where everyone who loved Manya had gathered the grim silence dragged on. They were listening intently to the sounds and sighs. In the daytime everyone had entertained hopes. But the night had brought premonitions and a sense of menace. And the bright lights that were on in all the rooms could not overcome the dread that had crept into their souls and that thrust its repulsive head out of all the hiding places, like a worm . . .

No one spoke. They all kept silent for so long and so tensely that the silence started to hum and ring in their ears. It simmered with a strange, elusive life.

And suddenly they clearly heard a voice, distant, weak, and impassive:

"Mark . . . Mark . . . Mark . . ."

Everyone gave a start and sat upright. Both doctors looked at each other with surprise, then bent over the bed.

Manya lay motionless.

Who had spoken the words? She? Whom was she calling? Whose name? Was it in her sleep? In a delirium?

The voice had also been audible in the drawing room, but it was even less comprehensible to those sitting there. And they all froze, seized with dread.

Half an hour passed. Or was it more? less?

Their hands and feet had grown numb because of their unaccustomed postures. Their blood hummed, pounding at their temples. Their breath involuntarily stopped.

And suddenly again . . .

"Mark . . . Mark . . . Mark . . ."

A voice from another world. Just as distant and weak as earlier, but terribly real, this time with a genuine tone of lifelike melancholy.

Perspiration glistened on Pyotr Sergeyevich's temples. Manya was motionless, her eyes closed.

Everyone involuntarily glanced around, looking for something in the room. Anya crossed herself.

Robert Yakovlevich suddenly rose and quietly opened the door to the drawing room.

"Who's this Mark?" he asked Sonya, barely moving his lips. "She's calling for Mark."

"Me?" the soundless question flared in Steinbach's wild eyes. He abruptly rose to his feet.

"Quiet!"

The host took him by his sleeve.

They entered the room on tiptoe. At first they couldn't see anything because it was too dark after the light in the drawing room.

"For God's sake! There's no need to be so upset!" Robert Yakovlevich whispered in Steinbach's ear. He was holding onto him firmly and could feel his body tremble. "She's probably sleeping . . ."

They stood motionless in the doorway, craning their necks and staring at the outline of the body in the bed.

"Who's he?" Pyotr Sergeyevich thought, noticing Steinbach for the first time. "Why's he here?"

No one could tell how much time passed as the silence again hummed and buzzed. Then the call came again, clear and distinct:

"Mark . . . Mark . . . Mark . . ."

Steinbach fell on his knees at the bedside. He did it so rapidly that Pyotr Sergeyevich got up, shaken.

"I'm here, Manya!!! I'm here!!"

Everyone heard this cry of despair.

It was as if the distant call reached him from the depths of the night in an endless desert. The call of a woman lost, perishing in the Infinity of a solitary soul. It was as if his cry of response wished to rend asunder the thick gloom, wished to overcome the boundless expanses, wished, with the power of love and despair, to keep a human being hovering over the abyss of non-being from falling in, slowly sinking into eternal Night and Nothingness. As if his voice, trembling and pulsing with his intense, passionate will, was the last branch over the abyss, the last board to hold onto in the ocean's depths. But that was all, all that she needed to be saved.

And the first tremor fluttered across Manya's immobile face.

Steinbach's lips clung to her hand. The eyelids of the dying woman twitched faintly.

"She's regaining consciousness," Robert Yakovlevich whispered, touching Steinbach's shoulder. "Quietly! For God's sake, be quiet!"

But instinct is more reliable than science in feeling its way in the darkness.

"Manya . . . Manya! I'm here! I love you! I'll never leave you!" he said forcefully, passionately, gazing in complete self-oblivion at Manya's dark, unrecognizable face.

And a miracle occurred, as if his voice had thrown a bridge from one shore to the other. Manya's soul slowly returned from the other world onto earth. From the realm of Silence and Shadows. From the endless remote expanse that had already unfolded its boundless horizons before the expiring eyes of her soul.

A weak light slid across her face. The shadow of a smile was followed by a deep, deep sigh.

Everyone froze, gripped with dread. It was frightful to look at Pyotr Sergeyevich.

But Robert Yakovlevich finally took command and placed his ear to her breast. "Shhh . . . quiet. She's sleeping."

He went out into the drawing room and took off his clouded glasses. And everyone saw the tears running down his face.

"Manya!" Sonya cried in a choking voice.

"Saved . . ."

The women threw themselves into each other's arms and sobbed.

"Quiet, for God's sake! You'll give her a relapse. Let her sleep in peace!"

In a letter to her Uncle, Sonya writes that the excessive dose of opium Manya consumed actually saved her life. She reports that Manya maintains complete silence and sleeps "like one dead," but always senses when Steinbach enters the room. A second letter follows, in which Sonya informs Uncle that she has abandoned her courses and that Manya shows signs of animation only in Steinbach's presence. Frau Kessler is enchanted by Steinbach and Pyotr Sergeyevich engages in lengthy conversations with him in the evenings. A month later Sonya lets Uncle know that Manya will be going to recuperate in Italy, accompanied by Frau Kessler and Steinbach.

Steinbach and Sonya were sitting by the fireplace. It was the last evening before the departure. A profound silence reigned over the house; the blinds were drawn. On a small table in front of Steinbach lay a folder containing papers and letters. He leafed through them, tearing up many of them, and burning a lot of them in the fireplace.

With reverent love Sonya observed his movements.

"Will you love her child?" she suddenly asked quietly, as if thinking out loud. He smiled.

"Oh, yes. Surely you don't doubt it?"

"What about jealousy? It is Nelidov's child, after all."

"It's first and foremost her child. It's her joy, her salvation. The first landmark in her new life, her new path. How can I not love it? If I could adopt the child, I'd consider myself the luckiest man in the world."

"And won't you be jealous?" Sonya repeated insistently.

"That's atavism. It's an old feeling that won't have a place in the new life, so we'll start with it. It's difficult to overcome the old, ramshackle person in oneself, Sofia Vasilievna. But that's as important a duty to oneself as, for example, self-respect. It's a conditio qua non. Whoever cannot overcome this in oneself isn't worthy to embark on the new way of life."

In the long silence that followed, there was the rustle of letters, so many of them!

"Mark Aleksandrovich, I have a favor to ask of you."

"I'm completely at your service, dear Sofya Vasilievna."

"No, not like that! No service, nothing official. It's difficult for me . . . to say it. But I'll do it anyway. First, call me Sonya, and let me call you Mark."

He threw down the letters, took her hand, and kissed it.

For a long time she didn't say a word, too agitated to speak.

"Then . . . you must write me. No less than once a week. And everything. You understand? And then . . . no, for God's sake, don't look at me, Mark Aleks . . ."

"Simply—Mark."

"Y-yes . . . Mark. Don't look at me or else I'll never bring myself to express my third request."

"I'm not looking, Sonya. But I'm listening."

"What are the letters that you've set aside? Are they important?"

"Very. I only received them yesterday and I didn't have the chance to destroy them in all the turmoil. People don't save letters like these."

"That means you'll burn them?"

"Yes. After I copy down the addresses I need. Why do you ask, Sonya?"

"I'd like . . . to do something for you."

"Thank you, my dear friend. But I don't want to expose you to danger."

"No . . . no. . . That's precisely what I want: danger, risk, struggle, sacrifice. Without that I don't understand love!"

Her cheeks flushed. She suddenly fell silent, frightened at her admission. But his immobility reassured her.

"I don't understand friendship without that," she said quickly. "Give me an assignment! Something important, something of value. Don't be afraid! I'm not that inexperienced, after all. When we were still girls Manya and I used to carry out assignments. And even very risky ones, for which our friend paid with a prison term and exile. We too were ready for anything then. And Lika trusts me now. But . . . you know, I don't share Lika's views. I'm ready to do anything to help your party!"

Steinbach firmly squeezed her icy hand.

"Thank you, Sonya. I'll remember that."

"I want to be a part of your life, Mark, not to be a supernumerary in it. To be close to you and useful. But, for God's sake, don't think that I'm doing it only out of my . . . friendship for you. That would mean belittling me. As long as I can remember, since I read *Les Misérables*, about Anjolerace, about the little hero Gavroche, I've said to myself: there's nothing higher than this! And Manya understood me. Yes, you don't know her. You don't see the fact that she's an esthete. We both dreamed of making our life bold and beautiful. Full of profound tragedy . . ."

Steinbach took a manuscript out of the folder. It was covered with fine handwriting, as precise as pearls.

"Do you know this handwriting, Sonya? Did you know Yan?"

"Oh, yes! I can't forget him."

"Any day now a book will be published abroad. I'm its publisher and Yan is the author."

"His book?!" Sonya stood up.

"Here's the original. They're setting it on the basis of a copy. The manuscript is so dear to me that I couldn't bring myself to part with it."

"Give it to me, Mark! Let me have a look!"

Profoundly agitated, she started leafing through the manuscript, gazing at the distinctive handwriting. Then she raised it to her lips, her eyes full of tears.

There was a long pause.

She sat, her elbows resting on her knees, her hands pressing against her temples, and staring into the fire.

"What are you thinking about, Sonya?"

"Mark . . . If he hadn't died, what would have happened with Manya? There wouldn't have been Nelidov. Nor you. Her whole life would have taken a different turn."

"Do you think so?"

His voice sounded so strange!

"Everything in this world is predetermined in advance. Everything is decided for us. We struggle against fate in vain, while Inevitability, concealed in the shadows, sinisterly ridicules our illusions."

"Mark! How can you possibly live with such feelings? What unrelieved gloom there is in your soul!"

"It's lived in terrible places," he said quietly and slowly, gazing into the fire. "And its refuge was in old tombs. It suffers from many sicknesses, and it has recollections of strange sins. It's wiser than we, and its wisdom is bitter. It fills us with unrealizable desires . . ."

"Who said that, Mark?" Sonya whispered.

"Oscar Wilde. And this is what he says about heredity: 'It entangled us in nets and inscribed the prophecy of our fate on the wall. We cannot follow it because it's inside us. We cannot see it. Only in the mirror of our soul can we guess what it looks like. It's Nemesis without a mask. That's the final and most horrible of fates. It's the only deity whose real name we know.'"

Sonya kept silent a long time, overwhelmed.

"Yan died, Sonya, but his ideas are deathless. And all of Manya's life should pass under his sign. He had a premonition of this when he wrote her his testament."

"What are you talking about? What testament?"

"Here's his manuscript. It's a vast piece of work. In it, from the proud height of his world philosophy, he touches on all aspects of our social life, our morality and religion, destroying one, creating another. But there are lyrical pages there devoted to womanhood. To you, Sonya, and to her. Do you want to hear them?"

"Oh, yes, Mark! Even now my heart's pounding. Read them! Do read . . . I'm waiting."

Yan's Testament

'Listen, you for whom love is the alpha and omega of life, its purpose, its ultimate meaning. You, for whom love is always drama, always destruction. It itself is fate.

Don't you think you've attained it? Don't you think that you've realized its worth? Erected a temple on earth to it?

You, who passionately appeal to love from the instant that your body and your soul mature; you, who die from grief when the man you love betrays you; you, who build the edifice of your happiness on sand. To you I say: you haven't known love!

More than once it stood timidly at your door and knocked at your soul. And in indignation you cried to it: "Go away!" More than once it lit a fire in each drop of your blood. And you responded in despair: "I mustn't!"

Pitiful slaves! Could you understand those who boldly followed the mysterious voice of desire along paths unknown to you? You cast stones at them. You taught your children to despise them. You taught your children to be ashamed of love. You shrouded the most wonderful creative act of nature in mystery. Branded it with contempt. How many of you renounced the world so as to leave love behind?

And yet you'll say that you loved love?

No. You loved a man. The first one to give you pleasure. The first one you came across whom you then took as your life's companion. You loved blindly and perished blindly when this man left you for another woman.

Is he worth your tears? Did you ever think about it? You never dared to open your eyes wide and look around you. Weren't there others at your side who were just as young and just as worthy? Just as ready to love? Were you so bold as to stretch out your hand to them and say to yourself: "Life is just as good as it was yesterday, when he loved me. I'll live and rejoice today, when another man loves me!"

But perhaps you loved his individual self? Something that the others don't have? Something that won't be repeated in this life? If so, then I say to you: You still didn't know love!

Love is an end in itself. It is self-sufficient. It doesn't know either good or evil, either obligations or betrayal. It has its own laws, its own mysterious paths. Who knows from where it'll come to us? When it will knock on our door?

Perhaps this evening, perhaps tomorrow morning? And who can tell when the enigmatic guest will leave us? Can you really know where, in which boundless space arose a whirlwind that races along the earth? And where it's racing to? And who can halt it?

Love is the same elemental force. Don't try to restrain it! It won't forgive you for that. Don't reproach it! It's deaf to all tears. Like the gods, it doesn't know pity. And who can tell? Perhaps tomorrow its laughter will ring out again under your window and will drown your soul in a golden wave of joy?

Send it nothing but blessings! Learn to obey its call blindly! Does it really make any difference who'll bring you this divine joy? Who'll pass you this intoxicating cup? Drain it to the bottom! And don't fear that joy will exhaust itself! It's all around you. It's in the world. It's immortal.

Here you are, sitting in a valley, a gloomy vale of sorrow, and you quietly rattle your chains. They're rusty from your tears and blood. They've sunk into your flesh. But you've grown to love your slavery. And with tears of tenderness you kiss your chains.

You've heard fairy tales, sparkling tales of happy Hellas. People lived in laughter, unashamed of their nakedness, composing hymns to nature. They erected temples to Aphrodite, with her golden curls.

You've heard other tales about the inspired age of Boccaccio and Raphael. People were bold. They dared to live fully, dared to love.

And the happy age of marquises and shepherdesses has preserved for you sweet legends of love as light as lace, carefree and laughing, like a sunspot on the path in a garden. But don't forget that these women also died on the scaffold.

Where is all this?

The romantic nineteenth century, satiated with love, will leave oppressive dreams as a heritage for future generations. Instead of a temple to Aphrodite with the golden curls it's raised one to Moloch-Love.* And it's sought to placate the insatiable divinity with bloody victims. The torments of jealousy, the tears of those deceived, the sufferings of the rejected, the curses of betrayal—those are the contemporary songs of love. Funeral hymns over the bodies of suicides.

Elemental drives perished. Souls perished.

What for?

And multifaceted Life, with its many resonances, with all the treasures of the unexplored, has passed you by.

Have you known the rapture of creative activity? The ecstasies of struggle? The sweetness of toil? The joy of achievement? What have you given the world, women? So little, so endlessly little of your selves! And do you really have nothing to say? Do you really not possess a rich, complex, and mysterious soul?

Wasn't what you call happiness an ominous quagmire for you, where all possibilities perished?

But tell me: perhaps you had moments of vague premonition, as happens in slumber, that all that was but a nightmare? And that daylight and freedom were ahead? Didn't you sometimes think that tears and curses would disappear from

KEYS TO HAPPINESS   127

FIGURE 6
Here the famed barefoot dancer Isadora Duncan poses
as the New Woman.

the world, just as nocturnal shadows vanish? If so, then you are thrice happy! Because you already are standing on the threshold.

Arise now! Follow me!

From the vale of gloom, hemmed in tightly by impregnable mountains, behind which shines the sun you do not know, I'll lead you to a tall tower.

The path there is hard. Are you hesitating? Are you trembling? So be it! There is no other route to freedom.

Do you see this door? It is forbidden, mysterious. I'll unlock it with magic keys. Come in. Don't be afraid! Breathe freely and deeply! Laugh at the sun! I'll spread before you boundless horizons. I present them to you as a gift—the sun, air, the golden distance! They're all yours!

Now look around you. What a free expanse! This is life summoning you to work for the sake of the new. Work for the common cause.

Where are your chains? Your torments? Everything that drained your personality of color? That turned your soul to ashes? Look below at what you've lived and suffered through. How petty and pallid all your sorrows of yesterday seem from this height! The mirages have vanished. The phantoms have dissipated! Rejoice!

And what of love?

Oh, it will come! You'll encounter it more than once as you move on. It will appear before you lightly garbed, unstained with tears and blood. It'll have a clear, shining forehead and proudly closed lips. Shhh! Don't frighten it away! No vows, contracts, and questions. Here it is—your inspiration! Your rest, your reward. Take it, with laughter and joy, as do children who know no sin! And with a smile of gratitude go farther on, where life calls each of us.

Remember one thing: you mustn't pause! You shouldn't look behind!

Greetings to you, the new woman!

To you, who have dared!

To you, who have cast off the yoke of love!'

BOOK THREE

SHAKY STEPS

IN MY DREAM I'D CATCH THE
VANISHING SHADOWS,
THE VANISHING SHADOWS OF THE
DAY THAT HAD FADED.
I'D ASCEND TO THE TOWER,
AND THE STEPS WOULD SHAKE,
AND THE STEPS WOULD SHAKE
BENEATH MY FEET.
AND THE HIGHER I CLIMBED,
THE CLEARER WERE OUTLINED,
THE CLEARER WERE OUTLINED
THE CONTOURS IN THE DISTANCE
AND SOME SOUNDS RESOUNDED
IN THE DISTANCE,
RESOUNDED AROUND ME FROM THE
HEAVENS AND THE EARTH.
—K. BALMONT

Writing to Sonya from Vienna during the winter, Steinbach describes their itinerary. He expresses his dislike of Europe as a "locked drawer," the haven of the bourgeoisie. Unable to fathom Manya's current psychological state or break through her apparent indifference, he hopes, nonetheless, to fashion a new Manya modeled on Yan's ideas. As he, Manya, and Frau Kessler travel by train through the Alps, Manya remains apathetic, sunk in landscape-inspired fantasies, while Steinbach worries about her and Frau Kessler waxes volubly enthusiastic about the gorgeous vistas they see from the train. Upon their arrival in Venice, Steinbach takes them by gondola to his palace, which looks out onto a canal.

Manya couldn't get used to the old palace. She was afraid of speaking loudly and walked on tiptoe. Everything delighted her: the mosaic floors and smooth marble walls; the priceless Giorgione frescoes on the decorated ceiling; the tapestries; the original crystal, which one couldn't find anywhere else in the world, the goblets and glass cups, fragile as a dream; the stained glass windows, with their arabesques, the intricate designs of the East. Even on sunny days they reduced the light, making it soft and mysterious, and strange shadows quivered on the floor. She gazed into the old, renowned Venetian mirrors, constructed of pieces, with bronze and silver frames. What eyes had looked in them! Such a mirror was once offered as a gift to the proud Anna of Austria as a rare treasure.

Steinbach serves as Manya's tour guide in the city, where everything enchants her and gradually awakens her to life. One evening they attend an open-air concert at the Piazza San Marco with Frau Kessler.

Beside Manya stood a group of women workers from the factories, tall, strong, and graceful. It was a pity their enormous shawls concealed their figures! They wore no kerchiefs on their heads, nor hats or lace, and had fashionable hairstyles, their hair luxurious and thick. Many of them had auburn hair, a hue that one would never find anywhere outside of Venice.

Suddenly Manya intercepted Steinbach's gaze as he examined the auburn-haired woman standing beside them. She was beautiful, with a dazzlingly milky skin. But why was he looking at her so strangely? His face had grown sharp and predatory, like a falcon's. Manya's heart contracted with pain. She couldn't breathe . . .

The Italian woman glanced around and blushed.

Did they know each other?

He raised his hat and said something to her. Her lashes drooped, and she laughed, showing strong white teeth.

"How lovely she is!" Frau Kessler whispered.

The Italian woman's face glowed with happiness. She said something quickly to Steinbach, looking around, shaking her finger at him, and with a movement of her chin indicating someone in the crowd. Steinbach glanced narrowly in that direction and shrugged his shoulders. He asked her something insistently.

She responded in utter confusion. Then, exchanging a quick, expressive glance with him, she nodded and blended with the crowd.

"They're going to meet," Manya thought. "He loves her. He lived here before he met me. This is his past, which I didn't know."

For a second longer Steinbach's sharp gaze sought the redhead in the crowd. Then he turned to Manya, and for the first time, with horror, she sensed something false in the increased tenderness of his voice.

It was as though a wall had arisen between them, and she no longer could see his face. She felt as though a pit had opened beneath her feet and any second she would fall into it.

"Are you tired? Do you want to sit down?"

She shook her head without a word.

Frau Kessler sensed a "romance" and smiled. It was a good thing, for what was the point of fruitless sufferings? Asceticism? Victims? Everything that deprives life of color and the soul of joy. He'd suffered too much in the sad incident with Manya not to have the right to "cheer up."

"Maybe you'd like to take my arm?" he asked, this time with profound tenderness. He saw the torment in her face, in her closed lids, her compressed brows, and her lips, which had grown pale. He forgot the woman who was a caprice, who'd revived memories of what affected him only physically. This one—inaccessible and sick—he loved selflessly, and the suffering in her face, the cause of which he didn't know, frightened him. And he slowly extinguished the flare of sensuality toward the other woman.

But Manya didn't believe him, she hadn't yet learned the great art of distinguishing love from desire. She was profoundly unhappy and turned away in hostility.

"You've got good taste, Mark Aleksandrovich," Frau Kessler laughed. His face suddenly grew cold.

"Yes, she's beautiful. She sat for a painter friend of mine two years ago. The painting was a success. She's married now."

"For whose benefit is he saying this? Why is he lying?"

Suddenly an infant in the arms of one of the working women standing beside them awakened and started screaming.

"Where are you going, Manya?"

But she waved her hand and ran across the piazza.

O solitude! Moonlight . . . Silence . . .

Tears gushed from her eyes. Her best illusions, her radiant faith, were dying in her heart. Let her soul be trampled in the dirt by him, the other, but she knew what it was worth. She'd believed that he loved her—sick, worn out, and faded as she was—that he was waiting, with patient selflessness, for her to awaken, that his eyes were closed to temptation, his soul impervious to temptation. She'd dreamed of rewarding him later. O this love of his! Her pride, her treasure. . . How rich she'd considered herself just yesterday! And now she was a pitiful beggar.

And what would slake the thirst in her soul now? What?

Mark and Manya tour Venice alone that night, but achieve no mutual understanding. When they return, Manya takes to her bed. Frau Kessler calls her ungrateful, remarks on Steinbach's devotion, and tells the tale of her own husband's infidelity.

"The human soul is rich and complex. And it's so profound that we often grow old and die without knowing what lies at the bottom of it. And everything in it that's enigmatic and dark, what slumbers there, and what we vaguely fear, is stimulated only by chance. My dear, you know that in the heart of the purest woman—provided she's a person of temperament—on a par with the loftiest feelings that seem to fill her whole life, there exist strange desires kept secret from other people and unacknowledged by her—dark caprices and sensual curiosity. Sometimes we repress that curiosity, but more often it represses us. Only for a time, of course, sometimes for just a moment. But it's an elemental force, and these moments are wonderful! And we remember them until we're old and gray."

Manya listened, not so much to the words as to the sounds. She looked at her companion's energetic face, now shrouded in reminiscences. Suddenly she moved closer to her and asked in a whisper:

"And what about . . . you?"

Frau Kessler bowed her head without a word.

Manya's lips moved soundlessly before she finally dared to ask:

"While your husband . . . whom you loved, was . . . still alive?"

"Yes."

Manya lay back against the cushions. Propping her head on her hand, she gazed out the window at the vivid sky.

She recalled her own past, caught between the two men whom she loved, loved equally strongly and passionately. So what if he had turned from her with scorn, in horror, as if from a monster. But could she herself repudiate her own past? Surely one's own past is the only thing that wholly belongs to one, as the poet said? The sole thing that doesn't betray one, doesn't deceive?

Frau Kessler mused:

"At times the wheat fields in Bavaria are all golden. As you stand looking at them on a summer's day, the air streams around you, and it seems as if God Himself is looking at the earth and blessing the peaceful field of grain. You walk along the field and suddenly come across poppies that are bright as blood. God, they're so gorgeous! You know only too well that they're nothing but weeds, and that they're out of place among the golden grain. But who sowed them here? Wasn't it the wind that swept by chance over the field? Who brought them to life? Wasn't it the sun, which nurtured the ears of grain? And what are the poppies guilty of—vivid poppies, which flame like blood . . . and please the eyes of passersby?"

"Mark, come in! Hello!"

"How thin she's grown . . ."

He kissed her hands. They were alone in the large room with high ceilings, where the sunset was fading.

"You didn't want to see me. Why not?"

"I won't ever tell you that, Mark."

"Surely I'll find the right words to help you over whatever's making you suffer?"

She smiled strangely.

"Don't you see?—I no longer believe in words."

He pulled up an armchair and, without releasing her hands, sat down beside her, alongside the bed.

"You've changed a great deal, Manya."

"Yes, Mark. I've become a different person. I've lost my love of life and . . . love."

"Why?"

"Because it wallows in filth. Because it lacks the ability to raise our souls above the common, beaten track. Because life makes a mockery of the soul."

He ruminated on her enigmatic words.

Suddenly, without any logic, she succumbed to impulse and drew him to her, asking in a whisper:

"Do you still feel the same?"

Oh, how searchingly she gazed at him!

"I can't change, Manya. My love is higher than life."

She continued to stare into his eyes and saw in them the reflection of a milk-white complexion, auburn hair, and a shapely figure.

"And I'm dark and sick. I've lost my figure. I'll soon be shapeless. Will his feelings withstand that?"

"And what if I were to . . . get smallpox?"

He smiled sadly and kissed her hair.

"I love your soul, Manya. Your soul, surely, can't change?"

"I don't want a love like that!" she felt like shouting. "Love and desire my body! That's the only thing one can trust. The only thing that's of value." But she didn't say a word, afraid of betraying her secret. And her heart was lacerated.

Why had Nelidov's sensuality offended her? She'd yearned for him to see and love her soul, to take her inner world into account, to be tender, like a brother.

But in this instance . . . she wanted complete control over this man—his desires, his impulses, his fantasy life.

"Tell me you love me!" she said somberly.

He knelt and kissed the edge of the blanket.

"Here's my answer!"

But his conviction that he'd satisfied her demands was misguided. His feeling was too elevated and pure! It resembled a prayer, and the image of the other woman loomed at its side—the auburn hair, the white skin. . . . She recalled her radiant love for Nelidov. Hadn't it sunk without a trace at Steinbach's first caress? At the first explosion of sensuality? That's where the power was, the elemental drive from which there was no salvation.

"Swear that you won't leave!" she said in despair.

"Leave to go where?"

"Anywhere . . ."

He heaved a profound sigh and sorrowfully shook his head again. Then he clasped her face in his hands and kissed her brow.

Manya awakens, believing she has heard a door slam. In the darkness, she makes her way to Steinbach's room, but finds his bed empty. Assuming that he has left for a night of pleasure with the redhead, she collapses in tears beside his bed. The next day she exacts a vow from Steinbach that he'll never leave the palazzo at night. She succumbs to the concerns of incipient maternity and decides to dedicate herself to her child. Sonya sends Steinbach a letter informing him that Nelidov, who has learned of Manya's suicide attempt, is now abroad. Steinbach, who welcomes being misperceived as the father of Manya's child and broadcasting her role as his mistress, ensures that Nelidov sees him in precisely that light.

From Manya's Diary

"Venice. December.

I've resumed writing after a long break. The last time was in high school. Sonya and I had met Mark for the first time at the station. And from that moment my entire life became nothing but a burning desire for him.

Why am I writing? Because I'm alone. Because I'm unhappy. Because tears are trembling in my heart and there's no one to whom I can confide my misery?

Who'll understand me? The demands I make on people are so high that everyone will find me ridiculous.

No, no! Even here, all on my own, there's no need to remember what I suffered through and what I became disillusioned with. I won't look back. After all, my life's ahead of me. My entire life, and I have to live it.

I used to love life, touchingly and trustingly, with ecstasy and passion. And it betrayed me, it pounced on me from a corner, at night. It cast my soul into the dirt, stifled my dreams, and robbed me of illusions. And so I'm lying here, robbed, degraded, and alone. Oh, so alone!

And now I can't even die! My child is small, helpless, it'll require that I answer for every step I take. I must live, even if my soul's full of despair. I need to get up and go on.

But go where?

Is there anyone in the whole wide world in whom I can believe?

Oh, you young and pure souls who'll never read these lines! You, who believed in life and dreamed of love: I extend my arms to you out of the depths of my fall. I weep for you as if for myself. Understand, if you can, that love doesn't exist! There's just desire. Our souls nurture a longing for the elevated, for boundless eternity. It's an echo from another world, it's the echo of a distant desert where our happy souls wandered before appearing in this world. These are the dreams of our souls, which cannot reconcile themselves to death and betrayal. And we women wish to realize these dreams on earth. But life makes a mockery of us. Do you hear what I'm saying? It also makes a mockery of you. People tell me that life is motion, a fast and unchecked race. A race through bodies that have been overthrown, through arms that are stretched out. Where do we race to? Who knows? A wave is carried toward a rock and breaks against it with its crest. Why? Who can say? We can't even see the meaning behind this, but it exists, though it's hidden from us. That's what I'm told. But can one's soul reconcile itself to this? Can a wave halt its course?

Life is the body, with its demands, caprices, passions, and special logic, which we don't understand. It's a deaf and dark force. A wonderful force, as Agatha says. How can our small soul, with its poor dreams, compare with it?

I'm afraid. Didn't I myself behave just like that?

Nelidov—there! I've uttered his name. It burned my lips and my soul, but I kept silent. Nelidov. . . Now I can say it loudly. I'm alone in the room, after all. And the whole household's asleep.

You were my love, my dream. My longing for the heavens. I was ready to give you everything, and asked for nothing in return. Nothing but a pure little caress. And I wanted you to lean down and gaze into my soul, and to see there the reflection of your image and my yearning to love you.

But my desire lived alongside this feeling. It lurked at the bottom of my 'I,' in that profound darkness where it's so frightening to peer in. Where many people don't peer until they've turned gray. And this desire wasn't you. Not you, but another! It lay in wait for me and would come over me suddenly, as it stifled love. And your image would drown in the tidal wave.

I'm not asking for forgiveness. No! I don't repent! No! Those vivid, sinful poppies were beautiful! Whoever covered the entire field with golden grain sowed them. How could I tear them out of my soul, destroy their beauty and joy? And there's probably a secret meaning, a mysterious law in this, but we don't see the purpose. Our eyes lack the necessary vision, and so we say it's fate.

But now I understand you. Now I know why you rejected me. Your soul harbored a great dream . . . and I destroyed it.

Farewell! We'll never meet again. You can't come to terms with something small and I've ruined your future. I deprived you of family, children, coziness, and the quiet joys of an uncomplicated life for which your simple soul yearned. I know you'll never forget me! But that thought brings me no satisfaction. I pray that fate will bring you happiness with another, someone who's better, more beautiful and stronger than I, for I'm weak and rebellious. I want you to meet a Liza from *A Nest of Gentlefolk*,* if such a creature still exists today. That's the only kind of woman you should love. Why did we ever meet, Nikolenka?

No! No! Why the tears? I don't want to be ungrateful. You brought me a lot of happiness. You gave me the gift of a child. And a mother, surely, can't be alone in the world. After all, won't a child fill our souls, stifle our longings, and realize our dreams?

But, my God, I feel so dreadful! Without illusions, my soul exposed and wounded, I have to go on. It's dark and cold. If only . . ."

Nelidov broods among the cliffs in Bretagne and writes to his mother that he wishes to forget "everything." For the umpteenth time he peruses a letter he has received from Moscow.

"December. Moscow.

You can not reply, but I can't remain silent. I'm Manya's closest friend, the only person who knows everything about her past between you and another. I don't know what Uncle told you. Do you know that for a long time the doctor feared for her sanity? That she lay between life and death? How did you interpret her suicide attempt? Was it her disillusionment with you or a lack of desire to go on living without your love? I didn't dare ask. She didn't say a word, and I won't touch upon that secret.

But there's another one. For a long time I hoped, for some reason, that you'd find out about it without me. But now I consider it my duty to reveal everything to you. Manya is with child. And the child is yours.

But why didn't she say a word about it? My God! I remember your words about heredity and degenerates that evening at our house in the country. Can one forgive such cruelty? Can one really reconcile oneself to such a verdict? She felt that you'd repudiate the child with horror as if it were degenerate. Your own child. She preferred to die with the child who was disowned and unwanted. Can you really not understand what she went through? People on the point of death don't lie, Mr. Nelidov. And if any doubts arise in your soul, dismiss them. Be an honorable man! After all, she entrusted her heart to you, didn't she?

But let's not dwell on that! I'm writing to you not so as to move you to pity or to justify her. Understand one thing: I don't blame her for anything! I simply refuse to understand her.

But I don't judge you either. In your place millions of people would have acted the same way. You're one of millions, then. And that can't be changed.

Don't think that I'm so naive as to expect remorse from you, that I consider you capable of an outburst of magnanimity. But here's what Frau Kessler writes me—I'm translating from German: 'Manya is depressed and losing weight. She cries for days on end and doesn't sleep at night. Her nerves are frayed. Where will she get the strength that she so badly needs? You know she's due in April. Any kind of upset is fatal for her and the baby. Surely she's not pining for Nelidov? She speaks so bitterly about love and shattered illusions! She hasn't uttered his name even once. But I sense that she hasn't fallen out of love with him. How unfortunate!'

Write a couple of words to her. Only a couple, telling her that you don't hate or despise her. So what if you've parted ways! Without any derision and bitterness, wish her solace in motherhood. You're a religious person, after all. Don't you think that she's atoned for her mistakes through her sufferings? Manya could die without having made peace with you. How will you feel then?

Farewell. I'm hurrying to make the post.

Each day is precious. Sofya Gorlenko.

Her address is: Manzoni Palace, Venice."

Nelidov travels to Venice and almost immediately catches sight of Steinbach. The two engage in a silent duel in which Steinbach effectively lays claim to Manya and so forever prevents Nelidov from making recompense. Steinbach rents a room at the Grand Hotel. Manya and Steinbach go to look at Italian art.

"That's not the way to do it, Manya," Steinbach remarked dryly. "You treat art like a tourist, a savage. I find it unpleasant. Do you want me to teach you the history of art? I dreamed of doing that when I brought you here to Italy."

"Oh, Mark. Don't be angry! You're right, of course."

That evening she said to him:

"I don't want to be a dilettante. Tell me about the origins of art. Tell me about Egypt, about the Chaldeans, and the East. Let's read every evening! Agatha, do you want to do that? Mark, my soul is on fire with the desire to learn everything, to submerge itself in antiquity, to dissolve in it. I have a premonition that in this world I'll find . . . myself."

And Steinbach spoke with passion about how in art the Aryan spirit struggled against the Semitic elements that infiltrated from the East. On the Turanian plateau, in that cradle of all nationalities, among the Persians and Hindu, for the first time awoke that rebellious Aryan spirit, that greedy, inquisitive idea that refused to submit and become petrified in archaic forms, as did science and art in Egypt and in Phoenicia, in China and among the Jews, and later among the Arabs.

"The Aryan principle consists of doubt, the search for an idea, the birth of philosophy and science . . . realism in art, its efflorescence. It's love of life, the struggle for the individual, political upheavals. It's active involvement. It's a striving for something. It's progress.

"The Semitic principle is fanaticism, intolerance, petrified dogmas, a passionate devotion to traditions. It's fear before the deity, and mistrust of nature, prompted by the barrenness and boundlessness of the desert. It's fear of life, mysticism in art, the absence of philosophical sweep. And those rebellions that do occur are exclusively religious. It's enslavement of the individual, the dissolution of one's own 'I' in the communal. It's awareness of one's own insignificance, prompted by the contemplation of the starry sky in the desert. The mute and enigmatic sky. It's asceticism and perpetual stagnation."

Steinbach paced about the room, pensively gazing at the mosaic floor. He spoke quickly, his passion flaring whenever the general idea would become clear to him, then slowing down his voice and his movements when the idea would slip away from him. Manya's eyes, dreamy and greedy, followed him, devouring his gestures, the sound of his voice, and his facial expressions.

"Throughout the history of humankind, this battle was waged between the two principles. In religion, politics, art, and science these two tendencies ran parallel, without ever merging. Where the Aryan principle triumphed we witness a republic, an educated people, proud and free, the rise of philosophical schools and the flourishing of science and art. That's what happened in Hellas. The Aryan spirit gave humanity the life-affirming, viable Greco-Roman culture. But the moment came when the gloomy East triumphed. It buried beauty and joy beneath the symbols of terror and retribution. The Semitic principle gave repressed nations despotism, theocratic domination, a life-inimical rejection of art, and persecution of philosophy and science. In the Middle Ages, these became the property of the elect. They hid in monasteries, just as in the East, where only high priests are sages and scholars. In the Middle Ages people were completely deprived of things spiritual. Everything was taken away from them."

While Manya listens enraptured, Steinbach expounds at considerable length on Semitism, aesthetics, and artistic masterpieces throughout world history. The two of them and Frau Kessler frequent museums and read art histories. Manya becomes obsessed with a portrait of Andrea Maria Lorenzo, Duke of Manzoni, and visits it nightly. The trio joins the crowds at the Piazza San Marco.

They sat down at a table outside the Cafe Florian. Frau Kessler glowed, happy at the crowds, noise, laughter, young faces, music, and almost springlike air. Manya seemed frantically, unnaturally cheerful. She kept gazing around, looking left and right, her eyes inquisitively searching among the crowd. She surreptitiously followed Steinbach's expressions and intercepted his glance.

Suddenly her spoon clattered against her cup and then fell onto the ground. Steinbach bent down to pick it up.

She was approaching, tall, shapely, with her luxurious auburn hair and the milk-white complexion unique to redheads.

"She has a wonderful figure! And he loves her." Manya didn't think that, but felt it with every fibre of her being. For a second her heart suddenly stopped beating and her vision dimmed.

She wasn't alone. Two working women, dark and vulgar, accompanied her, as well as two men, one middle-aged, the other younger. They looked like robbers, their faces thin and beardless, with rapacious profiles, bronzed cheeks, and intense eyes. All four were speaking loudly and quickly, laughing merrily, but she was silent and didn't even smile. She gazed directly at Steinbach, expectantly, with a secret question, her rosy lips half-open.

"He kissed them . . ."

They had drawn level when Steinbach raised his head and saw them.

Ah! His face quivered. True, only for a moment, but quiver it did. His lashes drooped and he made an imperceptible sign with his head as people do when some secret links them.

140   *Anastasya Verbitskaya*

"Your acquaintance!" Frau Kessler said naively. "Why has she turned away? Look, she's blushing!"

Teeth clenched, without raising his lids, and eyes fixed on the bottom of the cup from which he drank in slow mouthfuls, he replied:

"Don't draw attention to us, Frau Kessler! She's complained to me that her husband is jealous."

The group had moved off to the side, but stood nearby. Now Steinbach sat with his back to her. Manya could see her gestures and facial expression. She was laughing, the ringing sound clearly audible, but it was artificial laughter, with which she was trying to attract him. Would he turn around? What was he feeling? No. He sat calmly, his shoulders slightly hunched, and despite an aura of alertness in his brows and eyes, his gestures, as always, were languid.

Now Manya also started laughing. Her voice sparkled with hysterical notes, malicious and full of despair. She started telling Steinbach something, her arrogant, threatening, yet beseeching eyes flashing. Her hand touched Steinbach's shoulder coquettishly, playfully, as she pointed out to him someone in the crowd. She impatiently slapped his hand with her glove, intent on emphasizing her intimacy with him.

"It's the old Manya back in full force," Frau Kessler thought in surprise. "And looking so terrific, too!"

Steinbach observed her attentively, responding in his insinuating manner.

The redhead had stopped laughing. Only now did she seem to notice Manya, her youth, and her intimacy with Steinbach. Her brows arched in bewilderment, and, with an annoyed movement of her shoulder, she replied absentmindedly to a question from one of her female companions, who repeated her query.

As she passed them again, Manya suddenly stopped laughing and didn't even finish her sentence. Without turning round, Steinbach sensed the proximity of the other woman behind him. His nerves tightened, and, sitting as immobile as a piece of sculpture, he gazed into Manya's face. He clearly saw her brilliant, cutting glance, her arrogantly closed mouth.

"So that's it!" His head drooped, and he appeared to nibble quite calmly at the knob of his cane. But his heart was pounding.

"Would you like anything else?" he asked, after the palpitations had subsided, and even his voice had altered.

"No! I'm tired of sitting," Frau Kessler said.

"Prego, pagare," he said to a passing waiter.

The minute it took for the waiter to write out the bill and for Steinbach to pay it seemed endless to both him and her.

She had changed places and once again stood only ten paces away from them. The voices of her companions drowned out the music. She was probably watching him. Was she laughing again? Manya couldn't turn round to face her for fear of giving herself away completely.

She rose abruptly and took his arm.

"Let's get out of here!" she said, choking, as she tucked her hand inside his arm.

He wanted to turn back, but with extraordinary strength she pulled him toward the other woman. She clung to him as closely as possible.

"Is she trembling all over? Poor little thing. Surely she can't . . ."

And suddenly they were face to face, their dresses touching as Manya passed the redhead. She gazed at the pale, soft face that had caused her so much suffering, so many sleepless nights! She wanted to memorize all those lines, the shape of the gray-blue eyes, the curve of her lips, all the enchantment of the face that had captivated him and led him to betray his love . . . to grind her soul into the dirt, to shatter her illusions. To memorize them forever. Why? Oh, so as never, ever to harbor any faith! Never to abandon her soul! Never to know humiliation! Never cry. To seek happiness and strength in something else!

Steinbach walked past the woman with his leisurely, insinuating gait. His face dispassionate, he gazed coldly above the head with its luxuriant auburn curls, at the Procurator's colonades.

"O, wie schön, wie stolz!" Frau Kessler said, smiling at the redhead.

Manya wanted to assume a triumphant expression, to toss out a high-sounding phrase and give a carefree laugh. But her eyes were full of fear before the beauty of the working-class woman. And instead of smiling, her lips froze in a grimace of suffering.

Before they leave for Florence, Steinbach reads Manya's diary while she and Frau Kessler shop for souvenirs, and he learns of her suspicions and jealousy. The night before their departure, he witnesses her nocturnal visit to the portrait of Lorenzo, and, sleepless, he broods over the situation, realizing that she is climbing to the tower Yan foresaw in his philosophy.

In the meantime, Manya has a waking dream in which Lorenzo visits her and fills her with a terrible, unearthly joy.

La voix

"Viens! O, viens voyager dans les rêves,
Au-delà du possible, au-delà du connu!"
Je te répondis: "Oui, douce voix!" d'alors
Que je prends très souvent les faits pour des mensonges,
Et que les yeux au ciel, je tombe dans les trous.
Mais la Voix me console et dit: "Garde tes songes!"
"Les sages n'en ont pas d'aussi beaux que les foux."
—Ch. Baudelaire

"Mark. Why, that's the Kremlin tower!" Manya exclaimed, coming to a halt in front of the Palazzo Vecchio on Signori Square.

"Mmm! You noticed that? See what an impregnable fortress it is! You won't find such buildings anywhere in Europe. Even now you can see that a battle was fought on the streets here . . ."

"After Venice, the architecture seems so massive!" Frau Kessler said with a grimace.

"Yes, of course, but it has its own unique beauty. You just have to look attentively. I love this somber gray, the severity of line. Their architecture fully reflects the soul of the rebellious Tuscans. Manya, look up! See that little window over the clock on the tower? They say it's a prison and Savonarola was incarcerated there before his execution. They burnt him right on this square. And here's the stone on which, according to legend, Dante used to rest."

Manya looked around, her lips lightly quivering. She held a bouquet of yellow daisies, which also were tucked into the lapel of her coat. The first flowers . . .

From the moment they'd boarded the train that set off across the mountain pass through Apeppini to Florence, she'd started breathing more easily. They were leaving the cold, wind, and dampness behind and were coming to the south, the spring air, and sun. O, city of flowers and joy! No wonder there's a lily on your coat of arms. Whoever's suffering from heartache, whoever seeks oblivion, hurry here, to Florence!

They had settled into a palace on a narrow street where even in the daytime one could hear the sound of swords, where the Whites battled against the Blacks, and the Ghibellines against the Guelphs.

"I don't want a noisy hotel," Steinbach explained to the ladies. "This house belongs to friends of mine. They live in Paris. They lost their money a long time ago and constantly rent out the place. I got in touch with them by telegraph a month ago, and, fortunately, wasn't too late. There's little that's changed in the palace in five hundred years."

As they tour the city, Manya's rapture over various buildings and sculptures is accompanied by her awareness that her passion for Steinbach has vanished. He reads verses by Dante and Petrarch to her and, through her responses to the artworks they contemplate, attempts to gauge her frame of mind. They travel to Rome, which is packed with tourists. Steinbach reenacts his perennial role of cicerone and teacher of culture.

"Mark Aleksandrovich, I got a letter from Sonya."

"What does she say?"

"Nothing new. Nelidov is in Scotland."

"Ah . . ."

"Healthy and cheerful. But that's not the point. I want to talk to you about Manya."

"What's happened?"

"I'm frightened by her indifference! She sees that I receive letters from Sonya and Pyotr Sergeyevich. You'd expect her some time to ask how they're doing. 'They send their regards,' I tell her, or 'They send you kisses.' Not a word from her."

"Did you also speak to her about Nelidov?"

"What do you take me for? Of course not. But I'm disturbed by this coldness of hers, this complete alienation from the past. It's as if she's built a wall around herself to keep everyone away. She never says a word about Nelidov. All right, that I can understand. But I call her and ask, 'What should I tell Pyotr Sergeyevich?' She thinks a while, and then says listlessly, 'Tell him I love him.' She can see that I write him every day, but never wants to add even a word. Not a word."

"So-o-o-o. That's the way it is," Steinbach whispered, pacing alone in the darkness inside the inner courtyard and along the dazzlingly white flagstones of the corridor, listening intently to the drops of rain noisily drumming against the stone. "To repudiate the past, to start with the new. Not to let memories sink their claws into one's soul, the way a bur clings to one's dress. Whoever's like me has a soul like an artificial fruit. The worm's crawled away, but the fruit dries out. To be able to forget the face you loved . . . to forget your promises and break your vow. To meet with ecstasy the lips that reach out to yours, and to laugh at yesterday's sorrows. To bless your own tears. Of the past, to love only yourself and your thirst for happiness. To forge ahead, laughing and crying, deceiving and being deceived, in the mighty, instinctive impulse to live. And to manifest your 'I'—boldly, clearly, and joyfully. Oh, if only I could be like that!"

They continue to be enamored of the wonders that abound in Rome, strolling its streets, sitting in cafes, and looking at shopwindows.

A woman stood on the corner illuminated by the electric streetlamp. She was still young, but hunger and suffering seemed to have drained her of vitality and femininity. Her black eyes burned fiercely. She held a bundle of newspapers with hands blue from the cold, and she cried in a hoarse ravenlike voice: "Avanti . . . Avanti . . ."

She wore an old black dress with a torn scarf about her shoulders, and worn shoes.

Manya was walking across the square to the cafe and gaily chatting with Steinbach, when her gaze suddenly met those dark burning eyes. She stopped and fell silent, almost as if she were choking. "A terrible woman. . . Just like a shadow . . ."

"Avanti . . . Avanti!" the hoarse voice resounded.

Steinbach bought a newspaper from her. A moment later the woman caught up with him.

"You've made a mistake, signor. Take your gold!"

Mark's matte cheeks blazed. What did this mean?

"Forgive me. But I thought you needed it more than I . . ."

"Take your money, signor! I'm not a beggar. I earn my bread honestly . . ."

And that look . . . it held so much hatred! She seared their faces with eyes burning like coals.

Every evening Steinbach met the vendor, tipped his hat, and bought a newspaper. She proudly nodded her head at his greeting, and sometimes didn't even answer his bow, but only pursed her lips and turned away with a queenly gesture.

Once Manya looked back. The woman was watching them.

"Why does she hate us?" Manya asked in a whisper.

"She's a socialist. And in her eyes we're parasites."

Manya's eyes froze and the happiness faded from her face.

"Why aren't you drinking?"

"I don't feel like it, Mark."

Even her voice was dull.

All evening they were silent, as if a shadow had fallen on their life.

"What happened?" Manya thought on waking the next morning. "Why is my heart so heavy? Why don't I feel happy anymore?" The burning eyes had peered into her soul. Oh, how painfully they'd pierced her heart! "How dare she think that? And Mark says nothing. He shrinks like someone guilty. Where is his pride?"

The next day as she approached the corner, she turned away haughtily so as not to see the burning eyes and the scornful smile.

"Listen, Mark, how are we to take this? Aren't you a Social Democrat? Tell her."

"Manya, dear, be quiet, for God's sake! I'm embarrassed."

"But, after all, you belong to the party. Isn't that so?"

His face twisted painfully. "My child, don't you sense the tension and falsity here? What do she and I have in common? Don't you see the chasm separating us? What can fill it? Shared beliefs? A faith in the same gods? Even in Russia I was ashamed when a worker would turn to me and say 'Comrade.' He believed it, not I. Only a shared fate or ideal makes people comrades. And what is my ideal? Did you notice that woman's eyes? They burned with faith in the promised land. She foresees it. Even if she herself dies, she believes that her children will enter the world of her Dream. But where is the country of my aspirations?"

"Mark, I don't understand," she said passionately. "If you feel this way, why don't you start a new life?"

"Ah, do you still believe in one?"

"Yes, yes. . . If I felt that way, I'd give up everything, everything I had, for the right to reach for it . . ."

He smiled bitterly.

"Do you think it's easy to give things up? You need enormous character for this, and love for others, and I don't have this love. And will this really change anything on earth?"

She was silent, crushed. Where were her beautiful dreams? Why had life slipped behind a crystal wall?

There's news everywhere in the city of a strike, with the possibility that Rome will be isolated by it and go hungry. Frau Kessler insists that they leave; Steinbach has delayed, curious about what is happening. They manage to get tickets, but have some trouble at the train station because no porter will serve them. The newspapers blame the socialists for all the trouble. Manya, Steinbach, and Frau Kessler are able to travel as far as Milan.

To Sonya Gorlenko from Manya, Tyrol, June 1

"Morning . . . and what a glorious, fresh morning! I can see the Alps and some of the lake from my windows. Far off you can hear the jangling sound of bells. Those are cows pastured in the valley. They'll soon move off and it will be quiet.

I've a bundle of German newspapers before me. Mark got me this work. Right now I'm doing sketches for a humorous journal. Oh, how I love politics now! You wouldn't believe how deeply I've plunged into these waters! They pay me pretty well for caricatures. Sometimes there's a hitch and we go hungry. But it's really not terrible. Our life is so modest.

We'll live here until the first snowstorms, then we'll go elsewhere. Does it really matter where? Life will go on like the lake waters, now as yesterday, tomorrow as today.

In our little house there are only two rooms and a kitchen, where Agatha herself does the cooking. There are no servants. We can't afford them. We only pay for laundry, and that costs so much that we rarely eat meat. But that's also nonsense.

We have no carpets, pictures, silver, or porcelain. But for all that we have the mountains and the rosy snow on their peaks and the lilac forests beyond and the green meadows and the blue-eyed lakes and singing brooks.

Agatha and I came here to her homeland straight from Milan. Mark accompanied us and set us up, then left. I insisted on it. You know all this.

He's settled not far away in a neighboring town across the lake. He was constantly afraid that I'd die. He kept writing to Agatha. But I laughed at his fear. How could I die, when I love life so?

From here we watched spring come from beyond the mountains, how the days grew longer, and the earth began to breathe, shaking off its icy shroud. We heard the waterfalls roar, rushing into the abyss, and the brooks sing. 'Spring is coming!' they said. And we believed them, and waited for it. Then the first birds arrived and we greeted them like friends.

And spring came. It came down from the mountains, all asparkle in its transparent green cloak. It scattered handfuls of the first flowers on us in the valley. Overnight the trees in the forest quietly dressed themselves, and in the morning we saw this and laughed with joy.

And it was during one of those nights when the last storm was howling in the ravine, when winter was sobbing and taking a long leave of the valley, that spring brought me its best gift—my child.

It's not true that I was dying that night. Suffering is life. And I suffered. I knew that my life was necessary.

A toy cradle stands by my bed, decked out in lace and ribbons. In it a little princess lies sleeping. She was born with golden curls. She has a finely molded face, a proud profile, haughty lips. She's a refined type, just like her father. There's nothing of me in her. Even her ears, nails, and the shape of her fingers aren't mine. I recognize him in every turn of her little head, in the movements of her brows. Once he jokingly told me in passing that he always sleeps on his stomach. The princess sleeps the same way. When I saw this the first time, I fell on my knees in worship, as before a miracle. My entire life lies in her! All my happiness, my future . . .

Mark is horrified by my feelings. He calls them abnormal, mystical. He's afraid that they will devour my soul the way love once did.

Love?

Can it be true that I, bearing such a treasure in me, wanted to die on account of love? And die such an ugly, vulgar death! I, who dreamed to die beautifully. You saved me from that shame—you, Mark, and other friends. How I love you for this now! You didn't allow me to commit the most heinous crime. *She* had to come into the world, this new soul, this new woman. And who knows? It may be that all that I've done and strived for was an unconscious yearning to create this life . . .

Oh, to live! To live a simple, uncomplicated life, immured in this valley, among peasant folk! To listen to the ringing of the herds, the rustle of the forests above, the noise of the brooks rushing toward an unseen river. To see the dawn and twilight in solitude, and the sky covered with stars and the flight of birds. To read Mark's letters, saturated with tenderness. To think about you and Petya and Anya. To sit entire nights by the window, remembering Yan.

I must love someone. Give my soul to that person, my life. And believe that my soul will not be trampled, and that tears of hurt will not poison me as they did then. Only a child will give me such love. I know this now. And I take on my own shoulders the whole burden of life—humility, anonymity, loneliness, and even deprivation. But I'll make a paradise for *her* . . ."

Meanwhile Nelidov has returned home from Europe at the news of his mother's poor health. He revisits the Gorlenko estate and, in spite of himself, mourns the great love he lost there.

He struggled desperately with his ghosts. One of these evenings he saw Natalka in the park. She was hurrying from the garden, and her song resounded loudly. Her dark, bare legs flashed white in the twilight. He listened intently to her voice and suddenly seemed to remember something. He went to meet her.

The closer she came, the slower and more deliberate were his steps, and the tighter his whitened lips pressed together. When he finally reached her, his face was very white and his eyes were filled with a cruel and triumphant desire. She immediately understood. Her song broke off as his hands fell heavily on her shoulders. She stared into his arresting eyes helplessly, agitatedly, as if at the Inevitable.

Summer was passing. Work in the fields was at its peak. Nelidov gave himself no rest. Refreshed and happy, he rode out from the field to the construction site and returned hale and hungry. As he dined with his mother, he cast sparkling eyes on the silently gliding, barefoot Natasha, who served at table. She had grown pale and thinner. Nonsense! There behind Anna Lvovna's back she almost smiled at him. At night while the house slept, she'd come to him as always.

But in the evening he'd order his beloved Gilda saddled and ride to the Lizogubs, where Katya awaited him. He'd long been considering her. She was small and fragile. *That other one* had been strong, tall, and lithe, but he had to forget about her. And this one was convenient.

Why did he think that he needed a wife like Natasha Galagan—meek and embarrassed, with clear blue eyes and a chestnut braid? No. He was drawn to the playful, coquettish Katya. She had curly black hair almost like . . . but a little darker. And swarthy skin, without the same blush. But she was also pretty. Not as pretty, of course. No one could be prettier than *she!* But that one was, after all, far away. It was as if she had died, and he needed to forget her. Katya's eyes were also dark, but not quite as dark. No one else had such eyes! No one anywhere. . . But Katya had long, dark eyelashes and crimson lips. They weren't like flowers, like hers . . .

Ah, this was stupid! He'd forget her when Katya became his wife. He'd deal with the feeling that gripped his soul. He'd triumph over the life that had trapped him! He'd receive his inalienable share of simple happiness, as all do. He needed youth, happiness, laughter, dark eyes, crimson lips, a swarthy breast. He'd find it all with someone else and be happy, come what may!

Manya writes to Sonya from the Alps. She explains that she has not written before because she is so happy, completely immersed in the joys of nature and motherhood. Although she writes that she cannot breastfeed Nina (Frau Kessler declares that her breast was "made only for love"), she is already possessive of Nina, who is a temperamental little princess, very like Nelıdov's mother.

In Russia autumn has arrived . . .

"Ah, Nikolenka, it's quiet here!" Anna Lvovna declared. "If only there were children, laughter, youth. Sorrow stalks these rooms and I hear its steps. At least Natalka used to sing before, but now she weeps. Why don't you marry, Nikolenka?"

But he was still holding out, clinging to his freedom and his right to anguish, to be silent for days at a time and to roam about the bogs, accountable to no one for his days and young life. He clung to his right to remember, to curse, and to hate. When he married, he'd deny that right to himself in order to be honorable. To be faithful. When he kissed other women wasn't he kissing the face of that one and only, whom he could not forget? Didn't her starry eyes gaze at him in his dreams?

So he struggled. He wanted to conquer life, which had locked him in a secret, silent duel. He sought salvation in a fever of new plans, in new activity. And during the holidays he'd disappear with his rifle for entire days and return home wild, with blood on his hands, and the cruel look of an aroused animal. And once the house was asleep, he'd wait for Natalka.

He'd committed this vile act out of a feeling of self-preservation in his struggle with life. He didn't seek expiation. He'd done this consciously. And wasn't this happiness?

"Farewell, my lord! Don't think badly of me!" Natalka said to him tearfully at their last meeting, the evening before her wedding. A handsome young lad from a neighboring village was taking her for his wife, taking her without looking into her past, which was a secret to no one but Anna Lvovna. He'd been matched with her before, and now the old lady was giving her a handsome dowry.

But Nelidov knew that Natalka's tears were sincere. He understood that she was unhappy, too, and that, like him, she was desperately trying to piece together a broken life. That night, with uncharacteristic tenderness he pressed her poor trembling body to him, the body that had given him the illusion of oblivion and joy, and he thought: "She'll leave and I'll remain alone."

Nelidov arrives at the Lizogubs to propose.

The decision was made. He'd thought it over a long time. "Enough!" he told himself with proud spite. "I want to be happy and forget!" In fighting his love for Manya he was playing the trump card of marriage . . .

Poor Katya had grown up in the last six months while everyone around her whispered about her possible marriage. The girl who'd never cried now knew despair. How many times had she expected his proposal! How many times had she bitterly called herself mad! He couldn't forget that other one. . . That's why he'd aged ten years, and his eyes were so hard. Could one dare to hope that tenderness would ever shine in them? . . .

He took her hand silently. Katya shuddered, bowing her head.

"Dear girl," he said quietly and sadly, and softly kissed her fingers. "Dear Katya. . . You know why I'm here?"

She bowed her head even lower. Her lips trembled.

He embraced her by the waist very quietly, and her head lay now on his shoulder. She closed her eyes. Her heart was pounding so loudly. Fear or joy? Which was stronger?

He looked on in silence. Long dark lashes, and their shadow fell on her dark cheeks. Just as they had on *hers* . . .

The crimson lips parted. She was also beautiful. He leaned down and kissed her on the lips.

Katya's entire body trembled in his arms, but he held her firmly and kissed her lashes, eyelids, forehead, and brows very gently. Her brows were thin and lacelike. They weren't capricious, like *hers*. They were calm. All the better! He'd love these dark brows.

"I'm tormented by loneliness," he said. "Mama is sick, and can't wait for grandchildren. She wants to die in peace, amidst kindness and joy. And you'll be a good wife. I need that tenderness. I need a son, an heir to my estate. It's so gloomy in our house, Katya! But you're young! You laugh so melodiously, you have such joy in your soul. Warm us with your happiness! We've forgotten it."

"Not a word about love," Katya thought. "I guessed right . . ."

But what of it? What mad joy to be in his embrace! Her heart melted in her breast from his kisses. A longing for happiness made her head spin and her fear of him faded. She raised her lashes and looked up hungrily at his inclined face, his darkened eyes.

"Tell me that you love me!"

This burst from her unconsciously, pleadingly.

And he said softly and sadly: "I will love you, Katya. You'll drive away all the ghosts. You'll bring sun into my house. Your love will give me peace. I'm tired. I've gotten so tired this year!"

"That's all." In a wave of desperation she forgot her shyness, passionately embraced his head, and begged him, pressing her cheek to his: "Oh, tell me that you'll love me, only me, always... Swear to me. I so want happiness! I've also suffered."

With a trembling voice he spoke to her in anguish, firmly embracing her fragile body, which begged him to protect her from merciless life: "I will love you, Katya, tenderly, constantly, faithfully. The way a husband should love his wife. I give myself—my soul and my life—into these little hands. Don't destroy them thoughtlessly, as a child destroys a doll she no longer cares for. Don't let me be disappointed..."

His voice suddenly broke off. She lay still at his heart, her eyes open wide.

The two sense Manya between them, a ghost that will haunt their married lives forever...

About to leave her Alpine paradise during the cold winter months, Manya contemplates her future, deciding at this point that "art is higher than life," despite the sufferings of the masses. Meanwhile, Steinback is back in Moscow.

Steinbach knocked on the door to the furnished rooms on Petrovka.

"Who's there?" He heard a woman's soft voice, shaded with impatience.

"May I see you?"

There was a second of silence behind the door. Then, joyously:

"Ah, it's you? How wonderful!"

Steinbach smiled crookedly, taking off his glove.

"One second, Baron," a trembling voice said behind the door. "I'm only in my blouse."

"That doesn't matter, Lily."

"In a moment." The voice sounded more hoarse.

"Is she powdering herself or blackening her brows?" he thought.

The door flew open. On the threshold they looked each other in the eyes greedily and happily, each with his own hidden desire, the memory of past caresses.

When she shut the door, he extended his hands to her. But she impetuously hugged him and pressed her entire body against his.

"My God! How long it's been! Why?"

"Two months," he said, smiling calmly. With cold satisfaction he examined all the lines of the pliant young body that was so familiar to him, yet never failed to excite him. A soft flannel dressing gown fell in pretty folds, hiding nothing. There was a deep crease on her very white neck.

Lily was a blonde of medium height, a type who pleases men. She wasn't a beauty, but she possessed a feline grace, a softness of gesture and line. She was utterly feminine. When she grew agitated, a blush immediately covered her cheeks and her little nostrils flared. Her temperament had always attracted Steinbach.

They sat down on the soft couch.

"Your fingers are ink-stained. Have you been working, Lily? Am I disturbing you?"

"How can you say that! You inspire me. I'm finishing a story for a new newspaper. Have you heard of *The Road*?"

Steinbach frowned.

"Oh, Mr. Aristocrat! I can't be choosy. I've got to earn a living and make a name for myself."

"You've chosen a bad way for it, Lily. That 'road' will lead you into the mud."

She reflected for a minute. And Steinbach saw in her face the sadness that had so interested him three years ago, when he first espied her at a literary jubilee, a solitary, lost woman, a stranger to everyone. He'd come up to her and introduced himself. That evening he'd become her lover . . .

Steinbach proposes they go out for breakfast.

"I'll get dressed right away," she said flirtatiously from behind the screen. "Can you wait five minutes, dear Mark?"

"I'll wait," he replied and went up to the table where her manuscript lay. He heard the rustle of her dress, her movements. He looked over the lines written in the pretty English handwriting most institute students used. But he struggled to concentrate in vain. Blood was pounding in his temples. His solitude for the last two months, his meetings with a remote and indifferent Manya, which poisoned his soul—all this aroused in him a desire to forget, a sharp thirst for pleasure.

He threw the manuscript back on the table.

"Mark, wait!" she babbled. "I'm not ready."

"I've waited too long, Lily," he said hoarsely.

In a private room in a restaurant permeated with the sharp aroma of appetizers, plates of food grown cold, and sliced pineapple, Lily slowly drank champagne. Sitting on the couch with her elbows on the table, she gazed fixedly at Steinbach, who was smoking in the adjacent armchair.

Sometimes she maintained friendly relations with the men she'd been with out of need or for pleasure. Some of them she even treasured. But deep in her soul she scorned men. They were so avid for a caress, so "materialistic." They'd never done one thing for her gratis! And how many years had she struggled to be independent! How many years had she run about, afraid to miss an opportunity, like a hunter in the forest, ever alert to the game another might find.

FIGURE 7
K. F. Yuon's "Tver Boulevard" (1909) depicts Moscow nightlife.
State Tretyakov Gallery, Moscow.

She was tired. She was already thirty. She could hide her years, but life was passing by.

But the man before her was unusual, not like the others! And she loved him in her fashion—with tenderness and interest in his soul, which would always be inaccessible to her. Oh, of course, if he hadn't been a baron and so rich, his attraction wouldn't have been so great. And his aura as a social activist three years ago had driven her just as crazy as his looks.

He'd shown up unexpectedly again and again, each time attracting and intoxicating her, bringing with him a intense rush of happiness. He created some kind of exotic atmosphere for a day or two, tore her away from her routine, agitating her nerves, but giving her soul the illusion of happiness. And when he disappeared for long months, she resumed her work with a new spurt of energy, and forgave him his forgetfulness. And life again seemed alluring.

During these years she'd fallen in love so often! At the first hint she'd given her body and soul wholeheartedly to great Love. But there had been no real love. Her phantom had disappeared. Only desire gazed into her eyes—naked and without illusions. And she, tired and bitter, would leave the man or the men left her, carelessly, without concealing the chill in their soul and their squeamishness. And she remained alone.

He smiled.

"Your lips are twitching from curiosity, Lily."

"From interest, Mark. Curiosity is too vulgar."

"Admit it, you'd like to write about me!"

Lily has detected a great change in Steinbach, and he confesses that he is in love.

"Oh, you cynic! Who is she? A princess? A queen?"

His smile was faint.

"Yes, she's a princess, but her kingdom is not of this world. It's in her soul. And what does it matter? Isn't that better?"

"Is she a poet?" Lily cried.

"Don't ask. I'll say no more."

"Poor thing!"

"Oh, no! Don't pity me! Ever since I fell in love with this girl, my life has been filled with interest and substance. Don't you understand? I'm almost certain that if she loved me or was my faithful wife, boredom would settle in once more, like a housewife. I lacked just these sufferings, and she gave them to me. I lacked a woman's indifference, and now I know it. Isn't this a valuable lesson?"

He tossed away the extinguished cigarette, sat down beside the pensive Lily, and hugged her.

"It's better if we talk about you. With whom have you been in love? Have you met any interesting people?"

"Oh, yes. I knew one . . ."

"You're happier than I am. Who is he?"

"A writer. A talented novelist."

"Oho! And you, of course . . . loved him?"

He looked sharply and saw her entire face and even her forehead, under her sumptuous bangs, flood with color.

"I loved him madly. Ha! I was in love like a schoolgirl. Almost the same way I was with you, the first day we met."

He smiled ironically. "Thank you! I'm touched. . . When was this? Before our time together in July or later?"

"No, this was a year ago. Do you remember? When you went south to your estate and I ran off to Petersburg to find happiness in literature."

"Why didn't you tell me this at our last meeting?"

"Ah, Baron . . ."

"Mark . . ."

"All right, Mark. Remember, if you will, the conditions of our last meeting, which lasted all of one day. Rather, one night. Ha! You've poisoned me with your cynicism. You turn up from God knows where and for God knows how long. Personified darkness—the way Jupiter appeared to Juno. And you disappear into the unknown, leaving such heat behind you that one can't regain consciousness for three days . . ."

"You're flattering me."

"Alas! No. . . You've always swept me away. There's something in you."

"Let's talk about him, Lily. Have you forgotten?"

He responded to her hot, direct kiss, but his curiosity was piqued. "So?"

"He's a modernist."

"Of course. They're fashionable right now. Is he good-looking?"

"I-I don't know. He's charming."

"That's better. You still love him, Lily."

"No! Next to you, Mark? No."

"What's his name?" he asked seriously.

"Harold."

"Is it a pseudonym?"

"Of course."

"That means his surname is ugly. Is he Russian?"

"A Jew."

"Ahh."

"But he's a true European. He's studied abroad and has lived there a long time. He has the sort of cachet our writers don't."

"I don't recall his name. Where does he publish?"

"He's already put out a book of stories. But you don't follow literature!"

"Dear Lily, you can't follow everything."

"He's not everything. He's a poet of unearthly grace . . ."

"He also writes poetry?"

"Yes. He debuted two years ago with that book. He's a recognized talent."

"In your circle, Lily? That's easy fame."

"You're unfair, Mark. Who knew Verlaine, Baudelaire, Lisconte de Lisle, Heredia? These are select poets."

"But what has he written? In what genre? You're looking at me so strangely, Lily, as if you pitied me. Have I really grown so wild that I talk nonsense?"

"Dear Mark. You're amazingly behind the times! When you talk about contemporary writers, can you really ask *what* they wrote? Or *how* they write?"

"Ah, yes. The ordinary has died away. I forgot."

"Harold has short stories and poems in prose . . . all mood."

"Out of time and space?"

"Of course. All this is old stuff, Mark, like the Wanderers* in painting. And you—forgive me—you express yourself just like a critic from a thick journal."

"You've interested me. I'll have to buy his book. It probably sells very poorly . . ."

"Of course. They say that he is emulating Altenberg. But that's nonsense! He simply has the same mode of creation, if one can say that. But in general it's impossible these days not to be accused of imitating either Knut Hamsun or Altenberg."

"Why did you fall for him, Lily? Not for his poetry, surely?"

"You see . . . I met him at the height of the revolution in Petersburg. He was getting ready to go to Italy. He has weak lungs. But the strike began and he stayed."

"Cursing the revolution, no doubt?"

"He's generally indifferent to politics, Mark. But he suffered very sincerely when they closed the theaters and the journals were hanging on by a thread. Ha, ha! Can you imagine it? The respectable thick journals hanging by a thread. They also seemed useless then, like the books of the modernists. But for Harold this was a terrible drama, for his book of poems came out in September 1905."

"Y-yes. That wasn't a time for poems, Lily."

Her nostrils trembled. "But wasn't that a tragedy for all artists? To feel you're unnecessary, cast off."

"Who prevented you from joining the movement?"

She moved away and put her hands on his shoulders.

"Are you laughing at me, Mark? Can you imagine me as I am, an aesthete, as you say, passionately in love with form, for whom a book's style and mood are higher than anything. . . And suddenly I'm running around with illegal literature under my arm, looking for apartments, or agitating for the Mensheviks, like that Zina Lipenko, who imagines that she can serve two gods at once."

Steinbach admired Lily's flashing eyes and high color.

"I remember one evening. We'd all gathered at Z***. Everyone was depressed. Many of us were racing about the room. Don't laugh, Mark. We didn't know then that everything would settle down soon. We thought this was a watershed, that power had passed into the people's hands. We sincerely believed that there would be no more art in Russia."

"Do you think that a book is less dear to a working man than to you? The only difference is that you literati only read your own. But the workers read everything."

She was pensive.

"I didn't know. I didn't think that."

"You didn't know that a new reader has appeared? How else can you explain the evolution of the book market? The success of Gorky and Andreev?"

"Maybe, Mark. But then . . . don't you remember? Who needed belles lettres then? For many it was a matter of survival. Ah, I don't blame those who were committed to the revolution or who professed their love for the workers or joined the parties. That's the instinct of self-preservation. But in all that mess, in that convulsive desire to ride the waves, only one person in our circle stood to the side calmly, with a scornful smile on his lips . . ."

"Harold?"

"Yes. I remember his face as if it were yesterday when he said: 'You all have two options—go out on the street and merge with the crowd or stay true to yourself and be forgotten. I choose the latter.'"

"I like him, your Harold."

"Ah, Mark!" She kissed him impetuously. He didn't move.

"Are you angry?" she asked in a crestfallen voice.

"I don't respond out of delicacy to a kiss meant for someone else, Lily. So, that evening you and he . . ."

"Oh, what are you saying! I tell you, it was much later. At first he was terribly cold. And then . . . at that time he was living with someone else."

"As if this was some mistake? But go on. He eventually betrayed himself?"

"How you despise people! No, I tell you! I know that he had a very hard life at that time. He was starving. You don't believe it? Why are you smiling? The publishing houses had returned his enchanting novellas to him. One editor said straight out: 'Now, mister, that won't shag a dog out from under the stove!'"

"That's not bad. Ha, ha!"

"They were saying: 'Give us something about the pogroms, about the revolution. The public only wants to read about that.'"

"Well? It's a commercial business."

"But don't you understand how a real artist—not a craftsman—would suffer? This was the most vile coercion of our soul! And Harold fled Petersburg for an entire year. He went somewhere in the southwest and lived off his relatives. And there he wrote his book."

"For posterity?"

"Why for posterity? He's already well-known. But what it cost him to find a publisher when everyone was demanding 'Secrets of the boudoir' and pornography! And he writes with . . . such integrity. He got a pittance for this book."

"But he won much more—fame and your love, Lily."

She stared off into the distance, and he saw once more a lonely sadness in her eyes.

"Ah, Mark! What was my love to him? He loves only art. He loves the woman who lives in his soul, in his writer's brain. We're too ordinary. And prose, which you can't escape in any affair, oppressed him. He values only his moods."

They were silent for a long while.

Manya's face confronted Steinbach—her enormous eyes filling the entire world. Eyes filled with desire.

Why did he remember her just now?

"How old is he?" he asked suddenly.

"Twenty-five, twenty-seven . . ."

Steinbach sighed involuntarily.

"And were you unhappy, Lily?" he asked in a whisper, pulling her to him.

"Terribly, Mark! I was so tired of seeking people out and being deceived. You wouldn't believe how I threw myself at him at the very beginning! I dreamed that we would live together in two cozy, pretty rooms. My rooms have gotten so old with their soiled wallpaper, that bed so many previous tenants have slept on, that alien atmosphere permeating everything, that impersonal furniture . . ."

She suddenly grew quiet and leaned her head on his shoulder, as if asking him to defend her. He stroked her face tenderly.

"It's hard to be a Wandering Jew, Mark. The years go by and you begin to value what you rejected in your youth. I'm well acquainted with free love. I'm sated with it! If I were to meet a good man—you understand?—a good, simple man, who'd love me as I am, ah, what a true, tender wife I'd be to him!"

He guessed at the tears in her eyes. His hands were still. Hadn't he added to her cup of sorrow?

"In our base world, Mark, it's hardest of all for a woman to make her way in the world without a man. You need talent. But to hang on—to persist in the journals, to get reviews—there one needs ties, protection. Otherwise you're finished, and talent won't save you. But believe me, Mark, only the need for poetry drove me to Harold. I dreamed to merge with his soul, to work together."

"And . . ?"

"He told me that aside from certain moments, he couldn't even bear the breath of a stranger beside him. He needs a woman . . ."

"For pleasure?"

"No, more, for a mood. But only that. . . Our liaison lasted no longer than a month."

"Is he more demanding than I am?" Steinbach thought with amazement. And antagonism stirred in his soul.

He sat down in an armchair and asked for the check.

"Already? It's over?" the sad eyes asked. He felt ashamed.

"Would you like some coffee, Lily?"

"Yes, yes. Or are you in a hurry?"

He looked at his watch.

"I have an important meeting in an hour. But this evening we'll go to the theater and then have supper."

"At your place?" She looked at him provocatively.

He smiled.

"How many days are you giving me, Mark?"

He had excellent hearing, and he caught the almost imperceptible bitterness in that innocuous question.

"I'll be going abroad soon. I'm waiting for a telegram from my wife."

They served the coffee and liqueur. The waiter left.

"Sit beside me, Mark! And hug me tighter . . . this way. . . You were truly my greatest love."

"Don't people love but once, Lily?"

"No, I've loved a hundred times. Yes! It must depend on temperament. But it was always sincerely and passionately. The feeling lasted sometimes no more than a few days and nights."

"And for me?"

She looked at him reproachfully. Then she pressed against him with feline grace.

"You're special, not like the rest. And it was hard to refuse you."

"But tell me, Lily, if I had returned to you when you were with Harold, would you have shown me the door? No, tell the truth, without flattering me. I beg you! Let's be frank!"

He squeezed her hands and stared into her eyes. It was strange! As if he were jealous. Didn't he despise that feeling, consider it atavistic?

She blushed fiercely, but a moment later spoke meekly and firmly: "I'm a stupid, weak woman, Mark. I preach love as pleasure in my novellas—a gay, light love without obligation. But my soul, like the soul of the most average woman, dreams about an eternal, great love. And I can't give myself to two men at once, Mark. I couldn't live with two. . . And . . ."

"You'd have cast me off then?"

With a deep sigh she covered her eyes and embraced his head. She kissed his forehead and brows, seeking forgetfulness, seeking self-deception, even for a moment.

But he was silent, crushed. "Harold is younger than I," he thought. "The time has come for me to yield to others."

And he suddenly understood that he had long feared this moment—already five years ago he'd feared it, like a faded beauty whose only other rival in life has been love.

At the entrance to her rooms, he kissed her hand and suddenly remembered something.

"Yes. Your book, Lily. Don't hunt for a publisher, and don't worry! I'll take care of it."

She flushed hotly under her veil. But he was so used to paying for everything that he didn't even notice her embarrassment.

Steinbach and Lily part once more, she with sincere regret, he with the guilty sense of her "soiled" soul and inferiority to Manya.

While Steinbach is entertaining a radical colleague named Semyon Nikolayevich,

Harold, in the company of one Evdokia Mikhailovna Korovina, pays him a visit. Harold has lovely hands, although the fingers seem too long, and he is dressed like a dandy—in a top hat, a smoking jacket, gloves, and a golden bracelet. He is tall and thin, and has a long, pale, "non-Russian" face, thick, dark, short hair. His finest feature is his high forehead with indented temples and arched brows. Steinbach is impressed and confused. The aesthetic Harold has come to him with a proposal.

"This is a project for a new theater," said Harold, giving him the paper. "I hope to interest you in it."

Steinbach's brows knit painfully. Why did he speak? He had an accent and his voice was nasal and sharp.

"Another theater?" Semyon Nikolayevich burst out. "Are there so few of them?"

Harold explains that he wants this theater to put on the likes of Hauptmann and Maeterlinck. He wonders aloud why Russian society still hasn't learned to treasure art.

"We are the bearers and creators of a new beauty," Harold replied calmly. "Our motto is that art is higher than life. It is still understood as a reflection of reality, and that depreciates its soul."

"Are you an admirer of Oscar Wilde?" Steinbach interjected.

"We want to elevate art above traditions, parties, formulae, programs, and prejudices. If Oscar Wilde knew how neglected beauty was in Russia, what a pitiful serving role art plays, he'd long ago have given up on the Slavs."

"You stand, of course, for 'pure art'?" Semyon Nikolayevich asked with irony.

"Did you crawl out from under some rock?" Harold's smile said. "I don't understand either your question or your smile," he objected slowly. "I heard that in the '60s they rejected Pushkin. Isn't that funny to you now? Or do you seriously think that art could have some sort of goal? That it needs justification?"

"You'll have to do battle with the provinces," Semyon Nikolayevich smirked, nervously wiping his hands. "Your Petersburg is really a provincial city. When everyone out of boredom is avid for novelty, they break up into circles and there's incessant backbiting. Every circle has its idol, and runs to look at him and writes papers about him and publishes rave reviews. But in another circle that idol is toppled from his pedestal and smeared in the press. And everyone gets upset and yells, forgetting about the fact that Russia sprawls beyond the boundaries of this provincial town—enormous, mysterious, unknown, and useless to all of you. That's where the reader—that mysterious Someone none of you know—patiently and concentratedly reads from cover to cover what the capital throws his way—your poets, dramatists, novelists, philosophers, prophets. . . All the delirium of a sick society that's lost the few values left it after the storm."

"Are you also a literary man?" Harold interposed with a barely noticeable smile.

"But don't imagine that *you* are creating new values. And, in any event, even if you create them, the provinces will revalue them. You're all really working for them. Do you know the number of books sold in the capital? Ah! Of course, you're not interested in it. But you ought to know your public. There's no time to read in the capital. You've only time to look. The capital lives by visual impressions alone. There's a premiere now at the Maly, tomorrow at the Khudozhestvenny, and the day after tomorrow at the Chastnaya Opera. And Korsh is playing here, and there's a benefit there. My God! When is there time to read? To follow what's going on? When can one think about things? That ability is atrophying. One needs constant novelty and change. The soul is growing coarse. One gets one's opinions ready made from critical articles, from lead pieces. It's easier that way. There's no solitude and no need to look into oneself or anyone else. One gets used to being in a crowd and adopts a herd mentality. People are applauded and feted not because they please but because that's what's done. People are criticized and hounded not because they have no talent, but because that's what others do. A movie theater—that's what your capital needs! And if you want to get rich, forget your dreams about a *Studio* theater, and build yourself a movie house!"

"Thank you for your advice," Harold said in complete seriousness. "But I won't use it. And if all that you say about the capital's intelligentsia is true, then I count on our success all the more!"

"Oh, of course! You'll have the success of novelty until people are sick of you. Do you want to build on sand?"

"We'll try!"

"But beware of the provinces! Don't risk taking your propaganda to the provinces. No matter how removed you are from reality, you must have noticed the astounding, strange changes of the last years. Just look at a picture of the book market after 1905. It's so interesting that it demands the pen of a sociologist. Did you know, Mark Aleksandrovich, how N and Z quarreled after they'd invested all their capital in publishing a brochure?"

"It disappeared from the market in half a year."

"Mark Aleksandrovich, seriously, this was a spectacle that deserves closer study. It was like a stock exchange. Stocks rose and fell. Prices fell. Bankruptcy hung in the air."

Semyon Nikolayevich ran about the room, making beautiful, inspired gestures. He was embellishing a little.

"They publish journals in the capital, and wait trembling for subscriptions. The provinces decide—whether to be or not to be. And the reader stands to one side, just as enigmatic, opaque, and silent. The capital crowns literati and the provinces dethrone them. You toss out a slogan. The provinces will be mysteriously silent. They accept everything from you thoughtfully—tinsel with gold, glass with diamonds—and reject what's unnecessary, whatever doesn't answer their questions, slake their thirst, satisfy their quests. On occasion they even cast off pearls and diamonds, not because they don't know their worth, but because diamonds and pearls are cold in their beauty. These may be sparkling pieces of life. But the soul of today's reader, suffering after its illusions and dreams foundered against reality, longs for a reconciling synthesis, longs for an ideal. Form isn't necessary, understand, but essence! That's why not a single verbal artist can win the provinces. That's why they remain cold to all the new 'wonderful stars' our critics rain down on them. Their light is too weak to illuminate the darkness and murk of our lives. And note that even an artist like Lev Tolstoy had to renounce literature and become a prophet in order to win the soul of the Russian reader. I repeat: what's important to the Russian reader is not *how* something is said, but *what* is said. But do you have anything to say to him?"

"From all that you've said I see the absolute necessity of our *Studio* theater project. A people that doesn't value form and doesn't love its language is doomed to extinction. One needs to work on one's style, just as Cellini worked with his chisel. Have you been abroad?"

"Y-e-e-es."

"Have you seen Hibert's doors in the Baptistry in Florence?"

"N-nooo."

"Or the carved figures on the cathedral doors in Milan? I sense you haven't seen them. But you've overlooked masterpieces, the labor of an entire lifetime."

"But, if you please . . ."

"Excuse me. This time I haven't finished. An artist worked on one door twenty to thirty years."

"We live but once."

"And so? You want to say that it's mad to give your life to create a masterpiece?"

"I find your point of view alien."

"Oh, of course! But I didn't flatter myself to hope you would take my side."

"Stas! We'll be late."

"In a moment, we must finish. Mis-ter . . ."

"Semyon Nikolayevich," Steinbach quickly interjected. Harold remained unfazed.

"Semyon Nikolayevich says that we only learned to value Tolstoy when he stopped writing. And I remember from childhood that Karonin* and Machtet* were also some kind of prophets. I remember how my aunt went to study with one of them in order to straighten out her life. I was a child then, but the naivete of adults nevertheless astonished me."

"You already knew how to live your life?" Semyon Nikolayevich boldly smirked. Harold, however, didn't react.

"But that, after all, holds true for all of Russian society, which ignores the artist and demands the prophet. The intelligentsia needs schooling in aesthetics. It is underdeveloped. You ask if we have ideals? Oh, yes! We long to liberate the artist and resurrect art. *Studio* will give refuge to all those young playwrights whom contemporary directors don't understand, to all those innovative composers who have no place in our theaters. But the main thing is that we'll have ballet."

"Bal-let?"

Semyon Nikolayevich suddenly began to guffaw. His shoulders shook, his face reddened, and his hands trembled. Steinbach was abashed. The brunette laughed gaily. Harold was unmoved.

"You want to educate Russian society with ballet?"

Again he guffawed.

"If you hadn't laughed, I'd be upset. Your laughter cheers me."

"He really is interesting," thought Steinbach.

"Laughter, jeering, and abuse always cheer me. Name me one living idea that wasn't ridiculed."

"By the crowd?"

"Yes. But the more passionate its protests, the truer the conquest. Contemporary ballet best exposes the poverty and vulgarity of contemporary society. What has it done with the dance, rhythm, the music of gestures, songs without words?"

"Manya . . ." The memory pierced Steinbach. He shut his eyes and went pale. "I don't want Manya to meet Harold." This decision was instantaneous.

"You've seen Duncan, Baron?" the brunette interposed.

"Yes, and even her pupils."

"Our dancers will be younger, more beautiful, more shapely and grand than that Irish woman. Her achievement was to protest, to raise her voice first against routine and banality."

"But she tossed out the idea. Don't forget that!"

"We'll develop it. She alone was powerless to create the drama and tragedy of a new kind of dance. She gave us an accessible Chopin in her own way, and provoked indignation. A new dance requires new music and new gestures."

"But what a run on barefoot dancers! And they're all successful. The demand for aestheticized emotions has matured in our society. You're right."

"But raising one's arms in the shape of a Greek vase or flitting about the stage is not sufficient for expressing complex emotions. This will be an entire science."

"Oh, it will be so hard," the brunette sighed, and then laughed guiltily.

"You won't refuse us, Baron?"

"Not at all. I'm profoundly interested. Count me as your main patron."

A faint, half-suppressed exclamation burst out of Semyon Nikolayevich, but he remained in the shadows.

Harold was visibly embarrassed. He himself hadn't expected such an easy victory.

"Allow me to visit you tomorrow in order to clarify the details and map out a plan."

"Please. I'll expect you at seven."

After Harold leaves, Semyon Nikolayevich accuses Steinbach of betraying him and their shared prorevolutionary beliefs. Steinbach opts to ease the atmosphere.

FIGURE 8
Lev Bakst, "Portrait of Isadora Duncan" (1908). The barefoot American dancer incarnated the values of the New Woman and offered a model for Verbitskaya's heroine. State Pushkin Museum of Fine Arts, Moscow.

"Bring us wine and dessert! Semyon Nikolayevich, I'll always adore you. I completely understand why you played and continue to play such a visible role. You read souls—especially simple ones like mine. You have a rare temperament, the amazing temperament of a fighter! In it is your strength, but also your weakness. That's why hatred blinds you and prevents you from orienting yourself when you fall among the enemy. You're so accustomed to power."

"What does that mean?"

"Ah, my friend! We can speak freely with each other! You not only don't tolerate other power beside your own, you love only those who have no will, like me."

"But, excuse . . ."

"Yes, yes. I'm speaking without bitterness. I know my worth, too, Semyon Nikolayevich, and I believe you are sincere in your attachment to me. Every creator loves his creature."

"You're always ready to slip through my hands!"

"Ah, you give yourself away!"

Semyon Nikolayevich's face blazed like fire. But after a moment he laughed, showing his rapacious little teeth.

"You made quite an expressive gesture . . . ha, ha!"

The servant knocked and brought in the tray.

"Have you started to study gesture, Mark Aleksandrovich?"

"Drink, please. Oh, yes! I'm always interested in people who lose control over themselves. People seized by passion. Maybe that's because I have no temperament. Your temperament flares up all the time. The same thing captivated me in Harold."

"But that's someone who hasn't a drop of temperament! He barely flickered his eyelids. And he's depraved. You can feel it. Didn't you notice that he had a crooked face? The face of a degenerate?"

"He has a good forehead and brows. And his eyes are memorable."

"But his mouth? It's a composite of scorn and bitterness. And he's not even thirty. When I see a crooked face and a crooked mouth, I always think that this person must have some defect in his soul. But it's unlikely he has a soul. Only vanity and narcissism, and boundless assurance."

"There you go . . . it's just the power of your hatred that blinds you and doesn't allow you to make a dispassionate judgment when you meet people from the other camp."

"There's no camp there."

"Oh, there is! And it's a strong one. It may be that Harold's worldview is limited."

"From this tabletop . . ."

"But it's straight, whole. It must provoke interest. He—if you like—is even touching in his faith."

Semyon Nikolayevich filled his glass with wine, but his hand was trembling visibly.

"Since when have you become so sentimental? Listen, are you really going to let yourself be made a fool of by that bunch of adventurists?"

"I see a convinced man. For someone like me, who vacillates like a reed in the wind, such a clear outpouring of will and readiness to do battle are very touching."

"There . . . it's just that feature in you that drives me to despair! Mark Aleksandrovich, haven't I long been jealous of that anarchist's influence over you? And the influence of the famous Nadezhda Petrovna? I'm amazed how you've preserved yourself in this company! You even published his book!"

"Yes, there it is. My constant reference."

Semyon Nikolayevich drank his wine in silence. Then he quietly shook his head.

"I have to tell you that you have a malleable nature!"

"More likely I have no nature. I'm always seeking how to fill up a terminally boring life. And all that is dangerous and beautiful attracts me."

"Even an aesthetic worldview?"

"If you please, even that. You can say this without irony. And there's no reason to flash your eyes. Ha, ha! You're just like a tiger on a silk ribbon."

Steinbach and Semyon Nikolayevich go together to the theater, where they encounter Nelidov and his new wife, Katya. Steinbach discerns, nonetheless, that Nelidov has not forgotten Manya.

Steinbach seeks out Sonya, now a student in the Higher Courses for Women, and they discuss Manya and Nelidov in the privacy of his Moscow palace. He learns that Nelidov and others believe Manya's child is Steinbach's, and that everyone condemns Manya, thinking she is Steinbach's kept woman. Steinbach explains that he is taking Manya to Paris to study with the famous performing artist Iza Jimenez. He and Sonya realize that Manya must win fame herself in order to overcome her reputation as a fallen woman.

"Mark, do you want Manya to go on the stage?"

"Of course! Art will straighten her soul, heal her wounds, make her life rich, and open her to all possibilities. She'll be happy. Do you remember when we last sat together here?"

"That was almost a year ago. Oh, of course, I remember."

"Do you remember Yan's book? In which he summoned you women to a high tower and promised you the keys to happiness there, at the top?"

"Yes, Mark. I didn't manage to read the entire book, but I will."

"Manya will find her way by giving herself to art. And she'll gain the heights."

"Oh, Mark. That's so good! Do you remember how she danced? But what am I saying? You didn't see."

"I've seen," he said hoarsely.

She looked at him in amazement. His eyes were shut and his brows knit sorrowfully. She felt that he was suffering, and she didn't dare speak.

Suddenly a burning log crashed in the fireplace. The embers crackled and sparked. He opened his eyes.

"Goodbye, Mark."

"Goodbye, Sonya."

They had been in Vienna a week. Frau Kessler had rented two rooms in the suburbs near Schonbrunn, and had written to Steinbach in Moscow.

Gravel crunched under someone's heavy steps. People. What a shame! How can one save oneself from people?

Suddenly Manya stood up and her book fell to the ground.

"Mark! It's you!"

She ran to him in a burst of tenderness, without measuring her steps or her actions, thoughtlessly, like a flower, the way she had behaved in the mountains, yielding to the movements of her soul. She fell on Steinbach's breast and presented her face for his kiss. Ah, she'd gone for so long without a caress! She could hear his heart pounding.

He was shaken. This outburst momentarily deprived him of self-control. He kissed her face all over, and his hands trembled. He tried to speak several times, but couldn't.

"You were waiting for . . . me?"

"I don't know. I wasn't thinking about you. But when I saw you. . . Let's sit here! Kiss me once more, Mark. It's so good to feel your tenderness!"

What words! But why did his joy fade? He had no faith in himself. If it had been six months ago . . . but what had happened?

"Manya, I missed you madly. Not a single letter for a whole month! Aren't you ashamed?"

"Was it really a month?"

"She didn't notice . . ."

"Forgive me, Mark. I don't like to write."

She didn't see his smile. Weren't her letters to Sonya lying in his breastpocket?

"And I'm terribly lazy! Any obligation makes me suffer. Would such attention really be worth anything to you?"

"Better to be silent!" he thought, sighing, and he quietly drew her to him again.

"You're not curious about Nina, Mark?"

"I know everything."

"Ah, of course! But how did you find me here?"

He laughed and silently kissed her eyes.

"Have you been back for long? Where were you? Where did you stay?"

As before, a whole cascade of questions.

"I've just been in Moscow. And I stopped to see my wife."

"Is she all better now, after the operation?"

"She'll die soon."

Manya straightened up and involuntarily moved away. She looked into the sky with big eyes. Then she very quietly stroked Steinbach's hand.

FIGURE 9
Vasilii Milioti's "The Kiss" captures Manya Yeltsova's nature-framed trysts with both Nelidov and Steinbach. *Vesy* (1906, no. 9).

"Poor Mark! I'm sorry for her, too. It's terrible to die! I didn't feel that way in the mountains. I didn't fear death there."

He sat hunched over, as if all his bones had been removed. She watched him intently, with an amazement that made it seem as if she were just waking up. It was strange! His temples were gray. He must have suffered. How could she not have noticed those gray temples before?

They'd lived together for half a year, parting only rarely, and addressed each other with the familiar "you." They'd slept under the same roof, like sister and brother. They'd lived through everything together. All during the long and difficult evolution of her soul she could see him beside her, silent, effaced, near and, at the same time, remote.

She'd suffered a great deal on his account. Yes! But there'd come a moment of liberation. She remembered it. How could she forget? She'd fallen out of love with him, as she had with that . . . other one. She had stopped suffering.

And then they'd parted. The mysterious creature she bore in herself for a time absorbed all her strength and soul. Like the sleeping princess in the fairy tale, she had been bewitched. And life had passed without agitating or wounding her in her blessed sleep. Even when Nina was born and Mark had returned in order to love them both, she had lived without desires or dreams, passionately relinquishing herself to this new love, joyously sacrificing all her possibilities. Maternal happiness overwhelmed everything that had once seemed worthwhile. She didn't notice him at her side. Perhaps she had trampled his soul many times. What had he experienced? What remained from what had been?

She looked at him furtively. That profile, brows, that sorrowful mouth. How madly she had loved all this not so long ago! His mere touch had caused her to tremble from the expectation of happiness. And now he sat beside her, just as handsome. But why did her soul no longer feel that ecstasy? That trembling from his touch? Why didn't she feel as she once had, helpless, powerless, small beside him? Where had the enchantment gone? It was sad.

As if he had read her soul, he suddenly lifted his head and began to look at her—first at her legs, and then at her voluptuous breast. He also gazed into her soul. He didn't see the woman in this suffering being. Nina had been a charm, an enchanted circle fettering his will and desire. He couldn't pass into this circle.

Then he looked at her face. She had bloomed and strengthened, the way a young tree, tossed by winter storms, straightens up in the spring. She was beautiful. She was completely different. Her form was finished and stern. She had a different mouth, a different look.

For an instant their eyes met, and he turned pale with desire.

But she was far away. He was alien to her, it was clear. Was it possible to resurrect the past? Does life repeat itself?

"Manya, why don't you ask me any questions?"

She seemed to wake up.

"Did you see Petya, Anya? Are they well?"

He was waiting for other questions. About Sonya. But she was silent.

"I visited Pyotr Sergeyevich in the hospital. Everyone's well and happy for you. They know all the details from Frau Kessler. But your brother keeps asking what you want to make of your life."

"Well, what did you say?" Her voice grew dull.

"You must answer yourself, Manya. Your brother is right. Rest and care have put you back on your feet. You need to live, to open the door onto the street. Idleness is dangerous."

"Mark . . ."

"I know your aversion. But you need to walk along this street with head held high and find your own way. You can't live without prospects, Manya! Yan's book has lain before you all these months. Have you read it?"

"I know it by heart. I took it with me into the mountains. And it seemed to me that I heard his voice."

"And? Have you found your path?"

She slowly shook her head.

"Do you want to search for it together?"

She was silent. Her eyes did not blink and her lips compressed strangely. He'd never seen that expression before. It pained him. Had she grown so distant from him this year that she didn't even need his friendship?

"Do you have ambition, Manya?"

She thought and replied sincerely: "No."

"Have you ever dreamed of glory?"

She sat with hands clasped about her knees, bent slightly forward. Her eyes peered into the pale autumn sky.

"Never. I've always wanted only happiness."

"Only!" he thought with a smile. "I've sought it my whole life and am seeking it still."

"And how do you understand happiness . . . now?"

She spoke slowly, thoughtfully, as if finding her words at the bottom of her heart.

"It's to be free. That's the whole thing! To be free both externally and internally. To be loved, but not to love anyone."

Steinbach started, but restrained himself. "And Nina?"

"Nina is part of my own life. I'm talking about love. No! About desire."

"What's that?!"

"A lot has become clear to me, Mark. Before, Yan's words were a mystery. But then his book led me out of the woods into a clearing, and love no longer frightens me. I'd like to create a strange, but beautiful life for myself. Shall I tell you about it?"

"Yes . . . please."

"I imagine a house with empty rooms, without any things, sideboards, comfortable furniture, fine dishes or rugs. But inside there'd be marble statues, and flowers all around. And I'd contemplate them for hours at a time, lying on the floor by the fire."

"On a tigerskin, of course. That means there'll be a fireplace? That's no shabby apartment!"

Her left eyebrow arched.

"There, you see. Your lips are twisted. You think it's funny? Then why am I talking to you? Can you really understand?"

"No, Manichka . . . don't hide your soul from me!"

She was amazed at how despairingly he pressed her to his chest.

"Would there be people in this house, Manya?"

"It'd be good not to have them, Mark! But even among them I'd be alone. I'd come and go at will. Wander at night and sleep during the day. Because at night I'm an entirely different person. I love the stars, I madly love moonlit nights and the quiet of the sleeping city, and the silence of the fields. I love dark windows closed like eyes. Everyone is asleep, but dreams walk among them and give me wings. And I would stand oh so quietly and smile. Ah, Mark! On such nights the world belongs to me alone!"

"You are fortunate!"

"But during the day you have to dress yourself, drink coffee, read repulsive newspapers and think up drawings, talk soberly. During the day Nina cries and gets angry. And I feel insignificant and helpless. Agatha clicks a spoon against a tray to distract Nina and I immediately go crazy from the sound. It smells of diapers and they have to be changed. My God, what prose! Then I can't do anything, Mark—sew, fix things, brew coffee. I can't even light the lamps. And Agatha gets mad. 'You're sleeping in broad daylight,' she says."

He laughed and kissed her eyes passionately.

"I'll tell you a secret, Mark. I love Nina more at night when she's asleep. Then everything in that little room becomes terrifying and mystical. I fall to my knees beside her bed and watch her and am afraid to breathe loudly. I fear everything then. The walls themselves come alive at night and look at me and think something. And what's scariest of all is that all those things know more about Nina than I do. Then I run out of the house. I don't want that hostility, that hidden threat! I look at the stars and my horror fades away. I make peace again with life. I humbly accept everything it brings me. Isn't there Eternity and Immortality? Won't I meet Nina *there?*"

"She has already learned the torment of being a mother," he thought.

"Ah, Mark! I love these solitary night walks. Sometimes it seems to me that just then, around the corner, at the next turn I'll spy a shapely girl. She'll turn around hearing my footsteps. That will be Nina. We'll laugh and embrace like sisters. And then we'll walk farther, without fear or hesitation."

"Where?"

"It doesn't matter! Even to Death itself! If only we are together!"

She embraced his head.

"Mark! My dear friend! I'm so happy that I can tell someone at last all that fills my soul! Do you see? Agatha would never understand me. She keeps saying: 'Be sensible. Don't waste money! Don't give it away for nothing. We need it ourselves.' But I can't do this. I don't want to think about money. I want to earn only what is necessary. And dream, dream! And cherish my dreams like flowers . . . or perhaps sculpt or write verse for myself alone. And go to the mountains in the summertime. On first impulse, without regrets, I will give everything to the person who touches my soul. But there's no need for gratitude! Those are needless fetters on the soul."

"Your soul must be naked and empty?" he suddenly burst out with bitterness.

"Why? Don't I have my illusions? In my soul I open the doors and windows wide so that the sun can flood it with joy, so that it won't smell of decay. I'd like to forget everything and begin all over! That's how I understand happiness."

"You want to forget what you lived with me?" he wanted to cry out.

"When I was little and mama beat me . . . unfairly, without finding out why I was crying and what I wanted . . . and then in high school when the headmistress hounded me, I'd always hide myself in a dark corner and dream: if only I could disappear from the company of those people who scorn me and persecute me, and land on an island where no one knows me, and be born again with a new soul for a new life . . ."

Her voice intoxicated Steinbach. There was so much new in it! The old Manya didn't have such chesty, full sounds, such intonations.

"This dream about the new has always burned in my soul, this thirst to seek. I lived it in the mountains, Mark. Ah, I was so happy in the mountains!"

"You have to live, Manya," he said sadly.

"I know. But I'll never give up my dreams for anyone! They are my dearest possessions. They are my moods."

"Where have I heard these words?" Steinbach suddenly recalled.

"Who among us loves them? Who loves himself? Who treasures his soul? Who knows the joy of contemplating a statue or a flower for hours?"

"Harold," someone said clearly in Steinbach's soul. And, yielding to this foreboding, he hugged Manya tightly. He would give her to no one!

"Who of you knows what it means to be alone in the mountains and to listen to the quiet which is not of this earth? Or to stand in the forest silently, like a tree pierced by the sun, and cry from happiness? I know all this, Mark. And I wouldn't trade these moments for glory or wealth. I don't want to live like everyone else! And I won't. I need so little . . ."

"And so much, Manya! You're right. You can't buy this with millions. In general the only thing valuable in this world is what is not on the market. You've remained the same dreamer. But what of your path? The steps you've just taken?"

"I've two paths before me. Ah! Are you surprised? I knew it. The first is art, and I say to myself: 'Here! Kneel and contemplate. Study. Create. The joys of art are eternal. Creation lightens life's inevitable sorrows.'"

"And the second path? That's strange! I never thought you would hesitate."

"The second path is the one Yan took."

"Ah!"

"It frightens me, Mark."

"Why force yourself?" he interjected heatedly. "I wouldn't want that life for you."

"Oh, of course, I'll choose my path freely. Anything that doesn't come directly from the heart seems insignificant to me. But you know, Mark, I can't think rationally about that woman in Rome. Do you remember her?"

"N-no."

"Mark, how could you forget her eyes?"

"Wait. . . The newspaper vendor, yes?"

"Yes. She's stronger than I am, and richer. I think about her so often, and about so many other things. These are all parts of life, fragments that reach me. But beyond them I sense something enormous, oppressive. Maybe this is the path that leads us women to the heights and gives us the ultimate freedom?"

"You're not saying anything, Mark?" she asked a minute later, looking at his hunched shoulders.

"What can I say to you? You've grasped Yan's thought. All roads lead to Rome, to liberation. Choose your own . . ."

"I'll find it," she answered proudly, tossing her head with a familiar gesture, and her curls fell on her forehead.

"I don't know her at all," Steinbach thought with a strange feeling akin to fear.

"I see one blank spot in your vision of the future, Manya. There's no love."

She grew pensive and suddenly laughed gaily.

"Ah, no! That's difficult. You see how you've cheered me up! I want people to love me. But I myself . . . I can no longer suffer or weep or go mad or humiliate myself. I only want joy from love, and I'll take that joy."

"With someone else," gloomy jealousy wanted to cry out in him. But he didn't speak, clenching his teeth and lowering his head so that she wouldn't see his face. Wasn't everything clear without words?

But she said carelessly, without feeling her cruelty: "It's wild and strange to me that I can only see one face before me, as if I were hypnotized. That's well put in Yan's book. After all, there's a whole world around us. Isn't each new face I encounter a riddle? I remember one night in Venice . . ."

"What?" He quickly raised his head.

"I was suffering unbearably. But then healing came. That night I felt so clearly that my soul was empty, that it held no enslavement. Ah, it was so intoxicating, that feeling of freedom! I'll never forget it."

"Can you explain this to me?"

She laughed once more.

"No, Mark. You wouldn't understand me. I even know what you'll say: a nightmare, hallucinations. But the One who brought me this freedom bore my sadness away with Him."

She gazed at the sky, and ecstasy was in her eyes.

Her words seemed delirious to him. One thing was clear—he need spare her nothing. She'd bear the blow lightly.

They were silent for a long time. The leaves fell quietly, circling before them in the motionless air and falling on the earth with a strange submissiveness. They looked at them pensively.

"Have you thought about the stage, Manya? Would you like to be a performer?"

Her eyes sparkled. She pressed her head to his shoulder.

"That's my cherished dream. But how can I fulfill it? Agatha and I live very modestly on my drawings, and still we don't always have enough. Why are you looking at me that way? I know. I need only say the word to you or Petya. But even so, he's given me almost everything he had so that I could go abroad. And now mama needs a great deal. Agatha says that they've put her in the clinic again. Anya wrote that it would be better there for her than at home. You see? I know everything."

"Listen, Manya."

He told her about the imminent opening of *Studio*. He proposed that she go to Paris to study with Iza Jimenez. All that he would spend on her studies for that year or two she'd return to him after her debut in Paris. It was only there that they would value her first steps, her boldness. She'd conquer the crowd with her creative fantasy and temperament.

"And do you remember what power over the crowd means? You already felt it as a child."

"Mark, I've never thought about others when I danced. I only enjoyed myself. I was beyond life."

"That's where your world will be, Manya. You will live there, untouchable, far from sadness, impervious to slander and human pettiness. And only when your name is famous, when your picture is in all the newspapers, when you are independent and rich, only then you will return to Russia and come to me, stay at Lipovka. But not before, Manya! Come what may!"

The glow died on her face. She'd caught something in his tone, understood something in his eyes. He wanted to speak. His breath was taken away. He let go of her hands. But she clutched at him convulsively, and that gesture suddenly exposed all of her femininity, the depths of the despair that had enveloped her, a despair that rose up from the bottom of her heart and which she had not known until this minute.

"He's . . . dead?"

"No, no. What's the matter with you? I saw him in Moscow a few days ago, in the theater. But he's dead to you, Manya. That's true."

He didn't want, wasn't able to look at her. He couldn't look at her. But her fingers dug more painfully into his hands. When he stopped speaking, she made a convulsive gesture as if to say: "Tell me!"

"He wasn't alone in the theater. He was with his wife. He married Katya Lizogub."

Her hands suddenly weakened and fell to her knees.

He darted a look at her face. He would never forget those brows and that look, twisted by pain to the point of unrecognizability. He dropped his walking stick and hugged Manya.

"My child."

"Don't speak. Wait."

Her voice had become hoarse. Completely alien.

He listened to her irregular breathing. She wasn't crying, but it would be better if she were!

She raised her hands to her throat.

"Long ago?" It burst out at last. She spoke unclearly, through clenched teeth.

"Two weeks ago."

"Sonya said . . . nothing to him?"

"Nothing. She didn't see him for almost a year. If it makes it any easier, Manya, I can tell you that he's aged and looks ill. He has clearly suffered. He married in order to forget you, in order to live somehow, to make a family for himself."

"Can one really replace another?"

"Never! But he's struggling. And he's right. You mustn't perish on account of love. Life is stronger than dreams."

"Only they save us!"

What a cry of despair! Sobbing trembled in her voice.

But where were the words with which he'd hoped to heal her? Which he had promised Sonya? How pale they sounded now! They were like beggars who wait before the temple so that passersby would see them.

After a long pause she said dryly, drawing away from him: "Leave me now, Mark . . ."

Her face truly had aged. Her eyes stared fixedly.

He quietly kissed her hand and walked away almost on tiptoe, the way one walks away from a cemetery.

Wasn't she burying her last illusions?

"So be it!" he thought. "She's climbing to the heights. It will be easier for her now to make her ascent."

Steinbach's wife dies, and he must leave Vienna for a few days to attend to her funeral. He returns to accompany Manya, Nina, and Frau Kessler to Paris.

Manya and Frau Kessler opt to live apart from Steinbach in cheap, dreary rooms, yet Manya joins him often for sightseeing trips to the Louvre, the Valois Palace, and other places. Eventually the two women set up house in a little apartment with a garden and a terrace. Steinbach is impressed with Manya's refined tastes as she outfits her modest home.

Steinbach drives them in his automobile to Versailles, and the narrator gives us an extensive tour, replete with Manya's enthusiastic daydreams about the French aristocracy and outrage at the guide's antipathy to Marie Antoinette. Against this background Manya and Steinbach enter into a frank, painful discussion of their relationship, with Steinbach despairing of Manya's love, and Manya maintaining that she has transcended her love for Nelidov and her anguish over Steinbach's supposed "tryst" in Venice.

Steinbach also finds himself a little house to rent where he can create the illusion of "home," reflect his own "I."

Steinbach was anxious as he brought Manya to his housewarming. He'd driven over to pick her up. She would breakfast with him after a drive in the Boulogne woods.

She looked around her, enraptured.

"Do you like it, Manya?"

"You have wonderful taste, Mark. Where did you find these treasures? It feels as though you're in the castle of Saint Cloud or the Big Trianon, in Josephine's rooms. Where did you get that tapestry?"

"It was completely accidental. I visited all the antique shops. I bought all these pictures, furniture, carpets, and tapestries the other day."

And he added quietly: "I knew you'd come. I wanted you to come here and dream by the fireplace."

"What a marvelous clock! It looks like the one at Versailles."

"No wonder. It's from the same factory. It's already two hundred years old. And the factory disappeared long ago."

In the downstairs study the fireplace glowed. Centuries-old chestnut trees by the windows cast a shadow on the room. The door led out onto the terrace and into the garden.

"There's an empty fountain. How I'll love this house, Mark!"

She sat down by the fire.

"What do you do here alone all day? You're not afraid? There are no ghosts upstairs?"

"I have my valet with me from Moscow. I'm used to him. And I've written Uncle that he should come here. He's lonely without me. His melancholy has gotten worse."

Manya was silent. With a heavy feeling she remembered that terrifying figure she'd seen twice in her life.

Steinbach gazed at her little shoes, and blood beat in his temples.

"Mark, when will we go to see Iza?"

"That depends on you. You'll have to dance for her. Are you really ready?"

Clasping her knees, she stared pensively into the dying fire.

"I seem to be. I need to be in the mood for it. You understand. This is an improvisation. It's creating."

He took her hands and drew her to him. They were silent a long while. She closed her eyes.

"Manya, is that really possible? What will you portray?"

"Ssh! Don't frighten away with words what is rising up in my soul. They're troubled images, sad gestures. My God! It's so terrifying. They're slipping away. Mark . . . I'm happy. . . I see them again. . . Oh, I'm beginning to understand."

Lifting her head, she looked up at the cornice. A ray of the setting sun had crept through the leaves of the trees in the garden and the lacy curtains, and reflections broke up and danced on the wall.

He saw her world in her eyes—mysterious and holy. A tremor he'd never known before arose in his own soul.

"Manya," he whispered, and his throat tightened. "Do you know the meaning of this moment? Our souls touched just now. Our distant souls."

"Ssh! Oh, be silent . . ."

The November gloom entered silently and filled all the corners of the spacious room. It was already dark in the study. Steinbach rose and walked on tiptoe over to the window. He lowered the heavy draperies. Reflections of the fire fell on the gloomy furniture, and the gold shone dully. The hunting figures on the tapestry seemed like apparitions.

Steinbach knelt quietly. His soul trembled with ecstasy. If earlier his blood had burned with desire, now everything drowned in the selfless upsurge of the soul, the passionate striving to fuse himself once more with her secret soul, which he had touched for one short moment. If only she'd understand his anguish! If only she felt this thirst for the Infinite!

As if bewitched, against her will, losing her own sense of self under the hypnosis of his effort, she bowed her head and stared at him with the far-off, profound, and mysterious look of the soul, with the eyes of a poet who listens intently to the sounds of a song born somewhere within her. She didn't see him. He sensed it. He looked into those enormous eyes and said to himself: "I've met the mystery."

Timidly he embraced her. But she didn't even notice this gesture. He put his head on her knees and tears welled up in his breast. After an entire year's separation (though he had been near her physically) he held her close to his heart. But how remote she was once again!

He felt it, and his despair grew.

She stared at the fire with fixed eyes, amazed, agitated. She resembled a doe who listens to the echo of distant footsteps at the edge of the forest. Did she feel the anguish of his embrace? No. Did she grasp the import of this nearness? No.

Footsteps sounded, the footsteps of the Unknown God, the One they await and summon, Whom they seek everywhere. But His ways are mysterious. He enters the soul suddenly. And flowers grow beneath His feet.

Steinbach lifted his head and looked with anguish into her face. It was marvelous. Her eyes were so inspired that he wanted to shout: "Take me, a beggar in spirit, into your mansions!"

Her hands dropped limply to his shoulders.

Had he said anything? Asked for something? She didn't remember. With huge, mysterious eyes she peered into his pupils.

Why was he here with her at the loftiest moment of her life? What secret meaning resided in what was coming to pass? Who said that it had to be this way?

Their mouths were so close. Their breath commingled. He was silent, as was she. But in his face, eyes, and every fiber of his being were present the strained expectation and terror of joy.

That Terror was familiar to him.

She bent ever lower to his face, as if she were drawn by those hungry lips, those wild pupils of the strange, unfamiliar eyes. Why was he trembling all over, from head to toe? She strained like a taut string. A wave was cresting in her soul. A whirlwind rose up from her depths, ready to sweep away everything in its path! An all-destroying whirlwind, bearing a new life . . .

The wings of her soul fluttered and unfurled.

Oh, long awaited rapture! . . .

Who was weeping on her breast? Whose hands trembled at her heart? Whose embrace enclosed her in an iron ring?

Was it you, Unknown God? The god of inspiration and creativity? Oh, stay these minutes! Let me fathom the secret of your commands. Touch my heart once more, so that scarlet roses could grow there, flowers illuminated by a dream.

When Steinbach returns to Manya after this passionate interlude, she seems to have forgotten him, to his despair. Nevertheless, the two proceed to prepare together for Manya's dance audition, at which Steinbach will play her piano accompaniment.

"What are you thinking about, Manya?"

"It seems I've found. . . All that you played there goes against my mood. Have you heard 'The Ride of the Valkyries'? Do you have any Wagner?"

"N-no. . . I can send to the store immediately."

"But can you play this? Is it scored for piano? Ah, Mark, if I don't succeed. . . Did you telephone her?"

"Yes, don't fret."

He sat on the carpet by her feet. He hugged her and pressed his head to her breast. She remained still.

"I still don't know what you want to say with your dance."

"The story of my soul. Are you surprised?"

She embraced him with one arm, as if he were Petya, her brother or her friend.

"I don't know whether Iza will understand this. Or if she'll understand anything in general. But you must know. Your music will create the world. It will be the story of my soul."

"Of love?"

She moved away and gazed attentively at his searching eyes.

"No. Why love? Is there nothing else in life?"

"Oh, how much there was in that phrase. Farewell, Manya-girl! You'll never come back."

"My dance will be what was and what will be."

In despair he pressed his face to her breast. A mad desire grew in his soul. It sufficed for him to touch this body and an elemental passion clouded his consciousness. He embraced Manya tightly and painfully.

But her hand fondly rested on his face, so trustfully and tenderly. And she spoke in a trembling voice, the sort of heated and passionate voice that speaks words of love.

"I dream of presenting all that I've lived through in the dance, in gestures and mimicry . . . my love of life and my thirst for happiness . . . my love for Love. Do you understand? Then . . ."

"Is this the same person who was helpless before my caress?"

"Then death. That's the hardest part, Mark. I don't know whether I'll find beautiful and sorrowful images. Will they be tragic? Will you recognize them? I think . . ."

"What armor is she wearing? Where is her sensuality, which so enslaves me? Where did she find this strength? My desire is growing cold."

"I think one should only select tragic topics so as to elevate the dance to the heights, to the place it occupied in antiquity. It was once part of worship. The crowd has trivialized it. They've transformed it from a religion into an entertainment. But I want to serve this new religion!"

"She's stronger than I am. Her soul is on fire, but not for me. I can't fight the cold that breathes from her."

Suddenly she turned around and placed both hands on his shoulders.

"And just yesterday when we sat here together, I suddenly felt such strength in myself, such agitation, so many images surfaced. It seemed that I awoke just as you were . . . kissing me. Oh, Mark. I understood what inspiration is!"

She gazed into his pupils. Her eyes were once again big and mysterious. Then she quietly leaned down and kissed his forehead.

"I love you, Mark," she said. And it sounded like a prayer.

Powerless, destroyed, oppressed by her sense of self, he closed his eyes.

Now everything was clear. In a single instant the eyes of his suffering soul glimpsed the entire future of their love. She would take him in rare moments of spiritual uplift. His passion would be that music without which she could not create her images. Then he would remain in the shadows, and she would return to art.

Would she renounce this new interest? Oh, no! He had to be prepared for that! Everything that enriched her soul, everything that caused her creativity to flourish, had to be dear to him. There'd be no agreements, no vows. He would wait. Would she come back?

"Oh, Mark! Will I be able to express what's been born in me? Will I be able to captivate you and her? Do I have any talent?"

Manya and Steinbach go to meet the famous Spanish dancer, Iza Jimenez, who has retired from the stage on account of illness and receives them in a studio strangely decorated with old mementos, talking parrots, and little dogs. Manya takes an initial dislike to these surroundings and finds Iza "unlofty."

"Don't you want to begin?" Iza pointed to the piano.

"Oh, madame, another time. I beg your pardon. I'm too overwhelmed with impressions."

"What does this mean? She hasn't reconsidered?" said the black eyes of their hostess. And a hungry fire burned in them.

Bowing her head and smoothing the folds in her skirt, Manya told Steinbach coldly in Russian: "I'll never be able to dance in these circumstances, among dogs and parrots. Explain this to her. Invite her to your place tomorrow. Let her set the time!"

Steinbach thought for a second. Then, without altering a single word, he told the artist what Manya had said.

"Madame, I can only work at night," Manya said firmly. "During the day my soul is dull. As an artist you'll understand this. And if you agree . . ."

Iza is intrigued and agrees to these conditions. Manya dances for her at Steinbach's house, to the music of Grieg and Wagner. Iza is overwhelmed. Afterward . . .

"She moved me," Steinbach said, sitting by the couch on the rug and kissing Manya's cold hand. "I never expected her to be so direct. That's what it means to be a real artist! But you were amazing, Manya. No. I'll say no more. You know it all."

Her fingers weakly stroked his face.

"Mark. I owe you my success. I'm nothing without you!"

"What are you saying? Are you laughing at me?"

"You played so marvelously! You guessed everything that I thought as I stood in the middle of the room and waited . . . waited for what I had lived through a long time ago, and only with you. As if your soul was whispering with mine. And I understood what I needed to do."

They were silent for a long while.

"Manya," he said with an agitation he tried in vain to control. "In a year you'll be an artist. Do you remember? Not long ago you said that you'd like to . . . pay me somehow for my love. It requires no reward, of course. And I'm not asking for repayment."

"Mark... Why are you trembling? What are you afraid of?"

"Your answer, Manya. You know that my life belongs to you. But I'd like an intimacy of a different sort. Not for myself, but in order to protect you from dirt. Up to now you've lived behind a glass wall, and you don't know what life is like. It will mangle you with its paws if you and Nina remain alone. You need a friend, a defender. It's harder for a female artist than for anyone else to be alone. All around you there'll be slander and gossip. My God! I know that world so well! Here, in the twentieth century, we still haven't learned how to respect women. And the higher a woman rises on the strength of her talent, the more maliciously they slander her."

She held her fingers to his lips.

"In a word, you're asking me to be your wife?"

She sensed that he hung on her answer. But she was silent for a long time, tired and overwhelmed by reality after her waking dream.

"No, Mark, I can't."

"Why?" he asked barely audibly.

"I can't right now. I love my freedom too much."

"But have I . . ."

"Ah, I know! You're delicate, well-bred. You've shown that. But my life has already taken shape in my dreams."

"Where there's no room for me?"

"Under the same roof? No . . ."

"That's nothing, Manya! I'm ready to fulfill your maddest fantasies."

"I may love another, Mark. Neither gratitude nor compassion will stop me. I want to realize my dreams here on earth, to pursue all possibilities, make my life a poem . . ."

She saw his sorrowful smile, which she had once so loved.

"I've gone through so much with you, Manya. And I'm ready for everything. How can you frighten me?"

"With suffering, Mark."

"I've loved you for that suffering, Manya."

"Don't take so much on yourself, Mark! A taut string breaks in the end. I know this from my own experience."

He smiled bitterly.

"I'm too old for you, my child. And I know we're not a couple. You're a talented, exceptional woman, and I'm the most ordinary sort, remarkable only for the fact that I have money made by my ancestors. But I have one talent that the fairies forgot to put in your cradle . . ."

She raised herself up on her elbow and stared into his dark, matte eyes.

"I know how to love."

These words reached a soul depressed by daily concerns. She laid her head back on the pillow, and her hand tenderly fell on his shoulder.

She spoke after a pause, sadly looking upward:

"Dear Mark. Life is beginning. Dreams are departing. . . Here I am again at the crossroads. Alone."

"With me!" he added despairingly.

She turned her gaze on him, and looked intently, thoughtfully, and sternly, seeking something forgotten in those once-loved features. He was terrified by that gaze. He felt that his fate was being decided in this moment of silence.

"With you," she said with a strange intonation.

And closed her eyes with a sigh.

The silence continued. One could hear the crackle of the burning coals in the fireplace.

His heart was pounding with such pain that sweat beaded his temples. But he was afraid to move. She may have fallen asleep.

Suddenly she made a movement.

"Fine, Mark. I'll be your wife. But not now, no . . ."

"Why, Manya? Tell me why?"

He kissed her hands and the blanket covering her knees. He was trembling with happiness. Hadn't he thought that all was lost?

"I thought somehow that you'd understand immediately. Apparently, even the most loving man is incapable of penetrating our soul. I want to ascend to the heights myself, Mark. To the heights I dream of. Without your help. Without your name and . . . your money. I want to become something before the doors open wide for Steinbach's wife. I wouldn't respect myself if I felt differently. Don't be angry, Mark! And wait . . . it will only be a little while longer."

In her voice there was profound fatigue.

"I'll wait," he answered quietly. "I know how to wait."

BOOK FOUR

> I learned how to catch the
> departing shadows,
> The departing shadows
> of the dying day.
> And I rose ever higher,
> and the steps shook,
> And the steps shook
> beneath my feet.
> —K. Balmont

Manya proceeds to study with Iza, whom she has come to like. On holidays Steinbach takes Manya, Frau Kessler, and Nina to his place for sumptuous dinners. Steinbach's uncle, who now lives with him, is obsessed with Manya, who reminds him of his dead sister, Sarra.

Class was held next to Iza Jimenez's yellow salon. The room was empty, without carpeting or furniture, and had a single piano and one mirror-lined wall. Behind it was a bathroom. Its walls were draped with gauzy blue ballet skirts and flesh-colored tricot. A number was nailed under each costume. These were traditional ballet costumes with a flat open bodice, costumes that exposed the student's body. At a single glance the teacher had to be able to see all the body's contours and bends—the legs beginning at the hip, the knees, the feet, the shoulders. Here there were no obscuring decorations. Every movement or tension of the muscles was important. Everything had to be natural and seem easy, lending the dance grace and beauty.

Madame Fredau supervised the class on ballet gymnastics—that is, the most difficult steps beginning with the "positions," which are as boring and necessary for dancers as scales are for pianists, and vocal exercises are for singers. She was a retired ballerina, dry and sharp, who wore a red wig but no makeup on her faded face. She'd also change into a short wool dress that reached a little below her knees. If one only saw her figure and straight, elegantly covered legs, one would take her for a girl.

Manya quickly and easily mastered all the difficulties of these first steps, which proved almost impossible for many adults. "She already has her pointes," Iza said in amazement to her helper. This meant that Manya could dance freely on her toes. She was the only one of forty pupils who had this talent—something as rare as the naturally great voice of a singer. Many of the students thought the exercises oppressive. But Manya felt everything was important. She realized now what a difficult art dance was. When a ballerina slips across the stage, light as a shadow, barely touching the floor, the uninitiated would never suspect how hard it was to achieve this lightness and what torments this grace cost! And how many tears and doubts were concealed by her generic smile! This required little talent, but years of patience, persistence, and hard, unseen work.

Yet Manya was naturally agile. She'd guessed all the basic movements of the dance instinctively. Manya'd easily achieved *opposition*—that is, the movement of the hands and the reverse movements of the feet, which is fundamental to the art of the dance and which the clumsy Americans and vulgar Jewesses couldn't manage. It sufficed to see her standing on pointe, bent forward in a grand *arabesque*, ready to fly away, or standing in a proud *attitude*, with her arms uplifted as she strained upward in frozen motion.

One could feel that the dance was her element, and that nothing in it was beyond her ability.

In six months she'd so mastered all the complicated movements that compose dances—the *jeté, glissé, chassé, balance, pirouette*, etc.—that Iza permitted her to practice them only at home. Manya would practice for four hours straight, sometimes to the point of exhaustion.

"You'll end up with a heart attack," said Frau Kessler, when Manya, completely pale, fell on the bed. "Why are you killing yourself?"

"I want to be an artist, not a dilettante... That won't give me satisfaction."

"But Duncan? Iza? What did they study?"

"Duncan is a genius, and Iza has enormous talent. But she confessed to me that she'd always regretted not having learned classical French ballet as a child. And do you remember how Duncan would turn her arms about? It was terrible to watch! It violated the laws of plastic movement. I'm driving myself to master the basis of everything, Agatha. You can't become a pianist without learning harmony and you can't compose an opera without knowing counterpoint. The same way with ballet. Mark just told me that all these difficult steps were already familiar to dancers in ancient Greece."

"That can't be!"

"There's an entire study of it. Why are you surprised, Agatha? If a trade like prostitution required girls in the Orient to start training when they were seven years old, then wouldn't an art like the dance require more knowledge and practice?"

The school includes French and Russian aristocrats, "crude" American girls, and Jewesses, but only a few girls as poor as Manya. All the pupils are impressed, however, by the rich Steinbach's devotion to her.

Iza also had a few male students—no more than ten. There were grown-up Americans—some handsome and blond, others built like butchers, with heavy jaws and square red faces. There were also waspish, sharp Frenchmen. Manya noticed that they and the female students didn't flirt. On the contrary, a kind of professional envy and competition could be glimpsed in their relations, which in no way softened their manners. Everyone studied everyone else with mocking eyes and forgave no mistakes.

"Come tomorrow evening," Iza told Manya. "I've a pantomime class, and you'll see Nils."

Ah! His name was on everyone's lips. No one spoke indifferently about him. Manya was interested.

"But lock up your heart!" the Creole laughed, shaking her head and waving her finger. Her earrings were shaking, too, and her bracelets jingled.

The next day at exactly six o'clock, Manya walked up the staircase. Even through the door she could hear the impassioned sounds of the *fandango*. "Can I be late? Ah, what music!"

She quickly took off her coat in the anteroom. The dry, passionate clack of the castanets was luring her in.

"What a sultry sound! It burns..."

She pushed her way through the crowd of female students gathered at the entrance. There Iza caught sight of her. She nodded and clapped her hands at the accompanist.

"From the beginning. Nils, take your place! Maude, your shawl has come untied."

Nils—a Spaniard with a dark shaven face—turned around and spied Manya. "Ah, there she is!" He'd also heard a great deal about her. He smiled, and it seemed as though his sparkling teeth lightened his face. He bowed from afar. What a graceful gesture!

"Gorgeous!" thought Manya, gazing at his energetic profile. "Is he really Russian? And what legs he has, what a body!"

Maude was an American. She was a stylish blonde, and her costume suited her. Nils was above average height. Short, cloth pants covered long, muscular legs. A wide crimson belt girded his lithe figure. On his head was a red silk kerchief, the end of which hung over his shoulder.

They were dancing. The castanets clicked, and Manya's heart pounded. Was it possible to dance more beautifully, with greater passion and brilliance?

"I'm madly in love," Manya told herself. "Will I ever dance this dance with him? That would be pure delight!"

The lesson had finished, but she was still daydreaming with open eyes. About what? What a wave of creativity had crested in her soul! She couldn't remember when that had last happened to her. Images swarmed and poses took shape... An entire drama without words rushed by in her head...

In the corridor she bumped into him.

He was saying something, leaning casually against the wall. Before him stood a delicate blonde, dressed modestly as a milliner. She was gazing at him with love-struck eyes and she fussed with a pleat in his belt.

"You'll be coming soon?" she asked him in Russian in a ringing, childlike voice.

"If you want us to leave together, wait a moment, Milochka. Only change your clothes or you'll catch cold."

He spied Manya and fell silent.

She walked past without taking her eyes off him. He saw such fiery, open rapture in those dark, enormous eyes.

His face trembled. He bowed to Manya shyly. She blushed and bowed her head. With darkened eyes he watched her go.

Behind the door Manya heard the blonde's jealous question: "Who's that? A new one? You don't know each other?"

All night she saw his face in her dreams. The sound of the castanets haunted her even when she was awake.

Manya and Nils, the stage name for Pyotr Likhachov, are introduced by the wiley Iza. Nils becomes infatuated, but Manya is disenchanted by his normal, sweet demeanor. He invites her home to meet the wife and daughter. Manya realizes that she is only in love with him when she watches him perform on stage.

Manya continues to excel, and although her classmates try to court her, she refuses to socialize. Iza is tender only with her, and teaches her special classes in mimicry and dance at Steinbach's house. Manya asks Iza to address her as "Marion" rather than "Marie," because the latter name awakens painful memories of Nelidov.

Meanwhile the school is abuzz when they learn that Manya has a child and therefore a "past."

Manya's days were so full that there remained no time for love. But Steinbach didn't complain. Didn't she belong to him completely, him alone? Not even the shadow of a rival hovered on the horizon. Only Nelidov had threatened him. But that, after all, was over. And even if they met again, Manya would then be his wife.

Of course, that guaranteed nothing. He was too experienced to trust women, especially those who lived by their feelings. But Nelidov had thrown down an impassable chasm between himself and Manya when he married. People of that stripe don't betray their duty. "As long as she never finds out that he was in Venice!" Steinbach would tell himself.

Sometimes—very rarely—Manya would suddenly come up to him pale and upset, with darkened eyes. . . "Kiss me!" she'd say hoarsely, and would close her eyes with the expression of someone conquered from without, someone yielding to a higher force. And her face then would be tragic, and her love dark.

Steinbach would long relive these moments in his memory. These transports were magnificent. There was something elemental in this woman's passion. Some terrifying secret stared at him from her half-closed eyes.

And he could never forget her smile. It was bliss bordering on suffering. It distorted her features, and, at the same time, strangely enlivened her pale face. One couldn't help believing that this was the submission of someone in a battle beyond her strength.

But these moments passed, and Steinbach once again saw the distant gaze, the mocking lips. She'd part with him indifferently, letting herself be kissed, and hurry toward the door. Even at the threshold her soul was already preoccupied with another. She had her own interests, her own life.

And if he tried to detain her, he'd feel her resistance, even her antagonism. As if she'd given in to the enemy and despised herself for her weakness. "She's just like a man," he thought bitterly.

Once he couldn't restrain himself and told her so. She laughed.

"You've made me happy, Mark. I've always wanted to love the way you do . . ."

"I??"

"Why, yes. . . You're no better than the others." (She added this last when she noticed a strange break in his furrowed brows.) "And believe me, Mark. Now" (she accentuated this word) "I give you credit for that."

"I'm very touched," he interjected, twisting his lips. "But I don't entirely understand what is to my credit?"

"Knowing how to love without drama . . . lightly and joyfully."

"Ah!"

"You men have grabbed the keys to happiness. The puzzle that we women still anguish over you solved easily and long ago. But just wait. We'll get it, too!"

"A la bonne heure!"

He swung open the door before her. She left, and he remained alone with his thoughts.

To love lightly and joyfully. What irony! But obviously Manya sincerely believed that he could love this way. She hadn't forgiven him the redheaded Venetian. She was still convinced that he'd spent that night with her when he'd gone to meet Nelidov at the train station, and had wrested his happiness from him in a silent duel. But Manya's soul had been reborn since then. The trusting girl had died, and now there was this woman who wanted to laugh at illusions and take only pleasure from love without sacrificing anything. That was the program she'd set for herself. Did she have the strength for it? "We'll see, we'll see . . ."

"It's a tragic battle," he thought. "One can create for oneself a new worldview and preach the freedom of love and freedom *from love*. . . One can believe in that dogma passionately and consider oneself a new woman. But what does one do with the old feelings that have been cultivated for centuries? What does one do with the instinct of Femininity—that fateful instinct slumbering in the most precious depths of the female organism, beyond the dark threshold where thought doesn't penetrate? What does one do with the need to submit and sacrifice, a need that has been cultivated in the female psyche for thousands of years?

"To free one's soul from the yoke of passion. To fill that soul with a great striving upward. To rise to a lofty goal, seizing love like rest and joy. To relegate that love to second place in one's life. Those are the keys to happiness which Yan promised women.

"But should he have laid out this testament for woman alone? Isn't love the same sort of drama for me? Haven't I put it at the center of my life? Isn't it a kind of cult?

"'You have a feminine soul,' Manya's said that to me several times. Isn't that the secret of my own weakness? And if I lose Manya now . . ."

Steinbach does all he can to make himself indispensable to Manya. One of his strategies is to mesmerize her with lectures about the history of the dance, which, he says, began in the mysterious East. He describes its origins in Egypt, then its evolution in Greece, where it became a part of life itself. He talks about the modest birth of ballet in Rome during the reign of Augustus, and shows her his rare books on the dance. When he complains that present-day Western society exploits and does not serve art, Manya passionately agrees. They both want art to be "for the people."

Frau Kessler declares that she's appalled by Iza's mistreatment of her black servant, Mimi. But Manya counters that Mimi must be happy to love her so devotedly and selflessly. Manya is also not dismayed by Iza's greedy exploitation of the rich, or by her excessive love for her dog.

Frau Kessler was right to be jealous of the Creole. All that was fantastic and mystical in Manya's soul—her forebodings, superstitions, yearning to create, rapturous transports, everything that was alien to sober Agatha's soul and that Manya experienced alone—all this she found in Iza. To a great extent she recognized herself when Iza cried over a lost card game or when she was thrilled, like a child, by sunshine and a walk in the woods. Both of them loved fairy tales, daydreamed wide awake, and believed in their dreams. They valued their moods above all else in life. To steal away suddenly from home and sit all day in the forest, on a secluded path, without speaking or thinking, like an animal. To watch the golden leaves fall and spider webs drift through the air and onto one's face. To forget about dinner and those who were waiting at home. To cut loose from oneself and feel with every fiber of one's being how one fused with nature. Ah, Iza understood that! She never called her crazy. Like Manya, she had no habits and no respect for the customs of civilized people. Iza was like Mimi. "And like me," Manya thought. "Didn't Nikolenka call me little pagan?"

In the Creole's yellow salon Manya found what she'd missed in Steinbach's stylish rooms. She found herself.

Sometimes they understood each other with a half-word. Their souls were close even in silence. That's why Manya liked to drive through the woods with Iza, ride with her to the opera or the theater. She loved to sit silently beside her fireplace and to listen to her chattering over a steaming cup of cocoa.

In these conversations or in the woods or on walks or at lessons (especially) Manya experienced rare and precious moments. Then the quotidian, the petty, and the repellent fell away from Iza's soul—all the rubbish that had accumulated in her during her long years of hardship and then her fight for fame; in clashes with the impresario who exploited her talent, and with the commercial press and with the vulgar and sensual love of her admirers. Her soul suddenly stood before Manya as pure as in childhood, open to marvelous transports, full of life and gaiety, despite the illness that had removed her from the stage! Only in this untidy room did the face of a great artist suddenly emerge from under the veil of the everyday. One could only find the real Iza here—Iza the child, Iza the poet.

The Creole was attached to her student with the sort of turbulent feeling specific to hysterics—a feeling that strangely blended ecstasy and irritability, envy and tenderness, the yearning to rule and the yearning to worship, jealousy and a mysterious fear of Manya who sometimes seemed to Iza to be a person from another planet.

Often after a lesson, when the door closed on the last pupil, Iza would turn to Manya with glittering eyes: "Tu restes?" It would turn out that Iza had bought new postcards, and needed to look them over. She adored them and collected them.

And Mimi would bring them fruit, liqueur, and biscuits. Settled deep in the armchairs by the lamp, they'd meditate on an Algerian street or a moonlit Egyptian desert or the Sea of Gethsemane in the pale rosy smoke of dawn, with a flock of sheep and the pensive lonely figure of a shepherd. Everything here was as it had been two thousand years ago, and both women yielded to the pleasure of contemplation, understanding each other without words.

But sometimes Iza got spiteful, and on those days she really did hurl plates at Mimi's face. She'd get carried away, cursing unrestrainedly at Manya if she was fifteen minutes late. And Manya'd look at her with compassion, as if she were mad. Goodness and cruelty, enthusiasm and pettiness strangely mingled together in that soul.

But Manya understood the reason for her sorrow and outbursts of despair. This talented artist had abandoned the stage at the height of her career on account of an incurable disease. What had caused it? Hadn't it been the struggle for life and fame?

"Don't cry," Manya would say, hugging the artist and stroking her coarse hair. "You need to fight this and seek out new happiness."

"What happiness? I'm already forty-five. Illness has crippled me. Even when I teach you, I'm gasping for breath. And what lies ahead? Old age. Loneliness. You're easily consoled because you're only twenty and fame and love await you. You'll conquer life. But it's destroyed me."

"And you think it has spared me? No, Iza. . . It got me by the throat, too, and threw me to the ground. But you see? I've gotten up and I'm walking once more, walking up to the heights. Don't cry! We'll seek it together. Maybe we'll find that happiness."

"Marya Sergeyevna . . ."

"No, no, for God's sake! To you . . . and everyone else I'm only Marion."

"Marion. . . Marvelous, glorious Marion . . . you're driving me mad!"

He said this as he stood beside her in the half-lit corridor outside of class, seizing a moment of break time. Beyond the door one could hear the buzz of voices, as in a beehive, and then a sharp cry. That was Iza scolding one of the dancers in the pantomime they were learning. The Americans danced with their fingers spread wide, and that was intolerable. One's hands had to be graceful, with fingers bent in the right image. There should be no corners, only curves. Manya'd felt that with the sensitivity of an artist. They'd never criticize her. She found it funny.

"Vous êtes toutes des grenouilles! (You're all frogs!)" Iza shouted, burring her "r's" in despair.

Manya chuckled, but Likhachov was upset. Iza'd finished her tirade, and they started coming out.

Both Likhachov and Manya were in Spanish costumes. In her greasepaint and outfit, Manya'd become a beauty. The asymmetry of her features was erased when one saw those enormous, amazed eyes and sparkling smile. Likhachov was also extraordinarily striking, and he knew how to carry off his costume. The ecstasy Manya'd felt dancing with him had not yet faded from her eyes.

"How you danced just now, Marion! I'm madly in love with you. You're laughing again?"

"Yes. I'm always tickled when you talk of love."

"Cruel one! Do you like to torment me?"

Manya laughed resoundingly.

"Torment you? Ah, dear Nils! Don't use such sad words. . . Dear Lord, that's not your style. I so envy you your clear soul!"

"But you're simply laughing at me! My soul's broken in two. I don't sleep nights. Why did you taunt me yesterday?"

"I? You??"

"Yesterday during our dance, when I whispered 'I love you. . .' You replied 'I do, too.' Are you toying with me?"

"Not at all. I do love you, but only on stage when you're in this costume."

"Isn't that the same? It's still me, after all."

"No, it's not you! Not you. . . It's someone else. Don't you understand that life is one thing and theater is another?"

Likhachov cracked his knuckles. He'd like to grab her and kiss her right now! The serpent . . . she'd slipped through his fingers!

Iza's shouting had stopped. Footsteps were coming nearer. The door was flung open. Wicked grins and astonished looks seemed to embrace the pair. Likhachov's face was angry and embarrassed. Manya held back the wave of curiosity with a calm smile.

Nodding to Nils, she went off to change. Classes were over.

Likhachov caught up to Manya on the street. She looked around, and disappointment showed in her face.

"Can't you see that I'm suffering?" he told her in the capricious tone of someone unused to rejection. "Anything's possible. I've lost my head. I could ruin the role."

"Be quiet, Nils! Art should profit, not lose, by our experiences. Otherwise we're dilettantes, not artists. And then you make a mistake. Or do I know you better than you know yourself? The stage is your element. You're happier and stronger than I. And you're also mistaken in your feeling for me. You love your wife as a woman, but me . . . be quiet! I know. You love me as beauty, as inspiration. That's why I laugh happily when you speak to me of love. I'm proud of it. I'm happy. There's my tram. Goodbye, Nils! 'Til tomorrow."

He gazed after her with darkened eyes. She'd said goodbye with such a voice—just like someone in love who can't wait for a kiss. It wasn't a game. A voice like that can't tremble on command. But what was it, then? What?

Nelidov and Katya return home to their estate, where Anna Lvovna still insists on running the household and letting Katya live "without care." Nelidov finds it a great relief to be alone, although he is grateful to Katya for a kind of sensual oblivion and, of course, for her devoted love. He remembers his last night in the summerhouse with Manya, and reaches the same tragic conclusions he'd confronted in the past.

Back in Paris, Manya decides to take all her lessons at Iza's studio and soon distinguishes how her nature and style differ from her teacher's.

She'd quickly grasped the one-sidedness and simplicity of Iza's art. That was the Creole's strength, but also her weakness. She'd perfected the art of the "gesture"—the most difficult and complex art. She was built for pantomime. Her hands spoke as passionately and articulately as her face. Iza inimitably conveyed all that was clear and direct, all the strong movements of the soul—anger, fear, despair, hatred, and especially jealousy. She'd discovered amazing gestures for love, and an unforgettable mimicry of passion. There was something elemental, threatening, and intoxicating in her work. She was a great artist in entr'actes, in such Spanish dances as the malagueña, the bolero, and the fandango, which required temperament, above all. And Manya understood that she'd never achieve that perfection.

But anything refined or mystical, the sort of thing that enraptured Steinbach in Manya's work, was inaccessible to the Creole. She and Manya were of two different worlds, two different origins: Dionysus and Apollo. And that difference, which Iza felt at least subconsciously, filled her soul with a strange agitation, the almost superstitious fear a child or savage feels before an unknown natural phenomenon.

Iza's temperament oppressed and thrilled Manya. But her critical sense never died away. She strived proudly and passionately to throw off the charms of Iza's individualism, to free herself from the yoke of Iza's images, to become free in her creative work. Wasn't freedom the most essential thing of all?

When she studied some dance or pantomime, Manya infused it with part of her own soul, some new and complex psychological refinements. The image Iza had created would disappear, and a new one would form, which required new gestures, new mimicry. Nothing would remain of the old role and everything unexpectedly brightened with a strangely changed perspective. The main thing was effaced, and from the shadows there emerged previously unremarked features, the finest nuances, those secondary features that Iza didn't think it necessary to accentuate. And there obtained the impression of a familiar landscape that we see for the first time in the moonlight. Everything became new, mysterious, unreal. Instead of familiar contours, the eye saw only deep shadow full of mystery. But those objects we pass by indifferently a hundred times a day emerged from the darkness in a ghostly light.

And if Iza's work torched all the images, feelings, and events of the pantomime with the Bengal fire of blinding fireworks, then Manya's work was moonlight, which created a fairy tale world out of the everyday.

The clock was striking eleven. Katya opened her eyes.

She was alone in the room, in their wide double bed. Nikolenka was gone. Where was he? What a nuisance! She'd overslept. The guests had left so late.

This was the best room in the entire old wing, and Katya loved every little thing in it. With loving eyes she gazed at her husband's pajamas, thrown over the back of a chair, at his tie, tossed onto the bedside table, at his boots over there on the carpet. She'd have kissed everything . . .

She closed her eyes and smiled blissfully. What a night!

Here they'd been married five months, and she was crazy in love, as if it were the first day of their marriage. Oh, no! She loved him more. Now her entire life was in him, in his nearness, his caress. How could she have thought that she'd be bored in the country with him around? To wake mornings and gaze so quietly at his face as he slept. To catch the flutter of his eyelids, and then with a cry of rapture entwine her arms around his neck.

She liked to sleep, but she got up early for him. It was so much fun to listen as he washed! He was always embarrassed, and went behind the screen. What a strange fellow! But she felt no shame before him. Weren't they husband and wife?

"Wife," she repeated aloud. "Madame Nelidova." And she laughed loudly, hiding her face in the pillow.

She chattered almost without pause, joking, laughing. He loved her laughter. He was always silent. She talked for two. "A canary," her mother-in-law called her. Ah, she was very solicitous and kind! But her touch was cold. Katya sensed the jealousy of a rival. These mothers were so strange! In their eyes their son was always a prince, for whom there was no deserving woman in this world.

The door creaked.

"Katya! You're not still asleep?"

She rose up in bed with a joyful cry.

"Come here! Here . . . quickly! Kiss me . . ."

"Breakfast soon, Katya. I've already had my coffee."

"Without me? And you're not ashamed?" she interjected bitterly. "Well, then . . . you've ruined the entire day for me . . ."

He smiled faintly and kissed the swarthy nape of her neck. She stretched voluptuously, just like a little cat whose ear's been scratched.

"You'll drink another with me. I'll be ready right away. Why didn't you wake me?"

She dangled her thin legs over the side of the bed. She liked the fact that he saw them. She always wanted to see desire in his eyes. But he turned around quickly and went to the door.

"I'll send Odarka to you. She'll bring some hot water."

Katya was irritated. That was simply amazing! It was as if there were two people in him—one during the day, and the other at night. One was proper, tired, absentminded, indifferent, she'd say, if it weren't for those nights . . . those mad nights. Earlier she'd been so frightened by his rough and hungry caresses! Now she loved them. She waited for them. She'd wait all day, dreaming sweetly about nighttime. And if her hopes were dashed, she cried quietly so as not to awaken him. She so regretted the moments that passed without these joys.

She entered the dining room obediently, like a student in a boarding school.

Anna Lvovna smiled fondly. Katya kissed her hand.

Nikolenka was reading a newspaper aloud. Katya moved about as silently as a mouse. There were such tasty rusks on the table. Her little eyes sparkled as she drank the aromatic coffee.

Life was so fine! They were going to the Galagans today. There'd be blintzes, and then sledding. In the evening there'd be dancing.

They were saying something . . . about some new French novel. There was a review in the paper.

"Is it interesting, Nikolenka?" she asked in a ringing little voice.

"No. You mustn't read it," he replied simply.

Well, what of it? If she mustn't, she mustn't! Were there so few books in the world? Natasha Galagan would be offended by such "supervision." That amazing Natasha! Didn't she understand what it was to be a married woman?

Katya left the dining room on tiptoe so that she could go tidy up the skirts thrown about the bedroom. Odarka would be rummaging around, and Nikolenka would get angry. He liked order.

Yesterday, after the blintzes, while the men were drinking their coffee, Katya'd brought her friend into their bedroom. Natasha had blushed when she saw the bed. What a strange girl! What was there to be ashamed of, if they were husband and wife?

Natasha had said a great deal about a writer who was in vogue. She was enraptured with his talent. "Nikolenka can't stand him," Katya had objected. "He doesn't want me to read him." And Natasha couldn't restrain herself. "What terrible despotism! And you submit? You're not a little girl, after all . . ."

Silly Natasha! What did it matter, since Nikolenka loved her to be just that way?

Last night after the guests had gone home, she couldn't be still and she'd told him the entire conversation. And he'd said to her then. . . What had he told her? "I want you to be entirely mine—with my thoughts, my desires, my dreams. You need nothing of your own—neither tastes nor opinions. Everything should be mine. . ." Oh, how his face looked when he was saying this! His voice . . .

Katya stood frowning, her lace kerchief dropped on the floor. And what else had he said? "You must forget what you knew and valued, and learn everything new from me, from me alone. . ." But she'd meekly asked him: "Then you'll love me? Always? Always, Nikolenka?" And he'd answered: "Always!"

That had been yesterday, right here in this very room. And he'd embraced her then. He'd taken her as his own thing, trembling and submissive, always submissive. Wasn't her entire life in his? In his caress? In his love?

Back in Paris Iza explains to Manya that she loves money because it gives her security for a very uncertain old age. She grew up starving, and her one great love beat her and took her earnings, even as he betrayed her with other women. She attacked him with a knife, but her impassioned testimony at the trial led to her acquittal. Iza had many other affairs afterward, but never loved again, and she maintains that all men are alike—they promise everything until they get what they want, and then they can't hide their satiation. Iza also lectures Manya on the obligation to please her audience, a Faustian bargain Manya finds wholly unacceptable. She longs for an audience that would treat the theater as a temple and share her dreams.

Iza's yearly program usually attracts the press, because her studio has produced so many stars. This is all the more true now that dancing barefoot à la Duncan is the mode. Manya and Nils take the audience by storm with their passionate Spanish dance.

Manya and Likhachov had endless curtain calls. Iza was radiant. She hadn't directed the scene that way, but what difference did it make? And it had been done well.

Steinbach was gloomily silent. The theme of the dance was clear to him. He wasn't jealous of Likhachov. No. He believed in Manya's deep indifference to everything that wasn't art. And if her eyes burned with languor and if that sensual smile he loved so madly parted her lips just now, he knew very well that this wasn't for Likhachov. Manya had turned into her role. Let Nils and others adore her! As long as Manya was ascending to the heights, as long as her soul was preoccupied with ambition and struggle, nothing frightened him. It would be ridiculous to anguish over the fact that they seemed madly in love while they danced. He knew that.

But there had been something new and terrible in that dance. It wasn't entirely clear. He'd have to think it over. It was as if she'd suddenly revealed the secret places in her soul in her dance that evening, what she herself probably didn't realize. It was her terror in the face of love, her powerlessness before it. Her burning, deliberately repressed dream.

The newspapers published reviews the next day. Nils was declared to be a first-class artist. He'd already received several profitable engagements. They pronounced Marion a rising star.

Steinbach read all these reviews to Manya and Frau Kessler. He'd already made up a scrapbook with "Marion" engraved on the cover. He himself clipped these first reviews and pasted them into the album.

Manya smiled gently. She was thoughtful and seemingly happy.

"And who are you sending those to?" asked Frau Kessler, seeing Steinbach open up a second set of papers and begin to clip reviews.

"I'm sending these to Sonya and . . . Fyodor Filippovich."

Katya's life had darkened. Katya was unhappy. She had the impression that a gray cloud had covered the sun on a summer noon. There was the sense of an impending storm.

What on earth had happened?

She'd been at the Galagans the second day of Easter. At dinner were the Gorlenkos, Fyodor Filippovich, and Sonya, who'd just come from Moscow.

Nikolenka had grown pale when he saw her. Yes, Katya recalled this clearly. And he'd been silent all through dinner. He hadn't smiled once.

Why was he so pale? Why did Sonya purse her lips so scornfully? She'd nodded to him like a princess. Worthless girl! How dared she behave this way with her husband?

Katya's face was burning.

Over dessert that repulsive Fyodor Filippovich had extracted some papers from his billfold.

"Mesdames et messieurs," he said, slyly twinkling, "who of you remembers Manya Yeltsova?"

All the voices hushed at once. The ladies squeamishly pursed their lips. The men were startled. Katya bowed her head low. She was terrified of looking at her husband.

Waiting out the pause, as if he were relishing the effect of his words, Fyodor Filippovich declared: "And here's what they write about her in the Paris newspapers."

And he read them aloud. He read a great deal. It was true . . . the reviews were sensational. She was a rising ballet star.

"And here's her picture."

The newspaper passed from hand to hand.

"But she seems . . . rather skimpily clad?" the hostess whispered in embarrassment, scrutinizing Manya's figure through her lorgnette.

"Naked, pure and simple," Lizogub guffawed.

"Mon cher, that's an ancient Greek costume," Uncle condescended to correct him. "Haven't you seen Duncan? Marion really has a statuesque figure."

The ladies studied the portrait, shaking their heads. They wore an expression of wanting to hush an indecent conversation.

"Where did you get this?" Madame Lizogub shouted with hostility across the table at Uncle. She'd noticed her daughter's embarrassment and Nelidov's pallor. But he was squinting disdainfully and peeling an apple very carefully for his wife.

Suddenly Sonya's sonorous and cold voice rang out.

"Her fiancé sent it to us."

"She's getting married?" Galagan's son, the elegant law student, quickly interposed.

"Yes, to Baron Steinbach."

"Ah!"

It was as if a sigh passed through the room. Natasha held the newspaper in her hands. Leaning over her table, the men examined the barefoot dancer.

"She's very interesting!" Natasha spoke loudly, deliberately emphasizing her delight. Katya understood very well that this was deliberate. And tears were already trembling in her breast.

"What legs!" the law student cried. The men's nostrils flared as they took the newspaper and went over to the window.

"A striking woman."

"I'd never have recognized her. She has a completely different face. She's stern somehow."

"And here's a postcard," Uncle said. "She and Nils, another celebrity. They're both in a Spanish dance."

"Show us! Give it here!"

"That's her! I know her," Lizogub shouted playfully, without noticing his wife's fury. "Look how she's curved herself! How much languor there is in her eyes! Oh, devil take it, what a woman!"

"He's also extraordinarily handsome!" Natasha interjected. "Fyodor Filippovich, give me this postcard."

"With pleasure. Sonya has another copy."

"I'd never believe that he'd marry!" Madame Lizogub suddenly announced, her contralto overwhelming the general hubbub. "Why'd he want to marry, that Steinbach? And who marries such women?"

"Why?" Sonya cried.

"Ah, ma petite! Who is keeping her?"

"She makes her own living. She sketches for illustrated journals."

These words provoked general guffaws. Sonya stared about her with blazing cheeks.

"We know what sorts of journals those are!" Lizogub interposed. "With Steinbach's millions . . ."

Sonya pushed her chair back sharply and stood up. Now her round face was pale.

"Gentlemen, that's enough!" her high voice rang through the entire room. "I ask you not to forget that Manya Yeltsova is my best friend, and that if you all throw stones at her . . ."

"Tsk, tsk. Qu'est-ce qu'elle dit?"

"And since I will not give her up . . ."

"Are you in your right mind, girl?" Gorlenko asked his daughter from across the table.

"I can't remain in a house where my friends are insulted!" Sonya shouted hysterically and pounded her fist on the table. "I'll leave immediately."

"What's wrong with you, Sonya?"

"What lack of self-control! Vous êtes folle?"

"They insult a defenseless, lonely girl!" Sonya was already sobbing. "Uncle, aren't you ashamed to be silent?"

Uncle comically spread out his hands.

"Well, now. . . Now I'm guilty."

"Give her some water!" the hostess shouted. Everyone jumped up.

"Sophie, ma chèrie," Galagan said softly, kissing her head as she sobbed on his chest. "Calm yourself. Who's insulted her? Let her do her dances! We're very happy for her . . ."

"Come with me," Natasha said tenderly, embracing Sonya about the waist and leading her to her room.

In the dining room everyone fell silent, embarrassed and distracted. The men forced themselves to smoke. The ladies ate fruit.

"She's overtired from all those exams," Vera Filippovna explained gently. "She's completely ruined her nerves."

The law student knew about Nelidov's brief romance.

"Do you want to look?" he asked courteously, proffering him the newspaper.

"If you please," Nelidov answered carelessly.

Now Katya lifted her eyes for the first time. She couldn't keep herself from looking at her husband. Even if her soul's salvation depended on it, she wouldn't have been able to stop. And she saw. . . What? Nothing, others would say. But she knew. She believed the heart that trembled in her breast. Nikolenka cast only one glance on that "Manka." A fleeting one. But it was so keen, so voracious. And his mouth opened. He immediately passed the paper along and began to peel an orange.

That was all. They left soon after. Her head had begun to ache.

He was silent all the way home, as if he didn't see her sitting beside him, didn't see that she was terrified, that she awaited his caress.

Naturally enough, Katya begins to be jealous. When Nelidov asks her when they will have children, she realizes that a child will bind him to her.

Meanwhile Manya puts off Likhachov once more, alienated by his vulgarity now that he is earning real money. During their last meal together before he goes off on tour, Manya assures him that she won't forget him, and that she wants him to participate in Studio, *a proposition Steinbach has already made him. She also reiterates that he pleases her only on the stage.*

> Be far from the earth, and eternally glide
> On your snow-white wing
> In the pure realms of celestial ways.
> Succumb to heedless thoughts,
> Weep and dream,
> Fly away from the evil earth. . .
> It's better to wander about the cold and snowy heights,
> To gaze ever on beauty. . .
> It's better to suffer . . . but to suffer at such a height
> With a stormy breath.
> So take flight, that the earth might be barely visible in the distance . . .
> —K. Balmont

It was only the end of March, but Paris was already hot and dusty. Men walked about in suitjackets. Chambermaids and laundresses wore flowers in their hair instead of caps. These flowers dotted every corner: violets, yellow chamomile, stock. Stylish ladies still wore fur and muffs, but these were decorated with bouquets of cut flowers.

Children's voices and laughter rang out in the square near Notre Dame. Two female figures slowly crossed the square and stopped near the portals.

"So this is Notre Dame?" Sonya asked in a whisper, staring at the stained glass rose window.

"Yes . . . isn't it fine?"

"Finer than I'd imagined. Do you remember how we used to read Victor Hugo at night?"

"Once you've looked your fill, let's turn right toward that bridge. And there you'll see ghosts."

They turned right, and stood a long while on the bridge, with their heads tilted back.

Sonya held binoculars.

"What a horrid mix of the mystical and the cynical!" She looked around and then stared at the other bank of the Seine. "And what sort of palace is that?"

"The Palais de Justice. Have you seen anything more marvelous, Sonya? It was the old residence of the Capets—their court and their prison. There they were born, loved, avenged themselves, and died. Such strange and picturesque towers on the corners! This is my favorite corner, Sonya. I sit here for hours on my days off, alone in the square. And what images rise up in my soul! Let's go to the square. There's my bench."

"How delightful!" Sonya cried when the flower market unfolded before them, sparkling with color.

"And to think that there's deep snow and frost in Moscow now . . ."

Manya bought them each an enormous bouquet of yellow chamomile blossoms. They sat down on the bench, and Manya kissed the flowers.

"I love them—these especially. They're like the sun."

Sonya fell silent, overwhelmed with impressions. She'd only arrived yesterday evening. Steinbach and Manya had met her at the Gare du Nord. They'd embraced warmly, and the meeting had been a joyous one. They'd ridden straight from the station to the Nelly district, where Manya lived. There Frau Kessler had greeted her with hot coffee and a homey dinner. Sonya'd stayed with them. The four had chatted with each other almost until dawn, and then Mark had left.

"And your little Nina?" Sonya remembered just before going to bed.

Manya put a finger to her lips and led her on tiptoe into her room. A nightlamp faintly lit the cradle. Sonya leaned over it with involuntary reverence, for there before her lay a miracle—a love child.

It was only in the morning that Sonya managed to get her fill of that refined little face with its proud lips and gray eyes. She blushed involuntarily when she kissed the little hand, but Manya laughed.

"Her father's daughter, no?"

Sonya said nothing, losing her footing. Had Manya really fallen out of love with Nelidov? And as if in response to her thought, Manya added calmly: "She'll be very good-looking. Breeding tells."

"Enough about breeding. If only she has a heart . . ." Frau Kessler interjected.

"But, Agatha, why do you think he's heartless? No, he's even magnanimous and noble. Why judge him so severely? He's only . . . a normal man. . . Of course, I hope Nina will be more interesting and more complicated than her father."

"She's fallen out of love! Thank God!" thought Sonya.

They'd been sightseeing since morning. At two they were supposed to meet at Mark's for breakfast—that's what they'd decided the night before. Every minute was precious to Sonya. She'd managed only two weeks away, and she'd paid for the trip with one hundred and fifty rubles earned giving lessons. It had been so hard to convince her mother and father! Especially her father. She'd always spent Easter in Lysogory. But the main thing was that she had "traded them in." For whom?—for Steinbach's kept woman!

Sonya's cheeks burned every time she remembered those cruel words. Yesterday she'd found out everything from Frau Kessler. It was true that Manya earned little at this point, since her training took up so much time. And they'd never have been able to survive without Pyotr Sergeyevich's help. Were they in need? Oh, no—not now. Pyotr Sergeyevich sent them sixty rubles the first of every month. Of course, they didn't waste a single kopeck. And Frau Kessler kept house. They often had candies, cakes, pineapples, and bananas, but those were all Steinbach's contribution.

Manya was terribly proud. She always pretended that everything was satisfactory, and never allowed him to inspect her life too closely. Yet Frau Kessler knew how it anguished her to take money from her brother to live on, and money from her fiancé for her schooling. But soon it would all be over. Manya would go on the stage.

Manya stood up suddenly, and Sonya's thoughts scattered like the pigeons at her feet.

"Caught your breath?" Manya inquired, arching her left eyebrow. And again Sonya glimpsed for a single moment the former girl in the new Manya's face.

"Yes, dear, let's go!" With a rush of love Sonya squeezed her friend's hand.

"Now this way," Manya said. And suddenly her brows moved, her eyes widened, and Sonya felt something mystical approaching—much as it had been in the natatorium at their old boarding school, where water dripped and echoed in the silent night, and they, agitated and exhausted, were studying for an exam and were afraid to look around, because the floorboards were cracking and someone breathed coldly down the backs of their necks.

"I come here, too, almost every day," Manya whispered, as if afraid she would be overheard.

Sonya followed her as if in her sleep. A little further. . . They turned the corner, and there before them stood a low, strange building without windows on its front wall. The door was open. Some were going in, and others were coming out. They all seemed like simple people. There were many mothers with infants in their arms, or with little girls clinging to their skirts.

"What is this, Manya? Where are we?"

"It's the morgue. Follow me."

The room to the left was lit by a large window. Corpses had been placed along the wall opposite the entrance, under the window. There were five—three men and two women. They had no names. Therefore everyone had the right to look them over. Maybe someone would recognize them, and then bury them?

They lay in the clothes they'd put on the last morning of their lives. They were remote and alien to everyone, and they expected no more from the living.

How Manya loved to guess the last thoughts and feelings that had been imprinted on their frozen features! Those dulled pupils, secret smiles so intrigued her—with such overwhelming power! Eternity gazed on her from these dead faces. Eternity spoke with her through these closed mouths . . .

Sonya turned away involuntarily, but Manya kept staring.

There was a woman who'd been lying here for several days unclaimed. And she was to be buried tomorrow. She was still young. One could glimpse her greenish swarthy body through her shirt. How expressive her mouth was! All the lines in her sunken features breathed humility. Her half-opened glassy eyes shone sadly. "She killed herself," Manya thought. "She took leave of life, like someone superfluous, defeated. Out of need? Love? Loneliness? Who sent you to your death?"

Manya points out another corpse to Sonya, an old man who has no mark on him:

"This is the third time I've visited him, Sonya. He reconciles me with death. And all of them do the same. Is there really anything terrible in their faces? Look closely! I love to come here. We carry on a silent conversation. I ask and they answer. By the time I leave, all my sorrow and doubt seem so small to me. And I've already come to love this old man. I see immortality shining in his eyes, and I'm no longer afraid to live. I tell myself: if I weary of the struggle, if I lose my faith . . . if the One I summon breaks me, then there is always this way out. Why live without dreams and aspirations?"

"You didn't speak this way before," Sonya whispered. "You simply lived and enjoyed yourself."

"That was before. Now I think: it's better to die than to be untrue to yourself!"

As they exited, they bumped into some workers. During their short lunch break, these men had hurried to the morgue. One wave replaced another. Exhausted, careworn, and embittered in the struggle to live, they ran to look at those who'd been defeated. They were drawn here by that secret denied mortals in life.

Manya and Sonya pay a visit to Zhenya Lipenko, a Russian medical student who speaks frankly about the ghetto of Russian students in Paris, and laments the lack of love in her life. Manya objects to her self-criticism, arguing the importance of a woman's vocation and a woman's need "to love joyfully and easily," to conquer the enemy of her femininity.

After this interesting conversation, Manya and Sonya deliver a letter to Nina Glinskaya, a Russian writer who has earned a high reputation among French workers. As they ride the tram to Glinskaya's residence, Manya announces to Sonya that she knows her friend has really come to Paris because she loves Steinbach. Sonya protests that her work is more important than any romantic love.

Glinskaya was a shapely woman of medium height, about thirty-five years of age. Her clothes were severe, entirely black. Her light hair had been smoothed with a ribbon along cheeks that were thin and had lost their bloom. Her eyes were light and cold. She had an intelligent forehead, dashing eyebrows darker than her hair, and a subtle smile.

She led them through a modest dining room into her study. This was a large and gloomy room, completely stripped of feminine adornments and coquettish trifles. Everything was dark, severe, solid—a man's study. A green-shaded lamp illuminated the worktable, which was heaped with books and manuscripts. The gilded bindings of these books reflected in the glass of her dresser. Portraits of Elisée Reclus* and Kropotkin* hung on the wall. A piano stood in the depths of the room.

"She loves music. Perhaps she herself plays and sings," thought Manya.

"Sit down, please," Glinskaya offered kindly, bringing up a leather chair. "I'll glance through the letter right now."

The girls looked around with curiosity and embarrassment. They both unconsciously felt timid before this woman. Hadn't she managed to order her life in a new way? Hadn't she rejected the beaten path? Wasn't she, alone and proud, moving forward in accord with her convictions, feelings, and calling? Her lodging was bourgeois. Yes. . . "But it was paid for by her own labors," Sonya mused. "Every chair, every cup in this apartment was bought with her earnings. And if she loves comfort, who'd dare to reproach her? Doesn't every worker strive to beautify his life with the adornments of the petty bourgeoisie? Isn't that merely the satisfaction of the most legitimate aesthetic needs?"

"Are you here for long?" Glinskaya asked obligingly, putting the letter away and carefully locking it up.

"Alas! I've only a week. And Paris is immense!"

Nina Glinskaya laughed and became more feminine.

"It's true, one can lose oneself here. Can't I help you? What would you like to see?"

Sonya opened her mouth, and helplessly spread out her hands.

"Everything!" she cried.

Manya couldn't help laughing. Glinskaya also laughed loudly and looked ten years younger.

"But you have to choose a little from that *everything*. You've really revealed yourself to me through this one word. What most interests you abroad? People? Or things? By that I mean cathedrals, museums, monuments."

"People, of course!" Sonya exclaimed.

"But for me, of course, it's things . . ." Manya thought.

"Well, we've settled it! Have you been in the Ecole Libre? The Sorbonne?"

"We're visiting both places tomorrow."

"But tomorrow evening there's a general meeting of the Feminist League, Les droits des Femmes. Would you like to go with me?"

"Would I! I'd be thrilled!"

"But isn't it boring?" Manya asked, arching her left eyebrow.

"It depends for whom," Glinskaya responded, smiling subtly. "I've found this league terribly interesting since it's been infiltrated by a new wave of women workers—against the wishes of its founders and president."

"This means it's not a bourgeois league, like the one we have in Russia?" Sonya queried, leaning forward intently.

From her table Glinskaya took a pretty letter opener of black wood and began to play with it. She sank deep into her armchair. With delight Manya spied her small, stylishly shod foot.

"This woman wants to please," she reflected.

"Here, too, the league was bourgeois for some time, for the first five years. And now its president is an aristocrat, and the secretary a lady from high society. By the way, she's an educated, talented woman. And the president's companion is a learned bourgeoise. The core of the group, of course, is all bourgeois. They were all attracted to the idea of philanthropy—nurseries, shelters for children and old women, an exemplary laundry. But, as things developed, the league confronted the working-class element when it petitioned the government for a shorter working day for women . . ."

"Ah, is that so! They've even taken it to the Parliament?"

"What did you think? The president isn't much loved, but you can't deny she has energy, and ties. Now the league is recognized. Its meetings are attended by representatives from the press, the city, the ministry. You'll see yourselves."

"That's so interesting! But you were saying something about the workers?"

"Yes. . . I was saying that now the women workers themselves are interested in the league. They're joining up. They've formed a stable, united opposition group. They know absolutely what they want and where they want to go. It's hard for the ruling committee to deal with this new movement. These women don't want the patronage of ladies. You should hear how they talk! It may be that the president will resign her post on account of their antagonism. Everything will be become clear tomorrow."

"So the League, then, is essentially democratic?" Sonya cried.

"I wouldn't say that now. But it's doubtless going to be."

Sonya plied Glinskaya with questions. She wanted to see everything, go everywhere—especially to those meeting places in Batipol and Montmartre, those worker universities she'd heard about from Zina Lipenko.

Manya was silent, peering at the books in their light jackets. They lay in a pile on the edge of the table. Manya stretched out her hand and asked:

"*Amour libre* . . . what is this?"

Glinskaya turned around quickly and flushed.

"It's my play."

And Manya heard how tenderly and timidly her voice sounded.

"Ah! Here's your Achilles heel!" Manya thought.

"You write plays?"

"Yes . . . for the workers. I publish them myself. And they perform them in their clubs."

"You lucky woman! I envy you."

Manya said this so passionately and quickly that Sonya turned around to face her.

"That is . . . what do you envy? That I write, in general? That I write for the theater?"

"No, that you have such a public."

Glinskaya involuntarily moved forward. Her gaze was intent and profound. An entirely manly gaze.

"I'm studying dance," Manya explained, nervously leafing through the yellow booklet. "I'll be finishing up soon, and will have my debut."

"Here?" Glinskaya's brows rose.

"Yes. . . Here in the Gaîté Theater. But, unfortunately, my public is not like yours."

There was a short pause. It was as if both women froze, staring at Manya.

"What do you perform?" Glinskaya asked very quietly. "Are you a singer?"

"I'll be dancing character dances, Spanish and others. I perform pantomime. But the main thing is that I convey in dance what rises up in my soul under the influence of the music."

Glinskaya emitted a short cry of amazement. Without realizing it, she'd raised the lampshade so that she could have a good look at Manya.

"But my public will stare at me coldly, without understanding anything. And the reviewers who make or break an artist's reputation will come—people who are so removed from and indifferent to art, who are such ignoramuses. And I must entertain these people with empty souls and consider their applause a favor."

"I understand you," Glinskaya uttered vehemently. Impulsively, she extended her hand to Manya.

"What is she saying?" Sonya thought in fright.

"You do understand me," Manya smiled. "But you alone understand me. When I start talking about this with close friends, they say that I'm mad, that I myself don't know what I truly need."

"Is she talking about Mark?"

Sonya's mouth dropped. But Glinskaya interrupted her.

"Still, if you've recognized this yourself, why not go further?"

"Meaning?"

"Why not become an artist for the masses?"

"Where?"

"In one of the public theaters. Yes, of course there aren't many of them," Glinskaya added after a short pause. "And their repertoire is coarse, uninspired, and vulgar. All melodramas."

"Oh! Are melodramas so bad? Children love them. The masses should love them, too."

Glinskaya smiled. This thought pleased her.

"But . . . you see the problem?" Manya continued, confusedly picking at the yellow booklet. "I'm not sure my art will appeal to workers. Unfortunately, I don't know them. Only one thing is clear to me. No impresario will undertake something that doesn't guarantee him big profits. And only altruistic, idealistic people can work for the masses." ("Like you," she wanted to say, but could not, out of embarrassment.) "But the main thing. . ." Manya suddenly raised her head, her face confused, and almost tragic. "The main thing is that I need money myself—a lot of it. I'm studying on someone else's money. I'm living here on my brother's money. For me to feel completely free, I have to rid myself of these debts. And I'll get a lot of money at the Gaîté. I've also had a great many offers."

"But this money is from your fiancé, after all!" Sonya interrupted in agitation.

Manya stared straight into her eyes.

"Isn't it all the same? I want to be accountable to myself alone."

"And you're right!" Glinskaya exclaimed. "That's the first condition of freedom."

"I'm glad you've understood me," Manya said, smiling and pale. "I've other reasons to earn a living—a good living—which only the owners of bourgeois theaters can give me. But now that you've understood the main thing, the rest isn't important. Please give me your play! It's piqued my interest."

Glinskaya blushed.

"Both of you take a copy! Read it and let me know what you think. That's always valuable. You'll tell me at the meeting. And you can write me from Moscow."

"One more question," Sonya spoke shyly. "Are you a socialist?"

"No. When I escaped exile ten years ago, I was a desperate Social Democrat. But three years later my views changed. I'm an individualist. Above all I value the individual personality and its rights." She gazed at the portrait of Kropotkin. "There's the one who turned around my soul and my life."

"You don't recognize terror?" Sonya cried out.

"Why do you think so? Of course not. Isn't terror force? And isn't anarchism only terror?"

The doorbell rang in the entryway. The guests rose. Sonya was clearly disappointed. In her opinion the only interesting people were Social Democrats.

"Excuse us for keeping you . . ."

"Ah, I'm very pleased!" Glinskaya said sincerely, following them into the entryway.

"Qui est là?" she anxiously asked through the door, putting the chain on.

"Lise Durand."

Glinskaya quickly opened the door and the girls saw a thin lady in a coat and a hat.

"Entrez, Lise. . . Je suis seule. . . Well, goodbye! Until tomorrow. Here's the League's address." She handed Sonya a printed notice. "It's an open meeting. It begins at eight. We'll meet there. By the way . . . let me know when your debut will be. . . Send me an announcement. I'll come watch you. You've really interested me. Bonjour, Lise!"

As they went out, the girls noticed how reverently and tenderly this young, fair-haired woman gazed at Glinskaya.

Sonya and Manya attend the League meeting, where the women workers accuse the governing ladies of being out of touch with life, whereas the working women are proud to be equal with men, to not be parasites, and demand good daycare for their children. There is talk of birth control, of nurseries for working women's illegitimate children (these are not admitted in subsidized nurseries). The president recognizes the justice of these arguments and steps down from her post. Manya is impressed with this dramatic gesture of a well-dressed old aristocrat.

Frau Kessler had gone to bed long ago, and Sonya was also falling asleep. They'd returned from the Grand Opera, and Steinbach had gone home an hour ago.

Manya sat on her bed, dressed only in her nightgown, as motionless as a piece of sculpture, and white as a sheet in the soft light of the night lamp.

"I'm sorry, Sonya. I know you're tired! But you are leaving tomorrow . . ."

"What's the matter? What is it?"

"It's nonsense. I . . . I've got to ask you. . . You're not angry, are you?"

"What on earth do you mean, Manya! Of course not! I'll get all the sleep I need on the way home. I'd like to have a talk myself."

Sonya yawned luxuriously.

"Sonya, have you seen Nelidov?" The shy question sounded like the rustling of leaves.

Sonya's sleepiness instantly dissipated, and she propped herself up on her elbow. How expressive Manya's figure was! Her whole body drooped, shoulders hunched over, hands resting submissively in her lap. Her hair cascaded onto her shoulders, while her gaze was unseeing. The clock chimed two o'clock. Did that mean she hadn't slept at all? And she continued to think of him.

"You remember, I wrote to you when Ninochka was born . . ."

"Y-yes?"

"I wrote that I don't feel any hatred toward him, that I'm . . . grateful to him for everything . . ."

Sonya sat up on the bed, her heart grown numb.

"You didn't say anything to him, then?"

She raised her head then. Oh, what a piteous little face! The eyes of a wounded deer. Pride no longer flashed in them. Where was her smile? She'd been so cheerful all evening, had laughed so animatedly. She'd seemed so invulnerable. Sonya suddenly felt terrified.

"No, Manya, I didn't say anything to him. He was getting married then. And, besides, I hated him for so long. It was only when Mark wrote me that you'd forgotten him and that you were going on the stage that I agreed to meet him. This was a year ago, at Easter. He paid us a visit with his wife. But I hardly spoke with him, only with Katya. Uncle and Papa often visit them." (Sonya fell silent and waited.) "What else do you want to know? Go ahead and ask."

"Is Katya happy?"

Sonya saw Manya flex her hands and crack the joints of her fingers. What could she say? She couldn't throw in Manya's face all the "intimacies" to which Katya had shamelessly made her privy. She felt conscience-stricken just remembering them. These women bared their souls to an incredible degree! Of course, Katya could have lied on purpose, calculating that Manya would hear about it all. And she'd spoken precisely with that goal in mind.

"Katerina is terribly superficial! Of course, she's all aglow. She's made such a match. She was even ready to marry Klimov. It makes no difference to her. I can't stomach her . . . that laugh of hers . . . her voice . . ."

Sonya made a dismissive gesture and lay down.

"Sleep, Manichka! You've got to get up early tomorrow for your lesson. What about you? Will you be marrying Mark soon?"

Manya didn't answer, and Sonya felt terrible.

"Do you love him, Manya?"

"Whom?"

"Why, Mark, of course!"

"Yes, I do . . ."

"And you'll never fall out of love with him? It's really forever?" Sonya asked with severity and passion.

"Yes, yes. I won't love anyone else. All that's over."

"Well, thank God! It's time to forget that nonsense. You have such a wonderful life ahead of you. The stage, fame . . . and wealth, Manya! That means a lot, too. One can do so much good with money. You have a daughter, a friend like Frau Kessler. And Mark . . . he's an angel, and he loves you."

"And you?" The quiet question came after a long pause. Sonya turned round quickly.

"What about me?"

"You're not jealous?"

"What a fanciful notion!"

"Not the slightest?"

"I'm—organically incapable of it, truly!"

"Lucky you!"

"I suffer only when I think you—hurt him. And then . . . it's true, I hate you then. Manya, dear, don't torment him! Marry him as soon as possible. You can't imagine how painful I find it when. . . Of course, one should be above people and their gossip. But when you love someone, you involuntarily suffer from every vile hint. For example, you're the one who's postponing the wedding, yet there they say that . . . that Mark doesn't want to marry. And that he'll never marry you!"

"Nelidov?" The question escaped Manya's lips, and she paled.

"Of course not! Nelidov's a gentleman, nonetheless, and won't lower himself to gossip. But everyone's talking: Uncle, Father, Mama, Klimov. Even Lika. She becomes petty when the talk turns to you."

"I don't care!"

"But I do!" Sonya countered passionately, sitting up and dangling her bare feet. "They want to degrade you . . . and Mark. No one wants to believe that you earn money by working for German magazines."

"Right now I'm hardly earning anything. There was a time . . ."

"But you get money to live on from your brother, after all."

"Of course."

"But they don't want to know anything about that!" Sonya pounded the pillow with her fist. "So much vileness, so much malice!"

"I don't care," Manya said wearily.

"When I get back I'll tell them everything. That in three months you'll make your debut here and that you've already been invited on a two-year tour for a hundred thousand francs. But Mark turned down the offer on your behalf. How much is that in our money?"

"Thirty-seven thousand," Manya replied indifferently.

She lay down and covered herself with the blanket. All signs of life had vanished from her face.

"That means he's counting on your getting better terms?"

"Yes. Just as much in a single year."

"I'll tell them everything. Also that you'll pay off your debts first thing. Ah, that hateful Katya! And even Uncle doesn't shrink from gossip. He believes in your talent, but he's not capable of appreciating Mark's love. You should send me all the posters, all the reviews of your debut. I'll throw all of that in their faces. And if after that anyone dares call you" (she wanted to say "a kept woman," but caught herself in time), "I'll break off all relations with that person."

Manya didn't respond for a long time. It struck three o'clock. Sonya started dozing again.

Suddenly an unsteady, heavy sigh, resembling a moan, reached her. She opened her eyes.

"Manya, are you crying?"

"No, no. You go to sleep."

"What are you thinking about, Manichka? Surely, surely it's not that you can't forget?"

"Tell me this, Sonya. Does he know I have a child?"

"Yes, of course he does. I wrote and told him."

Silent and white as a phantom, Manya again sat up in bed.

"You wrote him? When?"

"When you left for Venice."

Manya lifted her hands to her throat. Sonya lowered her lashes so as not to see her gaze. Was it love or pride? Why was she suffering so much?

"He didn't reply. And I only found out from Uncle that he'd gone abroad. He returned in the spring and got married in October."

Manya was silent, her head lowered, crushed by this news.

"You see how easily he's settled for less! He needs a female like Katya . . . sensual, foolish, and submissive. He'll be able to do anything he wants with her.

I can imagine what a drama would have unfolded had you got married then! You'd have left him in a year! And it would have been even worse had you stayed. It would have been fatal—you'd have lost your talent and your beauty. It worked out for the best, Manichka! Mark lives for you and through you. Whereas there you'd have lived through Nelidov, and everything worthwhile in you would have imperceptibly died. Manichka, dear, forgive me! Perhaps it's cruel on my part to say this to you, but I'll do it anyway. I heard it from Uncle. Nelidov's convinced that Ninochka is Steinbach's child."

Manya made an impetuous movement, then controlled herself and lay down, her face buried in the pillow.

"For God's sake, don't be angry! And forget about Nelidov. What's he to you now? It's all over. He's got a wife and his own life. He keeps dreaming of an heir. Let him think that she's Mark's daughter! It's even better that way! Let him think you've eliminated him from your life! After all, aren't you the happiest woman in the world right now?"

For a long time she waited for a response, but Manya was silent.

The next morning Manya alternates between limp gloom and feverish animation. Sonya realizes that Manya hasn't forgotten Nelidov, and she is concerned for Mark. Manya dances for everyone, with Mark accompanying her on the piano, then says farewell to Sonya, whom Mark drives to the railroad station. Manya remains alone, sobbing, but finds comfort in the silent embrace of Mark's "crazy" uncle.

At Iza's, Manya meets the director of the theater where she'll debut. Iza realizes that Steinbach is behind Manya's rapid rise to fame as Marion. As rehearsals begin, Manya becomes "unaccountably moody," and mourns the fatal difficulties of an artist's lot. At the dress rehearsal she refuses to dance until stifled laughter stimulates her hatred, whereupon, in self-oblivious "inspiration," she conquers the crowd by her stupendous dancing.

Meanwhile, Nelidov has paid off his debts, enjoyed a luxurious honeymoon with Katya in Moscow and Petersburg, built their home, and settled into physical labor in the fields. Katya, pregnant and jealous of his past, is both capricious and panic-stricken. Lika finds herself attracted to Nelidov as she calms him down during Katya's protracted delivery. On learning that he has a son, Nelidov tearfully kisses Lika's hands.

Manya's "democratic" passions at her debut lead her to insist that the stage workers be allowed to watch her performance. She manages to triumph in the duel between "talent and the masses" and conquers the jaded Parisian crowd. Her refusal to give encores leaves the wildly applauding audience stunned, while she remains in the inner world of her dreams.

In a letter to Sonya, Steinbach reports at length on Manya's phenomenal success, attributing it to her ability to draw artistically on her "sufferings." She is now the talk of Paris, and Steinbach urges Sonya to ensure that Nelidov and Katya see all the rave reviews. He sends Sonya the few postcards of Manya that the city has not bought up.

In her diary Manya bids adieu to her old life.

Six months later, while Manya, Frau Kessler, and Nina are driving through Paris, a bomb kills two young men. When the women go to investigate, Manya is recognized as the famous Marion. She has been renting a villa and dancing to Steinbach's accompaniment; now only "Art" binds them. She wishes to withdraw from public attention and refuses to see the artistic director when he arrives, leaving Steinbach to deal with him.

"Have they gone?" Manya asked half an hour later, when the door opened. She was still lying down, but now her face was tranquil.

"It'll be a big scandal, Manya. But I informed both of them, irrevocably, that you're unwell, that you'll pay them compensation and are leaving Paris."

She gazed at him, her eyes sparkling, and smiled.

He paced about the room, thoughtful and uneasy.

"Do you know what an employee at Matin told me? 'I'm not surprised,' he said. 'I saw madame's face yesterday as she looked at the corpse. It left a mark on her nerves. She shouldn't have looked into the dead man's face.'"

Manya rose. "He understood that? He!"

"As you can see . . ."

"And tomorrow . . . will he tell all Paris that?"

"Of course."

With a gesture of revulsion she closed her eyes.

"Where can one get away from people, Mark?" she whispered with melancholy.

"We'll leave now for the Tyrol! We have two weeks before your London performance. You'll rest up . . ."

She thought for a while, then her gaze fell on the magazine illustration.

"No, Mark. Let's wait a little . . . a little longer."

Frau Kessler entered, without knocking or being announced, together with the babysitter holding Nina in her arms.

"We're going to the woods. The weather's marvelous," Frau Kessler said, greeting Steinbach.

Nina reached out for him, her little feet angrily kicking at the babysitter's stomach because she was making for the couch.

"Ma . . . Ma . . . (Mark)," she shouted and smiled in delight.

Steinbach took her from the babysitter. Nina fastened her hands in his beard and gave a resounding laugh of triumph.

"As always!" Manya whispered jealously, lowering the arms she'd stretched out to the child.

He brought the little girl over to the couch and lowered her toward Manya, who was angry.

"Now kiss Mu," he told the child conciliatorily.

"With your permission?" Manya tossed at him, eyes flashing.

"Mu . . . (Mutter)," the child lisped condescendingly and presented her cheek to be kissed.

"There's no need!" Manya said, coldly avoiding contact.

"You're all upset now!" he observed in chagrin. "But why vent your nerves on the child?"

The little girl turned away indifferently from her mother and wound her little arms tightly around Steinbach's neck. He showered her with kisses, then lowered her to the floor. The babysitter adjusted the little girl's dress. She self-importantly gave Frau Kessler her hand, and went off without a backward glance.

"A real woman!" Manya burst out bitterly.

"Just like her mother," Steinbach seconded her, and his lips twisted.

Manya suddenly leaped to her feet.

"Nina! Ninochka!" she shouted plaintively, and rushed to the door.

It was open, and Steinbach witnessed a strange scene.

In the salon, Manya fell to her knees before the little girl and passionately embraced her. She covered her face with kisses full of such despair, as if the child were everything she had left in life.

"It's more serious, then, than I supposed," Steinbach thought with growing alarm.

"Mu-u-" Ninochka protested, unhappy that her swan's down had been crushed.

"Why are you crying, you little fool?" Frau Kessler asked in German. "What sort of scene is this to enact in front of a child?"

Manya waved her hand, and, running back into the library, fell face-down on the couch, her shoulders quivering.

Steinbach paced thoughtfully about the room. Everything in the house had grown quiet. They were both silent, but the sense of alarm deepened.

How terrible was every unknown thing that threatened to take this woman, and her capricious feeling, away from him! Everything that threatened to disrupt his habits. Oh, the sweetness of habit, familiar only to tired people! This fear of novelty and change.

Prompted by newspaper reports about the anarchists, Steinbach urges Manya to escape to the safer area of the Tyrol. They argue about the anarchists—Steinbach declaring them cruel terrorists, and Manya discovering passion and beauty in them.

Steinbach receives a visit from Xavier, a friend of Yan's and a revolutionary, whom Manya saw when the bomb exploded in the Paris streets. Xavier is puzzled by Manya's/Marion's dissatisfaction with life, in view of her success.

"Have you seen me perform?" she suddenly asked unevenly.

A faint flush stained his cheeks. Not a smile, but a shadow of one, ran across his face and instantly disappeared.

"What a strange question! As though our theaters are accessible to people like me. Aren't we, after all, people from different planets, who have run into each other by chance?"

Manya's nostrils twitched. She rose and took several paces about the room.

"You reject art, Monsieur . . . Monsieur Xavier?"

"Simply Xavier. For me and millions like me it's just meaningless words. Yan in his book talks very well about this. The more talented and celebrated the artist, the more remote he is from the people."

Manya walked up to the desk and nervously leafed through the book with the expensive binding bordered in gold.

"Show me where that place is. Where does he say that?"

Xavier got up, then bent over the desk. They stood side by side, and their hands fleetingly touched. Wasn't he right that an abyss yawned between them, that they were people speaking two different languages?

"It's this page here—'On Art.' Have you read Yan's book?"

"Yes."

"Then you didn't read it well. Nor did Steinbach, though he'll keep it on his table. But that's the fatal destiny of all writers, especially ones like Yan. People read them. People wax ecstatic over them . . . yet continue to live as they'd lived. Mark Aleksandrovich is building the theater *Studio* in Petersburg, so as to provide entertainment for the nobility. And a girl as joyful as the morning gives all her talent to these people."

Manya's face flooded with color and she haughtily tossed her head. Their eyes met, hers filled with suppressed hostility, his with contempt. Yes, indeed—contempt! She had no doubt that that's what it was, and he had no wish to conceal it.

"To reject art is to be a barbarian! It means reverting. Art doesn't recognize any goal or ethics. The fact that it's inaccessible to the masses doesn't diminish its significance. Are you a Tolstoyan?"

He smiled faintly again.

"Why use labels? I'll give you an answer. The people need art and joy no less than the so-called intelligentsia. But, like everything nowadays, these joys fall to the lot of the rich and bypass the poor. Why do you think that the poor need only bread and work, and not poetry and beauty? And there's no need to take offense at my words. If Yan wasn't mistaken in you, if you're really the girl to whom he dedicated his life's work, then you already feel, however subconsciously, that I'm speaking the truth. Think of how to justify your life!"

"What?? What did you say??"

Quietly but insistently, he repeated:

"Think of how to justify your life."

For a second she was stunned, as if she'd gone blind.

"What nonsense! That's sectarianism! I live! As if that weren't enough! Why should I need to justify that? Doesn't a flower have the right to bloom, a bird to sing?" (She walked about the room in agitation.) "Your words smack of darkness and oppression! Yan never spoke to me about this."

"You were an insignificant girl without talent. A flower or a bird. But when someone possesses a lot, as you do . . ."

"You think that a person should be everyone's servant?" Manya interrupted heatedly. "An artist is free . . ."

FIGURE 10
The allure of art and spectatorship so central to the period of aesthetic revival is captured in this illustration by Grigorii Zolotov for an article by G. Pavlutsky, "On the Usefulness of Art and the History of Art," *Iskusstvo i pechatnoe delo* (1909, nos. 11–12).

"That's not true. She's the rabble's slave, and doesn't have the right to despise it."

The words of denial suddenly died on her lips.

Stretching out her hands, her fingers entwined, she gazed at a single spot with the expression that had so frightened Mark and Agatha.

Steinbach entered. He noticed Manya's strange expression, and she quickly veiled her eyes.

"Goodbye, Mark Aleksandrovich," Xavier said, approaching him. "Thank you for Nadezhda Petrovna!"

Manya extended her hand to Xavier.

"If I was curt with you, forgive me," she said in a subdued voice. "I'm not at all responsible for my actions these days . . ."

And she suddenly noticed his smile, or, rather, the shadow of a smile.

"Do you really think you can offend me?" his expression said.

Manya's hand fell, and she paled all the way to her lips.

He bowed to her from the threshold. The heavy curtains fell behind him.

"I'll just see him out," Steinbach said. "Wait . . ."

When he returned to the study ten minutes later, she was still standing in the same pose by the window, the blinds pulled aside, and gazing into the semi-darkness. Her face looked ill, eyes empty, her white teeth clenched in bitterness.

Manya's Letter to Harold

"The Tyrol

Harold, I don't know you and I've never seen your face. As recently as yesterday you were nobody to me. How did it happen that today you're occupying such a large place in my soul?

Yesterday I stood at the crossroads again. Not for the first time, Life—a Sphinx with everything that's gloomy in it, with the self-satisfied effrontery of conquerors and the slavishness and poverty of the vanquished—appeared before me and posed the fatal question: 'Whom do you serve?'

I have only one answer: 'I serve those who exult.'

And this answer clipped the wings of my feeble soul. The steps I've taken toward the peak during these years, trying not to think or look back, were radical. But I fell and crashed. And, choking in the dust of the wide road ahead, I told myself, 'It's the end. There's no point in living now.'

I read your *Fairy Tale*. It searched for me a long time.

Like a prisoner, half-blind from the darkness, who suddenly, through a fortuitous fissure in the wall, sees the open sweep of the sky, so through the prism of your *Fairy Tale*, immured in the walls of a duty that hereafter will be alien to me, the vistas of creativity once again opened up before me.

You, Harold, are one of the elect. You have the power to create imperishable images that are unknown to life from lackluster words, but are more vivid than it (Life). What is my modest dancer's talent compared with your wonderful gift? Like a shadow vanishing from the screen without a trace, I, too, vanish from people's memory once I leave the stage. Your verses, however, will live on.

But my grateful soul no longer harbors bitterness and melancholy!

Yesterday I was a dead instrument, languishing in the dust. Today my soul resounds. I'm a violin. You're the artist. Obedient to your will, I sing songs once again. They're for you . . .

I know that I, too, have been given power. And I've also been given joy. The images created by my facial expressions and my body movements should be precious to me, like a holy place. Whether they're pallid or vivid makes no difference. And the secret of my creative activity, however remote it may be from the people, will die with me without being divined by anyone else. And it'll never be repeated.

Harold, you've taught me to see a person's human worth only in what's unique, what's unrepeatable. You've once again confirmed the truth, which sounded in my soul long ago, in my youth—that the only worthwhile goal for a person is to find the form that will fully incarnate her individuality. And once the form is there, it's not important whether the person trudges along her narrow path unknown, or whether she walks along the wide road of Fame to the thunder of applause. Both roads are the way of Humankind.

Harold, will our lives' paths ever cross?

Or will the beautiful flowers sown in my soul by the poetry of your *Fairy Tale* blossom and fade without being plucked by you?

Marion"

In Petersburg, the writer Dora, who ekes out a living writing feuilletons, receives a visit from her friend Zina. The two exchange confidences and discuss "the Russian character," Harold, and love. Their conversation emphasizes the material and amorous tribulations of "women's lot." In the meantime, Manya decides to visit her siblings.

There was a deafening ring in the hall. Anna Sergeyevna threw down the dusty rag she'd been holding and rushed into the hall.

"What is it?" Pyotr Sergeyevich inquired, emerging from the study.

Full of trepidation, Anna Sergeyevna asked, "Who's there?" without opening the door.

"It's me! Me!" a young voice, full of the joy of life, rang out.

For a second Anna Sergeyevna was struck dumb.

"Why, that's Manya!" Pyotr Sergeyevich exclaimed, and, with a hysterical shriek of "Manichka!" he pushed back the bolt. He frantically embraced his sister, who threw herself into his arms.

Anna Sergeyevna cried as she stood in the rear, stroking Manya's shoulders. At last they could see one another! My God, it had been so long since they'd seen one another!

"An eternity! An eternity!" Manya repeated over and over again. Her eyes were full of tears, but her face glowed.

"What a beauty! Let me look at you! Ah, you've taken wholly after Mother! You look just like her now. Isn't that so, Petya?"

"The similarity's there, but she's got a lot that's purely Manya," he laughed. He'd grown as wrinkled as an old man.

"Where is she?" Manya asked anxiously.

"In Doctor L's sanatorium. It's wonderful for her there. Better, of course, than living here with us. Take off your hat! Why are we standing here?"

"What a hat! Look, Petya! Gorgeous feathers. So, what would you like? Coffee? Tea?"

"Give me some tea. So you stayed here?" Manya asked, looking around the dining room.

"We'd got used to it," Pyotr Sergeyevich said.

"How are things with you, Petya? Do you have a practice?"

"It's going all right. I work a lot. I defended my dissertation not long ago."

"It went brilliantly!" Anna Sergeyevna cried, running off into the kitchen.

They went into the study. Manya was touched by the modest furniture. He'd denied himself everything so as to support her for almost three years. They sat down on the couch upholstered in American oilcloth. With a wordless, passionate caress, Manya embraced her brother and pressed her cheek to his face.

"Lazybones," Pyotr Sergeyevich said, stroking her cheek. "If it hadn't been for Mark Aleksandrovich and Frau Kessler, we'd have known nothing about you. Two letters a year. Shame on you."

"Petechka, dear, life wasn't easy for me. I didn't want to upset you and I don't know how to lie."

"Why was it hard? Didn't I send you enough? Why didn't you say something? I'd have taken out a loan . . ."

"Ahh! That's not it! Not at all. As if I've ever . . . I've never cared anything about having to do without."

"What else, then?" the question escaped him with a quivering sound. Gently withdrawing, he intently examined her drooping face. She'd changed completely, and in essence nothing remained of the former Manya. Her mouth was different. And so were her eyes . . .

"Ah, Petya. Later . . . some time . . . I'll come back here in a month. I'll be on tour here, in N**'s enterprise. You'll see how I work."

He smiled involuntarily at the technical term. Manya noticed. How odd he was! Perhaps, like so many, he thought her craft was easy. Easier than any other?

"Are you here for long?"

"I'm leaving this evening for Petersburg, on tour at the *Studio*."

"Will you get paid a lot for it?"

She laughed, spreading the fingers of both her hands.

"What does that mean? How much?"

"Twenty thousand for two months there and here."

Pyotr Sergeyevich rose, thunderstruck, while she laughed.

"Outrageous!" he said, lifting his shoulders. "To throw such money away on the theater. In such a poor country as Russia."

Her head lowered, Manya examined her rings. Her cheeks paled slightly as she recalled Xavier and the upset she'd recently endured. "Think about justifying your life."

When she finally raised her head, her face seemed to have aged. But she smiled gently at her brother.

"Come here, come! I want to kiss you. You move me, Petya. You're just the same as before. But, don't you see . . . if people didn't love it so passionately—no, not art—but if they didn't love a spectacle, then I wouldn't have been able to pay back my debt to you and settle my account with Mark."

"Ah! That's good! Good that you've paid back what you owed him. You could have waited as far as I was concerned. That's in the family. I know I'm not consistent." Cracking his knuckles, he started pacing about the room again. "Anya and I were amazed to get such a large sum from you at one go. As if the money had dropped into our laps. Whee! Phew! What a celebrity!"

He smiled, looking her over as if examining a stranger from a distance. She wore a velvet gown and a string of pearls around her neck—a gift from her London admirers—with a striking, stylish hairdo, and a thousand rings on her hands. His face crinkled again and he resembled an old man.

"Come on—tea's ready!" called Anna Sergeyevna.

When they were already in the dining room, Manya said:

"Why haven't you asked me about Ninochka?"

"That's right! Where is she? In Moscow?"

"Mark and Frau Kessler are about to arrive and they'll be bringing her."

Her brother and sister exchanged glances. They'd long suspected that Steinbach was Manya's lover, and she didn't seem to wish to hide the fact.

Manya went up to the window and peered out into the side street.

Manya involuntarily recalls the evening she had waited here for Nikolenka. Mark and Frau Kessler arrive with little Nina.

"An angel. She's an angel!" as if through her sleep she heard Anna Sergeyevna's tearful voice. "Golden locks, blue eyes. What a marvelous child!"

Pyotr Sergeyevich twirled his beard in embarrassment. He'd seen Nelidov only once, but the little girl was the spitting image of him.

The dining room was instantly filled with noise. Frau Kessler talked nonstop, complaining about Manya. What a spendthrift! Terrible! Some Russian kursistkas* had come to her in Paris and she'd given them a thousand francs. Then some more came from the dining halls, and she gave five hundred francs!

"Why, that's good," Pyotr Sergeyevich smiled, stroking and kissing Ninochka's little hand. His soul was filled with melancholy and profound emotion.

"Not so good. You can't feed everybody. And what if she breaks a leg or falls ill? What then? No, I've come to my senses now, and I take the money from her and deposit it in Nina's name. She'll need savings. A child in her position . . ."

"What?" Manya interrupted in a quivering voice and set down the cup that she'd raised to her lips. "Repeat what you just said . . ."

Everyone in the room froze. "What eyes!" Steinbach thought. "Both threatening and imploring . . ."

"Don't be a bourgeoise, Agatha," Manya said coldly after a moment's silence. "Artists don't work for years, perfecting their performance and creating, only to submit to the prejudices and habits of the masses in their personal lives. No one dared ask Sarah Bernhardt who the father of her Morris was. He had a mother and that was enough."

Pyotr Sergeyevich stretched his hand across the table and stroked Manya's fingers. A loud sigh of relief escaped him. He smiled with satisfaction. "That's really well said! Good for you, Manichka!"

Manya drank her tea in silence, not taking part in the conversation that was now under Mark's control. She didn't notice his cursory sharp glances.

As they left, Manya said:

"I'll expect both of you for dinner at six in my hotel."

"We'll drink champagne," Frau Kessler laughed.

Pyotr Sergeyevich raised his brows.

"What's the occasion?"

"What a strange question," Steinbach replied. "Hasn't Maria Sergeyevna accomplished everything she dreamed of? Didn't she go through a long and arduous time before she reached her goal? You might think that she's just lucky, one of the chosen. Yes, that's so, but it's not only talent that gives us the strength for life's battles. Only hard work allows us to overcome in those struggles. Persistent hard work and faith in one's god. That god is Art."

"Bravo! Bravo!" Frau Kessler seconded him merrily.

And Pyotr Sergeyevich suddenly recalled the evening at the boarding school when little Manya had danced before an enraptured audience. Hadn't he himself dreamed of a new direction for the child? Hadn't he yearned to find a different god in her soul? Not love.

And, as if answering his thought, Steinbach completed it.

"A wide road has opened up before Maria Sergeyevna. Fame, the public's love, independence, creativity. We'll wish that she go down this road with her head held high, the way conquerors do! Not knowing any hesitation, scorning doubts, triumphing over the nondescript sorrows and little joys of the average woman . . . free from their illusions and disillusionments. And in this new life let's wish her a new happiness, quite unlike the one that she lived by *yesterday* and by which thousands of others will live *tomorrow!*"

Manya was putting on her hat in front of the mirror. Her hands shook and froze above her head.

"What a strange tone! Triumphant and bitter. Did he read my soul right now? There are no secrets from him. It's dreadful!"

A group of workers from the theater Studio *meet Manya when she arrives in Petersburg by train, but Harold is absent. While Mark takes care of preparations for Manya's performance and maintains close contact with Frau Kessler and Ninochka, Manya languishes on the couch, fantasizing about Harold.*

Filled with trepidation, Manya aims to pay a secret visit to Harold in his rooms, but finds he is not in. She spends the rest of the morning driving around the city in search of Harold's books and portraits. She learns that his works have sold out and that he enjoys extraordinary popularity, especially among women. She buys a postcard with his portrait, and compares him to Eugene Onegin as depicted in the opera! Back at the hotel, Manya lies to Steinbach that she had merely gone out for some fresh air.

Harold returned half an hour later.

The bellboy handed him *Marion*'s card.

Lips tightened, Harold looked at it, frowning, as if he wanted to see behind those six letters the image that they symbolized.

He sat down to work.

But it was difficult to concentrate. He was annoyed.

With a tremendous effort of the will he nonetheless got control of his consciousness, and gradually reality receded. The mysterious byways of the imagination that he now trod with an uncertain step lured him farther and farther . . .

And the walls enclosing the horizon fell . . .

It struck one.

He pushed away the paper, settled back in the armchair, and closed his eyes.

The mysterious byways vanished in the mist. And once again he stood face to face with everyday reality.

He needed to have breakfast, then to go from the restaurant to the editor's office to negotiate with Blagin about a story. He'd promised to give it to *The Voice*. From there he'd drop by Dora's, whom he'd not seen for three days.

The woman attracted him like a riddle. Once he understood her, the fascination would disappear. And that would be a pity . . .

Marion . . . he suddenly remembered. And he got up, brows twitching.

He should leave her his card. Right now? Yes, now, while she was at rehearsal. He didn't want to meet her.

Harold changed his clothes slowly, carefully considering all aspects of his outfit, starting with the tie and ending with the shoes.

Marion . . . remembered Harold. And again a strange unease seized him. He boldly confronted the feeling.

Everything unmediated was alien to him. And these lines emanated an intense heat. The words of the letter were simple and sincere. And that was why they seemed suspicious to him and hostile to the entire makeup of his soul. Just as what's valuable in art is not the depiction of reality, but the reflection in it of the artist's soul, so in life what's of value are not instincts but our struggle with them, our victory.

"There are many reasons that I don't want her see her now," he thought as he left the apartment. "As an artist, she'll captivate me, and will give me a lot of colors and images. And I'm waiting for her debut with bated breath. But we mustn't meet offstage. All fascination will disappear. I know myself.

"Take Likhachov, for instance. Onstage he's as splendid as a god. I see his feet, his torso, his movements. He excites me. Why would I debase this image? Once he's offstage, this semi-divine being will dress like me. . . No, much worse. . . He'll start saying banal things, invite me to dinner and, perhaps, will have too much to drink . . . the way Russians drink is unappealing in general. I don't want to see him like that. Or Tinskaya, the blonde with the virginal look. How insistently she keeps inviting me to see her when I go backstage to have a look at her! But I'm afraid of going. . . She's an exemplary family woman. In her small apartment I'll smell the fumes of the samovar, hear her children crying. She may receive me in a dirty housecoat, with her everyday face. . . And later, when she glides from the wings as a graceful fairy and gives me a melancholy, mysterious smile, will I be able to forget her worried home face and the banality of her situation? No, these experiences are dangerous for viewers like me."

He'd reached the side street. He needed to turn off to get to the tall, dreary box of a house where the editor's office was located, about five hundred feet away. But Harold went past it, hurrying to Nevsky Avenue.

It was already two. In the hotel he asked whether Marion was in her rooms.

"She left for the theater half an hour ago," the desk clerk told him kindly.

"Please give her my card."

With a sense of relief Harold left the building.

He needed to turn left to catch the editor at this hour. But instead he set off for the Neva. He was mulling something over, glancing at the tips of his shoes. (As a European, he scorned galoshes even in autumn.)

Harold stopped in front of the window of an art store. Marion's portraits were exhibited to everyone in the front of the window. Many people kept coming up and admiring them.

"She really is splendid," Harold thought. "Perhaps it's only makeup that makes the eyes seem so fascinating. But does it matter? Off the stage an artist can even be ugly. Life is nothing. The only thing that's important is art and illusion."

His lips tightened, Harold gazed into her face, full of intense heat and bliss, at her snakelike figure, so boldly curved in the sensual dance. And his uneasiness grew . . .

Why play the hypocrite with himself? The woman attracted him.

Without knowing her yet, without seeing her eyes or hearing her voice, even at a distance he felt them fierily and painfully vibrating his nerves. She aroused a cruel curiosity, sultry desire, youthful impulses—everything against which he struggled in the name of a higher goal, everything which had no place in his rigorous life! Passion distorts the personality. Passion is the enemy of creativity. He had to avoid this woman! The instinct of self-preservation had told him as much in the first moment he held her letter in his hands.

He approached another store window.

Manya lay on the ground in the pose of the Sphinx, her huge, mystical eyes gazing at him. She wore a light tunic, her hair caught in a Greek knot. Her dark brows were tragically knitted. Slightly raised on her elbows, her chin resting on her palm, she gazed into his soul . . . frightful, enigmatic, full of menace and challenge.

And Harold stood motionless, fully in her power.

There she was—Woman! Ever alien, ever inimical! A riddle comprehended by no one. An elemental, dark force . . .

Our happiness lies with her. . . But so does the doom of all possibilities, doesn't it?

Isn't it she who stands there, on all the roads and crossroads, lying in wait for the moment of weariness, reading in the wayfarer's pupils his craving for rest?

Isn't it she who, with a cruel laugh at whoever lies in the dust, places her foot on the chest of the vanquished?

Her hands are prehensile, and her lips thirsty . . .

She is a symbol of her sex, and the enemy of personality . . .

You who are climbing upward—beware of her!

BOOK FIVE

After seeking Harold in vain, Manya performs in one of his plays at the pioneering Studio.

Backstage at the *Studio* Steinbach saw the tall figure of Harold, and walked up to him.

"At last! Marion has been asking for you constantly."

Harold gave a restrained bow.

"She wanted to know your opinion. You're a strange author! You're not at all interested in the interpretation of your ideas?"

Steinbach caught himself using a false intonation that was alien to him, as if he were trying to ingratiate himself with the man.

"Forgive me, Baron, perhaps this will seem impertinent to you, but I'm always disillusioned when I see a play on stage."

"Your own play? Why's that?"

"No, other people's too, if I've read the play earlier. It's like having a dream that you try to recount the next morning. The facts seem the same, but the mystery's gone."

In the semidarkness backstage Steinbach attentively examined the other's cold face, the elongated forehead with indented temples, the firm outline of his lips, and the stubborn line of his chin. He felt terror. Was it that the restrained strength the man emanated made an impression or was it a presentiment . . .

"May I see Marion?"

"Yes, let's go to her dressing room. No. She'll be out in a minute. You saw her just now, I hope, in your pantomime?"

"She was splendid. I wanted to thank her."

Steinbach suddenly halted.

"Harold, I'm asking you not to say to her what you just did to me. The comparison with a dream that's recounted."

"Oh, Baron. You don't need to worry."

"Speaking frankly, I'm surprised. In my view, Marion was poetic and moving. I can't imagine that anyone could convey it any better . . ."

"From the stage? Yes. I take into account the conventions and realism of the theater, Baron. Everything that can be done Marion did. But, you see, I'm the author, and other images live in my soul. My soul contains dreams, here we have life. Of course, I won't tell her this."

"He doesn't like her," Steinbach thought. "All the better!" He knocked on the door of the dressing room. "Are you ready, Marion?"

"Is that you, Mark?" responded an indifferent voice from within.

"She doesn't love him," thought Harold.

"The author of *Fairy Tale* is here. He wishes to meet you."

There was a moment's silence. Subsequently, neither Harold nor Steinbach could ever forget that moment.

FIGURE 11
N. N. Gerardov, poster for the Fairy-tale Ball, St. Petersburg.
This poster shows the fin de siècle's embrace of folklore and witchcraft as a cultural expression of the ineffable, mysterious, and otherworldly that characterize Harold's stage production, "Fairy Tale."

Then the sound of impetuous steps, and the door to the dressing room swung wide open.

Manya stood on the threshold in her grayish-blue, semitransparent tunic, feet bare, her dark arms exposed.

"Almost naked," Steinbach thought. And why had he not noticed that earlier?

Manya's eyes, anxious and burning, fastened like a stinger onto Harold's face. Her lashes swept up, her brows arched, and her lips were half-parted.

Here he was, at last! He, about whom she'd thought all those months. She'd thought about him persistently, merging with his thoughts, metamorphosing into his images, trying to understand him in this strange *Fairy Tale*!

What a cold face! Impenetrable and alien. . . How tightly his lips were compressed! His appearance emanated strength and contempt. No, that's not how she imagined the poet.

Harold's eyes slid quickly over her face and figure, and he immediately bowed his head respectfully.

She unconsciously extended her hand, and he kissed it, barely touching it with his clean-shaven, dry lips. She saw the white line where his black hair was parted on the side.

Harold straightened and looked intently at her with his sunken eyes, which didn't have a trace of a smile. She was younger than he'd thought and more beautiful than in her portraits. No, she was no predator. There was a kind of helplessness and bewilderment in her gaze and gestures.

"I came to express my delight to you. Every author . . ."

An unpleasant, shrill voice. And how strangely he spoke! Too firmly. That's how people speak onstage. She listened but didn't hear. This wasn't it . . . not it at all. . . Was this how she'd imagined their first encounter? Why was he mouthing banalities?

She looked back at Steinbach and cracked her knuckles. Ah, they weren't alone! If they had been, she would shout directly in his face, "Stop! Surely you can feel that's not what I'm expecting from you?" Yes, that's what she'd say to him: "You were my inspiration." How often she'd said these words when she was alone! Without listening to Harold's polished phrases till the end, she nodded casually to him.

"Forgive me. I'm tired. We'll see each other tomorrow, I hope! Oh, yes," she passed her hand over her face, as if waking up. "We need to settle something right now. If you have any comments . . ."

"Why is she unhappy?" Harold wondered.

". . . I'd appreciate your letting me know them right now."

Steinbach felt fear. Something had happened. She was suddenly in a bad mood.

"Tomorrow it'll be too late," she finished limply.

A faint smile suddenly parted her lips. Her eyes were big and radiant. She gazed raptly, with a peculiar intentness, into Harold's eyes.

"Mystical eyes," Harold thought. "What's in them? A confession? A promise? A challenge?"

And now something stirred in his soul, yes—in his soul and also in his face. And Manya felt it. Ah! Finally . . .

"Until tomorrow!" she said faintly, gently, and disappeared.

The key turned in the lock. "She wants to be alone!" Steinbach thought. "She doesn't wish to see me. What did she promise Harold with that long, strange glance?"

Steinbach was pale. In the semidarkness backstage the two men walked toward the exit, exchanging polite half-phrases, sharply observing each other.

His lips twisting in a gracious smile, Steinbach thought:

"If both of us were to shed the veneer of culture and give free rein to instinct, wouldn't I take him by the throat on the spot, like a caveman with his rival?"

And Harold thought: "She's complex. This isn't your usual little actress. And I made an error in saying all those banal things to her that dozens of women would have been satisfied with. She deserves the truth."

"Goodbye, Baron!"

His dry lips compressed, Harold made his way down the corridor, tall, arrogant, and elegant. He held his top hat in his hands.

"Steinbach finds me unpleasant. Perhaps it's a case of jealousy? Does he know about her letter? This moment just now was beautiful. I love the first minutes of an encounter, there's nothing like them. These impressions, which are never repeated. I love this mystery of first glances."

He left the building, avoiding the group of women waiting for him in the vestibule.

The first lines of a sonnet, inspired by Marion's image, sounded in his soul. He listened to them reverently as to a distant, beloved voice. And so as not to disturb these delicate sounds, he walked slowly, pressing his walking stick to his lips and gazing ahead with unseeing eyes. He walked carefully, almost on tiptoe.

The theater was full, despite the tripled prices or, rather, thanks to them. It was a real spectacle-gala.

There were an unusual number of beautiful women in the theater today. Everywhere one could see bare shoulders, bright dresses, sable and ermine, fresh flowers, imitation pearls, and genuine diamonds. That was because all the ballerinas who were not engaged that evening had come to look at the famous barefoot dancer. And ballerinas were the capital's most beautiful and desirable women.

Indeed, it was a vanity fair! Everyone there knew one another as if they'd met in a drawing room. They greeted each other graciously, the women giving a cursory but sharp glance at how the others were dressed. Smiles lie, but the eyes cannot hide one's real feelings. Once their backs were turned, they maliciously slandered them and laughed vindictively. The artists consisted not only of women enamored of their own bodies or their own fame. The men were as petty, envious, and vain. One couldn't meet such feminine men anywhere but in this exotic milieu of artists, journalists, and actors at such gala performances. How many sexless beings, profoundly indifferent to each other, ran into one another here! They had no strong passions, no temperament. If they came together, then it was out of self-interest or vanity, and all their connections were ephemeral. For this audience, everything was superficial. There were only two strong motivations: envy and vanity, the exclusive passions that drove the will of the sexless, refined their abilities, filled their souls, and ruled their lives. And woe to a genuinely talented actress or painter! Men and women alike didn't forgive them their success.

Manya delays appearing on stage, and only her fellow-dancer, Nils, inspires her to go out and, once again, enthrall the audience. Manya is handed a bouquet of roses from "the author," and shortly thereafter Harold receives an unsigned telegram, inviting him to a masked ball the following day. Intrigued yet irritated, he loses himself in composing verses. Steinbach suspects Manya's advances to Harold.

"I've received a telegram, Manya, and am leaving this evening."

"Nina? My God! What's happened?"

"No, no. I'm going on business. This evening."

Unnoticed, Steinbach observed the expressions on her face. But Manya was in control of herself, and only the slight color that vanished from her cheeks told of her joy. Oh, to be alone, and especially now—not to feel that gaze, which lay in wait for her every move.

"Will you be gone long?" she asked, playing with her rings.

"I can't say. I'll let you know."

She was thinking about something, eyes slitted as she gazed down at the glittering ruby on her little finger. It was her favorite stone.

"Mark, send me a telegram as soon as you arrive. That very day. Will you?"

She raised her eyes and he saw something dark and ominous in them.

"What for?" the question escaped him involuntarily. "You speak every day with Frau Kessler on the telephone."

"No, no. You must send me a telegram."

He gazed intently into her eyes and suddenly smiled. And she felt her hands grow cold.

Steinbach leaves, and Manya realizes that he has done so purposely, knowing of her intentions regarding Harold.

No, she hadn't stopped loving him. Only now, having grown cold to his sensual caresses, did she appreciate his nature and love his soul. He'd become close, dear, and necessary to her. Could she imagine her future life without him?

No! No! Not for a single moment. Never, for anyone's sake, would she agree to leave Mark. "Not for anyone!" she said loudly, passionately, as if throwing out a challenge to someone. Nina, Mark, and art—that was everything on which her life depended. There was no one else like him in the whole world! And she would not find such a feeling anywhere. Ah, why, why had she let him leave without letting him know how much tenderness and melancholy lay in her heart? O, that glance with which he'd looked at her just then, as if bidding her farewell forever.

Manya roams about the apartment, now bemoaning Steinbach's absence, and spends the night sleeping on his bed. Mark sends a laconic telegram and Manya cheers up, anticipating her meeting with Harold. At the masquerade, a red monk follows Manya and Harold as she attempts to engage the writer in talk of love; we are led to believe that this spying monk is Steinbach. While she insists on the primacy of love, Harold acknowledges Art as his main passion.

"Are you afraid of me, Harold?"

He didn't reply immediately.

"Yes."

She hadn't expected such a bold admission and was disconcerted.

"What you portend for me is probably vivid and unforgettable. But, Marion, I already have my life's goal. I don't want to share my soul, and I don't know how to. I have my own world, Marion. Mysterious and wordless, like Böcklin's* sacred grove. Why allow the dark and hostile force called passion to destroy this peace? Chase away the radiant spirits that are dancing under the trees in the moonlight? Remember the shepherd and the maid in my *Fairy Tale*! Yes, I'm afraid of you, Marion. This elemental power gazes at me out of your eyes, and I don't accept your challenge. But it's not cowardice. No—it's a great love within me speaking, which isn't afraid of sacrifice."

She heard him out and closed her eyes in sorrow. The color slowly drained from her face.

"Farewell," she said silently.

And, head bowed, she moved off quickly, quickly, almost at a run. As the sobs rose to her throat, she clenched her teeth. God! She simply couldn't cry in front of everyone! She didn't see the dark eyes of the monk at the entrance who was watching them. To get out into the fresh air as fast as possible! To be alone!

Harold rose and stared after her, stunned.

What an elemental nature! He'd never met its like.

And, once again, harmonies began to sing in his soul. He was happy, for the evening had brought him a great deal.

He made his way through the halls without looking left or right, carefully carrying through the crowd, as if afraid of spilling, the magic goblet filled to the brim.

Passion had seized Manya. It had unexpectedly entered her soul again, like an invading barbarian, burning and laying waste everything in its path, toppling the altars of alien gods, trampling on values that were needless and incomprehensible to it. And Manya gazed with horror at this devastation. What would survive in this catastrophe?

Nina? She hadn't even given her a thought the whole night long.

Mark?

She straightened in the armchair in which, half-dressed, she'd sat until morning. Only now, when Polina brought in some chocolate and there was the sound of a broom knocking in the corridor, did she recall the figure of the red monk.

And again she grew chilled.

Manya learns that Steinbach is not in Moscow with Agatha and Nina, and, alarmed, ruminates on her "sufferings." Harold sends her a letter confirming his friendship and telling her, as Steinbach had done earlier, that she does not have "a woman's soul." Steinbach finally arrives in Moscow, and, walking along the street, recalls the time spent there with Manya.

He heard a soft exclamation:

"Wait, wait a moment."

Who was speaking? A weak, almost childish voice. . . Steinbach stopped.

A small, fragile figure stood in front of him. One could mistake her for a girl in her early teens, were it not for her long dress. She wore a short black jacket of Persian lamb. Shaded by her wide-brimmed lambskin hat, her face, with its enormous eyes, seemed very small and ghostly. She timidly placed her hand in its warm glove on Steinbach's sleeve and said in a faint voice:

"You're so beautiful! Let me look at you again and remember your features!"

He looked intently at her and felt the predatoriness of his own gaze. No, she didn't look at all like a woman seeking adventure. She held a violin case in one hand. What a pity she wasn't attractive! For an instant they gazed silently into each other's eyes, and he read everything clearly in her face. Yes . . . yes . . . there could be no mistake. Dreaminess was what gazed at him out of the girl's eyes.

Steinbach offers the girl his arm, and, as they walk down the street, her conversation reminds him of the young Manya, who loved him.

"It's so strange!" she said, sitting beside him on a bench. "When I awoke this morning, my pillow was soaked in tears. I was crying from joy. And since the morning I've been expecting something momentous, something special. Wait. Why did you smile? You think I'm abnormal?"

"No, no. Go on."

"I was tired from walking, and decided to return home. But some voice whispered to me: 'Take one last turn around the block, just one.' I went, and met you. Do you believe in premonitions?"

"Yes."

She fell silent and gazed at him in rapture.

"She's not as unattractive as I first thought," reflected Steinbach. "She's got irregular, crumpled features and puffy lips. But what lovely eyes! Mysterious, bottomless, ominous, and with a knowledge of something that others can't know. The eyes of a hysteric. They make her little face significant and unusual."

As Steinbach prolongs the exchange with the girl, Lia, he becomes convinced that she is psychologically unbalanced. At her apartment, where she lives with her grandmother, Lia notes that his presence there must be kept secret. She coughs repeatedly, they drink hot tea, and she confides that Harold is her favorite poet. She plays the violin, delighting and moving Steinbach. He learns that she is half-Jewish, called Liubov (Love) Grinevich, and spends most of her days practicing on the violin. As he leaves, promising to return, he realizes that she is in love with him, but he is not cheered by the thought. Their relationship becomes intimate, Steinbach cognizant that she is merely substituting for Manya in his thoughts. He tells Lia that Manya has first claims on him. Manya, meanwhile, cannot forget Harold.

"What do you need?" Manya asked herself. "Look into your soul and be honest and frank! Confess! What do you want? To control him? To control him completely, as you do Mark? To control his thoughts, his life, to make him your wordless slave? Yes! Yes!" she said loudly, and the words fell heavily.

"Do you want his caresses? Do you want to see passion in those dark, sunken eyes? Do you want to arouse his desire? Yes. Yes. But you know he told you that intimacy will kill all illusions. Don't you want to be his inspiration any longer?"

For several moments she sat, lips compressed, in a complete stupor. Then she suddenly rose and threw her arms behind her head in utter despair. "No! It's he who should serve me, not I him! His love should inspire me. His passion should nurture my soul. I'm a pathetic beggar woman without that love. Where is my strength? My pride? My creativity?"

Harold unexpectedly visits her, and asks whether she plans to marry Steinbach. She admits to indecision on that count, and he notices that she is suffering.

"Harold," she said in a profound voice. "In the short note you sent me there's one significant phrase. You said that I have a masculine soul. There's a lot of truth in that. If I were feminine, I'd start an alluring game with you, with a prelude to intimacy, full of innuendos, halftones, with the entire gamut of moods. I'd lie to you and to myself. I'd display my mysteriousness. I'd watch my own unapproachability with pleasure. If you coldly rejected this game, I could find consolation in flirting with another. But I have no interest in such cheap and vulgar coquetry. I confess honestly and boldly: I love you, Harold."

She intercepted his movement and raised her hand, leaning forward:

"Let me finish! I know that in the common view these avowals are obscene. A woman, after all, is doomed to wait in silence. She can't dare to choose and fight for happiness. But you don't subscribe to the common view. You're the chosen from thousands of people. You're the most daring and strong. And I turn to you as to a fellow-artist, as to my equal. Give me some support! I'm perishing. Everything by which I lived before our meeting, which I strived for so passionately—where has it vanished? I'm at a crossroads once more. And there's horror, horror in my soul. I see nothing ahead . . . only your face. I know, I can feel that you don't love me. You don't even understand the passion that's seized me. Where will I find the words to make you understand this horror, my sense of insult, my sufferings? See, you've lowered your head and fear to look at me. Harold, be a man. Look me in the eyes! Can't you see how they're filled with despair? What's frightening, Harold, isn't that my passion is unreciprocated, but that I, who believed so much in myself, after having almost escaped to freedom, find myself once again in a prison. O, how I despise myself! I wanted to laugh at love. And now love is laughing at me."

When Harold offers his friendship, Manya points out that she cannot be his friend, for, if anything, she feels hostility toward him.

"What do you want from me? Your words sound more like a challenge. Your entreaties sound like threats."

"You're right, Harold. This is a challenge, and in this duel someone must be killed. Either I or my passion. The world cannot accommodate us both. You, who love art, you, who have given your soul and your life to this idol, should understand me. Until very recently I lived only for that idol. I proudly rejected all temptations. Ah! What am I saying? They didn't exist for me. I laughed at the desire that others involuntarily experienced. 'What's desire?' I said to myself, laughing. 'Does it make any difference? If not this one, then that one's fine.' And I even have a lover. Consequently, no one scares me. But to love? O, my God! I had something to fill my soul—my child and my creative work. That was my world. Why did it all fall in ruins, Harold? Why did this dark passion have to seize me and carry me away, the way the wind whirls a wood chip about? Try to understand, Harold: this feeling I have for you brings me no joy, but only suffering. Furthermore, it's my debasement, an unbearable sense of insult. Having proudly challenged life, I am once again vanquished. Once again I'm down in the dust, with no strength to get up and go any farther. I'm not an artist now, but a pitiful puppet. For years I built my castle and considered it indestructible. Then you passed by—and now it's all in ruins. And I don't have the strength to start building anew.

"I'm not pleading with you for tenderness or love. I'm not proposing that you walk hand in hand with me through life. I myself want to be free from all contracts and responsibilities. And at the same time. . . O, I'll be completely frank! I'll be merciless with myself. Harold, the sight of that woman's face in your theater box tormented me. Both of you appear before me day and night. O, if you only knew how I'm suffering! I tell myself: 'Why doesn't he, the only man I need, not need me?' There's only one answer: there's another woman. My God! It's degrading to speak like this, to admit this, to offer oneself like this."

"Have you loved before, Marion?" His voice sounded soft, like the touch of a gentle hand on a wound.

"Twice."

"In the same way as now?"

"Oh, no! Completely, completely differently."

"I believe you. Your voice had such a moving quiver just now. Tell me, don't you recall your previous sadness and your previous joys with indifference now? Aren't these feelings completely a thing of the past?"

"No. I'll never stop loving Mark and never . . ." 'forget Nelidov,' she was going to say, but suddenly fell silent.

Harold was thunderstruck.

"It's not likely I'll become Mark's wife. But we loved each other too intensely. We suffered together too much for me to be able to forget him. Such a feeling is a higher value in and of itself. But something else also bound us. If I'm worth anything now and if I'm alive—I owe all that to Mark. I'll never, ever leave him unless he repudiates me. Ah! You're surprised? 'What's my role here?' you're thinking! But surely, Harold, our soul isn't so paltry and insignificant that its happiness is satisfied with gratitude and memories of the past? Doesn't it have facets in which other heights are reflected? Don't you yourself get carried away with a beautiful face? And, if you love me, as you claim, are you really indifferent to the woman who was with you in the box?"

"So you're offering me . . ."

"Shh! Be quiet! There's no need for irony. Look deep into my eyes, Harold. I'm perishing. And a joke is out of place when one's life is on the line. Transcend your pride and listen to everything I have to say! Oh, you're probably right in thinking that this isn't love. It's a sickness, it's madness, a mania. But don't maniacs commit suicide? Will this madness last long? I don't know. Perhaps once I've slaked this thirst I'll immediately become healthy and strong. But I don't want to lie even at this moment, which is so frightening for me. Harold, I want to take everything from you and I won't sacrifice anything for you."

"Is this how you loved earlier, Marion?"

"No. Oh, no! My love for Mark was a hymn to life. My love for . . . another was a prayer. In both cases I obliterated myself in this feeling, and I blessed this self-oblivion. Both times I loved selflessly, crying from tenderness, accepting insults with a smile. In my love I thirsted for exploits and sacrifices. My love was even free of desire, Harold. But that time has passed. I'm no longer a girl and I've learned to value myself. I won't yield to love a single inch of what I've gained! I want only joy from you. I seek only inspiration in this feeling. I know that it'll vanish when I achieve reciprocity. And when it vanishes, I'll become myself again. There! I've said everything. You can take offense and leave."

"Take offense?" He shrugged his shoulders. "At what, Marion? You and I have the same views about the nature of love in our lives. It's what gives life its color, but it's not its goal. Did I understand you correctly?"

"Yes, yes. I knew that you, you of all people, would understand me."

"But there are some things in which we diverge significantly, like two polar extremes. I, too, value myself highly, Marion. I, too, recognize neither sacrifices nor responsibilities, nor self-violation. And I value the freedom of my soul above all else in the world. Finally, I see in love the source of creativity and of higher earthly experiences. An element that creates life, not destroys it, as passion does. What prevents us from reaching out to each other? Why do both of us—and I have to admit to this—feel this latent hostility to each other? It's profound and elemental. Marion! Don't hide your face! Now you should have the courage to look me in the eyes—you, a proud, strong woman! Surely you can feel that I, too, should hate you, though I'm curbing this feeling? Surely you understand that you—with your temperament, talent, worldview, and all your elementalness—are my enemy. But what's more important, you're the enemy of what I value above all else in the world—my own creativity."

He moved toward her, looking into her pale face, with its lowered lids.

"Truth in exchange for truth. I respect you too much to indulge in word games or deception. I'm afraid of you, Marion. I'm more afraid of you than you are of me. You're elemental, I'm not. You awaken in me all the dark and frightful elements from which you yourself are suffering so terribly and fruitlessly right now, from the invasion of which I jealously guarded my soul until today. For that soul is consecrated to art. You know that. But it's dangerous to muddy pure sources, Marion. From our first meeting I felt the danger. I told myself: 'This woman will be your ruin.'"

She rose. Her eyes looked ardent in her pale face.

"That's why you avoided me? Is that right?"

He bowed his head in silence.

She leaned with one hand on the little table, while her other covered her eyes as if she'd been blinded. She heard his words as if in a dream.

"You described it well right now, when speaking about your earliest feelings, when you were very young. It was your soul's prayer. You knew real love, Marion. Bless life for having known that!

"In you I love my own inspiration. I love you when you're remote and elusive, with a sad smile, as you were just a moment ago, as you are only on the stage. And when I've hidden somewhere in the theater, lost in the crowds, I see your eyes, full of yearning for the impossible, my heart weeps with tenderness. I'm familiar with this wonderful yearning for that which the earth is powerless to give and our body is powerless to realize. Like the shepherd in my *Fairy Tale*, gazing at us from afar, I hear the mysterious words of strange and distant songs. People only hear them in their dreams, and on waking they forget them. But I'm a poet. In my cramped room, at my desk, my power summons these voices anew from non-being. And in this process your image rules, Marion. Surely that power is enough for you? I'm the one who should be entreating you, not the other way round: do not destroy this world! You've created it. Don't duplicate in life the sad ending of my *Fairy Tale*. My love-dream will turn into hatred the moment you submit to the dark power of instinct and destroy my soul's equilibrium. I attained it after years of unabating effort. I don't want to lie, Marion. I won't refuse you. No. And I'm weak-willed before this elemental attraction to you. But remember: intimacy will kill love. And I'll leave. All your charm will be powerless to hold me back."

He took her hand and respectfully, almost tenderly, kissed it with his dry, firm lips.

She was silent, her head bent in painful reflection.

For a long time after the door closed behind Harold she sat motionless, her body frozen.

Steinbach sends a telegram, reassuring Manya that her daughter is well and telling her that she should be happy, which she interprets as offering her license to pursue Harold. She goes to Harold's apartment, where their "inimical passion" is consummated. As a consequence, Manya blooms, while Harold feels drained of his creative powers. In the meantime, Lia, mindlessly in love with Steinbach, meets him daily in museums and at exhibits, joins him for walks, and in this way "revives" Stein-

bach's chilled "soul." When Manya telephones, he at once realizes the source of the joy in her voice. Lia offers to ease his sufferings by any and all means, but he nobly refuses.

During these days Mark's soul dozed, lulled to sleep by young love, intoxicated by the pure caresses of a swarthy young girl. His soul was at peace, and slept. His dreams were without sin.

At the sound of Lia's violin his sorrow faded and the dark receded. And the poisonous serpent of jealousy concealed itself deep down at the bottom of his heart. Here a meek David played on his harp, and a gloomy Saul listened to him, weeping.

Every morning upon awakening he dimly sensed his faint joy, and as he opened his eyes, he'd say to himself: "I'm beloved. It's not all behind me. I'm beloved."

Every day when the clock hands indicated the hour of two, he'd say to himself: "We'll be together soon, and I'll see her eyes. I'll see in them the dream I've realized here on earth."

And when the clock struck three, reality died away and the fairy tale began. He left his past behind, and without thinking or hesitating he went off to meet the new. He left the house full of strength and joy. Faint joy, to be sure, but had he ever known any other?

And then his eyes met those mysterious dark eyes, and his hard heart softened. They'd go to the old house on Ostozhenko. No one disturbed their rendezvous. No one violated their solitude. And a profound secret shrouded his life as before.

Sometimes they went strolling on moonlit nights. By day they'd usually meet at an exhibit or in the empty rooms of the Rumyantsev Museum or in the Tretyakov Gallery. But most often they'd sit together by the fire, he in an armchair and she at his feet, without noticing their silence, each with a separate world in their souls.

Going to bed, Steinbach would say to himself: "We'll meet again tomorrow."
He waited for these hours as rest.

Frau Kessler espies Steinbach with Lia, and is anxious that Manya return from her engagement in Saint Petersburg. In the meantime a telephone conversation with Manya conveys to Steinbach all he needs to know about her affair with Harold. He nearly insists on finding oblivion in Lia's embrace, but then controls himself for the girl's sake. He confesses to her that he remains a slave of his passion for Manya.

Frau Kessler to Manya

"Crazy woman, if you don't want to lose Mark, come back immediately. I've seen him myself with some girl. He meets with her every day on the boulevard and disappears for the evening. Is art so dear to you that you'd destroy your future with your own hands? I'm rushing to post this. He's come home. Don't tell on me. Nina has been sick, and now she's better. He didn't want me to write you.

Agatha"

When she received this letter, Manya stared long and fixedly before her.

Poor Mark! Even if he'd consoled himself a little, it was all the better! She feared no rival. And Agatha had sounded the alarm in vain. Could his love for her be threatened by these little distractions he sought to ease the pain?

Of course, I'll never dare mention that girl to him.

But as she dressed to go to the theater, Manya for the first time felt easy in her thoughts about Steinbach. She smiled the whole way there. Now it was easier to live.

Harold sat at his desk, trying to concentrate. His mind was not working with its usual agility. Only pale and banal words emerged from his pen. The main thing was missing: analogies and symbols. Only a craftsman writes this way. He'd not descend to that level.

He tossed his pen aside and threw himself into a chair. His face had sunken, his eyes were more deep-set.

It had been one week. One week of idleness and ecstasy. And he was already out of the groove and couldn't right himself.

And hadn't he foreseen this as he avoided Marion? She'd charged into his life like a thunderstorm. And, like a thunderstorm, she'd trampled the flowers he'd cultivated. Now, like the shepherd in his *Fairy Tale*, he was hunting for the scattered petals in vain. He'd not be able to collect them. Everything had perished.

But this could not last. He had to triumph in this duel he'd begun so bravely in order to kill his passion with his sensuality. This was the true path. He knew it. And it was no accident that Marion's daring masculine soul had pursued the same path instinctively in order to liberate itself and quench her body's thirst. One had to pass through this if one wanted to create calmly. One can't work with a fever in the blood.

Already he could see how the wilderness of enchanted forest was thinning out. High time to enter the clearing! To breathe deeply. To know once more the joy of solitude, the joy of silence at one's writing desk, within the four walls of a quiet room.

He went up to the table and grabbed his pen.

His glance fell on the clock and he sighed.

She was waiting to breakfast. She'd wrested this promise from him yesterday, without considering the fact that he needed to finish this story. "Does she really consider anything?" he thought bitterly. She wanted to see him not only in the theater, but at rehearsals. She constantly expected him for breakfast and dinner.

After the performance she'd summon him to her, like the conqueror his spoils, leaving him not a single free minute, treating him like a thing. She was a seductive, ever new, life-loving Delilah.

And in her room, at the sound of her laughter or passionate whispering, under the caresses of her marvelous hands, filled with the scent of her intoxicating perfume, he felt how his personality dissolved, how his "I" drowned under the hypnosis of another's will.

Was this love—this dark, elemental attraction, full of cruelty and so resembling hatred, that melded their bodies into a convulsive embrace? It only had to do with the body. Not the soul. This difference, which so frightened Harold and attracted Marion, would never disappear. And it peered out from their eyes with a mysterious threat in the most intimate and most sacred moments.

Yes, this woman knew how to intoxicate. She was like a natural force that induced trembling and concealed doom. But perhaps also rebirth? She knew no banal words, no vulgar gestures. Her face in those moments was full of mystical mysteriousness, like the face of an ancient priestess. And then she was marvelous! Somewhat later, when everything had settled in his soul, he'd realize that this face had given him a tremendous upsurge of creativity, a wealth of images he'd never known before. If he could only conquer and flee. If he could only break out into open space.

It was only from afar that he could protest, rebel. He could hate her for this constant violation, this informal intrusion into his life. What was it? A disdain for his personality or the unconscious life force of her soul?

"It's time to break this off . . . the sooner, the better!" the voice of reason pronounced masterfully. And he would be paralyzed, listening to it.

Never before had life granted him so much beauty. How vulgar and pale were all other women before her!

But still, still, he'd leave her.

Silk rustled behind him, and before he could turn around, a scented hand, still smelling of leather gloves, closed his eyes. He could hear tender laughter behind his back.

"What's keeping you so busy? I knocked twice. Hello!"

He took her hand and kissed its palm. A stream of fresh air entered the room with her. The scent of her familiar perfume reminded him of a time he needed to forget if he wanted to go forward.

He fell back into the armchair, holding her by the hands, and he gazed up at her from below. Her eyes were sparkling, her cheeks were crimson, her teeth flashed. Her left brow arched up. Her young lips smiled craftily. This was life, life itself, breaking through to him. Triumphant, merciless, all-powerful.

But there was no space for her in the room of the poet who stood above life.

"Why are you staring at me this way, Harold? What do you want to say? Let's go have breakfast right now. They held me up at rehearsal. Oh, it's so good that I thought to drive over!"

"I've no time, Manya. I have to write."

She laughed loudly and tossed his manuscripts about the table.

"What nonsense! This really won't get done?"

"This work has a deadline," he answered shortly and sadly. "It's my bread and butter."

Her gaze fell on the envelope: "To Boruch Isaakovich Mendel."

Raising her eyebrows in amazement, she looked first at his forehead, then at the envelope.

"What's your given name, Harold?" she asked in a subdued voice.

Smiling, he pushed the envelope toward her. Her left brow had frozen in a capricious expression.

"Is your name Boris?" she persisted.

"No, not Boris, but Boruch."

"Boris Aleksandrovich?" she raised her voice capriciously.

He laughed. This came so unexpectedly that she dropped her muff.

"My name is Boruch Isaakovich Mendel," he enunciated clearly.

And he suddenly stopped laughing.

"Your first disillusionment?" he asked after a pause, gazing at her fixed expression.

And, strange as it might seem, it was only now that her ear clearly caught the accent that at first made Steinbach frown and Nils laugh.

She stared at him with big, transparent eyes.

"But I've never pretended to be Russian," he said coldly, playing with the ivory knife. "I chose a pseudonym because it sounded pretty and shielded me from the crowd and its curiosity. But I don't like to be an imposter in my private life. Why is Boruch worse than Boris? But even if it is worse, it's my name. You'll have to reconcile yourself to this."

She was no longer listening to his words or his voice, but his accent. She looked about the room and its familiar walls with cold, curious eyes. Why had these walls moved today? And this magic room suddenly become cramped?

"Are we going out, Harold?" she asked, pulling on her glove. And a chill sounded in her voice.

But he understood her when he heard that voice. She'd never spoken with him that way. And her face was too expressive.

Hiding a sense of involuntary alienation and pain behind a mask of worldly civility, he walked out after her, grabbing his gloves and top hat from the table, pale, with pursed lips, looking hostilely ahead at the train of her dress.

Harold arouses Manya's jealousy by paying court to his ex-lover Dora. After initial rage and despair, Manya realizes that what she enjoyed with Harold was only passion, not love. Harold takes his leave, settles down to write, and forgets his various obligations to others. He has already forgotten Manya, and is in love with her fictionalized image in his novella, when Manya comes knocking on his door at two in the morning.

How pale she was! He could only see the enormous eyes of a "wounded deer" in her face. And he recalled the girl in his *Fairy Tale* as she went to her death.

She threw off her veil. He kissed her hand.

"Are you writing?" she asked meekly and sat down as if suddenly faint.

Her face was ill, pinched-looking. Her lips were dry and she had dark shadows under her eyes.

"Yes. I'm glad I'll be able to finish this before I go."

"Are you really leaving?"

"Tomorrow evening. My uncle died. My mother wants me there."

"My God!" she burst out. But, clenching her hands, she queried almost calmly: "And after that?"

"Then I'm thinking of going to Egypt. I've long dreamed of the Orient. And my doctor advises me to go. I've overtaxed myself a bit. And my lungs have gotten weaker."

"Your lungs?" she repeated in horror. "Were you ever seriously ill?"

"I've twice suffered from inflammation of the lungs. I spent one winter in Davos. They forbade me to overwork, get agitated, fall in love." A sad smile flickered in his eyes and then disappeared. "I'm a fragile vessel, Marion. My appearance is deceptive."

She stretched out a burning hand and tenderly squeezed his fingers.

"Don't talk that way. I feel like a criminal."

She pressed his hand to her cheek with a sweet childlike gesture. Then she kissed it.

He shuddered, just as if he'd been burned. All the blood rushed to his heart. He suddenly felt a mighty wave of sweet, unknown tenderness rising up in his heart. And it was beating, huge, agitated, happy.

"What are you doing, Marion? Dear Marion . . ."

"Don't! I feel good this way. Sit beside me! Hug me! This way. And we'll be silent for a little while. Oh, it's so wonderful to be together! Harold, why haven't we had these moments before?"

"Are you ill, poor Marion?" he asked after a long and strangely sweet pause, as he stroked her cheek and the hand that had fallen helplessly on his knee.

Her lips trembled.

"Ah . . . you're happy, Harold!"

He could hear the tears in her voice. This was so new. She was completely quiet and sad. He felt sorry for her. This was such a terrible, paralyzing feeling! Oh, if only he didn't succumb to it! Otherwise all was lost.

"Why are you unhappy, Marion?"

She placed her hands on his shoulders and studied his face for a long time.

"It's as if she's saying goodbye," he thought.

"Go on. Why are you silent, Harold? Say this: 'After all, you yourself wanted it, and I warned you. I loved you like a dream. You've destroyed this happiness yourself.' I know, Harold, I know. But could I have done anything differently?

"The wave crashed down on my head and bore me off. I didn't struggle against it. I knew that it would bring me to the shore. But you got there before me. You've already freed yourself, Harold. Here you are sitting at your desk, happy and proud. But I'm still struggling with the waves."

"You'll make the shore as well, Marion. People like you do not perish."

"Thank you for those words! I'm still an adversary worthy of respect. And you shouldn't think of me with scorn once we part. And if I succumb once more to this dark force, and hit bottom once again, you'll still understand, Harold? You give your word?"

Without answering, he held her head with both hands and kissed her eyes. He'd never kissed her that way before. Only Dora. But what was Dora to him now, when he stood before this woman, magnificent and powerful as Life itself? His soul had never sung out as it did now.

She went up to the desk and skimmed the lines of his narrative poem.

"This is where your strength lies, Harold. This is what distinguishes you from the crowd. And what I, a madwoman, struggled against."

Her voice broke. She took out a handkerchief.

"Are you weeping, Marion?" he cried.

She brushed the tears away and once again gave him a tender, sad smile, an enchanting smile he'd never known before.

"No, these are happy tears. They make things easier. I look on these lines with reverence. And I'm ashamed. It pains me that I prevented you from working."

"Don't talk that way, Marion! Two days of work have made up for everything. Who knows? Maybe this pause, this ecstasy was essential, valuable."

She gazed on him with shining eyes.

"You still doubt this? Ah, Harold, I know that my passion enriched you! Do you remember my letter from the Tyrol? Do you remember what you were for my work? Now I've repaid you. And this recompenses me for all my suffering these last few days. The sufferings will pass away. But your verses will endure."

She took the paper from his desk and kissed it.

"Marion. What does this mean?" he asked in agitation.

"I'm here, nonetheless!" she said proudly, striking the manuscript with her hand. "And you won't forget me."

She lowered her veil and went to the door.

"You're more magnificent in your sorrow than in your passion," he thought. "And if this draws me to you once more, I'm finished."

But—without expecting it himself—he asked her:

"Will you be home this evening?"

She silently lowered her head.

"But won't you call me, Marion?" he blurted out anxiously.

"No, Harold, I won't call you. Now you'll come of your own accord. But I'm prepared for anything after the night I just lived through. Even your imminent departure doesn't surprise me. I knew this, too. And I feel nothing. Something has died in my soul."

"That's victory, Marion."

"A Pyrrhic victory," she said with a bitter smile.

He escorted her to the stairs. "This is our last meeting. The final weakness," he mused.

He returned to his apartment. And suddenly felt the walls around him, something he hadn't noticed before. It was stuffy, cramped.

He sat down at his desk. The white paper gleamed coldly. He didn't feel like writing. His thoughts ran after the woman who'd trailed the scent of her perfume behind her and a bit of her soul. Their souls had touched just now, souls that hadn't seen each other beneath the blind, suffocating cloak of passion. They'd revealed their sad faces at last. And Harold's heart froze when he suddenly sensed the beauty of that complicated and stormy soul.

"I mustn't think of this!" he told himself, seizing his pen. "It's the trap of an enemy who never sleeps. Oh, it's imperative to be on guard, so that the enemy doesn't catch me unaware!"

He wrote. Then he suddenly threw the pen down and stood up.

Everything was finished. His mood was ruined. The chain had broken. He could string only flaccid words together. But an hour ago he'd strung a pearl necklace. His head was empty. All his blood had gone to his heart, which now for the first time pitied the one he'd feared.

"She is beauty!" someone said distinctly and severely. "She is beauty and life. And you've renounced her."

"And I renounce her still," Harold thought. "I renounce happiness in the name of a higher goal."

But for the first time it seemed to him that the sacrifice was enormous.

The clock struck four. He put his manuscript in the desk decisively, picked up his top hat, and went out.

She was free until seven. When he'd come in, she'd smile. Ah, that smile! How often he'd seen her in his dreams with that sad, meek smile! But never in reality, until this day.

"And I'd thought that I'd exhausted her completely."

His heart was pounding as he walked along the corridor of the hotel where Manya was staying. "If this is love, then I am lost," he told himself.

He turned pale as he opened the door. He'd even forgotten to knock, for the agitation that gripped him was so strong and new.

She stood by the fireplace, sorrowful, solitary.

"Harold!" she cried, rushing toward him.

How long afterward did he hear that cry!

And he spoke to her in a trembling voice he'd never used before; he said the words Manya'd waited for long and in vain; he put meaning into them that he hadn't known until this day.

"I love you, Marion."

Manya and Harold experience a miraculous night together, when both their bodies and souls become as one, after which Manya telegrams Steinbach to return. Stein-

bach hastens to be with her, although he must part with Lia, who suffers terribly in consequence, and he has a premonition of her death.

Manya pens a farewell to Harold, in which she declares that she is leaving him so as not to jeopardize their one beautiful moment together. She concludes that they both worship the god of creativity over ephemeral personal happiness, and, besides, her one true partner in this life is Steinbach.

Upon his return, Steinbach finds Manya in a state of terrible apathy.

"Where is Harold?"

"He's left. We'll never see each other again. And I was the one who made the decision to part."

The last phrase confounded Steinbach. He kept trying to speak. His lips were trembling.

Distant and silent, she didn't notice his agitation, and sat as she had before, hugging her knees and staring at the carpet.

"I knew this would happen, and that you'd come to the end of your infatuation."

"Why did you go away, if you knew?" she asked dispassionately.

"But weren't you grateful for this? Look in your heart and answer. Can you reproach me? There's no need to reply! I already know it all. But I wasn't afraid of Harold, Manya. Do you want me to tell the truth? I wasn't afraid of him. I knew that you'd return to me, tormented and unsatisfied. Yes. The way you are now—you don't need a man. You need a slave."

She lifted her head. The sorrow in his voice reached her consciousness. But then he controlled himself.

"You don't have a woman's soul, Manya. You're not made for the yoke, like thousands of ordinary women. You need power, freedom. You demand adoration, submission. You're used to it. For the last few years your life has been a battle for recognition, for your place in the world. All this hindered the development of femininity in your soul. And this enemy of yours, the most terrible enemy of a talented personality—femininity—was still sleeping. It wasn't time for it to awaken and destroy your life."

Now Manya gazed attentively at Steinbach. What he was saying and how he was saying it were slowly driving away the paralysis of her soul.

"So you're surmising that it nevertheless will awaken?"

"No! God forbid! I don't think this. I envision nothing. Sometimes words get away from me. Don't pay any attention! My nerves are a bit frayed."

She was expecting something, on alert.

"I remember your love affair with Nelidov."

"I knew you were going to talk about this," Manya thought, lowering her eyes.

"Your passion for him was no accident. No. It was fatal. You have to look deep to discover the secret of your attraction to him, your desire to be a slave to him."

"I discovered this," Manya uttered quietly.

He looked at her sharply from a distance.

"You know, I've thought a lot about the past this month."

He suddenly fell silent.

"You're afraid, Mark, that if we meet again sometime . . ."

She wanted to smile, but a grimace came out. With a face suddenly contorted by pain he interjected:

"On the contrary, I deeply believe that if you've found creativity within and you constantly work on yourself in this direction, you'll finally triumph as a personality. The femininity in you will die away imperceptibly, that woman who needed men, who sought sacrifice and submission. You've Nina for this kind of love. And this whole affair with Harold only bears out my words. He was . . . how can I say this? He was a cliff against which the wave of your feelings and passions pounded. You understood instinctively that you wouldn't be his goal, as you are for me, but only a means, that he'd draw from you all that he needed. And once he'd sated himself, he'd move on, with no spark left for you in his soul—his proud and cold soul. In a word, he treated you as you treat everyone else who loves you. Isn't that true? Didn't I immediately grasp and weigh all the threat of your attraction? My fight for you could only be carried out through submission, patience, and self-restraint. You weren't to know of my sufferings and jealousy. That only makes people like you more cruel. I knew what I was doing when I got out of your way. I won by leaving. If I'd stayed here, I would have lost everything."

"I never stopped loving you, Mark," she said, and the satiny sound of her voice seemed to warm him.

"I'm very touched," he replied with a smile, and once more placed her cold hand on the breast of his jacket.

"May I ask some questions, Manya?" he queried after a short pause.

She nodded silently.

"Why are you unhappy?"

The crackle of the embers could be heard in the long, strained silence. Steinbach's legs suddenly grew weak. He sat down in the armchair by the fireplace.

"Haven't you attained all that you aimed for? Your happy voice, your laughter when you spoke with me over the phone didn't fool me. I believed that once you'd indulged yourself completely, you, like all artists, would extract all the strength and fire from your passion that your talent and temperament needed—just like a flame that eternally feeds on direct sensation. I thought it through. And understood. You're not the only one like this. All artists, if they're not petty bourgeois in nature, need some nervous agitation. What happened? Why are you sick and tormented? And why have you cooled toward art once more? Or are you still infatuated with Harold? Why, then, did you decide to part? Manya, answer, for God's sake! I'm also in pain. And ignorance is worst of all."

She lifted her head without changing her pose.

"It wasn't a whim or an infatuation. It was love."

His body, strained in anticipation of her answer, helplessly lowered into the chair. A silence ensued. But Manya didn't want to break it. Everything had died in her soul—even pity for the one sitting crushed by the fireplace.

"Are you surprised, Mark? I sense you are. It was a blow even for me. At the very minute when it seemed that I was cured of my passion, I felt what I fear most in the world: tenderness, pity, the desire to sacrifice myself—in short, love. And I summoned you, Mark. You understood this correctly. It was a drowning man's cry. Because for someone like me, love and death are the same."

"I'm listening to you, and it seems like a dream. A terrible, but marvelous dream. And the same Manya is speaking who at one time, suffering from love, saw death as her only outlet? Do you yourself feel how much you've grown during these years? Do you grasp the significance of this victory? This is the final step to the tower. Now you're at the summit. The world lies before you."

She nodded bitterly.

"Such conquerors are pathetic."

"It all will come back, Manya. Be brave! I tell you sincerely now that I'm not afraid for you."

Steinbach rose and walked about the room.

"But there's still something here that I don't understand. You loved. What about him?"

"Yes, it's strange. His love, which he so feared, was born out of hatred. And, take note that he loved me as I am, without illusions, knowing all the weaknesses that bothered him before. He loved me, me, and not his fantasy. It was marvelous and terrible. Terrible because I still want to live. I want to struggle, and work, and not disappear in Harold, not dissolve in my feeling. It must have been the instinct for self-preservation speaking in me. And I decided to break it off."

"But how could he renounce you?!"

"He left without knowing about my decision. When he returns, I'll be far away. Oh, I know very well that Harold needs a slave, a vestal virgin who is obliged to tend his holy flame day and night. But this role is not for me, Mark. I've my own calling. It summons me to a new life. But my past is richer and fuller than what he promises me. What in this new life could equal the beauty of my struggle and my achievement? Tell me, what? Love? Oh, yes! That's happiness. But how long will it last? And I've already known this feeling. Need I experience jealousy once more? Lose my illusions again? Travel that sorrowful path? No! I can't do it again . . ."

"You never loved him!" Steinbach burst out with conviction. "Don't object, and don't argue! This was a cerebral feeling. Let us call real love, if you will, 'organic'—a love that doesn't judge, doesn't weigh things, doesn't fear sacrifice. It simply doesn't notice such things. You've only really loved Nelidov."

A faint smile trembled on her face.

"I don't remember who said that cerebral feelings are the strongest."

Steinbach froze at the other end of the room.

"Don't you see, Mark? I no longer believe in love. 'All or nothing' used to be my motto. I long for the same thing even now. But this is the cry of the heart. And my reason says something else. I'm no longer a girl, Mark. I've aged in my soul. I've matured. When I love as I do now, I already have the end in sight, as if it were the steppe at night, and there's a bonfire in it. But I don't know when the bonfire will be extinguished, and night will once more avidly embrace me and suffocate me. And now I'm in that night, Mark. I still haven't forgotten its mute face. Remember when I went silent and alone into Eternity . . ."

"Be still! For God's sake, be still!"

In an instant he was sitting beside her and grasping her cold hands.

"And now, after my confession, what will our relationship be, Mark?" she asked, smiling sadly.

He moved away involuntarily.

"I don't understand your question."

"What's your decision?"

"You're laughing at me! What sort of decision can I make? Didn't I renounce my will long ago? I want only one thing—to stay by your side, in any capacity. As a friend, a brother, a lover . . ." this last he wanted to add, but he fell silent. "As your impresario or your majordomo."

"Why suffer so, Mark?"

He stood up, clutching his head.

"What suffering? With utter clarity I see that I have no goal, no life, without you and Nina. Maybe you scorn me for this? I scorn myself, too. Do you think that I haven't thought about breaking off these ties? That I haven't tried to forget you?"

She lowered her head still more so that he couldn't see her face.

"My efforts were in vain! Whatever you do, however you abase me, even if you gave yourself to someone new each day, it's all the same! Without you my life has no meaning. I'm bewitched."

She raised her face. Her numbness had disappeared.

"And you've never tried to start a new life?"

She saw how he trembled.

"Never," he said firmly after a moment's pause. "Without you? Never. It's better to be unhappy with you than be happy without you!"

Oh, how light she became with these words, at the sound of his voice! Her soul, tormented by loneliness, made cruel by her struggle, suddenly softened. And it was as if triumphant joy flung open the doors and windows to warmth and light in her dark, boarded-up house. At last! He hadn't stopped loving her. He'd never stop loving her. Everything was as before.

But this lasted only an instant. Her face fell. Exhaustion tugged at her strained muscles. With a sigh of relief she lay down on the couch, hugging a pillow and pressing it to her cheek.

Steinbach approached quietly and sat down beside her. Without opening her eyes, she stretched out her hands and embraced his head.

He cuddled up to her like a child upset at being punished, when a cruel, but beloved hand suddenly strokes him on the head. Manya's heart was beating. He could hear it. For whom was it beating now?

"Manya, I'll tell you one thing more . . ."

"Tell me!"

"When you stopped loving me . . ."

"I never stopped loving you, Mark."

"No matter. When I left you with Harold," he said, involuntarily whispering, "I tried to understand what bound us together. Why did you speak with me over the phone if you loved another? Why, when you were upset about him, did you remember me? And I understood, Manya, that you summoned me like a master, and that I returned like a slave. Do you want me to tell you?"

She nodded, her eyes still closed.

"In our love you are the man. I am the woman. You order, and I obey. And if I can't live without you, Manya, then you . . ."

She opened her eyes for an instant and smiled a faint and tender smile.

It was so good that he spoke so assuredly, with such force! Let him think for both of them! Let him fight for them both. Let him decide. She was tired. She'd exhausted herself. She was happy to submit. Some resolution had to be found. He'd find it. While Mark was with her, everything was fine. His hand was firm and his heart true.

"You want to sleep?" he asked quietly.

"Yes, but don't go away. Sit near me. Hug me. I'm cold, Mark."

Unable to control an upsurge of sorrow and tenderness, he buried his face in her breast.

Once more they were together, embraced tightly, as they had before the face of Death. He knew this. He knew that she'd summon him again when those mysterious steps once more sounded nearby and the terror of loneliness seized her.

He thought as he shut his eyes: "Thank you, life, for preserving at least these minutes for me."

And, as if she'd guessed his thoughts, Manya suddenly opened eyes full of darkness and anxiety. And she asked: "You won't leave me, Mark? Never? Not for anyone?"

"Never. Not for anyone."

They were silent a long while, embracing each other still more tightly and sadly.

"She's fallen asleep," he thought.

Suddenly she spoke in a half-whisper, as if she were delirious.

"Is this all a dream, Mark?"

A scene from the past suddenly rose up before him. A Ukrainian night. The summerhouse. Stars above. A heated embrace. And passionate whispering.

"A dream," he said barely audibly. And his heart was pounding. He waited for the next words like a spell.

And he heard once more the sad whisper.

"Only death will part us?"

"Only death," he replied like an echo, fully enthralled to the past.

Steinbach suddenly feels guilty in his neglect of Lia, and he has a suspicious dream in which mute, cold Lia visits him in his bedroom. He is generally exhausted by yet another effort at resurrecting Manya.

Some time later Manya and Steinbach return to Moscow, where Manya passionately rushes to Nina and Steinbach to Lia, and Steinbach discovers that his friend had died just as he'd dreamed of her. She has left him a letter in which she declares that she knew he was leaving her and she therefore summoned Death. Steinbach is overwhelmed by anguish, hopelessness, and oncoming old age.

BOOK SIX

Manya and Steinbach are back in Moscow, where they have divided up the living space in his home, and Manya's family and friends have become caught up in her stage success. But Manya, slowly erasing Harold from her heart, succumbs to memories of Nelidov.

After the performance Manya returned to Steinbach's house. The moon was already high in the sky, and the shadow of the iron railing was sharply etched on the snow of the deserted street.

As Manya got out of the car, she caught sight of this shadow and immediately stopped. She didn't follow the car through the gates and didn't notice the caretaker, who was looking about with the night watchman in amazement, but stared now at this dark lacy shadow on the snow, now at the patterned railing and the house illuminated by bright snow in the distance. The house resembled a knight's castle, stylish and austere. Beyond its towers stood the dark naked trees of the garden.

Manya suddenly remembered the evening she'd first entered this house. This had been a fateful hour in her life, one that made her break with Nelidov inexorable. From this moment on her life had taken a different path. Oh, God! How long ago that had been! And nevertheless—how could she forget for a minute that her fate had been decided in this house?

With an eerie feeling she walked up the steps to the porch and rang the bell. She looked around in the spacious front hall, her eyes wide. She felt the antagonism emanating from the dark walls, from the grand staircase leading upward. She walked slowly, trying to remember something.

She'd felt something important then in this house. Had it been a premonition of a fateful denouement, of her suicide attempt? What was the source of this mystical terror and cold which had dogged her heels that evening and followed her even to her brother's apartment? And hadn't her resolve been born that night? Hadn't it been the next morning that she'd taken advantage of her brother's absence and stolen the poison from him?

The servant turned on the staircase lights. But she didn't want to go upstairs to her room. She had to think something through, explain something.

"Mark Aleksandrovich hasn't returned?"

"No."

"And Joseph Lvovich?"

"His grace is sleeping."

Manya slipped silently past the uncle's room and went into the study. She quickly flipped on the light switch near the door. She was all atremble inside. If she spent one more instant in the darkness, she would scream in terror, so clear did it seem to her that she was not alone.

Nevertheless, the room was empty. Mark had moved into it, leaving her his upstairs study. All his furniture remained there. This room held only his desk, his chair and . . .

From the threshold Manya saw the portrait on the easel. Across the room, from out of the heavy gilded frame the sorrowful face of a woman stared at her as if alive. Bluish black hair smoothed by a ribbon lay along the satiny white cheeks. The thin, winged eyebrows and the compressed bitter lines of the mouth expressed the eloquent tragic air of someone conquered by life. The bottomless eyes, filled with darkness, peered out at Manya, as if threatening her.

"Me?" Manya whispered involuntarily, craning her neck and fearing to go closer. "You're threatening me? With what? What do you know?"

From out of the gilded frame those bottomless pupils still peered at her ominously. Manya walked over to the window and then turned around to look at the portrait. The eyes followed her as if they were alive.

Manya's temples were immediately damp. "What am I afraid of? This is only an illusion." She tried to laugh. No! She couldn't forget the mysterious terror she'd first felt before this portrait. It had been exactly a week later that she'd poisoned herself.

She went to the door. The eyes followed her hostilely.

She didn't have the strength to turn out the light and walk along the dark corridor. A minute more, and she was already running as if someone were chasing her. She rushed to the light of the illuminated staircase.

Suddenly the door opened. It was the uncle's dark silhouette.

She threw herself on the old man and buried her face in his chest.

"I'm terrified!" she cried plaintively.

"There you are. I sensed it. I always know when misfortune is upon you."

She threw back her head and stared into his eyes, which were just as mysterious and fathomless as those in the portrait.

"Do you know how she died?" whispered Manya.

"Who?"

"Your sister, Mark's mother. Tell me! Did she commit suicide? Yes? You're not saying? Why? You do know? Ah! Now I understand. Now I understand everything!"

He closed her eyes with the palm of his hand.

"You mustn't think about this! You mustn't!"

Everyone in the Steinbach household, except little Nina, is preoccupied with his or her own sorrows and ruminations. Manya finds some comfort in the time she spends with Steinbach's uncle, who, we learn, has long suffered from melancholia.

Manya in her gloomy anguish couldn't perceive the changes in Steinbach. He wasn't living. He was only existing.

Although he showered the same attentions on her, his uncle, Agatha, and Ninochka, his heart wasn't in it. His soul was somehow paralyzed. "Not on my account," Manya perceived with her characteristic acuity. "He has his own wound. His own secret."

They saw each other only rarely now. He didn't accompany Manya to rehearsals. He only drove out for her performances, and then not always. Every day from three to six, until the dinner hour, he sat shut up in his study.

The clock would strike four. The thought would flit by: "It's time! She's waiting for me. It's freezing out. She'll catch cold."

He'd rise. And then the bewitchment would pass away.

There was nowhere to rush to. Nothing to fear. She lay in the frozen earth, fettered by unearthly cold, the eternal seal of death. And she didn't fear cold or storms or deceit or betrayal. Or all the sorrows of the world.

Sometimes he'd walk out along Ostozhenko to Lia's room. He had his own key to the apartment. Lia's grandmother would knock at the door and offer him tea. He'd thank her and decline. She'd walk away on tiptoe and hush the servant.

If Manya had seen his face when he sat there for hours in the darkness, staring at the burning fire, she would be shocked by how much he resembled his uncle. It wasn't only an external resemblance. Now his eyes showed the same expression of undying sorrow that Manya had spied that first memorable evening in Lipovka, when the crazy old man walked by her, staring off at the setting sun as if seeking the departing shadows of those who'd gladdened him on this earth.

A month passed before Steinbach at last decided to light the candles and open Lia's desk.

The key turned with a faint noise. The scent of dried roses wafted in Steinbach's face. The whole drawer was full of them.

Steinbach discovers Lia's diary, in which she professes that her real talent lies in loving, not in creating art. He finds comfort in reading it.

She'd have waited for him, of course. But who could say when he'd return? And if he'd come back, who knew if this young love would have seemed so beautiful and necessary. Wouldn't it have been an extra burden for his already sated, tired soul? Lia's death now was a cruel happenstance. But she wouldn't have wanted to live through his cooling off and break with her. Love is always tragic for people like Lia.

"She died without cursing me. It's better so!"

Manya returns with Steinbach to Paris and Iza, and is at first reinvigorated by her contact with her old teacher and the prospect of working on new projects. She sits with Iza, Mimi, and Nils in Iza's studio.

Manya looked about her with a sweet, tormenting feeling. She recalled the first evening she came here with Mark and danced for Iza. There was the same dust on the wreaths, the same discolored ribbons, the same portraits on the walls. Not a single chair had been moved. Only a whirlwind had passed through her own soul. Had she grown up since that day? Or had she become poorer?

"Ah, just wait until I see you in *Fairy Tale*! I'm getting excited already. And what did the impresario pay you?" Iza asked.

She clapped her hands together when she heard the sum.

"They didn't pay that kind of money in my day," she said thoughtfully, gulping down the cooled chocolate. "Now everyone's crazy about ballet. It's a kind of mania. Well, you're off to America then, Mani-ya? *Figaro* writes that both of you have been offered a tour?"

"I haven't decided yet," Manya replied, as if she'd just awakened. "We'll be here until March, then we'll go to London, and from there to Monte Carlo. Beyond that I don't know. You see, I'm terribly tired. It must be old age."

"Ha, ha! You eccentric! And your baron? You haven't dumped him yet?"

Manya stared wide-eyed at Iza.

Nils responded with a malicious smile.

"The baron and his uncle have probably cut their throats somewhere."

"You aren't marrying him? Ah, don't be stupid, Mani-ya! An artist should always be free."

Under the noise of the conversation Manya once more looked about her, completely entranced by the mood that gripped her inside these walls. She remembered the evenings she'd spent alone here with Iza, their conversations about art, their dreams about the future, their aimless daydreams about exotic postcards depicting the Orient and Egypt; their dreams about the Sphinx in the moonlight; about the silence of the desert, about the leafy palms crowding about the Nile. She'd been poor then and had been striving for all these inaccessible miracles. Now the world lay open to her. And Harold was there in that mysterious Orient. Alone and sick. Perhaps he was dying. But her soul did not fly off to the Sphinx or the desert or those palms. It didn't even fly to the man she had once loved. She thought indifferently about the man who'd only recently filled her dreams and desires. Everything had passed. She had been as rich as Croesus when she'd walked about in broken-down shoes. Now she wore pearls on her neck, and her hands were covered with diamonds. But her soul was empty.

"There've been no changes in the school?" she asked distractedly, standing up. "I'll go look in on the classes."

Manya watched all the classes silently. Here she'd worked, dreamed, strived, struggled. And it seemed to her that the entire beauty of life lay only in this struggle and achievement.

And once again day followed day, quickly and feverishly amidst rehearsals, performances, and stressful work at home before the mirror, at the dressmaker's and the hairdresser's, among photographers and artists, among flattering journalists who now were even admitted into her dressing room. They were powerless to harm her fame. She didn't need to lower herself to winning them over and being ingratiating.

And now it was easy to create. Harold's image had dimmed in Manya's soul, and she gave herself completely to her work. She created new roles. She studied Gluck and Wagner. She won enormous success in dramatic pantomime. She read all the librettos proposed to her, and consulted with Nils and Mark. She suggested that the authors change what she herself didn't "feel." And she dreamed of writing herself.

It was strange! This feverish work and strained creativity simply destroyed the woman in her. Her desires lay dormant. Her dreams did not torment her.

Since the night she'd parted with Harold, her lips hadn't touched Mark's. They met now as comrades. They were living apart once again, although they saw each other every day. Manya had realized her dream. In the house she'd rented for the next three years Agatha and Nina lived downstairs and there she had her bedroom, boudoir, and dining room. But the entire upstairs with its enormous windows was divided into her reception room and studio. She was studying sculpting, as she'd once dreamed of doing in the Neapolitan Museum. She spent all her free moments in the studio. It was her temple. And here was everything she'd seen in her girlish dreams: the fireplace with the tigerskin rug before it and the rare marble statues along the walls. And flowers everywhere. Here she admitted only the famous sculptor Chapelaine, her teacher, sometimes Nils, and Mark.

Manya discovers a gorgeous Italian street musician, Enrico, who reminds her of the portrait of Lorenzo in the museum in Venice. She insists on sculpting him—both in period dress and nude—but eventually is disillusioned by the fact that he is too young, passionate, and vulgar, and she lets him go when he insists on an affair.

"How sad it is!" Manya told Steinbach. She'd dropped in on him after her rehearsal, and she sat down on the ottoman without taking off her hat and fur, with her muff still in hand. "Now I've got to abandon his sculpture and go back to work on my 'Nymph'."

"I'd expected a different ending," he said with his crooked, unpleasant smile, standing at the other end of the room by the fireplace.

"And that was . . . ?" she interrupted sharply, and her cheeks were burning.

"He's so handsome!"

She waited, staring at him severely.

"Don't women indulge in sensual caprices?"

"As far as I know, until now this has been the privilege of men."

"But haven't you transcended these prejudices? It seems that you long ago freed yourself from the bonds our morals and public opinion impose on women."

"Unfortunately, no," she replied, leaning her elbows on the embroidered pillow and nervously tapping the tips of her shoes on the carpet. "You've overestimated me, Mark. I very much regret that I've not been your worthy pupil."

"My pupil?"

"Yours or others'. I'm talking about the men who write the laws that give us an example of virtue and create a double standard—one for themselves, and the other for us women. For when you squawk about our treachery, you're always afraid of the phantom of a broken home and illegitimate children borne by unfaithful wives. But we performing artists are independent. We stand on our own two feet, and we often don't have legal husbands. And how can you argue against our right to give of ourselves as we please?"

"Have I ever judged you?" Steinbach interposed.

She waved her hand, and a malicious smile spread over her face.

"You've not judged, but. . . Let's put an end to this discussion! I sense that you've not yet forgiven me Harold."

"Forgiven? By what right?"

"Don't play the fool, Mark!" she exclaimed, pounding the pillow with her fist. And he could hear how her voice gave her away. "I'll be more frank than you. I've also not forgiven you my shattered illusions, although I'm obliged to thank you and . . . Nelidov," she uttered with difficulty, "for the education you've given me. In love and in my entire worldview I am, of course, your creature."

"You're equating me with Nelidov?" he asked in a trembling voice.

"No, I'm not equating you. He's not on your level. And you've left us both in the dust with your magnanimity. But this was later, later. I only want to say— Nelidov taught me well how to be satisfied with little in love. How easy it is to console oneself, once you've lost your beloved."

"But, as far as you know, I've not married another woman."

She threw off her muff angrily.

"Why should you marry—when you have lovers in every city? Will you deny it?" It was a hysterical outburst.

He looked at her sharply, trying to guess the hidden reason for this. He tried to stay cool, but his heart was beating an alarm. He still preferred to wait it out. Let her say her piece this time!

"You also know how to find solace when your beloved betrays you. And you know that, even if you love someone else, you can find pleasure in kissing another. This doesn't interfere with love. This is from a completely different sphere. This is the two-faced truth with which you poison our souls both in life and in books. I thought that I'd die of grief when I read Knut Hamsun's *Pan*. A flood of filth washed over my soul. You can love the one, and possess the other at the same time without loving her! If it had been a mad passion, a mad infatuation, as it was in Balzac's *The Lily of the Valley*, along with a spiritual love for another, then I'd understand. My God! I experienced this myself, when I loved you both at the same time. But to do this without love, as you do, just for the sake of a sensual caprice? How simply you men solve all the dilemmas of love!"

"I don't understand anything," he interrupted, frightened by her fury. "What's wrong, Manya? May I sit beside you?"

"Sit down, sit down! But that won't make it any easier for me."

He couldn't restrain a smile. It seemed to him that for an instant he could hear the voice of the former girl in that passionate cry. And this warmed his soul. The high wall that had separated them for three months was wavering. He hugged her.

"Manechka, why are you angry?"

But she was crying and pressing her hand against his chest.

"It'd be better to strike me than insult me. How could you think that I'd give myself to Enrico?"

"Where's the insult, Manya? Beauty creates favorites. And passion doesn't bother with the pedigree of the person who makes our heart beat faster."

"That's what you all say! We don't know how to do that. We've not developed to that point! We still need our illusions. We need to love in order to give ourselves to someone. And I also don't know how to do that. I still can't cross that boundary. Cursed femininity interferes. Our stupid idealism."

Smiling, he twisted his lips.

"Oh, no! That's also a prejudice. Women are always materialistic, always calculating. Your 'idealism' is nothing more than atavism."

She listened to him, now lying completely quiet on his breast.

"We men give our love like tsars. We don't bargain with our feelings. And if the beauty of a peasant girl fires our soul, we raise that woman up to our level. We know we can do this, that our declaration won't injure us or our love. For this reason the social status of the one we choose doesn't concern us. Whether she be a café singer or a gypsy or a laundress or a factory worker—what does it matter, so long as she is beautiful? When we desire her, we don't pass her by. We don't fear public opinion. And if the whim turns into passion, we give her our name, and society accepts her with open arms. You women are inevitably humiliated by this kind of liaison and you get no tangible benefits. You must be a queen or an influential person in order to make people bow before a stable hand. That's how women on the throne managed it. There was nothing for them to fear. But for you, mere mortals, these relationships were not advantageous. You lost everything, and got nothing in exchange. That's the secret of the idealism you've elevated to a virtue. And if you were logical . . ."

"I'd give myself to Enrico—you want to say? No! No! I didn't need him, but the mood he created. But you'll never understand this. You judge from your own experience. Let me go! I'm hot. And it's time for me to leave. I don't love you, Mark! I came to you as a friend, and you . . ."

Her lips were trembling. She took out her handkerchief.

"Manya, I swear to you! I didn't want to insult you. I've told you my views honestly. For me desire is always holy and beautiful. It's a spark of godly fire dispersed in the world. What laws or boundaries can there be? Harold or Enrico? Isn't it all the same when this sacred spark flares up? What summons a tremor in the human soul? A lovely profile or a sonorous sonnet? Life itself is a goal. And passion needs no justification."

"So why are you jealous?" she asked pitifully, and helplessly wept.

"You shouldn't worry about that, Manya," he responded with a bitter smile. "That's yet another one of those despised prejudices that interfere with life. One shouldn't get angry with a person who cries as they cut off his shattered leg."

"But I don't need him, your Enrico!" she said passionately, trying in vain to extract herself from his embrace. "I never wanted him. I never dreamed about him. Why do you tie me to him? What are your intentions?"

He suddenly laughed. It was so unexpected for her. She fell silent in confusion. Closing her eyes, she felt his lips touching hers.

Oh, at last! She clutched his head and pressed herself to him in a passionate urge to forget everything that tore them apart, that had separated them all these long, long days.

Oh, what joy to be together again! To hear the beating of his heart. To feel his caresses. Everything would pass. If only fate didn't take away this happiness from her!

<blockquote>From Manya Yeltsova to Sonya Gorlenko

"London</blockquote>

I'm in England again, the birthplace of Byron and George Eliot. Do you remember how we cried when we read *Mill on the Floss* at boarding school? Do you remember the frivolous heroine who perished tragically in *Adam Bede*? You always said that I was like her.

When I was here the first time, it was fresh, green summertime. It was the peak of the season. Everyone had driven in from the provinces in order to enjoy life. And every evening, day after day, over the course of that month I had to give the same performance. It was awful! I turned into an artisan. I waited for the evening with revulsion. But the days were so fine! Mark and I would cruise the country backways near London in the automobile. They were full of poetry, peace, and quiet. When you drive past these flowering gardens and ivy-covered cottages, or past ancient castles with their gloomy, mossy walls, where there is standing water in deep moats, you can't believe that in this same land of plenty people die every day of hunger.

Now my soul no longer resonates. The city is wrapped in yellow fog and soot. You breathe it, and it permeates everything. Every two hours I look in the mirror. My nostrils are black, my nails are black. It's disgusting! And it's sad. I can never get warm, although they keep the fires lit all day. I'm depressed. I ask myself: what's driving me from city to city, from one crowd of strangers to another? Why did I leave Paris, where the spring sun is now shining, why did I leave my studio and the work I'd begun? I can't live without sun, Sonya! What demons drove me into this fog? Greed? But I have money. I have everything money can buy. And Nina's future is assured, even if I die tomorrow. I've arranged for Mama's life to be very comfortable until the end of her days. And she may live a long time. I left ten thousand rubles in my sister Anna's name when I was leaving Russia. Fame? But this never tempted me. With my need for contemplation, my love of nature, my fear of people, I ought to live in anonymity and alone, guarded from life by a high wall. But fate has thrown me into the cauldron, where alien passions bubble up. How I envy those artists and writers who don't have to be in contact with their public on a daily basis, who don't feel the burdensome dependence on them we performing artists do!

What strikes me most here, Sonya, is the sense of the human herd. You think that the English understand anything in ballet? Decidedly nothing! But the world is caught up in balletomania, and the English don't want to lag behind the others.

The other day I was presented to the queen in her box at Covent Garden.

Note that this is an opera theater usually closed until the fall season. But the success of the Russian ballet has forced the English to break with tradition. The queen gave me a marvelous sapphire necklace, and Nils a blue diamond ring. Now we're showered with flowers and gifts. My tour with Nils across Europe is a tour of triumph. But nowhere have we met with the sort of worship we've received here in stuck-up London. They give banquets in our honor. People compete and fight with each other on our account. If we agree to present tableaux vivants at Duchess Leicester's, the next day Lady Littleton moves heaven and earth to secure our promise to dance at her private residence."

Manya interjects here that she is not swayed by this flattery, and instead behaves capriciously and rudely on purpose. She knows these people would never accept her and Nils as equals if they were not fashionable performers.

"Nelidov made friends with all these people and felt 'at home' here. And if he brought his wife here, they'd also accept her, that vulgar Katya Lizogub. But all my talent and Nil's genius cannot save us from humiliation.

They're also polite with Mark. But they only tolerate him. His millions impress even the aristocrats. And then he's met these people at all the world's spas, where they bring the anguish and cold of their empty days. But they'd never accept Mark as their own. I'm not even interested if they know anything about our relations. We are living apart, we get separate invitations. But he manages always to be where I am. My bad behavior shocks him. He doesn't want to understand me. We're quarreling.

Only Nils comforts me. He remains true to himself everywhere. But to do so he is unbearably proud and delightfully audacious. I sense that they're afraid of him. I know that if he enters into intimate relations with the two beautiful ladies who flirt with him like queens with a stable hand, recklessly, aware of their impunity—then how maliciously he'll manage to humiliate them! He's always the master of the situation."

It turns out that Manya has returned to London to get acquainted with Nelidov's ex-lover, the society woman, Lady Hamilton. She guesses, too, that Lady Hamilton and Mark were once lovers. Recalling her one beautiful night with Nelidov, Manya swears that she'd relinquish all that she possesses—talent, fame, wealth, and adoration—to spend one more such night with him.

Manya is asked by the Russian Jewish political journalist N to do a benefit performance for striking workers in London. At first she refuses, citing her hatred for her public, but when Mark suggests an arrangement that would make free tickets available to the striking workers and Russian émigrés, she agrees with passionate enthusiasm. She writes to Sonya about the performance.

"I've just returned from the theater. It was attended by a public that had never been to a ballet, had never seen me and Nils, for whom this evening will shine like a star in the darkness of their impoverished lives. Tomorrow Mark will send you the reviews. You'll hear what ovations Nils and I received. But you'll never know from these reviews how inspired my performance was! You'll never learn what happy tears I shed when I answered the curtain calls. And how agitated I was in the wings, waiting for my entrance. Here am I, the one who controls herself always and everywhere because I don't respect or fear my public! I don't respect or fear the press, either. Before the performance Mark came into my dressing room and said: 'N and his family are sitting in a box. There are a lot of émigrés here. And if this audience doesn't satisfy you . . .'

Sonya, this was the same N, Yan's teacher, the one that stern Xavier read, whose name we dared not utter at boarding school. He's never seen his homeland, and, like Herzen, he'll die in exile. His book is banned at home. His worldview is a nightmare for any government official, be he rightist or leftist.

But when Mark proposed to introduce us, I shouted, 'No! No!' I ran off into my dressing room and started sobbing. Are you surprised? But why? This time I felt and acted logically. This was self-preservation. A year ago Xavier told me: 'How can you justify your life?' And I had no answer. It's hard for me to meet him. Every time I recall these words, the old discord rises up in my soul.

I myself know that the joy and beauty I expend in the service of the rich should be accessible to all. An artist belongs to the people. And a work that has no roots in the people will perish. If I could justify myself before, because I was striving to rise up out of the dirt I'd been trampled in by those to whom I gave my body and soul, and because I was struggling for a place in a society that rejected me—how can I justify myself now?

Sonya, my heart tells me that if my life up to this minute was an ascent to a high tower, then I'm standing now on the final step. And soon the moonlit distance will spread out before me. I don't know how this will be. What will it be? But my heart is beating from sweet anticipation. And I feel like shouting: 'At last!'"

Manya returns to Paris and pays a visit to Nina Glinskaya, where she encounters the famous radical Nadezhda Petrovna Storozhenko. Storozhenko is delighted to make Manya's acquaintance, and tells her of her political friendship with both Yan (Prince Sitsky, as it turns out) and Steinbach. She disguised herself as a religious pilgrim in order to make her way through Ukraine, and both men aided her in this. Storozhenko dreams of returning to Ukraine to see her sister.

Manya also has a long, serious talk with Glinskaya, who tells her about her new book, The Crisis of Love, *in which she sorts through and evaluates different sorts of passion and love.*

From Manya Yeltsova to Sonya Gorlenko

"Bologna

I'm going to surprise you, dear Sonya. I'm leaving the stage. 'Why,' you'll cry. I've seen this cry in everyone's face, in all the papers. 'Poor dear!' Nils told me. 'Are you so sick?' Mark says nothing, but thinks the same way. I can imagine Iza's rage! I hear Agatha's reproaches. Oh, my God! Who'll understand me? Where is the person who will extend me his hand in this difficult moment?

If you think this is temporary insanity, or a whim, or a hysterical fit, then you're as mistaken as everyone else. If you say I don't love art, that'll be slander. It has given me the loftiest joys in my life, and I was born to be a performing artist. But where is the audience that can stir my heart?

I saw it once, that intimate audience for whom art is a holiday and the artist is a magician who brings oblivion, who has the power to make peace with reality. And the memory of this audience haunts me. I even see it in my dreams. Long ago I dimly foresaw meeting it. And if I didn't dream what I lived through in London . . .

Listen, Sonya! This crisis has been long in the making. When I've gone to the theater, I've always comforted myself with the thought that there are cheap seats (more or less, of course) and that these seats will be occupied by the poor—poets, students, clerks, porters. I thought of them while I performed. I lived and burned brightly on stage for this little group of people. When I answered curtain calls, I always looked up. But the more famous I became, the wider grew the gap between me and these people because they didn't have the enormous sums to attend. Remember, Sonya, who my public is: those sumptuous ladies with their muffs, those boring bald young men in smoking jackets, those polished military men, those bald, flabby tycoons. Chekhov's plays, Maeterlinck's fairy tales, Scriabin's inspired music, Isadora Duncan's dance of genius, Moissy's performances, Gorky's lines written in blood—all of this is entertainment for them! And the impertinent faces of the journalists? Can these people really penetrate the soul of a creator? Can they approach another's work with respect? This is what they can do—spit on others, humiliate them, whistle at them, drag them in the mud. This is the only thing they want to do.

'So much bitterness!' you're thinking. 'Ungrateful Manya!' Yes, I'm a lucky person. But I've only recently learned from Iza what it cost Mark (approximately, according to her calculations, he denies it all out of delicacy) to advertise me in all the cities where I perform. Without advertising neither my talent nor my passionate love of art would have made me successful. But advertising also makes mediocrity successful. And the hypnotized petty bourgeoisie accept this with the same respect they accord genuine artists. What good is their assessment?

Mark and Nils are still hoping for something. In vain. I'll pay an enormous forfeit and maybe I'll be poor once again. The papers will print a series of ridiculous articles. And with this scandal my artistic career will end.

But I want to dance the dance of the savages. I'm happy, happy! Only recently two paths lay before me—love and enslavement or freedom and art. I chose the latter. You don't know this page of my life. They're drenched in the blood of my heart. It's not worth remembering! Everything has passed. And life is once more before me. I'm standing on the heights and looking down. Countless paths run out in all directions. They're beckoning me. They're luring me into the unknown. Which will I choose? Which one will I take? I know one thing: each one leads me to a new life. I know one thing: there's no road back!"

Her decision made, Manya is gratified, momentarily, to receive a formal proposal from one of the members of the "stuck-up" British aristocracy, Nelidov's equals.

"Am I disturbing you? Excuse me! I'm so happy that you're feeling better at last."

Lord Littleton was a well-proportioned, elegant, dark-haired man with a refined, well-bred face. One wouldn't say he was fifty. He spoke excellent French, with a barely perceptible accent. His cold gray eyes rested on Manya's face with unconcealed rapture. And Manya liked this. When she was thanking him for the flowers, she was upset that her cheeks flushed. She wanted to exert more self-control. But she strived in vain to feel hostility for this Englishman. His passion had won her over.

The lord was shocked by her decision to leave the stage. Dared he ask why?

She replied evasively. She explained it all as a matter of exhaustion. She was noticeably agitated. It was wonderful that he controlled himself so well and conducted the discussion with such tact!

She answered distractedly, irrelevantly. Mark would be returning from Nice soon for breakfast. They shouldn't meet.

Suddenly he stopped talking, and Manya grew frightened. Now there'd take place what had long been in the making. Lord! If only she could disappear, fall through the floor . . .

"Miss Marion, you've guessed what I want to ask you?"

Manya bowed her head low. She could hear the tremor in that restrained, always dry voice. But why was she ashamed and feeling sorry? Why didn't she feel like reveling in her triumph?

"You've too refined a nature, miss, not to guess why I've been following you from city to city. Why I allow myself to dog you with my worship and make a display of it. I am asking you to be my wife, Marion . . ."

There they were, these words she'd so passionately pursued only a month ago with a refined, calculated flirtation. Why? To use him to humiliate Lady Fife and Lady Hamilton and all these haughty and stuck-up people who saw her and Nils as mere entertainment, as lesser beings? Oh, how remote and pale her injuries seemed to her now! Would Lady Hamilton hear of this confession of love? What did it matter now?

She raised her head with a tender, guilty smile and placed her hand affectionately on his coat sleeve.

"Milord, forgive me! There's some misunderstanding here. If I'd known . . ."

She saw how he turned pale. He was clenching his dry, sharp teeth. "My God! What have I done, base thing that I am! Why?"

"A misunderstanding? What do you mean to say?"

"You . . . you haven't heard? I've long been engaged to be married."

He made a movement.

"To Baron Steinbach?"

"Yes. It's such a pity that I didn't tell you then! But you didn't ask. Forgive me. Are you angry? Are you in pain?"

Almost weeping, she peered into his stony face.

His face softened. He stared at her thoughtfully. Then he took her hand and held it tenderly in his. And for the first time Manya felt the charm that emanated from this man. For the first time she felt their souls touch.

"Will you try to forget me?" she asked plaintively. "Will it be hard for you to remember me?"

"On the contrary. Allow me to write you from time to time. Leave me a small corner in your memory! I don't want to believe that you won't return to the stage. It would be too heavy a blow for me and an irreplaceable loss for art."

After he took his leave, kissing her hand with deference and tenderness, Manya listened to the ever quieter sound of his retreating footsteps. And she wept quietly. Over what? She was afraid to admit to herself that she was terribly sorry for. . . An opportunity that was forever lost? A page suddenly torn from her life? The words of love she didn't hear enough, that she could never get enough of? The intoxicating joy of conquering another's soul? My God! Why did they have to part now, when they'd first felt their souls' nearness? When she'd first recognized her attraction?

She could have experienced many marvelous minutes with this refined, educated, charming person.

Now this could not be. They wouldn't meet again. The game of love was finished. There was no freedom. One had to bring oneself in line. To constantly clip the soul's wings. Mark was jealous. Mark was suffering. Her infatuation with Harold had cost him dearly. He now clearly suffered from a heart ailment. A famous doctor had told him so in London. Any upset could kill him. And she'd never survive this loss!

"Why are you crying?" She heard Steinbach's voice.

"Ah, you've come back, Mark! It's nothing. . . Don't pay any attention. Kiss me, Mark! I'll smile right now."

But Steinbach was cold. His brows were furrowed

"I met Lord Littleton on the way. Was he here?"

"Yes, yes. He came to say goodbye. He's going away."

Steinbach sat down at a distance and thought gloomily about something.

"Why were you weeping? Were you sorry to part with him?"

She was silent, scrutinizing her fingers. She'd stopped crying. His cold stare and interrogation irritated her.

She'd felt such sweetness in making the sacrifice for him. Bitterness and anger rose up in her throat and began to choke her.

"Speak frankly. And please, don't have any mercy. What do you need? Dictate your terms. Are you ordering me to go away again?"

He let these words drop slowly, with an unpleasant smile. He'd posed a question and was waiting for the answer.

She got up suddenly with burning eyes.

"Go away! Go away! Don't you dare torment me. Don't you dare toy with me!"

"I'm toying with you?"

"Yes, you are. Yes! You toss me like some rag from Nelidov to Harold, and from Harold to Littleton, and even to some organ-grinder."

"Well put. It seems that I'm to blame?"

"Yes, you alone are to blame. Why do you suffer everything in silence? Why don't you get upset? Why don't you fight for your happiness? Or is it so cheap to you? Or do you think that I'll always come back to you, no matter what the circumstances? Yes? Or are you afraid to test your strength . . ."

"Or?"

"Or is this some devilish arrogance? You think I can't live a day without you? That the world will become empty without your love? Fine is the love that knows no jealousy!"

"Why do you think I'm not jealous?"

Manya leapt up with trembling lips.

"You're lying! You don't know how to love. You're incapable of jealousy. If Nils had been in your place, he'd have locked me up, or maybe have beaten me, he'd insult this lord, challenge him to a duel, kill him, me, and himself in the end! This is what jealous people do. But your soul is helpless and your feeling is weak. Yes! Yes!" she cried, staring defiantly as Steinbach slowly turned pale.

She herself had paled suddenly from the whirlwind of madness and despair that had swept her up. But she couldn't stop. It was as if demons had taken hold of her soul and shouted these cruel words for her.

"Well, know this, that he proposed to me, he asked me to be his wife. And I didn't reject him. You hear? I didn't reject him. I promised to think it over. Mark! Mark!" she shouted wildly, rushing after Steinbach. "Where are you going! Stop, what do you mean to do?"

"Does it really matter to you?"

"Wait, Mark . . . listen! My God! What's wrong with you? Your heart? Have I killed you? Mark . . . Mark. . . It's a lie. I've gone mad. I need no one but you. No one in the world!"

She rang the bell. Steinbach was already lying down on the couch, clutching at his heart. Sinister dark blue shadows appeared on his face.

"Call the doctor at once!" she shouted to the servant. And she poured out some water with trembling hands. "Drink this. Wait, where are the drops? Do you have them?"

She came back. She quickly and deftly made a compress from the clay Steinbach always had nearby.

Steinbach tried to smile.

"Mark! My happiness!" she whispered through her tears, dropping to her knees before him and kissing his hands. "How could you believe me? I'll never see him again. I love you, my treasure... Forgive me, madwoman that I am. I'll never grieve you again. I'll never make you suffer. Tell me what I should do to prove my love for you?"

"Marry me, Manya," he whispered in a barely audible voice. "Then I'll believe you."

She pressed her face into his shoulder and wept.

"Do you agree?"

"My God! Yes, if that's what you want! Aren't you and Nina my only happiness?"

From Manya Yeltsova to Sonya Gorlenko

"Dear Sonya, we've returned to Paris, and tomorrow is our wedding.

'At last!' you'll say, loving Mark as you do with such a lofty, radiant feeling, stripped of jealousy and unfathomable to me. But for me, believe me, this wedding is a surprise. I'd long ago stopped thinking about marriage to Mark. Could this really add anything to my feeling for him?

How did it happen? You see, while we were in London we poisoned each other's lives for days on end. I was madly jealous of one woman. I was simply beside myself with jealousy. And once I even struck him, for God's sake. Don't hate me. It was terrible, Sonya! If he'd gotten angry, it would've been easier. But he grabbed my hands and said in a tone that pierced my soul: 'Poor, poor child!' Then I suddenly felt guilty and started sobbing. Mark had compared me with a child who'd gotten hold of a knife. And this child was wounding herself, and shouting, and crying, and involuntarily wounding all those who wanted to disarm her and calm her down. There was no living spot in my soul. My God! It's so fortunate that this nightmare passed away!

Mark was also jealous on my account of a very interesting man, an aesthete and balletomane. You remember my pearls? Lord L. gave them to me as a present from him and a group of admirers during my first visit. Then he became my shadow and followed me from city to city. I gave Mark my word that we'd never meet again. And I've kept it. He told me: 'If it's a matter of a passing infatuation or a caprice, I'm always ready to go off for a while. I don't want to force anything. I'm afraid that you'll later regret the lost moment. Your happiness is dearer to me than my peace. But to be deprived of you altogether, to see you become another's wife—that means dying to me.' Can you understand his psychology? Such high-minded self-denial is foreign to me, for I'm jealous and passionate and greedy for joy.

We've avoided publicity. But the repulsive street still didn't spare us. There appeared articles about the marriage of a Russian millionaire to a famous barefoot dancer, with our pictures, etc. I tore them from the newspapers with a shudder, as if they were slippery and smelly frogs. Tomorrow evening a train will bear us far away from the spectators and the journalists, to some place in the mountains, in the wilderness where only Silence will greet us. We'll be alone together. We'll listen to the quiet. I'll press myself to his heart.

Agatha is rejoicing. Iza is angry. It's a good thing that Nils stayed in Monte-Carlo! I fear he'd beat me. . . .

I'm alone. I feel like crying. Why? I don't know. I'm gazing at Mark's picture. The magnificent eyebrows. The sad eyes. The sorrowful smile. Will I make him happy? He's asked for nothing. I've promised nothing. Ah, he's so smart not to set value by words and vows! But I sense that, like a true Semite by blood (despite the fact that he's an Aryan in his soul), he ascribes great meaning to rituals that, for me, are empty formalities. He thinks that marriage will bind us still closer. No. We're bound by these years of suffering, when we walked hand in hand along the steep path. And I vow never to abandon my true comrade—the noblest being on earth. I kiss his picture and weep. Sonya, you won't laugh at me. Why are we apart in these minutes when my heart is full of him alone? He's never seen such happy tears. He's never seen such an outburst of tenderness. And if right now . . ."

She suddenly got up, completely pale, and threw aside the pen.

In the middle of the night Steinbach heard the doorbell.

"A telegram," he thought, turning on the light. "Something important. From Petersburg. From Semyon Nikolayevich. Do I have to go there again? Leave Manya? How sad! I'm so tired."

There was a knock at the front door. Footsteps. A woman's steps, the rustle of a dress.

He sat up in bed. Manya? Nina? Had anything happened? His vision darkened, and his heart pounded fiercely.

"Is it you, Frau Kessler?" he cried at a light knock on the door. "Wait, I'll be out in a moment."

"It's I, Mark! I!"

Manya burst into the room like a force of nature. She fell on her knees beside his bed, in her hat and coat. He saw her tearstained eyes.

"Nina?" he whispered, clutching his heart.

"Mark, I had to see you. I had to tell you . . . I'll suffocate if I don't speak . . ."

"My God! What is it? Speak."

"I love you, Mark. I love you madly. And you alone. Do you hear? You alone in the whole world."

"Dear child! Why are you crying? Stand up."

"No, no, I'm so base, so vile, I've tortured you all these years. And here again. . . My God!"

"It's nothing. Give me some water! It will pass."

"I've killed you, Mark. You have heart disease."

"It's nerves. Don't cry."

"No, no, let me stand before you like this! It feels better to . . . repent so and . . . cry."

"There, you see, you yourself are in terrible shape. Why aren't you sleeping nights?"

"Oh, Mark, Mark! This has been such a happy night! And my tears have been so sweet. I wanted so madly to embrace you, to vow to you . . ."

"No vows are necessary."

She wrung her hands.

"There, you see, you don't want to believe me."

She fell face-down on the blanket.

"My beloved Manechka," he spoke sadly, seating her beside him. "I'm incredibly touched. Your outburst is so beautiful! I thank you for this."

She turned away and didn't let him kiss her tearstained face.

"You don't believe anything!" she burst out in despair. "If you believed me, you wouldn't thank me. You can't forgive me anything."

"Manechka, dear, I'm the happiest man. I thought that you'd changed, that there'd be no more such marvelous outbursts."

"Why? Why did you think so? Oh, Mark! Embrace me with trust. Forget the past. I swear to you that I'll make you suffer no more. I'm going to take care of your poor sick heart. It's my treasure. I'll tremble night and day over this treasure."

"Calm yourself, Manya. Drink some water! Wait, I'll give you some drops. Turn away."

"There's no need! Don't get up. Hold me close to your heart, like this, and listen, listen . . ."

"Yes."

"And believe my every word . . ."

"Yes."

"I swear on Nina's life," her voice sounded triumphant and passionate, and her eyes were filled with terror. "I swear by all that is sacred to me in this world that I will be your faithful wife."

"Manya, don't, be still."

". . . that I'll never deceive you, that I'll never cheat on you."

"Manechka, my God!"

". . . and even if I meet and fall in love with another, I'll joyfully . . ."

Groaning, he closed her lips with a kiss.

But she pulled away, pale and trembling, and concluded with a tragic gesture and tragic expression: ". . . I'll joyfully sacrifice my happiness for you, and you, Mark, will never know of this sacrifice!"

He pressed the sobbing Manya to him. It was good that she didn't see his sorrowful smile!

Back in Ukraine, Uncle visits Nelidov, and informs him that Manya has wed Steinbach. He also tells him about Nils's love for Marion and his wife's consequent suicide.

"A fatal woman," Nelidov said suddenly, coming to a halt at the table and looking with melancholy at the magazine that Uncle had insidiously covered with his elbow. "Don't you find that she's fatal? And could Nils possibly have forgiven her his wife's death?"

"But how is she to blame, Nikolay Yuryevich? Surely you don't blame the sun for the fact that it burns you? How can it not burn you?"

"That's terrible!" Nelidov said after a pause, passing his hand over his eyes. "Poor woman! What she lived through."

"And note that she was religious. Consequently, her soul's drama . . ."

Nelidov suddenly stopped in the middle of the room.

"It can't be! A religious person wouldn't dare take his life. He carries his cross in silence."

Uncle was so struck by the expression on his face and his intonation that for a second he didn't know what to say.

"Yes, yes, of course. He carries it while he has the strength to do so. And what if his strength gives out? Surely you allow the possibility of such a paroxysm of emotion that a person stops believing not only in people, but in God, too?"

"Then that's madness, acute insanity."

The two men disagree, and before leaving Nelidov takes one last glance at Manya's naked form. On his way home, Nelidov reminisces about his past with Manya. Upon arriving home, he turns to Katya with passion and resumes a sexual life with her. But Katya still has a presentiment of disaster.

Lika and Nelidov discuss local matters. In the meantime, Manya informs Iza that she is returning to the stage, but now as a folk artist. Not wishing to rely on Steinbach's money, she plans to fund her appearances by selling her villa and her jewelry. She and Mark return to the Tyrol for a month, but Manya cannot recapture her former sense of joy.

In France, Manya encounters Xavier, who commends her for having discovered a means of "justifying her life." Meeting Nadezhda Storozhenko, an activist originally from the Lipovka area, in Vienna, Manya and Steinbach leave with her, Frau Kessler, and Nina for Lipovka. Mme. Storozhenko's political activities necessitate that she travel incognito, as Manya's aunt.

It was almost evening by the time they drove past Likhoy Gai. The horses slowly made their way uphill as Vasily Petrovich turned round on the driver's seat and said:

"Here's where they shot at Nelidov in the spring."

"But they didn't kill him, did they?" Steinbach interrupted quickly.

"He escaped injury only by chance."

Manya closed her eyes and leaned heavily against the back of the carriage.

"Who's Nelidov?" Nadezhda Petrovna asked.

"The local representative of the nobility. He's waiting to be appointed governor. He has aspirations to becoming a minister, people say. Has strong connections. The people don't like him. An interesting character," Vasily Petrovich smiled, his lips twisting. "Tough and fearless. He'll end badly."

"So that's the state of affairs here!" Nadezhda Petrovna joined in gaily, looking intently into the depths of the gloomy forest.

Manya raised her eyelids. For the first time she looked at the woman who was so dear to her with alien, surprised eyes. Then she shifted her gaze to Mark. He was disconcerted and avoided her glance. He'd known that, and he'd kept it from her. She also gazed at the gnarled oak trees. And gradually she stopped hearing what the people around her were saying, while the forest seemed to whisper to her.

When they arrive at Steinbach's estate, they discover it and Ostap, Steinbach's old servant, unchanged.

Steinbach walked ahead with his wife, pressing her arm firmly against his body and kissing her fingers. Here it was, the moment for which he'd long been waiting, about which he'd dreamed so passionately!

Manya's face was pale. Her eyes gazed into the distance, at the dark clumps of trees in the park. Could there be anything more elevated than the moments she'd experienced there?

"I didn't expect anything like this," Frau Kessler said as she entered the double-lit hall.

But Manya and Steinbach were already running to the study.

He locked the door. From the gilded frame the eyes of the beautiful Jewess followed them with a mysterious menace. Lusterless, bottomless eyes that were familiar. But Manya didn't fear them now.

Her eyes moist, she took a long look around the room. It was here, that very evening, that she'd danced semi-naked. O, life! Wonderful, majestic life. You don't repeat yourself.

She cried upon Steinbach's chest.

He'd waited for this moment, he'd thirsted for those tears. He forgave her everything for shedding them, all the sufferings he'd endured and would endure again.

Manya visits all her old haunts, including Yan's grave, where she weeps and reminisces.

Then she sat on the bench at his grave.

Six years had passed since the morning when Yan said to her: "I'll give you the keys to happiness. The most valuable thing we have are our passions, our dreams. Wretched is the person who disavows them!"

Hugging her knees and clasping her fingers, she gazed into the lofty sky shining through the foliage, and thought:

"Well, Yan, I've come to you. I've returned to your grave after a hard and long journey to the top. I fulfilled your precept: I didn't disavow my dream, and I freed my soul from love. I weep over it as a loving collector weeps over a priceless vase that's been shattered into pieces. But I bless my tears. And I love my sufferings . . ."

"Yes," she thought, "My soul straightened out and my sorrows are forgotten. Perhaps the Dream for which I sacrificed happiness has paled, but another one is ignited. It will illuminate my whole life till the end, whenever it may come and wherever it may overtake me. The past is wonderful and love is wonderful. But what I've managed to win back from life is dearer to me than my delirium, than my madness, than what people call happiness. Are you pleased with me, Yan?"

Steinbach joins her, and, recalling the first stages of their liaison, observes how much Manya has changed.

They were having breakfast when the servant announced:

"Fyodor Filippych from Lysogory and the young lady."

Manya ran out to greet them, Steinbach hurrying after her.

"My dears! Dear friends!" Manya said joyfully, and, moving from Sonya's embrace, threw herself on the embarrassed Uncle's breast.

"I don't know what to call you now . . ."

"Manya, of course. Uncle, you're just as elegant!"

"Come, now! I've not kept up at all," Uncle protested flirtatiously, smoothing the graying hair at his temples. "But you've really become a beauty."

"Don't address me formally!" cried Manya, seizing his shoulders. "For you I want to be the young girl I was before."

Her left brow arched, her eyes sparkled, and one could see the dimples in her cheeks. Yet she wasn't the same as before. What a supple, shapely figure! And the dress . . . Sonya felt a trifle ashamed. The dress hugged her figure, without a single fold apart from a narrow train. It looked as if she wasn't wearing a skirt. And all the lines and forms of her body were visible through the fine material, as if Manya were naked. But Uncle was in ecstasy.

"It's the new fashion in Paris," Manya explained. "There's no skirt, only tights." Laughing, she raised her dress and showed her feet in the pale blue material and bright, small shoes.

Sonya blushed. The men roared with laughter.

"At least don't go out into the street in such a dress! The children will run after you," Sonya whispered. It was just as it had been in high school.

"My dear little puritan! I have no other dresses."

They led their guests into the dining room and introduced them to Uncle Joseph and Nadezhda Petrovna. Uncle Joseph at once stood up.

"Where are you going?" Manya asked in chagrin.

But the old man gently removed her hands and, stooped, made his way down the terrace steps. He disappeared around the turn of the tree-lined walk.

"He's got so gray!" Uncle thought with relief as he looked at Steinbach's temples. "His skin is still like ivory, but his eyes have completely lost their fire. Life with Manechka is evidently not easy. He looks so much like his uncle now! In the evening you couldn't tell them apart if they wore the same sort of hat!"

"My daughter," Steinbach said, lifting Ninochka by her arms from her highchair.

And Uncle grew embarrassed again. "Surely he can see that she's the spitting image of Nelidov?"

"What an enchanting child!" he babbled.

Sonya and Manya draw apart, and the former is surprised at Manya's newfound democratic attitudes. Uncle invites Manya and Steinbach to visit them the next day.

Steinbach and Uncle were holding a conversation beside the boiling samovar on the terrace in Lysogory. Vera Filippovna was nervous, her face splotched with color. Gorlenko was also perceptibly embarrassed, and smoked in silence, breathing heavily. Of course they were happy to see Manya. What had happened in the past was the past. She'd married, and that put an end to it. No one could deny they were good neighbors! And she'd also become a real beauty! One could only marvel. Vera Filippovna was even proud of her, and all the petty trifles and unpleasant things were forgotten. They'd remembered only the strange little girl—naive and kind—with the enormous eyes. And now this girl was a celebrity and Steinbach's wife. But her clothes struck them as outright indecent! She'd lifted her dress when she'd run down from the terrace, and under them there had been only tights. She seemed naked. "These women artists really have no shame," Vera Filippovna thought with a certain satisfaction.

Having gulped down a cup of tea and thrown off her picturesque hat with the enormous brim, Manya seized Sonya under the arm and ran off with her into the garden.

Here, too, Manya succumbs to the lure of memories about the past.

"Dear little girl. . . You have a wonderful face. And your smile is happy, it knows no grief. There's a whole world in your eyes. What's the secret of your joy—that elemental, blinding joy, which breathes through every cell of your thin body? Remember, however, remember—what did you expect from life? Love. The sun illuminated only one facet of your soul. The others were in sad darkness. And what did love bring you, except tears and sufferings? After losing that small joy, you wanted to repudiate the sun, laughter, and your transports and dreams. You sought death, poor girl."

Those were the thoughts of the celebrated Marion as she sat, eyes closed, seized by the irresistible enchantment of the past! And her very sorrows, the happy sorrows of youth, seemed dearer to her than all her joys and achievements.

When Manya joins the others, Sonya notices the change in her mood. They return to Steinbach's estate.

"What a beauty!" Nadezhda Petrovna said, her arm linked with Manya's as she paused in front of the portrait of Steinbach's mother. "She looks as if she's alive. What a wondrous portrait! Her eyes look tragic. She wasn't happy with your father, Mark Aleksandrovich!"

"That's right. She committed suicide."

Manya gazed intently into the mysterious eyes.

"Mark, why didn't I see this portrait here before?"

He turned round in surprise. Her voice had changed.

"Because six years ago you were here only once, in my study, and the portrait was in my bedroom."

"Sing us something, Mark Aleksandrovich," Nadezhda Petrovna requested. "You have such an enchanting voice!"

He sat down at the piano. The windows were open. The dark July night did not waft any coolness into the room, which was softly illuminated. It was so comfortable to listen, with eyes closed, as one lay back in the luxurious armchairs.

Steinbach was gloomy. And if Manya had not been so full of that strange, anguished, venomous melancholy that had poisoned her soul in the summerhouse in the park at Lysogory, she wouldn't have been able to bypass his unhappiness. He'd spent the entire day roaming around the park, recalling Lia and everything that he'd lost with her death. But what would be changed if she'd not died? Wasn't he chained to Manya's chariot as her pathetic slave?

He sat down at the piano and began to sing, his thoughts on Lia and the poor joy that her love had brought him. But the sounds of his genuinely enchanting voice, apart from the words, awakened in the soul of each listener the sorrow of unrealized desires, a yearning for what life hadn't given them. And the sweet pain stimulated tears that couldn't be shed. Words came to mind that could never be spoken. And for a long time after the last chord faded everyone was silent, overwhelmed. The yearning that had filled every sound of his deep voice involuntarily demanded silence. They spoke in whispers, and no one applauded.

One day, when Steinbach's uncle and Nina's nurse take the child out for a ride, she is almost run over by a carriage. Its passenger is Nelidov, who, upon learning from the nurse that Nina is Steinbach's daughter, returns, shaken, to his carriage.

But some power seemed to force him to look back. Ninochka was running toward the ditch, where some yellow flowers grew. She merrily chattered away in German. Nelidov took the little girl in his arms. For a moment his greedy, sick eyes gazed into the child's frightened face. Nina wanted to shout, but was afraid. He passionately kissed her eyes, her cheeks, and her convulsively distorted little mouth, then put her down again.

"A-a-ah," Ninochka shouted in resentment.

But he'd already leaped into the carriage and the horses were moving off. The gloomy old man gazed after him with tension and alarm.

The nurse makes much of the incident when they return to Steinbach's estate, while back home Nelidov finds himself unbearably agitated.

The little girl on the dusty road. Nothing but that little girl. Everything had perished: the structure of the life he'd worked out and the peace he'd bought so dearly. His lips still retained the scent of the delicate little face, the touch of her long eyelashes. His lashes. He smelled the perfume of those proud little lips on his own mouth. *Her* child. *His* child. How could he have any doubts? His son, the heir to his name, didn't resemble him in any respect. He'd taken completely after his mother, a little beetle, with enormous dark eyes. Whereas the little girl was a Nelidov. No, a Galitskaya, with his mother's chiseled features. Hidden somewhere in a cupboard was Anna Lvovna's old album, which she'd saved during the fire. And if one found in it the yellowed photograph of Nelidov, taken when he was five, then one would see the haughty little face of the blonde girl, whom his horse had almost killed that morning.

And suddenly reality vanished. A whirlwind emptied his soul, tormented by remorse, of everything by which he'd lived before. He saw before him Sonya's letter, saw himself at the train station in Venice. Hadn't he rushed there in a mad burst of love and pity, so as to consign everything to oblivion, so as to clasp this girl, the mother of his child, to his breast? Ah, why hadn't he succumbed to this burst of feeling completely? Wasn't she the sole love of his life? Wasn't she the first, the only one who'd found in his soul that great, rare treasure—Tenderness? And wasn't it from this tenderness that his vanquished heart had started trembling during that dark July night in the summerhouse, when he'd arrived at the rendezvous with her in the park at Lysogory?

To forget everything. To forgive everything. No! That he couldn't do. His wonderful burst of feeling would soon wane. And once again the dark figure, which he'd met at the pier in Venice, like an ominous symbol, would rise between them. He knew himself. He couldn't forget the past of the woman he loved.

Steinbach's calculation had been accurate. Nelidov had fallen into the trap set by his enemy. Blinded by jealousy and revenge, he'd lost his last possibility for reconciliation—the very thing he'd gone looking for after receiving Sonya's letter. It was then that he lost his way to happiness.

"Enough! Enough!" he tried to convince hiself. "What kind of happiness would it have been? A momentary reconciliation and hours of bitterness. Jealousy, reproaches, sufferings. Hatred and mistrust. Happiness is hardly possible without faith. And can one really have faith in someone like her? It's all for the best. I need to get a grip on myself. To forget the past, realize my responsibilities. Not be untrue to myself."

"Nikolenka-a-a," Katya's voice, as if in a dream, sounded from afar. "The manager's waiting for you."

The governor once again visits the area, and he and Steinbach discuss local unrest. The governor informs Steinbach of a report the authorities have received about him, and questions him about Nadezhda Petrovna. The governor notes that Steinbach's former gardener (Yan) was Prince Sitsky, who was wanted by the authorities. After the governor leaves, Lika, in a quick exchange with Nadezhda Petrovna, implicitly agrees to assassinate him. Steinbach ensures Nadezhda Petrovna's safe departure from his estate. In the meantime, Manya sees a strangely familiar face when she peers out at night into the darkness. And once, when out riding, she believes she espies Nelidov's silhouette. Steinbach's uncle informs Manya that his sister, Sarra, whom Manya resembles, died in precisely this area. Manya takes to roaming about the environs at all hours of the day and evening.

It was already growing dark when she approached the slope leading to the glen where the dam and pond separated Lysogory from the wide road to Lipovka.

Somewhere behind the poplars a horse neighed, and someone emerged soundlessly from the darkness.

"Don't be afraid!" she heard a familiar voice. "It's me."

She stopped and couldn't breathe. The blood rushed to her heart with such force, causing it to pound so madly, that Manya was deafened. What was he saying? What were the words he was uttering?

"Do you recognize me?" he asked timidly, stooping to look into her face.

"Yes, I recognize you. I've been waiting for you for a long time, Nikolenka."

He drew back as if she'd struck him in the chest.

"Is this a dream or not? I'll wake up any moment . . ." she thought.

"I also sought this meeting. I've thought about you a great deal. I'm terribly guilty before you."

"You? Before me?"

She was silent for a moment.

"What are you guilty of before me, Nikolenka?" she asked sadly, tenderly, after finally managing to get a grip on herself.

But horror seized Nelidov at that tender voice. He couldn't control an inner tremor.

"Why are you speaking *like that?* Why are you addressing me familiarly? You're another's wife. Don't call me Nikolenka."

She laughed quietly and sadly.

"How do you want me to call you now, when all these years when I thought of you that was what I called you?"

"All these years? What do you mean?"

She heard his breathing, saw his suffering gaze. Yet she couldn't awaken. A dream . . . a dream. None of it was waking reality. It was an embodied vision. The approaching night was practicing witchcraft. And she was afraid of even stirring, of speaking loudly.

"Marie, hear me out! Take the weight off my soul. The other day I ran into a little girl on the forest road . . ."

"That's your daughter, Nikolenka. Now do you believe it?"

She heard a strange noise resembling suppressed sobs.

"Ah. . . You'll never forgive me that baseness!"

She quietly went up to him and took his hand. She was terrified of waking up. No, this wasn't a dream! This was his hand, small, hot, and strong. But why was his whole body trembling? Why did he pull back his hand? A bottomless, boundless pity suddenly entered her soul and left its mark.

"I've forgiven everything, Nikolenka," she answered in a profound voice.

She wordlessly gazed at his face, which grew pale in the semidarkness, at the luxuriant wavy hair, at his capricious brows. He once again saw her unforgettable eyes and firmly clenched his teeth. He feared himself. Someone dark and frightening gazed out of his eyes at this alien woman, whom he had possessed. And he couldn't let him have his way. Not a word, not a movement!

Otherwise everything by which he'd lived would collapse and crush him under the debris.

Steinbach's uncle suddenly appears, but Manya tells him that Nelidov is Nina's father and won't harm her, then persuades him to leave. As Nelidov and Manya leave the area, Nelidov yearns to possess her again, and simultaneously thinks of death as a solution. They agree to meet at the same place the next day. At home, reviewing their encounter, Manya realizes that she has "come a long way" since the day she attempted suicide on account of Nelidov. When Manya tells Steinbach of her planned tryst with Nelidov, he fears the revelation of his having kept secret from Manya Nelidov's presence in Venice. Manya waits for Nelidov at their assignation point.

She rose, so strange, so exotic in her narrow white dress, which hugged all the lines of her body, leaving her neck and arms exposed—so enigmatic among the peaceful fields, resembling some troubled dream. She saw the greedy, amazed glance he cast over her figure. And a feeling of alienation suddenly crept in a cold stream into Manya's soul. "His wife wouldn't wear such a dress," the thought flashed through her mind. "But what do I care about his censure! And why are my cheeks burning like this? Even my eyes hurt."

He kissed her hand, which she extended to him with a regal air, all alien and haughty. His kiss was long and ardent. And her soul instantly grew dark. She recalled Katya. She recalled her own pain when he'd rejected her. And if his eyes flared with passion, she wouldn't allow him a single movement. "Men don't marry women like you," the cruel voice sounded from a distance. That's how he spoke with her. O, his passion wouldn't find an echo in her soul! "I no longer find it frightening. I've grown up. I'm strong."

"Forgive me for looking like this, but I've come straight from work. Have you been waiting long? Please excuse me. I didn't want the workers to see where I was going."

How timid his voice sounded! How uncertain his gestures! Her gaze softened. There was no need for hostility. This moment would pass, and they would never meet again.

"Let's sit down, Nikolenka!" she said with a sigh, sitting down on the hillock. "Let's stay here until the sun goes down."

"Marie, I acted like a madman. I shouldn't have summoned you here. We could be seen here at any moment."

"What are you afraid of, Nikolenka?"

"I should protect your name. You're married."

"Be quiet. Don't ruin my mood. I've been waiting a long time for you. I've waited six years for this meeting. Don't speak. Don't start reminiscing. Let me dream with my eyes open! Forget that I have a husband and that your wife is waiting for you. Surely you can feel that these are all phantoms? And the truth is only you and I, and this burial mound, and this sunset?"

"If only that were so!" the bitter exclamation was torn from him.

He looked around, but there was nobody in the area. Somewhere below, in the valley, a herd was moving along and there was the loud crack of a whip. In the distance one could see some geese, as if snow had fallen on the black, plowed field. A tiny barefoot little girl was chasing them in the direction of the farm.

Nelidov sat down at Manya's feet, on the dry grass that had turned brown, and from below stared at her face, alien and rosy in the sunset, with her new hairdo and her strange, dreamy expression. But it was a seductive, sinful face, intoxicating, like the scent of a tuberose that makes the heart pound and the head spin. He struggled with himself, squeezing his hands and clenching his teeth, trying to look away. But he lacked the strength, for the moment would vanish and the next day there'd be nothing left apart from a burning memory.

"Are you happy, Marie?" the words were involuntarily torn from him. "Do you love your husband?"

She was looking at the sun.

"Look, it's about to set! There's just a teeny-weeny bit left, just the edge . . ."

He timidly took her hand and kissed it passionately.

"How you've changed, Marie! To me you've become a new and alien woman."

"Look! Look!" With a tender movement she turned his head toward the sunset. "It's about to disappear . . ."

"Your face is completely different."

"And now it's gone," she said with a profound sigh.

And suddenly in her eyes, in her smile he saw once again the girl who had disappeared long ago—his Manya, whom he'd loved so passionately. It was as if she'd peered out of the window of a stranger's house and sadly smiled at him. His agitation was so acute that he couldn't say a word and, paling, shut his eyes.

"Do you remember, Nikolenka, our first meeting right here?" she asked dreamily, just as the former Manya would have done.

"Here? No, I don't. You're wrong . . ."

She gently moved away and coldly, sadly, looked at the fading strip of sun, at the clouds bathed in the sun's rays high above them in the sky.

"And now I've lost you again," he said with melancholy. "Once again I don't recognize you."

"Have I become better or worse?" she asked in a strange and matter-of-fact voice, without a trace of coquetry.

"I—don't know. I can't tell, Marie. It's a pleasure to look at you. And it's also terrible!"

She sat bolt upright and her lips quivered pitifully. What was happening? After all, she was strong, proud, and had grown up. He'd stayed the same. What did she have to fear now? But her innocent joy was disrupted. She could no longer yield to the spontaneous enjoyment of his proximity. A split started within her, and this strong and proud woman again gazed into her heart in alarm, where arose the mute phantom of the girl who had yearned for love and subjugation.

With difficulty, her lips instantly grown dry, she said:

"You've been happy all these years, Nikolenka. I know you love your wife, you have children, and your life is full . . ."

He raised his head and gazed at her in silence. And now for the first time she saw how emaciated he'd become and older, how sharp lines were scored around his once scarlet and now pale lips, how a deep wrinkle cut into his white brow, and what sadness lurked in his sunken eyes. If this was happiness . . .

"Nikolenka," she said in sudden fear, leaning over him, "Let's forget everything! Let's not say a word. Can you hear how quiet it is? What a world surrounds us. Why should we suffer? It's not as though we've done anything wrong. And was it really possible for us not to meet? O, Nikolenka, help me! Let's be like children. . . Value this moment. It won't ever return. Now we're alone, Nikolenka, alone in the whole wide world!"

Why was he so pale? Why did he look at her so strangely? And why was despair rising in her own soul, which began to waver and flicker, like a candle in the wind? He held her hands so tightly that they hurt. Her voice and her panic penetrated his blood like poison.

"Nikolenka," the words escaped her lips plaintively, helplessly. "Tell me that you're happy! I'll be pleased for you. Tell me that you're happy! All these years I saw you as happy, arrogant. Why aren't you?"

He pushed her hands aside and fell face-down on the ground at her feet.

For a moment she sat motionless, as if in a stupor, her lips half-parted, gazing at some spot before her.

"Is it that . . . you didn't stop loving me, Nikolenka?"

She heard muffled, tearless sobs.

Everything wilted in her soul. Everything was on the point of collapse. Everything dimmed. An enormous, dark wave arose, and she felt she was perishing.

He lay there, face down, his whole body shuddering.

"Nikolenka, my dear child . . ."

She had no words. Everything was powerless and vapid before the great burst of feeling that overcame her. She raised his head, pressed her face against his and stroked his hair. His long lashes tickled her cheeks. And her heart once again fluttered with profound feeling.

"Marie, I had reason to be afraid of you. You left, but you shattered my life."

"But don't you love Katya?"

"My God, no! No! I yearned to fool myself. I thought I loved her. All my life, all these years were a complete and utter lie. I dreamed of you . . . all those nights . . . all my dreams were only of you."

A mad yearning to nestle close to his heart, the elemental yearning for sacrifice, for *self-destruction* in love—all this was burgeoning in her soul, paralyzing her will. His darkened eyes beckoned her somewhere.

"I love you, Nikolenka," she whispered unconsciously.

"Marie, what did you say?"

She let him embrace her. He kissed her face, her lips. For a second she thought she would lose consciousness from the searing bliss. Wasn't this, in fact, the truth? The only truth in the world?

Sitting upright now, eyes closed, he remained at her feet.

Something had occurred just then, fatal and irreversible. Something enormous and awesome had loomed in his path and cast an ominous shadow on his soul; his transports faded instantly. Again, as had happened in Venice, he was standing at the outer edge, on some threshold. Just one step and—there'd be Silence.

She got up first and, staggering, completely shattered, leaned on his shoulder.

Hand in hand, they slowly made their way amidst the darkening fields without noticing their own silence.

Suddenly he stopped.

"Surely this isn't the last time we'll see each other, Marie?"

"That's impossible, Nikolenka! I'll die if you disappear from my life again. Once again, just once . . . I didn't say everything I wanted to. My soul is hungry. I should tell you how much I love you, my dear child, how madly I love you . . ."

"That's terrible, Marie! Terrible, yet it brings me happiness."

"My God! How can I go back home? How will I live through this night? Home! But where is my home?" She laughed painfully. "Isn't that wherever you are?"

She twined her arms around his neck and cried.

"Don't cry, Marie! It's terrible. It undermines my courage."

His hand stroked her hair. She grew calm beneath his caress, and smiled through her tears.

"Ah, this tenderness of yours—I dreamed of it so passionately once, tried to awaken it in you. You know, that's the most terrible thing, Nikolenka! I can remember everything coldly. I can forget everything. But this caress. . . What should I do now? What can I do? What?"

She started crying again, leaning into his shoulder, then suddenly lifted her head.

"Aren't you afraid now, Nikolenka?"

"Yes, I am. And I know why. Because I can't live without you, and I don't dare live with you."

"So you did finally sense that. Death always accompanies such a love. I know that, I've already experienced it."

He passionately clasped her to him.

"Let's die together, Marie!" she heard his voice, full of despair.

He brought his lips down on hers, and, shuddering with terror and rapture, she felt once again her lack of will where this man was concerned. It was as if the earth receded from beneath her feet. The dark voice of powerful instinct called her from the mysterious abyss. Dark waves rose and extinguished her consciousness. She remembered them. She knew what they meant. Her soul yearned for enslavement. There was no more freedom. It was over. Everything was over!

The creak of a carriage sounded. Someone was coming from the farm, and there was the sound of voices.

They broke their embrace, with, oh, such pain. Squeezing her hands, helpless to overcome her inner trembling, Manya peered tensely into the semidarkness. Had they recognized her? It made no difference.

The carriage drew level. Simple, unfamiliar faces. A simple, mysterious life. They removed their caps respectfully and humbly bowed their heads. The workday was over, and it was time to rest and sleep.

"Marie, it's grown completely dark, and we've got to go our separate ways today. It's awful, but we must. Your husband . . ."

"Be quiet! I don't have a husband. Surely you understood that, Nikolenka, now, during those moments? Surely you understood that I'm your wife before God, before the heavens above. And that there's nobody and nothing that can come between us?"

Shaken by her voice, he closed his eyes. And suddenly Katya, pitiful, deceived little Katya—so close and at the same time alien to him—seemed to gaze at him from out of the darkness.

Guessing his thoughts, Manya took his slack hand in hers.

"Nikolenka, tell me what I should do. Should I follow you? Should I disappear from your life? Give me your orders! I'll do everything you say. I'll find the strength. Don't think about me. There isn't a sacrifice I wouldn't be willing to make so as to see you happy, or at least peaceful, as you were all these years. After all, you managed to live without me. Tell me! My love won't flinch from anything! If only you don't suffer."

"Why did you come back, Marie?" the question was torn from him like a moan.

She embraced his head. She clasped him to her the way a mother would her child.

"Nikolenka, if only I'd ever surmised that you'd suffer. I felt that you hadn't forgotten me. You're not the sort to forget. But I thought that you could reconcile yourself. I see I was wrong. Nikolenka, what madness parted us, who were created for each other?"

She could smell the scent of his body, his dear breath. The taste of his kisses remained on her lips. But the yearning to give herself to him no longer drove her. A great tenderness and a great sorrow had engulfed her passion, the way a wave covers the shore, and had swept away the sufferings of an unsatisfied, sublimely beautiful burst of passion.

Manya vows that she is his in the only way that matters. They agree to meet the next evening at the precipice, and while he speaks of his passion for her, she docilely agrees to anything he may decide. They finally part and make their separate ways home.

"Where is he going? Home. To his wife? He's mine, body and soul. What will he do now? Have supper, then go to sleep beside his wife, filled only with yearning for me. And he won't defile his burst of passion by giving it to another woman, to that little Katya, who for some reason happens to be in his bed. He'll turn his back on her beseeching glance. He'll move away from her dark-skinned body. He's mine now! I've taken his soul, his thoughts, his desires. Will it be for long? It doesn't matter! He's grasped it with his heart, not his mind. But how criminal he feels now before this insignificant Katya! With what a guilty look he'll respond to her! Poor Nikolenka! Only now will he feel the chains that he willingly put on himself. And it won't occur to him to tear them apart and escape to freedom. What's freedom to someone like him? Nothing but words. And tomorrow, when we part, he'll despise himself and won't bless fate for a moment's joy. He'll try to forget me."

Barely able to make her slack limbs move, she walked through the wide courtyard past the flowerbeds and fountain. Someone's horse snorted nearby and the bay windows were lit up. Someone was visiting. O God! To shake the hands of people who were superfluous to her, to listen to conversations . . . now! After what she'd just experienced?

She approached the park grating.

"Where am I going now? Why am I going there? To see Mark's suffering face, his big, jealous eyes? To play the role of his wife in front of everyone? Why this charade? Who needs it? 'What of your vow?' he'll ask me. He'll ask without saying a word, with his cursory glance. And what can I answer? Did I seek a meeting? How can I avoid my fate? Didn't I have my own life—new, conscious, and wonderful? And is there anything left of all those proud plans and hopes? How pale and pitiful are all our efforts at deluding fate!"

"Is that you, Uncle? Where's Mark?"

"I don't know. I left. Some guests came, they're making a lot of noise. I'm frightened, Manya. I'm afraid of something again. Where were you? I've been waiting for you here for so long."

Manya tells Steinbach's uncle that she loves Nelidov and marrying Mark was a mistake. Avoiding a meeting with the visiting Sonya, Vera Filippovna, and Uncle, Manya retreats to her room, where she reminisces.

Yes, it was two years ago. She was swimming in the sea when suddenly the wind changed and it grew turbulent. Everyone had left the water, and she remained on her own. They shouted to her, and she laughed joyfully in response, intoxicated with the increasing alarm around her. Transparent green in color, like the bodies of jellyfish, the waves rose, lifted her, and gently deposited her. Suddenly she looked back and horror cut off her breath. A monstrous wave was approaching that covered the horizon, like a gray-green moving wall. "It's the end," Manya thought clearly. She lunged for the rope and convulsively grabbed hold of it. But at that very moment the mountain of water toppled onto her, blinding and choking her; it tore her away and, tossing her onto her back as easily as if she were a chip of wood, swept her into the open sea.

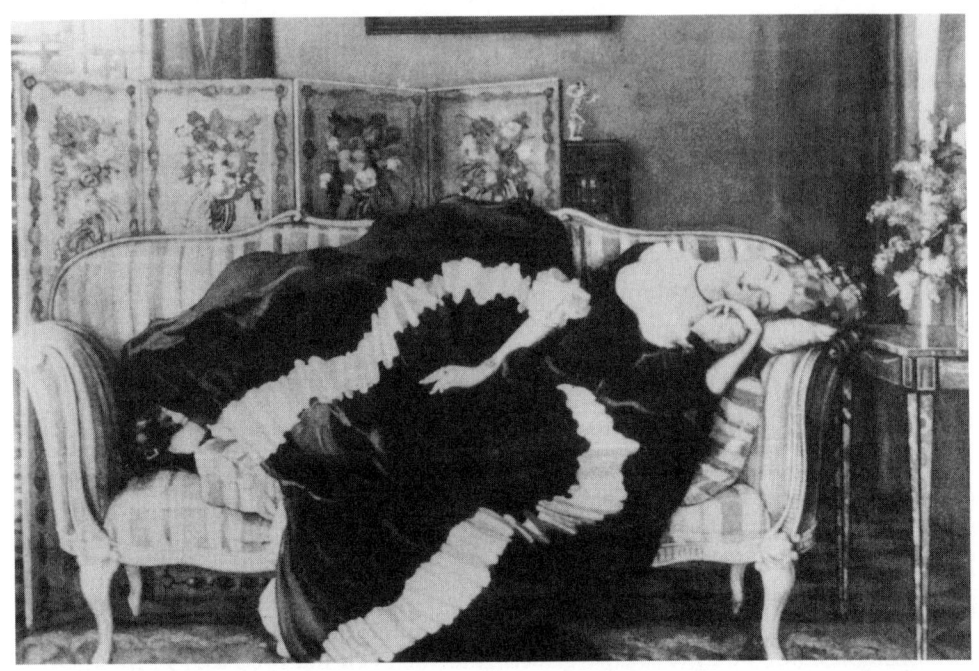

FIGURE 12

Konstantin Somov, "Sleeping Woman" (ca. 1911) reflects the era's obsession with supine female bodies—stretched out in sleep, sickness, or death—which Verbitskaya exploits in Manya's near-death scene, seduction scenarios, and moments of psycho-physical weakness. *Die Kunst* (1912–1913, no. 27).

They saved her with enormous difficulty. And it took her a long while to recover from her swoon and the shock.

Now she gazed in front of her, brows furrowed.

The same wave, fatal and irrevocable, suddenly had risen, carrying away and destroying everything that it had taken her years to build with love and faith, everything for which she'd struggled and worked with stubbornness and despair. The whole new order of her soul instantly collapsed under the pressure of this terrible wave. Its name was *Femininity*.

Isn't that the most powerful, the most treacherous instinct? It's what tramples the flowers that open at dawn. It's what extinguishes the fires on the altar. It's what mutely, in the darkness of our subconscious, in the silence of the night, stifles the great aspirations and elevated transports that are born in the daytime. It's what lies in wait for us on all the roads and crossroads. It attacks like a predator. And, twisting our arms, it cynically mocks our dreams and makes us follow it. Where? O, it understands everything. It sees only its own goal, for which we, with our pride and our ideals, are only a means. Woe to whoever is vanquished in this battle! The soul that has desired slavery cannot raise itself.

She lay with eyes closed, holding her breath. And a smile roamed over her lips. O, bliss! She recalled how she had pressed her face to his in a mighty surge of tenderness and how his long lashes had tickled her cheek. "Just like Nina's," she thought. Her soul rejoiced once again. And sweet tears again stung her eyes. Who, except for him, gave her such moments of sultry tenderness and boundless pity? Her child. Her Nina, when she kneeled beside her little bed, gazing at the sleeping little girl, and implored God to direct all of life's blows onto her own head so as to ward them off from that sweet little head. How pale the moments that she'd lived with Mark—the dark delight of sensuality—seemed now. And the cold joy of her love for Harold seemed even paler. A strange "rational" emotion. Nelidov had been and remained the master. He alone aroused the instinct of submission in her restless soul. With the others, she was in control; with him, she was the one being controlled. With the others, she took and demanded everything without giving anything back. With him she gave everything with submissiveness and joy. With the others she had been an individual. With him she was a woman.

"I'm tired," Manya thought. "I'm tired of struggling, tired of striving. I don't need to make an effort. Just to give all of myself. Submissively accept the common lot. Oh, if there's a long life ahead, I'd give all of it up so as to return to that wonderful, that terrible moment when he squeezed me in his arms and said to me, 'Let's die together.' I'll never recapture that moment! Never!"

Steinbach brings her a letter from Iza, and experiences relief that Manya has not learned of his role in her affair with Nelidov. He informs Manya of a riot at his factory that he must immediately resolve. She only now tells him that Izmail visited her and that she gave him a check. Izmail is suspected of the attempt on Nelidov's life, he and his corevolutionaries are being followed, and Nadezhda Petrovna has been arrested. Steinbach urges Manya to flee with Nina and Frau Kessler.

"... Manya, what's keeping you here? Is it that you want to see him once again?"

"Yes, Mark, I do, for the last time. Then I'll leave. I don't want to stay here any longer myself."

He clasped her tightly to his chest. "Finally!" his tormented face said. O, that final terrible wager! This final fatal skirmish with fate.

"When will you be back, Mark?"

"In the morning or tomorrow during the day. I'll send you a telegram."

"They won't kill you?"

"No one will touch me. I've no one to fear."

"Mark, hurry back as soon as possible! Don't leave me alone now, when I'm so afraid, when I've lost my way."

"Do you love him, Manya?"

"I didn't stop, Mark! That's the whole horror of it. If he summons me, I'll follow him to the ends of the earth. But I know, I feel that he won't summon me. He doesn't have the strength to do so. I need to get away, get away as soon as possible, to vanish from his memory. After all, he was happy without me all these years. Who knows? Everything passes, everything will be forgotten. I want him to be happy!"

Steinbach withdrew from her.

"She's thinking only of him. Not even of herself. She loves him with that great feeling with which I love her. I'm powerless here."

She pressed her face against his shoulder.

"Mark, Mark, forgive me for being cruel! But do I really need to tell lies? Can't you see everything yourself? You're so wise and so perceptive, you've always been able to read everything that's in my soul."

"No, no, don't cry!" he replied, stroking her face. "I value your truthfulness. Tell me everything. It'll be easier for both of us."

"Mark, remember that I made a vow . . ."

She sighed mournfully.

"I told you—there's no need for that. Words can't change life."

"Ah! You knew that. I didn't. I sincerely believed that I was prepared to sacrifice everything for you, that even meeting him wouldn't change anything. But I didn't know myself. See, I can't lie. You're wise, you know a woman's soul. Tell me: what can stop her in this rush to sacrifice herself? But you're as dear to me and as close as before, Mark. Oh, this is something completely different! I love you as a friend, as a brother, a faithful companion, as my strength and faith. For me you're above everyone else. Don't take your love away from me, Mark. Forgive me in advance everything that will happen. This is your last ordeal, Mark. We'll go away together, start a new life. I need something big, something radiant, so as to forget what I'm losing now."

As if speaking to herself, slowly and unevenly, Manya said:

"I've been lying here for a full hour, thinking, and trying to understand what happened. How could it have happened? Why he, specifically? He's so distant from my soul, so uncomplicated. You're much closer to me, Mark." "And Harold was closer, too," the thought flashed through her mind. "You both valued the individual in me. But he sees only a woman, and he despises Marion. He needs the submissive Marie. Can it really be that the whole secret of his attraction is this straightforwardness? Your love is elevated and lucid. His love is dark and primitive. But it's as powerful as death. I realized that now, I felt its fatality. I don't want to degrade it. I cry with emotion and happiness. It's the love of a nightingale for its mate. But surely even in a little bird passion isn't stronger than the life instinct? What a terrible power it is, Mark!"

"Terrible," he echoed with a strange submissiveness.

"And now, when we stood side by side, everything that was hidden in me unconsciously, everything that slumbered in my body, which I don't know or which I'd forgotten, all of it thirsted for him so powerfully that for a moment I couldn't even see anything. Mark, we were born for each other. What kept us apart?"

She fell face-down in a passionate burst of despair.

"Manya," he said quietly, sensing, with despair, the futility of his own words, "Nelidov's love, a new life with him would be the end of everything: of creative work, struggle, social involvement. It would be the death of all possibilities. Remember the years you worked on yourself, your sufferings, the development of your soul, the long, difficult uphill struggle. Remember all the values that you elaborated. Remember your wonderful renunciation of Harold. Surely all that can't go down the drain because instinct has spoken? I know it's difficult to conquer it; freedom of the soul doesn't come easily. But you've already emerged the victor from all your trials. Rise just one step higher! It's the last. And you'll have conquered life. Surely you must sense your victory—the greatest victory of the spirit—in your ability now to look at Nelidov from above, with a consciousness of your own superiority? And why do you think that your purpose is to subordinate yourself to him? Surely the past has proved that freedom is dearer to you than love? You've forgotten everything, Manya. But I have a good memory."

"The irony, the irony of it," Manya thought, still lying down, her face hidden. "What sort of victory is it, when I yearn to die for him, to be trampled upon by him? Ah, to give myself to him! That's what I should have done. Given myself to him and died."

Steinbach leaves, exacting her promise that she won't decide anything until his return. Close to midnight, as Manya and Frau Kessler on the terrace discuss their imminent departure, they hear footsteps in the darkness. Manya requests that Frau Kessler tell Steinbach, in case she "cannot," that he should destroy the house and give away the land on Lipovka to those who have the right to it. Alarming noises interrupt their exchange, and, armed with a flashlight, the two women find what turns out to be the body of a spy, killed by Zyama. Manya keeps her rendezvous with Nelidov.

He met her under the precipice, as he'd promised, when it was already dusk. Silent and trembling with agitation, hand in hand they walked the short distance to the forest. They exchanged neither glances nor caresses during those minutes, their lips mute and their souls apart. And their path to happiness was sad, as if they had neither choice nor a will of their own. They resembled two doomed people walking to the sacred grove of a goddess's gloomy temple so as to pacify fate with a sacrifice. Only when the oaks of Gai cast their shadows on them did Manya recognize the place where Nelidov had first taken her in his arms. Fate itself had led them there.

When they recovered their senses, it was already night, and the sky was lit with stars.

They sat in a close embrace, leaning against an old oak, which had witnessed the flowering of their love and which now witnessed the sunset of their happiness. The thirst for earthly happiness was slaked, and other voices sounded now. Now the harsh dictates that had been silent until then called out. A coldness that was the harbinger of parting stole into their souls. And, once more, in the distance glimmered the inevitable path that had been forgotten in their ecstasy of love—the sorrowful path along a dreary plain, with the soul solitary and oppressed by melancholy about what was impossible, with burning recollections of what was lost forever.

Eyes closed, Manya relived anew the moments that had flashed by. When she'd made her way to their meeting place, why had tears trembled in her breast? From a yearning for happiness? Yes. But, just as earlier, there'd hardly been any sensual passion. But in this self-oblivion, in this all-consuming tenderness and readiness her soul once again attained the highest fervor of feelings accessible to mortals. And shuddering from recollections of that sacred moment, she once again noticed with emotion how the years of suffering and yearning had spiritualized Nelidov's feelings. He no longer possessed that vivid spontaneity that had blinded and subjugated her. Passion no longer predominated in him. He was free of cruelty and the elemental thirst for destruction. His caresses were also permeated with melancholy and tenderness. And Manya once more believed in the great delusion of love, which promises the mystery of the union of souls in the embraces of the flesh.

Suddenly she heard his empty, monotonous, lifeless voice, which instantly tore her out of her sweet oblivion.

"It's already night. We have to part, Manya. Now we'll never see each other again."

At this her strength abandoned her and she burst into tears.

But this time, unlike yesterday, he didn't comfort her. He had no words of tenderness for her, nor caresses. He was gloomy, as if a wall of ice had suddenly risen between them. And the cold from it streamed into Manya's cooling soul.

"Nikolenka, forgive my weakness. These are the last tears I'll shed. I'll be brave. If you want me to disappear, I'll go away, and you'll never hear of me again. Tomorrow I'll go far, far away, I'll return to the stage and . . ."

"And into the arms of your loving husband?" he finished her sentence coldly. "Go on! Why did you stop?"

She shrank, wilting completely, as if he'd struck her.

"You're cruel. What do you want? Tell me! At just one word from you I'll leave Mark and be your mistress. If you don't leave your wife, I'll submit to that, too. Tell me . . ."

He kept silent, as gloomy and distant as before. She laid her hands on his shoulders, trying to discern his features.

"Let's look for a way out together, Nikolenka. We'll fight this . . ."

"In the name of what?" he asked harshly.

"Ah! You no longer believe in happiness."

"It doesn't exist without you. But I won't have it with you, either. When I met you six years ago, you were like wax in my hands, submissive and devoted."

"I'm the same, Nikolenka. Still the same . . ."

"No, you're wrong. It's not for nothing these years have passed. I've lost you irrevocably. I don't know you. Are you really my little Marie, who preferred death to a long life without me? You have something that can console you. Right now you'll leave, return home and resume your life, such a full, rich life, but without me and my love. And you'll recall this night, for which I'm ready to pay with my life, as ravings. See how far apart we've drifted? You forgot me and found happiness in another. I stayed the same madman. And only now do I understand what I lost in my meek little Marie, who loved me more than life itself. You can't bring anything back! Not anything."

Her sense of horror increased, and not so much from what he was saying as from the sound of his voice, which was lifeless.

In despair, she nestled against his breast, as if turning her back on a terrible premonition.

"Listen, Nikolenka! I went through a long and difficult time when I was far away from you, true! And I thought that our paths had drifted apart. I was mad not to understand that I was looking for you wherever I went. And do you see? Fate once again brought me to this forest and to you. Why? For a life with you? For death without you? I don't know. Perhaps you can tell me, Nikolenka? I attained the heights, but you called me, and I fell. And I'll never be able to climb back up. My place is here, at your side."

"You'll grow bored with me," he said in the same quiet, lifeless voice.

"No, no, no!" she replied, embracing his legs and pressing her face against him. "To love you, to serve you is my sole desire, that's my purpose here on earth. That's what I needed, Nikolenka! That's the one thing I needed!"

Nelidov is unbending, and insists that they part. He mentions that he followed her to Venice, saw Steinbach at the railroad station, and assumed that Nina was Steinbach's child. Manya senses that he is contemplating death, but wrings from him the promise of a meeting the following day. As Nelidov leaves, she hears Steinbach's voice. He escorts her, totally dazed, to the house, and cedes to her request that she be left alone. She falls asleep, and awakes to the sound of Steinbach's uncle knocking on the window. He urges her to follow him, so that he can show her where he found "him." They rush to the spot where she last met Nelidov, and the old man turns his flashlight on a figure lying on the ground.

"Look," the old man whispered, lifting his flashlight.

"Here . . ."

He lay on the ground, under the same oak where they had embraced six years ago, where they had sat together just recently.

She'd known this. She'd known this a long time ago.

She approached the body without a word and fell to her knees.

Nelidov lay in the peaceful pose of someone sleeping. One arm was outflung, his service cap fallen in the grass, exposing his pale forehead, with the tan line clearly marked. The light fell on his face, and Manya saw his half-open lifeless eyes, his long lashes, his pale, peacefully closed lips. His face, which such a short time ago had been distorted with suffering and despair, emanated tranquillity and peace.

She kissed his heavy hand. And only then did the awareness of the horror of what had happened pierce her. The unearthly, frightful coldness of his hand penetrated her heart. A pitiful moan escaped her.

"Sarra, Sarra, don't cry . . ."

"Who's that speaking?" she wondered.

"Ah, it's you, Uncle?"

"Let's go home. Let's hurry. It's frightening here . . ."

Home? But where was home? Where was the shelter that would hide her from impending Death? And wasn't her place here, beside the one who'd been earmarked for her by fate?

"Don't cry, Uncle. Don't be afraid for me. Nothing can frighten me now. You see? I'm not crying. I'm not hurting. It's fine now. Now I understand everything. Go over there. . . See that road? It goes straight, straight through the field, to the estate. He used to live there. He lived there with another and called her his wife. Don't you understand? It's a mistake, Uncle. I'm his wife. And Nina's our daughter. Hurry there and wake her. He shouldn't be lying here on the ground. Go on, and I'll stay with him. Don't be afraid. You'll come back for me. It'll be light soon. Go on, go . . ."

The long, uneasy rays of light from the flashlight ran forward, piercing the darkness. His footsteps died in the distance.

They were alone. O, at last! At last!

She lay down beside him, and, lifting his heavy head, laid it on her breast, embracing the motionless, rigid body and pressing her lips to the cold brow.

How often during these years she'd dreamed, the way a sinner does of inaccessible paradise, of spending a whole night alone with him; of lying like this by his side in a tight embrace; of hearing his heartbeat, feeling his breath, the flutter of his lashes on her cheek, of silently, with tears of tenderness, kissing his dear face. How often she'd dreamed, as if of an unattainable happiness, of waking up in his arms and greeting the dawn with a smile of gratitude! She'd needed so little, so very little to bless fate and die reconciled, having assuaged her soul's eternal hunger! And life, which had so lavishly gifted her with all the unnecessary blessings, had denied her this one, this sole joy.

"Here we are now, alone together," her disconnected thoughts ran. "Now to fall asleep together and not wake up again. Neither sufferings nor regrets, nor remorse. Here is my wedding night, about which I always dreamed when I was tired from a whole day's struggle and work. What did I struggle for? What was I aiming for? Of all that I gained, what do I need right now? Peace. Peace and silence."

She quietly kissed his dead face, but her lips were freezing. The chill of death again pierced her to her very heart. She remembered the heat of his body, the dear scent of his breath, so sweet, so memorable, and so special.

The clatter of wheels reached the glen. People's voices. . . Someone's hysterical shrieks. Surely they weren't coming here? Surely this wasn't the end?

For the last time she pressed her mouth to the pale, tightly closed lips, for the last time she kissed the pale brow, the golden curls, the small hands with their nails turned blue. Then she rose. Her foot stepped on something hard. Ah! His revolver. She picked it up and clutched it in her hand. Yes . . . Yes. . . It was all clear now. Everything was fine now.

She quickly left the forest, and as she reached the edge of it she looked back for the last time. The motionless outline showed dimly black in the grass. "Farewell, Nikolenka. I'll follow you."

As she made her way up the steep path to the top, she saw below the hazy figures of people, heard alarmed voices, and a woman's shrieks.

Faster, now, faster! To the place where peace and silence awaited her.

In her room she quietly locked the window and pulled down the blinds.

It was dawn.

She turned on the lights and approached the portrait.

Once more the two women, one alive, one dead, gazed into each other's eyes. But now there was no fear, no hostility, and no mystery. "I understand it all now," Manya thought. "I know why you were a threat to me. I know where you were calling me. We're sisters in spirit. We're both doomed. Vanquished, like you, I'm leaving this life, which I've not been able to master. Let others struggle with it! Let the strong emerge victorious, those with souls that burn with faith, with souls that are illuminated by an idea. I've reached my limit here, and I'll wake to a new life where there won't be any suffering on account of love and its slavery, where I'll learn to love freedom."

Manya kisses the portrait, then goes to Nina's room and kneels beside her bed.

"What's awaiting you, woman of the future? Surely not the same sufferings? Surely not the same delusions? The same slavery of love? Is it possible that a woman will never be able to be happy any other way? Is it possible that she'll never find in her soul the joy of yearning for that which doesn't delude, doesn't change, doesn't die? My little Ninochka," she thought, her lips touching the sleeping child's golden hair, "Will you find the road to freedom, which I didn't?

Will you obtain the keys to happiness, which I didn't know how to wield? O, if only you don't repeat my mistakes! If only your life doesn't pass under the dark sign of passion! If only you grow up proud and strong, unlike me! What can I, who have been vanquished by love, give you? Farewell, my Ninochka!" Manya whispered, kissing the child's hand, which was dangling over the side of the bed. "May God ensure that you never cry when you remember me! They'll tell you I was mad, they'll tell you I had no right to die. They'll condemn me. Don't defend me, my little girl! You, too, should condemn me in your heart! Call my rejection of life madness, for life is wonderful. For life as such is a blessing and has value for those who neither want to fall nor fear doing so; for those who have set high goals for themselves. And only the tired, only the doomed, like me, leave it voluntarily."

Manya quietly kissed the damp little forehead, made the sign of the cross over the little girl, and tiptoed to the door.

This time it closed without a sound.

It was completely light when Manya crossed the room. Birds were twittering in the park. The day was beginning, as bright and joyous as the one before, with a wealth of dew, with a blinding noon, with an amber-rosy sunset. She would see it from her fondest burial ground no more. She wouldn't see anything.

The drawn blinds made her room dark. Quickly, now! Quickly, while the ominous news still hadn't reached the estate.

She turned on the light and sat down at the desk.

Manya's last letter to Steinbach

"Mark, I am leaving. But I'm not summoning you to take this final journey with me. Forgive me this deception, my dear, my only friend! It's easier for me to die with the thought that Nina won't be left alone in this enormous, frightful world. It's so good to think that you'll clasp my little girl to your heart and protect her from the life that has killed me. Mark, I sense that this attachment will save you from despair. Teach Nina how to survive in the battle with love, with what to fill her soul to the brim, so that the mirages of the desert in which we, the vanquished, perish, don't lure her.

Another thing. Mark, I think with joy during these last moments that you and Iza will finish my life's work, which I started with such love and faith. Carry out all the things that you and I dreamed and argued about in the Tyrol. So what if it's utopian! So what if it's madness! Be mad! Don't fear the ridicule of the mob! Create the marvelous fairy tale on earth that I didn't have time to accomplish! And thousands of people will bless your name.

O my friend, my faithful companion, forgive me this last betrayal of you and myself! I'm crying right now as I recall how many years, with what self-sacrifice, you led me to the tall tower along the road bequeathed by Yan. With you at my side, I fell on those steps; with you at my side, I battled with tiredness and revulsion; with you at my side, I conquered and made my way up, higher and higher, to the secret pinnacle. But he whom I couldn't stop loving passed by, far below. He summoned me, and I fell and was shattered. I cannot rise again.

I don't reproach you for anything, dear Mark. I know that everything you did was done with the wish for my happiness. You weren't thinking of yourself when you kept us apart. And to you alone I'm indebted for all the elevated joys of creativity and my achievements. But the woman in me is stronger than the artist. I'm powerless before love. I had good reason to fear it! He is dead. And I'm following him. I can't stay behind.

Now I see clearly that all these years death and you battled for my soul. You were the victor once. But, hiding somewhere nearby, death dispassionately followed my desperate efforts, my tragic battle. It waited for its hour to sound. And that hour's come.

O, Mark, don't you, whom I'm abandoning, condemn me. Remember that my whole life was like one passionate cry; one longing for freedom; one burst of passion for that which is above the the earth and material things. Remember that this life was a dream about the impossible. And yet always, despite my insatiable thirst for joy, despite this yearning to keep moving forward, further and further along new and unfamiliar paths, in my soul—sometimes vaguely, sometimes clearly, sometimes subsiding, sometimes flaring up, there sounded, like a single incessant note, the persistent need to rest, to go to the limit, to fall silent, to close my eyes, to disappear. I know now that this was the voice of Eternity. It was the summons to another life, which awaits me, and where I'll awake with a joyful and renewed soul, one that doesn't know the chains of love.

Mark, when you read this letter, don't cry for me, don't pity me. I am departing from life while blessing it. So what if it has vanquished me! There's no bitterness in my heart. I leave life tired, but grateful for everything it's given me. And don't think that I'm afraid. Death is a liberation for those who, like me, lie on earth with their hearts bleeding after their final, fatal skirmish with the predator—love. Death has swung open the prison gates for me and the breath of infinity is already blowing in my face, and my eyes have a premonition of eternal light. But I wish to shout to everyone who tomorrow will see the earth's sun, the sky high above, and the diamond drops of dew: Love life! Appreciate life! Bless it for both good and evil, both happiness and suffering, both day and night, and for the peace that awaits us—the tired—, the peace that will never deceive us. Everything's full of mystery here, Mark. Yet there's nothing pointless, nothing senseless. There's no stopping and no disappearing. And I, too, won't die, dear friend! I'll not disappear from the world. I've always known this. Your Manya, who got tired of suffering, will die. But my free, my immortal soul, will arise.

Farewell! The door has opened slightly, and I'm standing on the threshold. I glance back and I see only you at my side on all the intricate paths. I'm taking your portrait from the desk and kissing your brows, your eyes and lips. You, who gave me so much earthly joy, you, who have loved me so selflessly, most noble of people, remember me in your faithful heart! I know that it won't beat again for another love. I know that you won't have long to roam alone in the twilight. And the night that will also finally bring peace to you, exhausted by love, is near.

One final request: bury me beside Yan—beside the beloved bench on which you and I sat that radiant morning when my heart first started to beat for you. And while you live, close the house and park, lock them up. Let the paths along which you and I walked to meet joy become overgrown! Let no one's laughter sound within the walls where I cried in your arms, where you loved me. Don't let the empty chatter of strangers disturb my final sleep beside Yan and frighten off the radiant shade of our past happiness."

EPILOGUE

"Telegram, Mark Aleksandrovich," the servant said as he entered Steinbach's study in Moscow.

Steinbach was burning letters and papers in the roaring fireplace. His valet Andrey moved about silently, packing the most essential things in his hand luggage.

The telegram was from Frau Kessler in Berlin:

"ARRIVED SAFELY. NINA IS WELL. TAKE CARE."

"Andrey, I'm entrusting my uncle to you. As soon as he feels better, take him to Paris. Did he sleep last night?"

"Very little, Mark Aleksandrovich. He's always delirious and crying."

"Give him a bromide. Have the doctor visit every day I'm gone. If something unforeseen happens, please don't get flustered! Here's a passport. And there's Uncle's passport. This wallet has everything—money and a letter of credit in my name. Hide it now. I put my trust in you."

"Don't worry, Mark Aleksandrovich!"

Suddenly they both fell silent. A bell shrilled downstairs. They looked at each other in agitation.

"May I, Mark Aleksandrovich?" A metallic, melodious, joyful voice spoke behind the door.

Semyon Nikolayevich entered and froze. He couldn't conceal his astonishment.

There was nothing left of the old Steinbach. Where were his good looks, his proud bearing? His face was immobile and lifeless. It seemed like a mask out of which his bottomless, opaque eyes looked darkly and even more mysteriously now, as if they'd looked into the beyond and had seen what was invisible to others. The imprint of terminal illness lay on his extinguished, fallen face. It had stooped his shoulders and silvered his hair. "You've survived her, but not for long," thought Semyon Nikolayevich. "I knew it'd be this way."

Both ate almost nothing at breakfast, but they drank a great deal. Semyon Nikolayevich told a lively story about the newspaper—about how hard it was to carry on for a cause. But this was nonsense! They hadn't laid down their arms. If there was money, then there was strength enough. And faith in oneself.

"By the way, about the money. I went to the bank yesterday, Semyon Nikolayevich, and made a deposit in your name. This sum will fund your cause for a long time to come."

"You'll be away a long time?"

"I'm never coming back."

"But what about your estate and your factory?" he inquired after a long silence.

"I've left everything in trusted hands. My will is all prepared and has been left with the notary. You'll be pleased with my arrangements," Steinbach smiled faintly. "My factory will pass over to the workers. I'm leaving the land to the peasants. I've willed one estate to my daughter. I'm in a hurry right now to fulfill my wife's last request and open a people's theater in her name in Paris."

"I'd like you to take on something grand and noble. Forgive me, but I'm so afraid for you."

"You're afraid I'll kill myself? You see, Semyon Nikolayevich, that would be much easier than living and suffering, than surviving what I've survived. But I dare not. I've a daughter. And I wish that Manya's name not be forgotten by those she loved so sincerely, by those she thought of at the height of her fame and in the last moments of her life. She didn't value what the crowd valued. She had no sense of property, of being settled. She sensed the breath of the Eternal in all that was instantaneous and passing. She lived to strive, she lived for beauty. She heard voices there where all is dead and mute for us. And the very madness of her quest is holy to me now."

"That's Love for you!" thought Semyon Nikolayevich, walking along the street and still stirred by his meeting. "It's a great and terrible power, destructive and creative at the same time, rending the soul and creating entire worlds."

The bell rang once more. Steinbach stood stock-still by the fireplace.

"May I?" Sonya cried behind the door and then immediately raced into the study.

Without greeting him, she stared distractedly for an instant at Steinbach's dead face. Covering her face with her hands, she burst into tears.

"What's happened? What is it?"

Steinbach opened the crumpled telegram.

"LIKA ARRESTED. SHE SHOT THE GOVERNOR. HE'S SERIOUSLY WOUNDED. ROZA ALSO ARRESTED."

For a long time Steinbach said nothing, staring at the weeping Sonya.

"Why did she do this?"

"It's crazy, isn't it?" Sonya said, sitting down on the couch and wringing her handkerchief. "Can this really help? Will this really change anything?"

Once again Sonya cried helplessly.

"What's in store for her now? Death . . . death. . . My God! And for what? What madness this terror is! She had such a rich, sensible, marvelous life filled with lofty joys and love. And just think if she comes to her senses and regrets what she's done?"

"She won't regret this. Lika has never been hysterical. She knew what she was doing."

The telephone on the table rang sharply. Steinbach went up to it and listened tensely.

"Yes, yes, thank you, I understand."

He put down the receiver and went up to Sonya.

"Leave now, dear friend. I thank you for everything!" He kissed her hands. "But you can't stay here a minute longer."

"What is it?"

"Izmail was arrested with Manya's check. I have to flee. There's probably a search underway right now at Lipovka, and there will be a search here tonight."

"My God! Let me take what you've left here! Give it to me!"

"I'm very touched, dear Sonya. But I've essentially destroyed almost everything. And that's not the real danger. Leave right now! Telephone me, only not from your place, but from some drugstore. You see, it's getting dark out. I can't guarantee that they won't follow you even now."

Sonya hesitated for a moment. Then she fell on his breast and wept. With the same dead, still expression that made him so ominously resemble his uncle, he stroked the hair of this girl who had loved him silently and selflessly all these years, who'd seen in him alone all the colors of her own severe, self-abnegating life, a life deprived of personal happiness.

Leaning back and holding him by the shoulders, Sonya stared at him with tearful eyes filled with selfless love.

"Mark, don't forget me! Write me. . . My life will be so empty without you!"

"Don't denigrate yourself, dear Sonya! Your life will be full and bright even without me and without what we're accustomed to calling 'happiness.' Before you lie lofty goals, a beloved cause, a vocation you've been preparing for for years. Farewell!" He held her face in both hands and kissed her on the forehead. "Work. Write to me. And come rest in Paris. We'll reminisce about the past. We'll talk about Manya."

It was already dark. The entire lane lay in slumber. The lights were extinguished in all the windows, and the moon had risen high in the sky. But a light still burned in Steinbach's second-floor study. A shadow was still moving about.

Other shadows, inconspicuously surrounding the house, followed it vigilantly. The gates were closed. The night watchman and the caretaker stood as if frozen by the iron railing.

Suddenly a door opened, and a tall stooping figure with a gray beard walked out onto the porch. From under a round hat gray curls fell on his temples. Mysterious dark eyes stared ahead lifelessly. A walking stick tapped along the flagstones of the courtyard.

"Who's that?" whispered one shadow, stretching its neck.

"The crazy master," the caretaker replied in a whisper.

"Why is he going out?"

"It's their habit to go walking every evening, your excellency . . ."

"And nothing comes of it?"

"Nothing, sir. We're used to it. They'll come back in an hour, maybe earlier. They're quiet."

"Let him pass."

Slowly the old man crossed the wide moonlit courtyard. He passed the gate. His lifeless gaze slipped over the strained faces of the people who stood concealed in the shadow of the railing and over the figures who'd frozen in surprise on the sidewalk opposite. Bent over, with lowered head, he walked down to Ostozhenko, tall, apathetic, eerie, and mysterious in the dead moonlight. His entire figure emanated sorrow and loneliness. The very rhythm of his footsteps and the dry knock of his stick along the stones seemed to say, "Old age, old age, old age."

Time passed. How much? The light still burned above. The shadows remained motionless by the railing. And random passersby shied from them in fright.

It struck midnight. "It's time!" a strong voice uttered. And the shadows moved into the moonlit courtyard. The sleeping house was seized by a living circle. There was a loud, extended, mighty ring at the door. Three minutes of silent waiting passed before the door opened.

They went upstairs to the study. It was empty. A half-drained glass stood on the table. An open bag was in the corner. Some torn newspapers lay on the carpet. The fire in the fireplace was smouldering. All the lamps were lit. And no one was there. They turned on all the lights and searched the entire upstairs, peering into the corners and cupboards. No one. It was as if the whole house had died. The cook, the maid, and the servant who'd opened the door were dishevelled, half-dressed, and terrified, and couldn't give them a single straight answer.

They went downstairs and—at last!—there was a locked door.

They knocked loudly and powerfully. There was the sound of bare feet on the floor. Andrey, sleepy, half-dressed, waved his hands.

"Quiet, quiet . . . you'll disturb the sick man. He's just fallen asleep."

A lamp with a dark-blue shade shed a faint light.

"Who's sleeping?"

"The master's sick uncle. What do you want?"

"What do you mean, the uncle? Why, that was just he, he only just. . . Turn on the light!" shouted the strong voice.

A bright light suddenly illuminated the room. With a cry the frightened old man started up in bed. His long gray beard fell on his breast. Gray curls clung to his damp temples. His mysterious eyes fixed in terror on these unfamiliar faces. His hands were trembling. He'd remembered something, something terrible.

"Sarra-a," he cried in a heartrending voice and hid his face in the pillow.

Everyone looked at each other in fright and disbelief.

Steinbach had disappeared.

Glossary

Parenthetical numbers following the entries refer to the book in which the item appears; the first occurrence is indicated in the body of the text with an asterisk.

Bakuninist: follower of Mikhail Bakunin (1814–76), revolutionary theorist of anarchy, ideologue of the Populist movement. (I)

Böcklin, Arnold (1827–1901): Swiss painter specializing in austere landscapes before turning to the themes of death and destruction. The grove in question appears in his *Sacred Wood* (1882). (V)

Borisov-Musatov, Viktor (1870–1905): Fin-de-siècle painter of evocative, wistful landscapes and garden scenes with elegantly dressed figures, who exhibited with the World of Art in 1906. (I)

Campanella, Tommaso (1568–1639): Italian theologian, philosopher, and poet. A rebel who hoped to establish a utopian communist state, in prison he wrote his famous political utopia *Città del sole* (*City of the Sun*, 1602). (II)

Charcot, Jean Martin (1825–93): French physician and neurologist, chair for nervous disorders at the hospital of Salpetriere, who investigated the "pathological" aspects of art and elaborated his notorious theory of female hysteria as womb-based. (II)

Class Matron: a residential, supervisory position in tsarist girls' institutes, one of the few paid positions open to institute graduates. (I)

***Crossing* and *The Golden Fleece*:** two Russian journals of literature and art at the turn of the century, then considered avant-garde. (I)

"Death of Ivan Ilyich" (1886): One of Leo Tolstoy's strongest stories about the trauma of death. (I)

Duma: an elected representative assembly with circumscribed legislative and budgetary rights and functions instituted by Tsar Nicholas II as a concession to popular demand after the 1905 revolution. (II)

Eternal Jew: possibly a reference to the Wandering Jew, a legendary character condemned to roam without rest because he struck Christ on the day of the Crucifixion. (I)

Ferri, Enrico: criminologist, pupil of Lombroso. (II)

Glahn: see *Phall and Glahn*.

Goland and Mélisande: characters in Maeterlinck's play *Pelléas et Mélisande* and the opera by Claude Debussy based on it. (I)

Hamsun, Knut (1859–1952): pseudonym of Knut Pedersen, Norwegian novelist, playwright, and poet, author of the novel *Pan* (1894), which treats the inner life of the individual. (I, III)

Higher Courses for Women: modeled after a two-year sequence of courses for women introduced in November 1872 within Moscow University under the directorship of Vladimir Guerrier. Although the Guerrier courses ceased in 1886, they set the example for other efforts at advanced education for women, most notably the Bestuzhev courses in St. Petersburg, which survived until the 1917 revolution. (I, III)

Jacquerie: specifically, the revolt in 1358 by peasants of Northern France against the nobles, but more generally, a peasant revolt. (I)

Karonin, S. (pseudonym of Nikolay Petropavlovsky, 1853–92): a populist Russian author of stories about the impact of reforms in the countryside and the intelligentsia's intellectual wanderings. (III)

Krafft-Ebing, Richard (1840–1902): Austrian neurologist, author of works on mental disease, notably *Psychopathia sexualis*, which influenced contemporary notions of degeneracy. (II)

Kropotkin, Pyotr Alekseyevich (1842–1921): Russian geographer and anarchist, whose *Paroles d'un révolté* (1885) extolled the propagandist purposes of art. (IV)

Kursistkas: young women attending the Higher Courses at university (formerly accessible only to men), whose image of emancipation consisted of unisex clothes, dark glasses, short hair, and an "unhealthy" desire to learn. (IV)

Lacrima Cristi: wine produced throughout Italy, usually quite fruity, overvalued on account of its evocative name (literally, "Christ's tears"). (II)

Little Russia: an alternate Russian name for Ukraine. (II)

Lombroso, Cesare (1836–1909): Italian physician and psychiatrist, author of *Genio e follia* (*Genius and Madness*, 1882) and *L'uomo di genio* (*The Man of Genius*, 1888). (II)

Machtet, Alexander (1852–1901): Russian populist poet. (III)

Maeterlinck, Maurice (1862–1949): Belgian symbolist poet and dramatist, on whose play *Pelléas et Mélisande* (1893) Claude Debussy based his opera by the same title (1902). (II)

Moloch: a deity whose worship required the sacrificial burning of children, thus generally identified with any phenomenon demanding appalling sacrifice. (II)

A Nest of Gentlefolk (1859): novel by Ivan Turgenev about the landed gentry's role in the national debate between Westernizers and Slavophiles. (I, III)

Pan (1894): novel by Knut Hamsun. (I)

Phall and Glahn: protagonists of Knut Hamsun's highly subjective novels, the latter from *Pan*. (I)

Rautendelein: a female character in Gerhart Hauptmann's fairy tale drama *Die versunkene Glocke* (*The Sunken Bell*, 1896). (I)

Reclus, Elisée: journalist, author of the article entitled "The Evolution of Cities" for *Contemporary Review* (1895). (IV)

Rusalka: mermaid or water nymph in Russian folklore, reputed to be the soul of a drowned maiden who committed suicide, famous for haunting and tickling unwary young men to death as she pulls them down into the water. Title of a poem by Alexander Pushkin and of the Alexander Dargomyzhsky opera based on it (1855). (I)

Sanin (1907): novel by Mikhail Artsybashev (1878–1927) that caused a sensation for its advocacy of following one's natural inclinations in all matters, particularly sexual desire. (I)

Senta: the "faithful woman" who redeems the Dutchman condemned to eternal wandering until his redemption in Richard Wagner's opera *The Flying Dutchman*. (I)

Social Democrats (SDs): Marxist radicals who formed their party in 1898 around G. Plekhanov, which split in 1903 into the Bolsheviks, who, led by Lenin, advocated a close-knit organization of professional revolutionaries, and the Mensheviks, who favored a broader and looser assocation. (I)

Socialist Revolutionaries (SRs): a party that formed in 1901 and represented the older populist tradition of Russian radicalism. Its extremists advocated terrorism and assassination to achieve its ends. (II)

Tarpeian rock: a section of the ancient Roman Capitol where malefactors were thrown down a deep ravine, named after Tarpeia, daughter of the governor of Rome's citadel. For the promise of trinkets she opened the city gates to the Sabines, who upon entering the city crushed her with their shields. (II)

"A Terrible Vengeance" (1832): Nikolai Gogol's lurid, folklore-steeped Gothic tale of demonism, incest, and bone-crushing revenge. (I)

Wanderers/Itinerants: artists belonging to the Association of Traveling Exhibitions, founded in 1870. It established realist painting, often with a social message. Members included Repin, Levitan, and Surikov. (III)

BETH HOLMGREN is Associate Professor of Russian and Polish Literatures at the University of North Carolina, Chapel Hill. She is the author of *Women's Works in Stalin's Time: On Lidiia Chukovskaia and Nadezhda Mandelstam* (1993) and *Rewriting Capitalism: Literature and the Market in Late Tsarist Russia and the Kingdom of Poland* (1998). She co-edited (with Helena Goscilo) *Russia • Women • Culture* (1996). Her current work focuses on Russian émigrés to the United States between the world wars.

HELENA GOSCILO is Professor of Slavics at the University of Pittsburgh. Her most recent publications include *Russia • Women • Culture* (co-edited with Beth Holmgren), *Dehexing Sex: Russian Womanhood during and after Glasnost*, and *The Explosive World of Tatyana N. Tolstaya's Fiction*. She is currently co-writing, with Nadezhda Azhgikhina, a cultural study of the New Russians, tentatively titled *Born Again: Entrepreneurship, New Russian Style*.